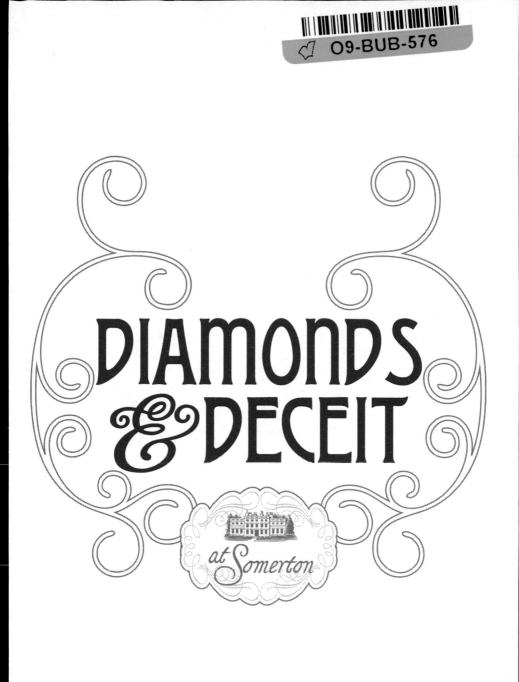

DIAMONDS & DECEIT

at Somerton

DIAMONDS & DECEIT

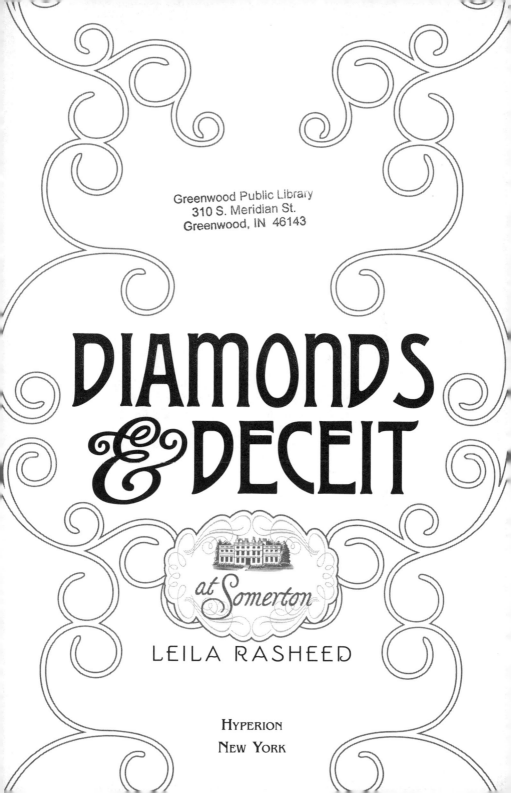

at Somerton

LEILA RASHEED

HYPERION
NEW YORK

First Edition
1 3 5 7 9 10 8 6 4 2
G475-5664-5-13288
Printed in the United States of America

This book is set in Palatino
Designed by Marci Senders

ISBN 978-1-4231-7118-8

Reinforced binding
Visit www.un-requiredreading.com

SUSTAINABLE FORESTRY INITIATIVE   Certified Sourcing
www.sfiprogram.org
SFI-00993

THIS LABEL APPLIES TO TEXT STOCK

ALWAYS FORGIVE YOUR ENEMIES—
NOTHING ANNOYS THEM SO MUCH.

—OSCAR WILDE

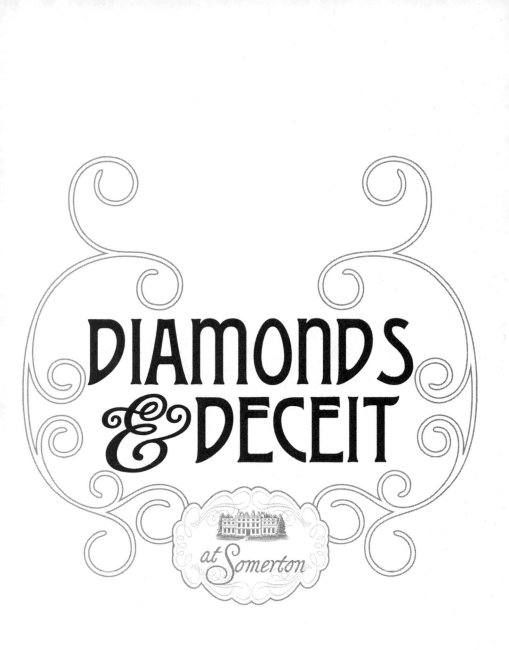

DIAMONDS & DECEIT

at Somerton

Act One

CHAPTER
One

The London Season, 1913

Ellen scurried along the servants' corridor, her aching arms stacked high with dirty dishes from the garden party outside. It was a blazing hot London day in May, but it seemed as if even the sunlight didn't dare enter the servants' passage for fear of getting under Cook's feet. The only rays came through a small, dirty window, sunk slightly below the level of the gardens, and screened by a box hedge. The sunbeam crossed Ellen's path like one of Cupid's golden arrows.

She paused at the sight of it, glancing back toward the kitchen. Mrs. Strong's voice echoed down the corridor, but no one was watching her. Shifting the tower of plates so they sat more securely on her hip, Ellen went up to the window and stood on tiptoes to peer through.

AT SOMERTON

At first she could see only ivy and whitewashed walls, but by squinting a little and craning her neck she was able to catch sight of one the season's unmissable events—the first Milborough House garden party since its mistress, Mrs. Fiona Templeton, one of the richest widows in London, had metamorphosed into the Countess of Westlake. Lady Westlake and her family now spent most of the year at the earl's estate, Somerton Court.

To Ellen it looked as if angels were gathered on the lawns, glowing in chiffon and delicately embroidered lace, with halos of flowers around their heads. Ellen was a country girl, and Lord and Lady Westlake's assembled guests reminded her of the stained-glass figures in the church she used to attend before she had gone into service: bright and far out of reach, people who lived in a happy land she could not even dream of setting foot in.

"Ellen!"

Ellen jumped as Cook's voice rang down the corridor.

"What are you dawdling over? Get down to the scullery with those plates!"

"Yes, Mrs. Strong!" Ellen scurried off. She wondered if the day would ever end. Her feet felt too tired to take another step. Tweenies like her—halfway between a house maid and a kitchen maid—got all the dirtiest, most tiring jobs loaded onto them. But like all the other staff at Milborough House, she was willing to work as hard as she had to so that this day could be a success. It *meant* something, to be the tweeny at Milborough House. It *meant* something to touch the angels, even if all you touched was the rim of their dirty plate. From the footman who handed out the champagne, to the chef who had given himself a migraine slicing cucumbers into discs so thin they were like transparent jade, to the gardener who had marshaled a team of fifteen men to whip the flower beds into shape in time for the big day, to the tiny insignificant dot that was Ellen ferrying plates back and forth along the Stygian corridor, all the staff at Milborough House felt this, and it pulled them together with a force stronger than gravity.

As Ellen approached the laundry room, she noticed that the door was ajar just a crack. Then she heard voices.

". . . the last time. I'm serious."

It took her a moment to work out that the man who had spoken could not be a servant. Not with such a voice. But that wasn't possible. The ladies and gentlemen were never to be found downstairs, any more than she was to be found in the drawing room. And what on earth would they be doing in the laundry room, besides? She slowed, unwilling to intrude.

"You know you don't mean that." A woman's voice this time, and an oddly familiar one.

"I do."

"Oh, Laurence"—a sweet, lilting laugh. "You say that"—a teasing sigh—"every time."

Ellen drew closer. She heard the whisper of silk. There were gasps. More sighs. Still not understanding what she was hearing, she looked through the chink of the door. She saw a mist of pink-and-white chiffon, tumbling blond hair. A man's hand was pressed into a bare white shoulder, half crushing a crimson silk rose adorning the woman's dress. Two golden heads, lips locked together, kissing passionately. That was all she glimpsed, then the man pulled away.

His eyes were pale and shrewd, his face was handsome, and more than that, aristocratic. The woman was facing toward him, away from Ellen. Ellen did not see her face, just the silken sheen of pearls against the nape of her bare neck as she reached up to draw her hair over her shoulder.

"This time I mean it," the man whispered furiously.

The woman was half laughing as she said: "You scold me so often, darling, I'm beginning to suspect we're married."

The gentleman—Ellen was sure she knew his voice, she had heard it behind the wainscoting a hundred times this season— reached for his hat and cane. The young lady caught his arm.

"Let me go," he said, but he did not pull away from her.

"Let you go? I don't force you to meet me like this. You are free to leave whenever you wish—if you can."

The man made an angry sound. He shook her off as violently as he had drawn her to him a moment earlier. The woman gasped. Ellen jumped back into the shadows, quivering with fear as the man pushed the door open, and glanced left and right down the corridor.

"Laurence!" the woman hissed. It was hard to tell if it was fury or love in her voice.

The man—Laurence—raised a hand to straighten his cravat. His face was set, hard, arrogant, as if he would cut down any challenger. Ellen knew he did not see her, in her drab clothes, stained with dishwater, a stray potato peel down her sleeve and her cap askew, her hair lank and sweaty from the kitchen. She blended into the shadows of the servants' corridor. But she saw Lord Fintan—the cut of his morning coat, the folds of his sunshine-colored cravat, the smooth line of his gloves as he pulled them on one by one. She saw the swing of his cane and heard the crack of his shoes walking away from her down the corridor toward the open back door. The sun blazing through it touched his golden hair like a halo, as if he were an angel returning to heaven, leaving behind nothing but a faint whiff of expensive cologne and some crimson silk petals scattered on the black-and-white-tiled floor.

CHAPTER
Two

"Rose, are you quite well?" Ada Averley placed a hand on her sister's arm and drew her to one side, looking into her face with concern. They were with a small group in the Arabian summer-house at the bottom of the gardens, where the ornamental fountains cast crystal music into the warm, scent-laden air.

Rose, beneath her Poiret hat, was wilting. She wanted to say: *No, I'm hot, and I have a headache, and I'm exhausted from the ball last night, and I wish the eternal din of London would fall silent for just one moment so that I could hear my own heart beat*—but she couldn't say that. Plain Rose Cliffe, housemaid, might have done it, but not Lady Rose, second daughter of the Earl of Westlake. Lady Rose had standards to uphold, a family who could be let down.

Instead she said, "Perfectly, just a little tired."

Ada smiled sympathetically. Her hand remained on Rose's arm as they turned back to the group. Rose steeled herself to face the sharp, amused eyes of Lady Gertrude de Vere, Lady Cynthia Fetheringale, and Lady Emily Maddox, three other debutantes. It seemed such a long time since she had been Ada's lady's maid, carrying secret letters between her and Ravi, the Indian student with whom Ada was in love. Not for the first time this season, she wondered how Ada was bearing the separation from him. Every time she tried to raise the subject—not often, for they were always in company, always watched; there was never the opportunity to be alone together as there had been when they were mistress and maid—Ada deflected her. Rose was puzzled, and worried.

"The gardens are simply exquisite," Lady Gertrude said, glancing about her. "I feel as if I were standing in a painting."

Rose smiled her agreement. The gardens of Milborough House were one of the seven wonders of the London world. It was Gertrude Jekyll who had designed them, creating bold, painterly sweeps of color around sinuous paths that led from lily-studded lakes to charming pergolas and secluded bowers. The best of the flowers were artfully designed to bloom and release their enticing, musky scent just at the height of the season.

"And such a delicious scent!" Ada agreed, as if she had read Rose's mind.

"A little tainted with washing soda, don't you think?" murmured Lady Cynthia, with a sidelong glance at her companion.

Lady Gertrude tittered. Rose's headache intensified, but she managed not to lose her polite smile. She tried to focus on the strains of the Russian string quartet mingling with the chatter and laughter of the guests. It seemed forever since she had been at a piano, and she knew the lack of practice was beginning to tell. She would once have found music in everything, in the morning birdsong at Somerton, in the wind in the trees, in the rattle of the housemaids' brushes and buckets. But music needed a backdrop of silence, and there was none in London.

"I think it's simply wonderful how my stepmother always manages to put on such a delightful party," Ada replied. Rose was grateful for her sister's tact; she did not feel she could have spoken so calmly.

"We are all wondering which celebrity she has invited to entertain us this evening," Lady Emily replied.

"Yes, indeed! After Nijinsky and Melba, it's hard to see who else she can surprise us with." Lady Cynthia had an extraordinary nose, a little like a shark's dorsal fin broaching the waters, and she had the habit of raising her chin so that she was looking down it at whomever she spoke to. She raised her chin now and directed her voice at Ada—despite being introduced, she had not yet spoken a word directly to Rose. "She is so lucky with her staff."

"We are very lucky indeed," Ada replied quietly.

"No doubt the servant question never bothers *your* family, Lady Ada." Lady Gertrude took up the theme. "My mother is quite concerned about the availability of housemaids these days. But I hear the Averleys have plenty of them—almost, one might say, too many."

"Oh, one can never have too many housemaids," Ada said cheerfully. Her hand was still on Rose's arm, a reassuring, strong presence. Rose was glad of it as she took a couple of good deep breaths and counted to ten. It seemed that everyone they met knew that Lady Rose Averley was the illegitimate daughter of Lord Westlake and his housekeeper—and that until a year ago she had been a mere housemaid at Somerton. *I might not be aware of the finer nuances of table manners and social calls,* she imagined herself retorting to Lady Gertrude, *but I have become expert in the fine distinctions between whispers, smirks, stares, sniggers, and outright jibes.*

"Rose, Ada, I don't think you've met the Duchess of Ellingborough." Rose turned, relieved to hear her father's voice interrupt the conversation. Lord Westlake joined them. With him was a tall, elegant lady wreathed in fox furs and pearls.

"But I have met Lady Ada," the duchess said, her voice piercing as an icicle. "I had the pleasure at your wedding, Edward. Lady Rose, however . . ." She turned a pale-blue gaze upon Rose, who just managed to stop herself from curtsying. "I don't think I have had the pleasure."

"It is my sister's first season," Ada said hastily.

"And yet your face does look familiar," the duchess continued.

That's because I carried your bathwater up five flights of stairs the night of my father's wedding, Rose thought. *You glanced at me long enough to scold me for dropping the soap.* She held out a hand. "I am very glad to make your acquaintance, my lady," she said.

The duchess's fine nostrils quivered as she examined Rose. "Odd that you were not at the wedding," she continued.

Lord Westlake coughed in embarrassment. Lady Gertrude and Lady Cynthia exchanged malicious glances.

"Oh, I think she *was*, Your Grace," Lady Gertrude said. "Only you might not have recognized her because—"

"Why, here he is!" Lord Westlake exclaimed in relief; and at the same moment Ada said, "Laurence! We wondered where you were."

Lord Fintan smiled as he joined them. His cheeks were slightly flushed, as if with the heat of the sun. "Lady Ellingborough, how delightful to see you after such a long time," he said, coming to stand at Ada's side. "My mother frequently asks after you—"

"I am quite well, thank you." The duchess raised a hand to her lorgnette and studied Rose. "I was just wondering why I had not had the pleasure of making Lady Rose's acquaintance at the wedding."

Rose began to realize why the upper classes were the upper classes. They didn't get embarrassed. They didn't take a hint. They just kept on drilling until people gave up in exhaustion and let them have their way. No wonder they'd won the battle of Waterloo.

Lord Westlake cleared his throat and lunged for a passing footman who had a tray full of drinks. "Champagne," he said. "I think we should have a toast."

"A toast?" The duchess raised her glass and her eyebrow.

"Yes, to my future son-in-law." Lord Westlake raised his glass to Fintan, who smiled and raised his own.

"Indeed!" The duchess finally looked away from Rose, to Ada.

Rose was startled. Ada was marrying Lord Fintan? She turned to her sister, but a small sound, the tiniest gasp, distracted her before she could speak. Rose looked toward the sound and saw that her stepsister, Charlotte Templeton, had joined them. She was standing as still as a photograph. Then her color returned. No one else seemed to have noticed.

Rose found her voice. "Ada, I had no idea. . . ."

A moment later, she was embarrassed at the lack of enthusiasm in her voice. She was pleased—of course she was pleased. The engagement had been expected by everyone—everyone, that is, who didn't know Ada as well as Rose did. Fintan would make her an excellent husband. He was clearly in love with her, they had so much in common, and . . . and she hoped she had sounded as happy as she knew she ought to feel.

"I'm hardly surprised," said Lady Emily, raising an eyebrow. "Ada and my brother make a natural couple."

"Of course, I simply . . ." Rose trailed off in confusion. Looking at Ada, she said, "Of course you will be very happy." She wished she could ask Ada if she was sure, very sure, she knew what she was doing. She remembered the way Ada's face had brightened when she opened a letter from Ravi, the passion with which she had spoken of him, the risks she had taken to meet him. Could Fintan really have replaced him so quickly?

Ada smiled back at her. "Who can doubt it?" she said.

"Did I miss an announcement?" Charlotte's smile embraced them all as she stepped into the circle. "Dear Ada, I wish you joy. And Laurence too, of course."

The others crowded in with congratulations, and Rose found herself, not for the first time, subtly edged out.

Ada glanced back over her shoulder with a small apologetic smile for Rose, and Rose made sure to make her answering smile as warm and glad as it could be. The last thing she wanted was for Ada to worry about her. She deserved to enjoy her happiness and not be burdened by Rose's discomfort.

She stepped back into the shade of the arbor, still watching the group she had just left. Ada, a slight figure in a dress the color of wisteria blossoms, framed by the heavy, dark figures of her father and Laurence. Rose noted the warmth between her sister and Lord Fintan as Ada placed her hand on his arm. There was the vivacity in her laugh as she echoed his jokes. And there was a slight flush on her cheeks and a slight glitter in her eye that could have meant many things.

Rose looked up to the great, elegant iceberg of Milborough House, the serene women draped in stone that framed the upper drawing-room windows.

Ada is as much the Averley family's face to society as this house is, she thought. It is a wonderful marriage, correct in every way. Of course Ravi was impossible. And yet, and yet . . . Rose played with a strand of her pearls, anxious without really knowing why. She thought again of Ada's smile when she'd received a letter from Ravi, compared it to the one she wore now. It was like comparing a real rose to the silk ones on Charlotte's dress.

"I just cannot understand why I should not have been introduced to Lady Rose at your wedding, Lord Westlake." The duchess's refined vowels sliced through the air. Rose closed her eyes and groaned gently to herself. She let the waves of the crowd usher her even farther away from her family's summerhouse. Perhaps it would be possible to find a spot in the gardens where there was some silence. At least it was no hardship to wander alone through the gardens of Milborough House, she thought, as she walked away from the group.

Rose strolled past the flower beds as the kiss of croquet balls echoed from a little farther away, mingled with shrieks of well-bred laughter. She smiled as she saw a very young couple walking together, under the discreet but careful gaze of their mothers. The girl seemed hardly older than fourteen, and the boy still had the pink cheeks and coltish long limbs of a schoolboy.

"Lady Helen Fairfax and dear Blanchford," a woman nearby commented to her friend. "Such a sweet couple. I expect they'll be engaged this season."

Rose was struck by the adoration with which Lady Helen looked up at the boy. Yes, she thought, that's how Ada used to look at Ravi. Rose glanced back toward the group, feeling troubled. But Ada was hidden by the crowd.

Rose walked on, unnoticed, trying to escape the snatches of lazy conversation that followed her: "Lady Verulam's ball is to finish the season. . . ." "Where is that amusing Sebastian Templeton . . . ?" "The situation in Europe is really quite grave. . . ." "What will replace the Russian craze . . . ?" "I long for a new couturier to break the monotony of Poiret. . . ." No matter how far she went, it was impossible to find silence.

At Somerton

She found herself near the servants' entrance, where the tables were spread out. The only things brighter than the footmen's white gloves were the ice swans weeping themselves away in the midst of the ruins of luncheon. She could see the inviting steps down to the kitchen. It was such hard work being a housemaid, but at least she'd had friends. She drew nearer, shielded by the hedge. A footman and a housemaid were laughing together, sharing a cigarette by a small, dirty window. Rose's slipper caught on the gravel, and the maid looked up and caught her eye. Rose felt a hopeful smile waver on her lips, but the maid's laughter was instantly replaced with a cold, professional mask. The footman dropped his cigarette, and both of them went back to wiping plates. A resentful silence bristled from them. Rose couldn't blame them. She'd have felt the same, if she had caught a lady seeming to spy on her. She turned away, an ache in her chest.

A certain change in the tone of the crowd caught her attention. Garlanded hats turned, like flowers to the sun, toward the house. Near Rose, one elderly dowager leaned to whisper to another. "It can't be!" replied the second woman, sounding disapproving.

Curious, Rose looked up at the terrace and saw a broad-shouldered young man standing on the top step, facing the crowd. He seemed to have just come through the open French windows. His hair was unfashionably long and tousled, the breeze plucked at his red-gold curls as if he stood on the bridge of a ship. Rose understood at once why people were staring and smiling. He wasn't dressed at all for a garden party. His long sleeves were stained with something gray and blue, and he wore no hat at all. She found herself feeling irritated. Whoever he was, he was clearly so certain he would be well received that he hadn't even bothered to dress correctly.

"The Duke of Huntleigh," announced the butler.

"My dear Alexander . . ." Rose's stepmother swept forward to welcome him, her brightest smile vying with her diamonds to out-dazzle the sun.

"Huntleigh!" exclaimed a lady nearby, and she and her neighbor glanced at each other. "Trust the countess to capture the season's roariest lion."

Rustles of excited whispers ran through the crowd like a forest fire. Clearly the Duke of Huntleigh was another desirable prize for the season's ladies to grapple over. Rose had met a few of these prizes—not for long, no one wanted to waste time on a former housemaid who did not even have a dowry to go with her new title—and had quickly decided that not even a hundred thousand a year could make up for a lifetime of having to make conversation with them over the tea table.

Rose glanced up at the Duke of Huntleigh again. He was just walking down the steps with the countess; his mouth curved into a small smile as he looked at the crowd. It wasn't a smile of happiness. There was something contemptuous in the way he waved away the footman who stepped forward to offer him a glass of champagne.

Rose turned away. But no doubt everyone thinks his fortune makes up for his arrogance, she thought. Oh how I hate this world, where no one's smile is real.

CHAPTER
Three

"Well!" Charlotte Templeton seated herself before the mirror, back straight and head held high. She removed the pins one by one from her hair and let the blond curls fall loose. "That was certainly eventful. How many more shocks to the system can this season stand, I wonder, Ward?"

Stella Ward, who was putting away the dress Charlotte had just stepped out of, didn't answer immediately. The footman had overheard the engagement announcement—there were always eyes, always ears—and seen Charlotte's expression. The rumor of Charlotte's old involvement with Lord Fintan had caught like a badly banked fire. The whisper had leapt from tongue to tongue in the servants' quarters and raced up the servants' stairs just as a real fire would have done, to Stella's bed-sitting room where she waited for her mistress to retire. Miss Templeton would be humiliated, Stella knew that. What she did not know was whether it was safe to talk about it. But since Charlotte had raised the matter herself . . .

"I'm very sorry, my lady," she said. She knew that Charlotte, unlike her stepsisters, was a mere Miss, but sometimes it was tactful to make a little mistake. "If it's any consolation, I'm sure he'll regret his choice. He—"

"I beg your pardon?" Charlotte's voice was cold as an iceberg, and Stella suddenly felt like the *Titanic*.

"That is—I thought—" She floundered. "Lord Fintan—" She saw Charlotte's eyes in the mirror. They were blue as Arctic water.

"I was not referring to Lord Fintan," said Charlotte, still watching Stella. "Why would you have imagined I was referring to Lord Fintan, Ward?"

Stella felt herself blushing with fear and anger. How could Miss Templeton be so hypocritical? Stella herself had arranged the assignation at Gravelley Park last season.

"I apologize, my lady. I must have made a mistake."

"Yes," Charlotte tilted her chin and removed her diamond earrings. She laid them in the silver tray, where they chinked against her other jewels. "You shouldn't listen to servant-hall gossip, Ward. It's not becoming."

As if you didn't wait greedily for me to bring you the latest scandal every night! Stella thought. Now she was angry, more angry than afraid. So she was to tell tales when it suited Miss Templeton but keep silent as a dressmaker's dummy when it didn't? Well, perhaps she had her own ideas about that.

"You're quite right, my lady. I do apologize again." She kept her eyes down as she folded her mistress's dress. The red silk rose that secured the shoulder was torn, she realized, and some petals were missing. She opened her mouth to mention it to her mistress, and then hesitated.

"I meant, of course," Charlotte went on, "the return of the prodigal son. Alexander Ross."

"The Duke of Huntleigh, miss?" Stella said. She carried the dress away to the wardrobe. Under cover of the shadows, she unpinned the rose and slipped it into her apron pocket.

"The much-hunted Duke of Huntleigh, yes." Stella went back to her mistress, who was leisurely removing the rest of her jewels.

"I must say I'm surprised to see him back," Charlotte continued. "We all thought he and his vast fortune had disappeared into Africa forever. It wouldn't have surprised me. There was always some scandal he was running from, wasn't there?"

Stella was not inclined to indulge her mistress; but on the other hand, it was not a good moment to annoy her. She took the silver-backed brushes and began to brush her mistress's hair.

"There was indeed, miss. There was that episode with Lady Antonia Wood. . . ."

"Is it true, then, that Lord Arden threatened to horsewhip him on the steps of his club?" Charlotte giggled.

"Well, I heard it from His Lordship's valet, who has no reason to lie, miss." Stella giggled too. "Lady Antonia had a bet, apparently, on one of the horses at Goodwood, and she wanted to see her horse run, so he took her down there."

"Out of school, wasn't it?"

"I believe so. I hear they behaved quite scandalously. They stopped at Pickering Castle, which is her brother, Lord Arden's, seat, and bribed the butler into giving them the keys to his cellar—"

"No! And Lord Arden is such a known collector of wines," Charlotte exclaimed.

"Exactly, my lady. I hear the champagne was entirely gone through by the time they had finished. So of course when they arrived at Goodwood they were in quite a shocking state, and ended up somehow in the presence of royalty. . . ."

Charlotte laughed and laughed. "How on earth did he extricate himself from that one?"

"To tell the truth, miss, I don't think he did. It was after that that his father—the late duke—sent him abroad."

"Yes, it must have been the very last straw," Charlotte said thoughtfully. "Sebastian tells me that ever since getting sent down from Oxford, the duke had been running through his allowance at a terrible rate. But where has he *been* for two years?"

"Well, miss, rumor has it he was in Paris living with an artist's model."

"How thrillingly scandalous!"

"Even better, I'm assured that there was a quarrel and the . . . *lady* stabbed him." Ward smirked.

"How exciting." Charlotte fingered the ropes of pink pearls that hung from the jewelry stand. "My mother was disappointed he didn't stay longer. I suppose he is still in mourning for his father."

"I don't think His Lordship pays much attention to convention," Ward said.

"And do you think he has pawned the parure yet?" Charlotte asked casually, playing with the jewels that were scattered on the dressing table in front of her.

"Certainly no one has seen it for a long time. The duchess, his mother, was the last one to wear it; but of course she was not seen in society for a long time before her death."

"So he is now the fifth duke and has the inheritance entirely in his hands?"

Stella nodded meaningfully.

Charlotte ran a finger through one of her blond curls and let it bounce up. "He always said he would never marry. But perhaps now that he is independent he has changed his mind."

Stella caught her eye. "I've no doubt that you would be able to persuade him, miss."

Charlotte smiled, or at least her mouth curved upward. "That will be all, Ward. You may go."

CHAPTER
Four

Charlotte watched until the door had closed behind her lady's maid and her pile of laundry. Then she ran her hands over her forehead, kneading the headache that lay there like a stone. But she couldn't knead away the pain. She astonished herself by bursting into tears.

It was humiliating! That was the one, hateful fact that burned inside her. Not simply to be pushed aside—Laurence had never rejected her before, not in three seasons—but to have him declare he would marry that dull little gray-eyed bookworm right in front of her, and worst of all, for Ward to know and pity her!

"Oh, it's unbearable!" she exclaimed, jumping up. She rubbed her hand fiercely across her face. Tears were not her style. Tears achieved nothing. The only thing that would erase the humiliation was revenge. And she had plenty of ammunition for that.

She sat down at her writing desk, took her writing case and pulled out a sheet of paper. She began writing with trembling fingers.

Dear Sir,

I think you will be interested to know the full details of Lady Ada Averley's relationship with a young Indian student, Ravi Sundaresan, which began in the spring of 1912. . . .

She stopped writing. No. She was moving too fast. She needed to think. This was too important to spoil for want of a little planning. It would certainly humiliate Laurence if she let everyone know about Ada's affair with that Indian student, and she had no doubt that, once humiliated, he would come running back to her. She smiled slightly. He was very welcome to come running. She was determined not to be there when he arrived.

She lifted her gaze and considered herself in the glass. Dolllike features, rosebud lips, eyes a little too small but artfully colored. Certainly Alexander Ross hadn't been immune to her charms two years ago. She remembered that Saturday-to-Monday at Gravelley Park very well, though he probably didn't. The cad had been drunk practically the entire time. And if anything, two years had improved her. She had lost none of her looks and was infinitely more experienced—while he, romancing around Montmartre with his paintbrush and his cocotte, had no idea how society worked. She sniffed contemptuously. Stabbing, indeed—how middle class.

Behind her the candle flickered. This was her third season. She had to marry *someone*, and that someone had to be rich. Even better if it was the only man in her circle that Laurence truly hated.

She folded the letter she had begun and carefully slipped it into her writing case, a plan forming in her mind. She put the case back in her desk drawer and opened the drawer just below it. Inside was a sketchbook, the cover slightly yellowed with age. She hadn't touched it for years, not since she had left the schoolroom, but as she flicked through the pages, she smiled. So the duke fancied himself an artist?

She always knew there had to be some point to those interminable drawing lessons.

CHAPTER Five

Much as she longed to slam it, Stella closed Miss Templeton's door softly behind her. Carrying the laundry and the mending, she walked down the corridor toward her own room. As she did so the door to Céline's room opened and Céline came out, carrying a pile of clean shifts, and started down the corridor toward Lady Ada's room. She was humming a soft melody under her breath, and she looked, irritatingly, far too bright and cheerful for three in the morning.

Stella's grip on the laundry tightened, her nails digging in. The French maid was the last straw. She was paid more simply because she was French, and she had a pert, insolent air about her that Stella simply could not stand. How dare she hum at this time of night, as if she actually enjoyed sitting up?

Stella deliberately swerved as Céline passed her and knocked the shifts from her hands. At least, that was what she meant to do. Céline, annoyingly, clung on to them and instead of the shifts tumbling to the floor, there was a loud ripping sound as a seam gave.

Stella recovered herself first.

"You'll have to sew that now," she said in a low fierce whisper. "Hope you're proud of yourself, working for a jumped-up housemaid."

Céline drew herself up and met Stella's eyes without the slightest sign of fear.

"At least I work for a *lady*," she said. "Miss Templeton isn't even that."

"Lady!" Stella spat out a laugh. "I don't think much of ladies that can be made that way. You can't carve them out of soap."

Céline shrugged indifferently. "All the nobility had to start somewhere," she said.

It was simply infuriating, Stella thought. Nothing she did seemed to have an impact on that pert little smile.

"I bet Miss Charlotte will be curtsying to Lady Rose before long."

Stella nearly choked. "Oh do you?" she managed. "Oh, do you indeed?"

"*Oui*," said Céline, with what seemed very close to a smirk. "I do. And now, if you'll excuse me—I am late to undress my lady."

She walked off down the corridor. There was the hint of a flounce in her walk as she opened the door to Lady Ada's room, and the smile she cast over her shoulder in Stella's direction could be called nothing but insolent.

"Oh!" Stella clenched her fists as the door closed, leaving her in the dimly lit corridor. She was furious, but there was nothing she could do but go on to her own room. The only thing that comforted her was the thought of the silk rose, still in her apron pocket. Those missing petals had to be somewhere.

Chapter Six

"I beg your pardon for being late, my ladies," Céline said as she came into the room. "One of the clean shifts seems to have been torn. It must have happened in the laundry."

"I'm sorry, Céline, that will be extra work for you," Rose said, turning to face her. She did feel sorry for the maid—she remembered very well how her fingers had been sore after stitching and darning night after night when she would rather have been in bed. But, she thought as she watched the maid begin to unfasten Ada's dress, Céline was a better lady's maid than she had been. She seemed to actually enjoy her work. She was constantly encouraging Rose—in the most deferential way, of course—to peruse some of the new catalogues and magazines from London's best dressmakers, to consider one trimming or another, to make a decision about lace or silk chiffon. The whole thing filled Rose with the deepest depression. Whatever she wore, Lady Gertrude and Lady Cynthia and all the rest of them would make sure she felt like a housemaid wearing it.

"It doesn't matter, my lady," Céline smiled, plucking hairpin after hairpin from Ada's hair.

"At last," Ada sighed with relief as her dress shimmered to the floor. Céline bent to pick it up and Ada seated herself in front of the mirror. She opened the drawer and took out a thick sheaf of papers, which she began to read. Rose glanced at them curiously.

She was exhausted, but she was also longing to talk to Ada about her engagement. She glanced across at Ada, but Ada was reading as Céline brushed her hair and did not look up. The candlelight glinted from Ada's deep brown hair, from the silver-backed brush, and from the jewels she still wore.

"Has mademoiselle given thought to her dress for the state ball?" Céline asked Rose, as she drew the brush down in long, soft strokes. "A sample arrived from Poiret—black and pink pearls and a fan of peacock feathers—"

"Oh, goodness." Rose stifled another yawn. "I haven't had a moment to think of anything important, let alone dresses."

"Mademoiselle, dresses are always important." Céline sounded shocked.

"Yes, of course they are," Rose said hastily.

"And particularly for *this* ball," Céline went on. Her pretty mouth seemed to be trying to suppress a smile.

Rose glanced at Ada, but Ada was still absorbed in her reading.

"What do you mean, Céline?" she asked.

"What I hear, my lady, is that the season is quite thrown into disarray, with the return of the Duke of Huntleigh from foreign parts," Céline said, folding up Ada's ribbons neatly. "Those ladies who have become engaged to be married are trying to disengage themselves, just in case. Those who have not are increasing their efforts toward the state ball. Poiret will be busy. Madame Lucille has not a single free appointment."

"Oh," Rose sighed and yawned at the same time. "Not the Duke of Huntleigh again. I seem to have heard nothing all evening but the scandals he's been involved in, the extent of his gambling, the reputations he's ruined. . . ."

"And the size of his parure," Céline murmured.

Rose coughed. "I beg your pardon?"

"The Huntleigh parure. A set of diamond jewelry, made for Marie Antoinette originally."

Ada glanced up. "The Huntleighs have some Bourbon in their blood," she said.

"Oh, I see. But he sounds awful—why is everyone so keen on him?"

"His father has just died."

"How sad." Rose was startled; tragedy didn't seem to fit with the image she had formed of the arrogant young duke.

"He has come into the dukedom and a very large fortune

besides," Ada said. "The Huntleigh reputation isn't good, but Huntleigh credit is." She added, "That will do, Céline, thank you."

"My lady," Céline bobbed a slight curtsy and turned to Rose's hair, her fast, deft fingers plucking out hairpins.

Rose glanced at Ada as she turned another page and it rustled. "Ada, what on earth are you reading? Aren't you tired?"

"It's the reform bill," Ada said distantly, her eyes on the paper. "I want to have the most important passages by heart in time for Laurence's speech."

Céline and Rose caught each other's eyes in the mirror.

"Do you think it's really necessary?" Rose spoke gently, but she was worried. There was a small frown line between Ada's eyes that had not been there before the start of the season. And now it seemed to be there all the time. "You get hardly enough sleep as it is. You will make yourself ill—isn't it better to wait till the season is over?"

"Oh!" Ada stood up, quickly and nervously. She crossed over to her bed, still staring at the paper, and lay down, her dark hair spilling in waves across the pillow. "No, I couldn't do that. I should go mad if I did nothing but visit and dance and dress for the next two months." She turned another page, seemingly absorbed.

Rose sighed. "Thank you, Céline," she said. "You may go now—you must be tired."

She turned to Ada as the door closed behind Céline. "Ada, really and truly, are you happy about this engagement?"

Ada looked up. Her eyes gave as little away as the carved eyes of the caryatids outside.

"Of course," she said lightly. "Laurence and I have so much in common. We are bound to be happy together."

Rose hardly knew what to say. She knew Ada was sending her certain messages: not to ask questions, to accept and smile. In the course of the season she had begun to realize that the veil Ada wore, of good breeding, tact, and grace, was a veil of steel, not silk. It protected her . . . and yet it also separated her. Not just from people like Lady Gertrude, but from Rose, in whom she had once confided everything.

"I mean . . ." Rose hesitated. "Do you love him?"

Ada's smile was brief. "Love grows, don't you think?"

"I suppose so," Rose said quietly.

Ada turned away, then seemed to think better of it and looked back. "Rose, I can do good as Lady Fintan," she said. "I can change England for the better. That's important, don't you think?"

Her gray gaze was level, and Rose knew that whether she agreed or not with Ada's decision, she had to respect it. "Of course," she said quietly. She stood up, pulling her Indian silk shawl around her shoulders. "Good night, Ada."

"Good night, Rose," Ada replied.

Back in her own bedroom, Rose found a fan of fashion magazines and illustrations on her dressing table. She sat down and flicked through them, reading Céline's neat annotations: *This velvet column is very elegant, no, mademoiselle? . . . This one is too ultra, I think. . . . The dull gold would be very flattering to your complexion. . . .* Rose put them down with a sigh. Céline was certainly an exemplary lady's maid, she thought. Even for someone whose job was to be attentive to the details of fashion, she seemed quite passionate about dressing Rose well. But what was the good of being dressed well, Rose thought—glancing at her jewel cases and fan cases, hat boxes and drawer after deep mahogany drawer of fur-lined, sequinned, beaded luxury—if it meant she couldn't be happy? If it meant Ada couldn't be happy?

She drew her writing case toward her. She had promised to write to Annie, and now was as good a time as any. It seemed like a lifetime ago that the two of them were maids together at Somerton. And yet nothing had changed for Annie.

Rose began to write, wishing she could say the things that were really in her heart. But that wasn't possible. Her life was an Eden compared to Annie's, and she knew it.

Writing to Annie took her longer than she had expected, and she was glad to slip, yawning, into bed just as it grew light. Even now there was no silence; the rattle of a cart in the street outside and distant street cries haunted her until she fell asleep.

CHAPTER Seven

Somerton

Annie Bailey came hurrying down the servants' stairs of Somerton Court, cap askew on her mousy hair. Five to eight, and she had time to snatch a piece of toast if she was lucky, before she had to fill the coal scuttles and carry them up four flights to the bedrooms. She could already hear Cook shouting orders, and swung to one side as the footmen hurried past with their silver trays held high, delicious smells of bacon and eggs and kidneys wafting out.

"Here," James paused to say, "have you heard the news? Lady Ada's engaged!"

"I'm miles ahead of you," Annie replied. "Saw the telegram when Mr. Cooper took it up."

"Good news, ain't it?"

"For our wages," Annie grinned. They all knew how close to the wind the family had been sailing—Lady Ada's marriage would put that right, at least for the moment.

"Get a move on, James! It's breakfast you're giving 'em, not lunch!" Cook shouted from the kitchen. James ran on up the stairs and Annie went down into the kitchen.

"Toast me some bread while I wash up, Martha," she told the scullery maid, and headed for the sink to rinse the ashes off her hands from laying the fire.

Martha went on talking to Thomas without pause as she moved from the washing up to the toasting fork. "It's like every night I can hear the scream, and the Horrible Thud," she said, shuddering.

"What are you on about?" Annie demanded, shaking her hands dry.

"The blinkin' murder, as usual. I wish you'd give it a rest, Martha," Thomas said. "Pass me that kedgeree." He grabbed it from Cook's hands and hurried back upstairs.

"I might rest, but his poor murdered spirit won't be so lucky," Martha said darkly.

"I don't know about his poor spirit." Annie checked her reflection in the piece of broken mirror lodged on the window-sill, and straightened her cap. "I met Simon Croker, and he was a nasty piece of work, I can tell you—not that I'd wish him dead. I think it's a shame about Oliver."

"So do I," said Cook, taking a moment to look up from her

breakfast-time preparations. "Poor lad. I can't imagine he'd be capable of murder."

Annie didn't reply at once. The kitchen door was ajar to let out the heat, and there was a view out across the courtyard to the stables. As Annie watched, a boy with tousled dark-blond hair and freckles crossed the cobbled, straw-strewn yard, leading Lady Georgiana's white mare, Beauty. He was so handsome that Annie couldn't help staring. The new stable boy, she thought. Of course, Mr. Cooper had mentioned engaging someone. He disappeared around the corner.

"What I'm wondering," Martha said behind her, "is whether he'll get murder or manslaughter. Murder's hanging. Here's yer toast, Annie." She banged a plate onto the table.

Annie turned away from the window and sat down to eat, still thinking about the handsome stable boy. It would be fun to go to the fair with him.

"I've never seen a hanging," Martha went on.

"You wouldn't go and watch!" Annie was half shocked, half fascinated.

"I'd feel I had to, just to get the sense that justice had been done," Martha said virtuously. "Did I say as how I hear his blood-curdling scream and hear his skull cracking against the stone floor every night like that jam pot James dropped last Sunday—"

"Yes," chorused everyone, "you did."

"And we wish you'd give over when we're trying to eat!" Annie said through a mouthful of toast. "Poor Oliver. He was a good valet to Mr. Templeton, for all I've heard, better than that Croker. Better looking too," she added sadly.

"But it's such a scandal for the house," Martha went on. "I can't go near the conservatory without a shudder—"

"And quite right too," said a firm, quiet voice from the doorway.

Annie jumped. Mrs. Cliffe was framed in the kitchen doorway, an elegant, sober figure in black. Annie dropped her eyes and an awkward silence fell. It was hard to be the same around Mrs. Cliffe these days, not now they knew all about her and Lord Westlake. And yet no one, she noticed, dared cheek her to her face.

"You have no reason to go anywhere near the conservatory," Mrs. Cliffe said, giving Martha her sternest glance. "A shudder is the least you ought to feel if you find yourself so far out of your place."

Annie glanced around at the others as Mrs. Cliffe went on down the corridor. Their expressions were resentful, except for Cook, who looked concerned.

"*She's* a nice one to talk about getting out of her place," Martha whispered with a rebellious snigger.

"That'll do, Martha." Cook wasn't laughing, and her voice was low.

The bell rang out, the new electric sound shrilling through the kitchen.

"Ugh!" Annie groaned and put her toast down. "Lady Georgiana? What does she want at this time?"

"Off you go, Annie." Martha grinned. "No rest for the wicked."

Annie ran for the stairs. The world might have turned upside down for Mrs. Cliffe and Rose, but for everyone else it was work, work, work as usual.

CHAPTER

Eight

"Oh, Annie," Georgiana Averley said, turning to the door of the music room as Annie entered. "Could you tell Cook it will be I who sees her at eleven, not Lady Edith? Lady Edith has a headache, I'm sorry to say." Georgiana winced at the lie, but she could hardly tell her that her cousin William's wife was drunk again. "And we are expecting Mr. Simmons, Papa's agent, for dinner, so there will be one more, but she needn't go to too much trouble—the fowl will stretch, I am sure, and perhaps there could be another vegetable dish—I leave it up to her."

"Yes, my lady." Annie dipped a curtsy and went out. Georgiana sighed and went to the piano. Her heart was hardly in the practicing. She missed Ada so much. She wondered how much longer she could keep Edith's drinking habits concealed. The servants would surely notice sooner or later.

Think about it later, she told herself. She closed her eyes and lost herself in the music. Waves of waltzes swept her along, then she swung into the new ragtime. In London they would be dancing to this, the beat of the feet on the pavements, the roar of the engines, the glare of the new electric lights around Piccadilly. She could have gone to London with her sisters. She *should* have gone to London. Plenty of girls her age were out, it wasn't fair. She was so much stronger now, her chest hardly ached at all when she ran—

"Georgie! There you are." The door banged open; her hands skidded into a discord. Michael Templeton strode in, the customary frown on his face. "What are you doing—oh, tinkling on that old thing." He flung himself down on the sofa, mud from his shoes scattering across the rug Annie had just cleaned. "Do you believe it? Your father just wrote that I am to go back to Eton. I know this is Mother's doing! Why can't the pair of them just leave me alone?"

Georgiana sighed. She loved her stepbrother. Just one smile from him—rare as those were these days—could make her heart race like a runaway train. But sometimes, she had to admit to herself, he was very annoying.

"Well, for what it's worth, I think they're both right," she said. Michael sat forward with an angry exclamation. Georgiana raised her voice to drown him out. "What on earth are you doing here but moping around and making yourself miserable? You must get something to do, and you're too young for the army—"

"Only by one year!" Michael protested.

"It doesn't matter. You must go to Oxford or Cambridge, there's no help for it. You're not going to inherit, you know," she added bluntly. "And you don't have a title, so I can't imagine any heiress marrying you."

Michael scowled. "I've told you a thousand times, I'm marrying Priya."

"Ssh!" Horrified, Georgiana got up and closed the door. "You mustn't say that so loud. Anyone could hear!"

"Why shouldn't I say it aloud? I don't care who knows it. I love her and I'm not ashamed of that. I'm proud."

Georgiana took a deep breath, struggling to contain her pain and annoyance. It was not simply that it hurt to be reminded that her own love was not requited. If the servants got wind of the fact that Michael and the nursemaid were secretly engaged, Priya's life would become very difficult.

"Really, Michael, you are terribly childish sometimes," she began. Michael interrupted her.

"That's rich, coming from you. You do nothing but flutter around after Mrs. Cliffe, with your head full of dinner menus and dramas about laundry lists."

Georgiana blushed angrily. "For your information, I'm trying to learn how to manage this house."

"Well, that's a waste of time," Michael sneered.

"How can you say that? So many people's lives are tied to this place."

"Mine isn't." Michael jumped to his feet. "You act as if Somerton is all there is, as if you'll be able to fritter your whole life away giving orders to Cook and entertaining the vicar to tea. But things aren't like that anymore. We've got automobiles and airships and telephones. There are a thousand things that a man with some energy can do. I'm going to get out of here, and earn my own living. Priya and I will live a real life, away from this . . . museum."

He stormed out of the door, leaving another set of muddy footprints going out.

"Oh, the silly—!" Georgiana broke off and rang the bell. Her face was hot, and she felt tears of annoyance prick at her eyes. If Michael ever bothered to think about anyone but himself, he would have considered that Somerton wasn't just a museum. For everyone who worked here, it was their whole life. That wasn't a responsibility that could be lightly thrown away. Michael might talk about the modern world, but Somerton was *her* world, here and now, and she was determined to make it a good one.

Chapter Nine

"Drunk again," Cook said when Annie gave her Lady Georgiana's message. She was up to her elbows in bread dough; flour dusted everything around her. "I feel sorry for Lady Georgiana. You can see she's trying her best, but she's only a girl."

"There was a man from London at the door the other day," Martha said, looking up from peeling the potatoes. "Cooper got rid of him. He didn't say, but I'm sure it was about Sir William's debts. He mentioned horses."

Cook shook her head as she began kneading again. Lord Westlake's nephew had always been trouble.

"It's a bad business altogether. I wish he wasn't the heir."

"Well, Lady Ada's marriage should sort things out," Annie said, only half listening.

Instead of going back to her work, she hovered at the back door, watching the stable boy as he worked.

"Don't think we don't know who you're looking at," Martha said over her shoulder.

Annie started and turned to face her. "And why shouldn't I?" she said, returning to the kitchen and pausing to glance in the greasy piece of mirror that sat above the sink. She tucked her hair in tidily, and set her cap on her head at a more flirtatious angle. At least as flirtatious as a housemaid's cap could be. Martha nudged her out of the way to tumble the potatoes into the sink.

"Give over yer primping," she scoffed. "He won't be interested in you."

"Want to bet?" Annie patted her hair and gave a little twirl. She didn't look so bad, she thought. She might not be a beauty like Rose, but she had a pretty nose and hardly any freckles. She glanced at the clock. She could steal five minutes just to pop over and say hello to him.

"Annie, love, a lad like that has his pick of the ladies."

"And he won't pick you, that's for sure!" Annie tossed over her shoulder as she went out into the courtyard. She held her head high and walked with a swing in her step toward the stables. Now that Rose wasn't here, Annie was certainly the prettiest of the housemaids. There was no reason the new stable boy wouldn't be interested in taking her to the fair.

She reached the stables and peeped coyly round the door. The boy was at the far end of the stable, filling the rack with hay.

He didn't look up as she came closer. Annie cleared her throat, making him look up.

"Hello," she said with a smile.

The boy grunted a greeting and went back to pitching hay. Annie gazed at his arms. They were like wood, she thought, like carved, hard oak. . . .

"Got something to say to me?" he asked.

"Oh!" Annie started and blushed. "I just thought I'd come over and say hello. You know what with you being new and all. What's your name?"

"Tobias."

Annie waited for him to ask hers, but he didn't. She went on: "Up from the West Country, are you?"

Tobias looked up for the first time, and smiled. Annie's knees weakened. He had the whitest teeth she'd ever seen.

"I am."

"You can hear it in your voice, it's like cream and honey," Annie fluttered, then blushed as she heard herself.

Tobias's smile broadened and he set the hayfork to one side. He brushed the hay from his hands and walked unhurriedly toward her. Annie felt her face turning bright red. She couldn't stop staring at him. His skin was the same golden color as the hay.

"Just a social call, is it?"

"Y—yes." Her voice had gone squeaky; she hastily brought it down. "Yes." Too low, she sounded like a man. She swallowed and started again. "Some of us are going to the fair this evening and I just wondered, I thought maybe, since you're new—" This was all going wrong. "If you'd like to come with us?" Her voice ended up squeaky again.

"I see." He was standing so close to her that she could smell the clean sweat on him. "That's a kind offer . . ."

"Annie."

"Annie, of course. Only I won't be taking you up on it."

Annie fell silent in disappointment. Tobias nodded toward a beam, where Annie now saw a photograph of a young lady that had been propped against a nail. Annie took it in at one glance; the elegant clothes, the gloves, the feathered hat, the large dark eyes, the small mouth parted in a smile to show teeth as white as the pearls on Lady Edith's best brooch . . . and the complete absence of a maid's uniform.

"See her? This is my young lady," Tobias announced. "She works in the haberdasher's in the village. Miss Sadie Billesley is her name."

Annie made no answer, but she had the feeling that someone had upset a jug of iced water in her insides.

"I'll be going to the fair with her. So can you think of any reason why I might go with a servant instead?" Tobias looked Annie up and down, and Annie was conscious as never before of her work-hardened hands, her ugly uniform, and the scent of the kitchen that hung about her. How could she compete with a young lady who worked in a shop, who was allowed to wear scent and jewelry and got called "miss" by the customers?

Annie was frozen for a second. Then she turned and fled. Her face was burning with mortification as she ran across the courtyard, back to the kitchen. Right now, being a servant felt like the worst thing in the world.

She slunk back into the kitchen, rubbing the tears from her eyes with the back of her hand. She hoped she could get through without anyone noticing and making fun of her. Luckily Martha was gutting fish at the sink and wasn't watching her. She edged past Sarah, the second housemaid, who was drinking her tea, toward the door to the servants' corridor. Before she reached it, it swung open and Thomas strode in with the post.

"Letter for you, Annie," he announced, tossing the envelope at her. Annie just caught it.

"For me?" The shock dried up her tears. No one wrote to her. Why would they? She couldn't read. She could, however, make out her own name at the top of the address. Thomas was right.

Annie stared at the letter in astonishment. A thousand wild fancies hovered in her head like specks of flour in the sunbeams. Maybe some long-lost relative had died and left her a fortune. Maybe some visiting duke had seen her and fallen in love. Maybe—

The bell shrilled out.

"Oh, I hate that noise!" she exclaimed.

"I'll go." Sarah put down her tea and jumped up. "You read your letter, Annie. It's not every day you get one of those."

"Thank you." Annie felt embarrassed. She didn't care to show that she couldn't read. She hesitated, then remembered. Priya, the nursemaid. She loved reading, and she wouldn't tell tales. Annie, full of excitement, ran out of the kitchen and up the servants' stairs to the nursery.

She found Priya standing by the crib, folding nappies while Augustus played on his rocking horse. Priya swung round, her eyes wide and scared, as Annie came in.

"You're jumpy," Annie laughed. "Got a guilty conscience?" She ran over to Priya. "I got a letter, look! It's addressed to me with a stamp and everything."

"That's wonderful!" Priya took it. "But what do you want me to do with it?"

Annie blushed. She hadn't thought to be embarrassed by asking Priya to read her letter, but now she realized how foolish she must look, asking for help from the Indian nursemaid. Typical housemaid, no education and no chance of a better life. Not like Miss Sadie Billesley. "Read it to me. I never had chance to get my ABC. Not that I need it." She tossed her head. "No time to waste on novels."

"Of course I'll read it for you," Priya said with a kind expression that only made Annie's face grow warmer. She opened the letter and scanned it. "It's from Rose!" she exclaimed.

"Rose!" Annie was startled and pleased. She hadn't expected Rose to write, not now that she was a fine lady. "What does she say?"

"That she misses you, and it's so busy down in London that she hasn't a moment to herself, but she thinks of the time you used to work together and she hasn't forgotten you, and she hopes you haven't forgotten her. And she sends her affectionate wishes to all." Priya smiled. "That's lovely, isn't it?"

"Rose was always kind," said Annie. She felt warm inside, and somehow her aching knees and hands didn't seem so bad . . . but then she caught a glimpse of herself in the mirror above the mantelpiece. Rose would be a fine lady now, all silks and satins and feathers and jewels. And here was she, drab and plain in her uniform, and no hope of going anywhere but up and down the stairs, up and down, up and down.

"Thank you, Priya." Annie took the letter back. "If I can do anything to help you, just ask."

"I . . ." Priya hesitated, then took a deep breath. "I did want to ask you if . . . never mind. It doesn't matter."

Now Annie was curious. "What?" She leaned in closer and lowered her voice. "Priya, you can ask me anything."

Priya looked terrified, but she took another breath and started again. "Well, have you ever found Sir William to be . . . to try and take liberties with you?"

Annie looked at her in shock. Priya was blushing, her thick eyelashes swept down to hide the expression in her eyes. Annie's shock turned to irritation. Did this girl really think she had caught the eye of the Earl of Westlake's heir? Did *everyone* in this house have delusions of grandeur?

"No," Annie said, drawing herself up. "And I can't imagine he would have any interest in . . . 'taking liberties,' as you say, with someone like *you*. I hope you haven't set your sights on him."

"No, I—"

"I mean, why would Sir William lower himself?" Annie went on, feeling more and more resentful as she spoke. "You ought to be grateful he's kind to you—grateful for all this family has done for you. After all," she sniffed, "think where you'd still be if they hadn't brought you to England with them."

She swept to the door. Priya might have her large soft eyes and her slim waist, but she, Annie, had moral dignity. The curate's sermon from last Sunday echoed in her ears: *Bless the squire and his relations, and always keep our proper stations.* Poor Priya, she thought as she went down the servants' stairs. If only she had had the advantages of being born in a Christian country, she would know that.

CHAPTER
Ten

London

Rose looked out of the window of Lord Westlake's motorcar as the chauffeur brought them to a halt before the entrance to Buckingham Palace. Liveried footmen as tall and solid as British oaks framed the grand doors. One of them, gold buttons glinting, stepped forward smartly to open the motorcar door. Rose gathered her skirts, and with a nervous glance at Ada, who sat beside her, stepped out. At once she was glad of her fur-lined opera cloak's soft hug. Even though it was a pleasant May evening, her ball dress was so delicate that the slightest breeze made her feel as if she were naked.

"I don't want to be covered in jewels as if I were a table at Garrard," she had begged Céline a week ago. "Please, find me something simple to wear."

"My lady, it is a state ball." Céline looked worried.

"And everyone there will know that I was once a housemaid. I don't want to give them more reason to mock." She had smiled at Céline in the mirror. "I place myself in your hands."

As she stepped from the motorcar, she hoped she had been right to trust her. She clutched the cloak around her, her heart sinking as she thought of the moment she would have to remove it. No matter how Céline had tried to convince her that the sapphire-blue silk was *meant to* hug and reveal her curves, that it was the fashion to have nothing but velvet ribbons skimming her bare shoulders, she couldn't help imagining her mother's face if she saw her in such a dress. Ugly as they were, at this moment Rose would far rather have been wearing a maid's uniform. It was as good as a cloak of invisibility.

She followed her father and the countess up the stairs to the palace. A blaze of electric light and the more muted, subtle tones of candles seemed to unroll a glowing carpet of gold for them to walk on. Ladies in their shimmering ball gowns, light turning their diamonds to fire, and gentlemen in top hats and tails as glossy black as their ebony canes were walking up the stairs, chatting and laughing. Rose thought it looked like the fairy tales she had been told as a child, the enchanted world under the mountain that enticed in travelers to dance and dance . . . and then wake in the cold dawn to a world changed beyond belief. She shivered, and quickly followed her family into the entrance hall. She swept into her curtsy to Queen Mary as elegantly as she knew how, and allowed the tide to pull her on into the ballroom.

At Somerton

Ahead of her, Lord Westlake said to his wife in an undertone, "I hope to see Rose dancing tonight, my dear."

Rose knew that the polite words masked a bitter conflict. The countess resented having to accompany her husband's illegitimate daughter, child of his housekeeper.

"Of course," the countess replied, raising her eyebrows as if surprised at the comment. "If anyone asks her, she is welcome to dance."

Rose knew that was the end of it. The countess always made sure to keep her out of the way of any dance partners. She sighed as the countess led them toward the chairs where Lady Gertrude and Lady Cynthia were already sitting with their chaperones. The orchestra was in full swing, but it was hard to enjoy the music, knowing that she wouldn't be dancing.

Ada slipped a hand under her arm as they went. "You must promise me you won't hang back tonight, Rose," Ada said softly. "You have as much right as anyone to be here. You are an Averley."

Rose smiled back, thinking how beautiful her sister looked. Her dress was shell-pink net over cloudy-gray silk, and pink pearls edged the neckline and the hem giving it a languorous, sensual weight. A diamond star nestled in her hair.

"I will try," she replied. Ahead of them the crowd parted to reveal the glistening sweep of the dance floor, couples moving back and forth across it like blossoms swaying in the wind.

Before Ada could answer, Fintan came up to them, smiling, and Rose knew that was the end of their private conversation for the evening.

"Will you dance, Ada?" he said.

Ada glanced at Rose, who quickly said, "Please do, I will be quite safe here."

"I—" Ada hesitated.

Rose mustered up her brightest smile and urged Ada toward Fintan. "Please, I wouldn't be happy if you sat out on my behalf," she said firmly, and turned away to join Charlotte, Gertrude, and Cynthia on the chairs.

Ada gave Rose a reassuring smile as they moved away, elegantly gliding as if on water.

Rose sat down, aware that the women were staring at her.

"Such an interesting dress," Lady Gertrude remarked, addressing her directly for the first time. Rose knew that *interesting* was no compliment. She glanced surreptitiously around, noting the other debutantes' dresses. Her heart sank. All were in pastels, soft and muted. The blue she had thought so beautiful in the haberdasher's, the shade of a painting of the Mediterranean sea she had once seen hanging on the drawing room wall at Somerton—and, according to Céline, the precise shade of her eyes—seemed to glow in contrast.

Rose felt the color flow into her cheeks.

"Yes, quite unconventional." Lady Cynthia covered a smile with her fan.

Rose tried to twitch the opera cloak over the velvet ribbons that were all that covered her shoulders. Others around them were staring and whispering. How could Céline have let her pick out that color? She should have realized there was a way to do things, and that to be different would only result in more ridicule.

"Rose *is*, though, isn't she?" Charlotte yawned.

Lady Emily twitched her fan like a cat twitching its tail. "I think it's delightfully daring," she murmured. Rose gave her a grateful glance, but Emily was looking over her shoulder, toward the crowd.

A moment later Lady Cynthia hissed, "There he is!"

Rose didn't have to look around to know who she was talking about. There was only one man who could make Lady Cynthia sound quite so much like an excitable viper. Charlotte snapped open her Spanish fan, and held it before her face, eyes moving above it to follow the Duke of Huntleigh as he crossed the room—mothers sticking to him like burrs to a jacket.

"Oh, do look, how unfair, Ethel Berridge is practically glued to his arm," whispered Lady Gertrude to Lady Cynthia.

"It's simply exasperating—oh, there goes the countess. She'll shake her off."

"And bring him over here, I hope."

Indeed, Rose saw that the countess had managed to detach the tenacious Ethel Berridge and was coming toward them with the force and determination of a jockey heading for the Grand National finish. The duke, though a head taller than she was, had no chance of resisting. He looked thoroughly annoyed. Suddenly Rose found herself in his gaze, and, taken by surprise, did not instantly look away. It could only have been a second in which their eyes met, but she felt heat touch her cheeks as if as if tinder had met flint.

Rose looked away swiftly. She hadn't meant to draw his

attention, and she was annoyed that she had done so. Now the story of the housemaid turned lady would scamper around the ballroom once again—only this time it would be of the house-maid turned fortune hunter.

"Charlotte!" the countess announced as she reached them. She was glowing with sapphires and self-satisfaction. "Alexander left our little party so quickly that I hadn't the chance to bring you together. But of course you remember each other. Alexander, I'm sure you know Lady Gertude, Lady Emily, Lady Cynthia—and this is Lady Rose."

Rose looked down with a wry smile while Lady Gertrude and Lady Cynthia twittered greetings. The countess might as well have inserted the word *unfortunately* in front of her name. She looked up and was disconcerted to see that he was still look-ing at her and would have seen her smile. He, on the other hand, looked as likely to smile as Buckingham Palace itself. She quickly glanced down again, playing with the tassel on her fan. A man with no sense of humor, how dull, she thought. But his eyes were deep green, dappled with gold like a sunlit forest.

"I must congratulate you on your recent marriage, Lady Westlake," the duke said. His voice was low and serious. His eyes fell on Charlotte, and his momentary look of confusion was quickly replaced by composure. "And of course I remember Charlotte very well."

"Yes, our first season was delightful, wasn't it?" Charlotte's eyes sparkled from behind her fan. "I particularly remember that Saturday-to-Monday at Gravelley Park—they have such a fine collection of Oriental vases. I did enjoy sketching them."

Rose was startled enough to look up from her fan. Charlotte, she was sure, would not notice an Oriental vase unless one hit her on the head. But Charlotte looked perfectly innocent, smiling sweetly at the duke.

"They certainly do," he replied with an answering smile. "Lord Fintan's home is delightful."

"It's such a pity he doesn't invite you more frequently. But then Laurence is a peacock who likes the stage to himself."

"Do you think we are rivals?" He glanced back at the floor where Fintan and Ada danced, gazing into each other's eyes.

"I think you were once." Charlotte's tone was almost flirtatious. Lady Gertude and Lady Cynthia exchanged glances.

The duke looked at her blankly, then, with a hint of embarrassment, said: "I must admit that my last London season is a . . . little hazy in my memory."

"Oh, I remember it very well." Charlotte smiled behind her fan, her eyes sparkling.

"Indeed?"

Rose was amused to hear the duke sounding quite nervous. He looked over Charlotte's shoulder, directly at Rose. Before she could do anything but blush and wish she were elsewhere, he said, "Lady Rose, are you engaged for this dance?"

There was an outraged rustle as all the women swung to face Rose. Rose found herself speared on at least three fierce gazes.

"Oh, *Lady* Rose doesn't *dance*," Lady Gertrude said with a high-pitched giggle.

"No?" The duke did not look away from Rose's face.

"No indeed. She has rather more practical accomplishments." Lady Cynthia fluttered her fan.

For the first time Rose had seen him, the duke looked intrigued. "I see. Are you political, Lady Rose? Is this a protest against the patriarchy of ballroom conventions? I'll agree it's unfair that the ladies have to wait to be picked."

The countess placed a hand on his arm. "Alexander," she said softly, "it would be kinder not to tease her. You can see how embarrassed she is by your attention—"

Rose found herself furious. She did not want to dance with the duke. It would only draw eyes to her. But she most certainly would not be told by the countess who she was allowed to dance with. Besides, hadn't Ada said it? She was as good as anyone there. She could dance with anyone who asked her. She clutched Ada's words to her like a lucky charm.

"Lady Gertrude is sadly misinformed," she said shortly. "I should be delighted to dance with you." She could feel the furious gazes of every woman upon her, cold and hard as diamonds. *You expect me to try to snare him,* she thought. *Well, I'll show you that even though I'm a housemaid, I have pride.* No one will be able to call me a fortune hunter. I shall dance with him, but I shan't speak to him, let alone flirt. But I shall have one dance, at least, this season.

She caught up her train and took the hand the duke extended. He raised one dark eyebrow, an ironic humor in his eyes, and swept Rose onto the dance floor.

CHAPTER
Eleven

Ada allowed Laurence to steer her across the dance floor. He was an assertive partner, and if only she could conquer the slight irritation she always felt at being led, it would have been delightful to dance with him.

"Happy, darling?" He broke the silence, looking keenly into her face.

Ada was slightly taken aback. It was not often that he enquired about her feelings, and she hesitated. Was she happy? Not without Ravi—not with an ocean separating them—but she had known right from the beginning that all that was impossible. She remembered the first night they had met, their first kiss. It had been on the boat back from India, the stars had been sharp and clear overhead as he drew her close. She had been so full of grand ideas, so naïve and innocent. Ravi had destroyed her illusions about India, but he had replaced them with something better—truth. He was the only man she had ever known who had treated her not as a lady, nor as a woman, but as an equal. In the few months they spent together, he had rewritten her heart. Even though she had neither seen nor heard from him for months, if she closed her eyes she could still imagine herself in his arms, not Laurence's.

"You certainly look happy," said Laurence. She opened her eyes with a start. Laurence was looking down at her, smiling. "Indeed," he went on, "I don't think I've ever seen you more beautiful than in this moment."

She blushed under his gaze, startled to realize that her heart was beating faster. She scolded herself for thinking of Ravi. She had told herself a long time ago that it was useless to think of him: too painful to remember the times they had kissed, the way he had made her feel. It was best to put those feelings away, to think instead of things that were in her power to do, things that could make a difference to her family and her country. Things like marrying Laurence.

Hastily she said, "What a crush tonight. I should think the whole of London is here."

"And they are all looking at us," he replied.

"Are they?"

"Of course." He reversed, smoothly gliding her past the orchestra. "They're saying what a well-matched couple we are."

"I suppose they are." She smiled at him.

"Do you agree with them?" His gaze did not leave her face, and she had a slight, uncomfortable desire to blink.

Dear Laurence, she thought. He wants me to love him so much. The thought twisted a guilty knife in her heart. No matter what she felt for Ravi, it would be inexcusable to allow Laurence to suspect that she might have cared for someone other than him. He did not deserve that.

"Of course," she said, and her voice was warm, and she drew closer to him. She breathed in the scent of his cologne and clean muslin. He smiled. There was no denying that he was very handsome. And he was in high spirits tonight. Maybe now was a good time to ask a question that had been nagging at her for some time. "Laurence," she began. "I've been wondering where exactly you stand on the Irish question. Your speeches—"

"Ada, please." His voice was pained. "Not tonight. Let's just enjoy ourselves, shall we? Like any other couple in love."

Abruptly he stopped dancing and drew her after him, off the dance floor, toward the open French windows that looked out over the gardens of St. James'. She followed him, but hesitated when he stepped outside into the warm night.

He turned back to smile at her.

"We *are* engaged," he said teasingly, stretching out an inviting hand.

Ada followed him out into the gardens. She crossed her arms, though it was not cold; the thin fabric of her ball gown shuddered in the breeze. Laurence led her out into the darkness, his shirtfront and cuffs shining white in the light from the ballroom.

When we're married, she thought, we'll be alone like this together all the time. Forever.

"We should go back," she said. "Rose—"

"Rose can take care of herself." His voice was low and seductive. He took her in, his gaze raking over her low neckline and the glittering diamonds at her throat. Wrapping an arm around her waist, he pulled her close to him. "I want tonight to be about us and us only."

Gently he took her face between his hands and kissed her. Aware that no one could see them in the shadows, she pressed closer, melting into him. The kiss deepened, and she felt his hands upon her waist, with nothing but the thin silk of her gown between them. She had never been kissed with such desperation. His kisses moved across her cheek, down her neck—and she pulled away, breathing fast, trembling.

"Engaged, Laurence, not married," she said, with an unsteady laugh. But her heart was beating fast, her face was flushed, and she had to admit that even though he was not Ravi . . .

"In love," he said, pulling her back to him. This time she met his lips boldly and as they kissed, she felt herself weaken and soften, whirled away like a leaf on a wild river.

"You mustn't keep me waiting." His voice was rough and tender at the same time, as he murmured in her ear. "When shall we be married?"

She felt a catch in her throat, and suddenly the passion was gone. This was too real.

"It depends upon my father," she said, drawing away.

"I'm not marrying *him*. Ada, when? Let's set a date. We can announce it tonight—"

"No," she said hastily. "That is, I—it's so soon. It feels as if we're moving so fast." Her voice shook. She rambled on. "It's Rose's first season. I want to be there for her. There are so many considerations—I don't think—I can't be sure."

She pulled away from him and walked back to the ball-room, sparing a single glance back at her betrothed. His face was obscured by the shadows, and she could not read his emotions. She wished she could at least read her own.

CHAPTER
Twelve

The duke was an excellent dancer. Rose realized this in a second, with relief. She had had dancing lessons all through the spring, but with so little practice during the season she had forgotten most of what she had learned.

Yet there was an awkward silence. Rose was beginning to feel a little abashed. She had expected the usual well-bred yawns about the weather, Cowes, and Goodwood. Either that, or—with the duke's reputation—an actual assault on her honor. Neither of these were forthcoming, and she was beginning to feel a little embarrassed for dancing with him out of pure bravado. Not such a fierce lion after all, she thought. Her thoughts drifted, as usual, to the unseen people in the room. The footmen standing silently at the doors, uncomplaining about their aching feet, the hidden army of lady's maids in the cloakrooms, waiting to dart into action should a lace petal fall from a hem. And for every lady, a maid waiting up, yawning, till her mistress deigned to come home; for every gentleman a valet doing the same. The queue of chauffeurs smoking outside. And then the cleaning, the dusting, the polishing, the—

"What are you thinking?" the duke said. His eyes were fixed on her face, sober and curious.

It was so unexpected. Not in half a season had she ever been asked that question. Before she had an instant to think she had answered, readily, "I was thinking those mirrors must be the very devil to clean."

She heard her own words with the most mortified shock. Color rushed into her face and she felt dizzy with horror. The duke burst out laughing. How could she have said that? How could she have exposed herself so horribly?

"B-but it's true!" she gabbled, hardly knowing what she was saying, simply feeling that she had to defend herself. "Look at that old man leaning against them. They pick up fingerprints like you wouldn't believe and some poor girl will be up all night scrubbing them."

He was still laughing. Heads turned as they passed to swing around at the top of the room, and the music swept them away again. Rose felt tears of embarrassment and anger start to her eyes. How dare he laugh? So many people's hard work had gone into creating this ball. Now she didn't care what he thought of her. She jerked her hands away from him; he misstepped and nearly tripped them into the path of the next couple. Rose tried to push him away but he held her wrists, his shoulders shaking with laughter.

"Have you any idea how much our supper cost?" she snapped. "And how much a housemaid earns? And how—"

"Some idea, yes." His green eyes were dancing. But he was *really* laughing. Not sneering. "You're quite right, of course, this entire event is ridiculous."

Rose felt as if her weapons had been tweaked out of her hands. "But . . ." she began. "I—" There really wasn't anything to do except agree with him.

He went on, with relish, "It's utterly decadent, entirely foolish, silly, destructive, idiotic, charmless—"

"Not charmless," she objected, with a small smile. "Did you not see Lady Gertrude's Brussels lace gloves? I've been informed that they add enough charm to the room to make up even for my appearance."

"Vapid, vicious—"

"No, no, not vicious." She shook her head at him solemnly, glancing around at the glittering crowds. "It's *fun*."

"In its way." His gaze skimmed the room. "But I sometimes wonder how long it can all go on."

"I think till four o'clock in the morning at least," Rose said unhappily. She caught his eye and they both started laughing again. "That's not what you meant, was it?"

"No, it wasn't," he said, steering her away from a nearby couple. "And you're right, it is fun. At least, it is now." He smiled down at Rose and, to her horror, she felt herself blush. "And I'm sorry for my melancholy outlook," he continued. "I shouldn't be casting a pall over the season."

"I forgot, your father died," Rose said. "I'm very sorry."

"Thank you," he said formally. They danced on in silence. Rose winced. How could she have put her foot in it so badly?

"At least he died in his bed," he added a second later. "He must be the first Huntleigh in centuries not to have been killed in battle. Bannockburn, Edgehill, Waterloo . . ." He grinned. "It's a sad sort of life, brought up with faces much like your own glooming down at you from dusty portraits, seeming to say, *Your turn next*. It's hard to escape your past."

Rose was silent. It was a shock to hear her own thoughts put into words.

He glanced down at her uncertainly.

"I—I'm being poetical, I'm afraid." He was *apologizing*. He thought she disapproved of him! "At least that's what Laurence always used to accuse me of. A great sin in his eyes."

"You know Lord Fintan well?" Rose glanced around, but she could see Ada and her fiancé nowhere.

"We were in the same year at Eton."

"Are you really rivals?"

"Oh, hardly. Laurence was always interested in politics, and I have no desire to go into the House." He smiled. "We have never really cared about the same things."

"Well, I like poetry," she said firmly.

He smiled. "I'm glad to hear it. But still, I shouldn't let my ancestry weigh on my spirits. After all, they had to die some way or other. Strawberry leaves are not the fruit of immortality, no matter what the Countess of Westlake thinks."

It took Rose a moment to realize he was joking, and then she laughed aloud. Heads turned. Rose quickly covered her mouth. She could see the countess glaring at her from the crowd.

"I must learn to laugh more discreetly," she said when she had recovered herself.

"No, please don't." His eyes shone as he looked at her. "We don't hear much laughter during the season. Not real laughter. Yours makes me feel—" He broke off, frowning. "I don't have a very good reputation, you know," he said gloomily.

Rose laughed again. It was impossible not to like him. He was such an odd mixture—droll and melancholy by turns. "You have a *terrible* reputation," she replied. "But no one seems to mind."

His mouth twitched again. "The Duke of Huntleigh is much in demand." He smiled. "But I sense not by you."

"Not in the least," she said firmly. It was best to establish that at once, she thought. She wouldn't give him any excuse to say she had flirted with him.

"I don't blame you." They were moving toward the crowd as the music slowed. "The Duke of Huntleigh is a dull chap."

He steered her forward. She was a little dizzy, and he steadied her, holding her close for an instant.

"Alexander Ross, though," he said, warm and soft in her ear. "I flatter myself you might get to like *him*."

Rose felt herself flush and could not stop the smile that

warmed her face. She wasn't sure if it was his words or the fact that his lips were so close to her ear. She felt the soft pressure of his body against hers. She had a wild, insane desire to sink into his arms. But instead she stepped away from him, breathing fast. Everyone was looking at them, she realized. He was still holding her hand, even though the music had begun again. And she wasn't letting go of his. She wasn't quite sure why.

She glanced toward the French windows. Before them stood Ada and Laurence. It seemed they had just entered. Laurence was frowning, a look on his face as if he had tasted something sour. Ada's expression was tense and anxious. They stood close together but apart, each seemingly lost in their own thoughts.

"Aren't we engaged for this dance, Alexander?" A voice disturbed Rose, and she turned to see Charlotte smiling as she raised her dance card. "I nearly forgot, I was so busy admiring that wonderful portrait in the corner. The Italians have such a gift for character."

The duke started and released Rose's hand. "We are." He bowed over Charlotte's.

Rose could only step back and watch as Charlotte, still talking enthusiastically about art, sailed away with the duke and was lost on the dance floor.

Chapter Thirteen

Palesbury

"Here." Sebastian Templeton leaned forward to speak through the sliding window as Jackson drove the De Dion–Bouton toward the stone gates of Palesbury Castle Gaol. Jackson obliged by drawing the car to a halt.

Sebastian tried not to look up at the high stone wall as he got out. Visitors from abroad who didn't know what this place was admired the picturesque ivy that grew up the walls. But he knew what it was. A prison.

"Wait for me in the village," he told Jackson.

As he walked toward the stone arch and the great wooden gates, he found himself shuddering. He did not want to see Oliver in here. He wanted this all to be a dream, for none of it to have happened—

At Somerton

"Mr. Templeton, sir!"

Sebastian started. The man who was in front of him—he must have been lurking in the shadows—had a coarse, familiar face, an insolent gaze. His collar was dirty and his coat out of style. He touched his hat briefly and smirked at Sebastian. "*The Daily Truth*, sir. Have your thoughts? Comments on the terrible tragedy, awful crime, depravity of modern society—"

"No," Sebastian said roughly. He pushed the journalist aside and hammered on the wooden door.

"No comments? Wasn't expecting to see you here. Good of you to trouble to look in on your valet. What does your countess mother think of it?"

The man looked him up and down, and Sebastian hammered again. He felt as if he were being crawled over by insects. At last, the window opened, and the turnkey looked out. Sebastian stepped back at the smell of his breath.

"Gerrout of here, you!" the turnkey bawled. Sebastian realized he was talking to the journalist. The man backed away but didn't leave, like a stray dog. Sebastian heard metal clanking and rattling, and the door creaked open. Sebastian hurried inside. He shivered in the cold damp air that met him.

"So sorry for the nuisance." The turnkey was an obsequious little man with rotten teeth and a beer belly. He ushered Sebastian along, the keys at his waist dangling and clanking like some kind of medieval torture instrument. "The prisoner's down here. Very good of you to take so much trouble over him. I've told him he should be grateful—"

"Here?" Sebastian strode ahead, down the stone passage. If one more person told him how good he was being he would scream. "It's very cold," he murmured.

"It is a gaol, sir. Can't have the felons getting off easy." The turnkey chuckled.

Doors creaked open, slammed shut. The metal bones of the keys jangled like witches' teeth. Sebastian had a strange feeling that he was heading deeper into a cave, into one of those old pagan burial sites, with long tunnels leading down deep into cold barrows where steel rusted and bones mouldered. He shuddered.

To either side were bars, and behind some of them were men. Some were silent, others muttered or shouted to themselves.

"It's this one, sir." The turnkey stopped. It was dark and Sebastian hesitated. He could see no one in the cell.

"No need for you to go farther, sir, if it takes you funny," the turnkey said. "It's not a place a gentleman would feel comfortable in."

Sebastian screwed up his courage and strode forward to the bars.

"Oliver?" he said.

For a moment he still could see no one in the shadows, and then his eyes grew used to the gloom and he saw Oliver standing in the center of the cell, arms folded. He looked the same, his dark eyes, his proud face, the hair Sebastian longed to run his fingers through. The only changes were a growth of stubble and the prison clothes that looked like a joke. Sebastian could not stop the smile that flooded over his face. He ran to the bars and Oliver did the same. Sebastian remembered himself enough to turn and say to the turnkey. "You may leave us now."

The man bowed and retreated. Sebastian moved closer to the bars, glad now of the darkness that covered them. His fingers and Oliver's clutched each other through the bars. They did not speak until the turnkey's footsteps had faded away completely and the only sound was the mice scrabbling inside the walls.

"How are you? How is it?" Sebastian whispered. His mouth was dry.

"I've known worse." Oliver smiled, but Sebastian saw the glint of pain in his eyes, and something else—fear.

"You must let me give myself up."

"We've been through all this. I forbid it entirely. You have much more to lose than I do."

"Yes, but I can't stand by and watch you go to court on my account!"

"It'll never come to that," Oliver said confidently. "The barrister will sort it all out—by the way, it was good of you to engage him."

"Don't be ridiculous. I couldn't have done less." Sebastian tightened his grip on Oliver's fingers. "What else can I do for you? Your family—they must want to know where you are."

"Never mind my family."

"But they must be frantic. I can get them here. I'll send Jackson to pick them up."

"Please, leave it."

"It doesn't matter about the cost. I'll pawn my cuff links—"

"I *have* no family!" Oliver almost shouted. His voice rang from the bars. Sebastian was shocked by the fury in it. The scrabbling of mice paused for an instant, then went on again. Oliver's voice softened. "Just you."

Sebastian looked into his eyes. They drew close together, and their lips touched through the bars. Sebastian closed his eyes, aching with the need to pull Oliver closer, remembering a summer lake, cold wine, a time of happiness and freedom before all this insanity had entered his life, a time that felt like a thousand years ago. A single act of violence could be the touchpaper that blew up the ground you stood on.

He heard footsteps approaching and pulled back. Oliver did the same. He backed away into the center of the cell.

"You'd better go," he said. His face was shadowed, but his voice told Sebastian everything he needed to know.

Sebastian pulled his gloves from his pocket and adjusted his hat before turning to the door just as it opened.

"Good afternoon, Mr. Brompton," he said, recognizing the barrister he had retained for Oliver.

"Mr. Templeton!" The barrister's jowly face wore an expression of startled displeasure. "I hadn't expected to see you here, sir."

Sebastian didn't reply immediately. Instead he placed a hand on the man's arm. "You must tell me if there is anything I can do, anything that you might need to make the case go well," he said in a low voice.

"Of course. Of course." Brompton still sounded troubled. He turned to follow Sebastian as he tried to walk on.

"I feel I must say something, sir. It's best for you not to come here."

Sebastian raised an eyebrow.

"There are newspaper men outside. It's become something of a cause célèbre in the gossip papers. You being so concerned about your valet . . . well, it's admirable of course, but it can lead to tittle-tattle." He avoided meeting Sebastian's gaze.

"Tittle-tattle." Sebastian gave a slight, mirthless laugh. "Well, if that's the worst the world can do, let them do it. Oliver's suffering is a lot worse than mine, and I will not cease to do what I can to lessen it."

He turned away before Brompton could reply and followed the turnkey up to the main gates. He hardly noticed the passage this time. He was seething with fury inside, at the world and its prying eyes, at himself and his impotence. Why the hell, he thought, can't everyone just leave other people alone?

He found Jackson and the car in front of Moss Booksellers. The window was filled with a display of a new novel by someone called R. J. Peak. Jackson was reading a copy himself—*A Duke for Daisy* the cover said—and seemed entirely engrossed in it. He jumped when Sebastian tapped his shoulder.

"Sorry, sir!"

"Somerton, please." Sebastian got into the car and settled back into the luxurious leather seats. As they drove away he sat suddenly forward. His brother, Michael, had just come out of the bookseller's, with a package wrapped in brown paper. Odd, he had never thought of the pup as a reader. His mother couldn't even get Michael to return to Eton. Maybe he had picked up the habit to impress some young lady. But Sebastian's thoughts quickly returned to Oliver and the storm of troubles headed their way.

CHAPTER
Fourteen

Somerton

"Thank you so much, Mrs. Grundy. We will be sure to let you know our decision as soon as we can."

Georgiana closed the door of the housekeeper's room after the latest applicant for Mrs. Cliffe's position, and turned to Mrs. Cliffe, who sat at the desk with her notes before her.

"Oh, my goodness," Georgiana said as soon as she was sure the woman was well out of hearing. "Did you smell her breath? Pure gin!"

"*Not* one we will be inviting for a second interview," Mrs. Cliffe said with a sigh. She leaned forward and made a cross next to Mrs. Grundy's name.

"I don't know how the agency can think it right to send them." Georgiana put her hands to her forehead, where a headache was beginning to pulse. She had never imagined that interviewing for a housekeeper could be so frustrating and exhausting. She looked around at the comfortable room, and heard the tick of the old clock pulsing like a heartbeat around it. It was impossible to imagine anyone but Mrs. Cliffe sitting here, ruling the household. What would Somerton do without her?

"There is a national servant crisis, I'm afraid, my lady," Mrs. Cliffe said.

"So I hear. I suppose it must be attractive to live in town, but I can't think a dirty, noisy factory a more pleasant place to work than Somerton." She furrowed her brow. "I hope we make things pleasant for the people who work here, Mrs. Cliffe. I certainly try to."

Mrs. Cliffe smiled at her, a warm, motherly smile that comforted Georgiana to the core.

"Everyone here feels lucky to work for the Averleys, my lady. You couldn't ask for more generous employers."

Georgiana smiled gratefully at her. It was nice to feel she was getting it right for once. It was so difficult with Papa and Ada away. Neither William nor Edith seemed to care about the estate, and she had found that if anything was to be done, she had to take charge.

"Thank you, Mrs. Cliffe," she said. "I must go and tell Lady Edith that this one didn't suit either. She won't be happy, but what can one do?"

"Nothing indeed, my lady," Mrs. Cliffe agreed. She followed her to the door, and held it open for her. "Somerton must have an excellent housekeeper, and I certainly will not leave until one is found."

Georgiana stepped out of the door, but hesitated. She turned to Mrs. Cliffe, wanting to express something of her gratitude for the support she had received.

"It will be very hard to replace you," she said. "In every way."

Mrs. Cliffe smiled. "Have no fear. We will find someone capable."

I do hope she is right, thought Georgiana as she hurried through the servants' passage and up the stairs to the green baize door. Or we'd have to manage it all ourselves, and a pretty pickle we should make of it! She felt she was just beginning to realize exactly how much work went into running Somerton. It was quite frightening—and yet it was pleasant to take on such a challenge, to feel, well . . . *needed*. She had been ill for so long, it was a nice change to be able to look after others for once.

As she entered the hall she saw Cooper opening the door to her older stepbrother. "Sebastian," she said in surprise. "I'm glad to see you, but I didn't know you were coming." She faltered, noticing that he looked tired and sad. "Is everything all right?"

"Yes . . ." He handed Cooper his hat and picked up the local newspaper, frowning at the headline before putting it down again and looking at her. "I've come directly from the gaol, that's all."

"Oh . . ." Guiltily Georgiana remembered what must have brought him to the area. "Poor Oliver. Did you see him? How is he?"

"As well as can be expected, I suppose." Sebastian's usually sparkling voice was flat. "If you'll excuse me, I have some letters to write."

"You're staying then?"

"Afraid not. I must go straight back to London. My mother gets restless if I am not at her side for the season."

"Of course." Georgiana followed him with her gaze as he trudged up the stairs to his room. She was touched at the obvious pain he seemed to be in. She turned to Cooper. "Will you see that something hot to eat and drink is sent up to Mr. Templeton?" she asked. "He looks as if he would like it but won't think to ask for it."

"Of course, my lady."

"Do you know how the case is progressing?" Georgiana asked. "It seems such a tragic thing. It must have been an accident, surely."

Cooper inclined his head. "All of us liked Oliver, my lady. An excellent servant and a pleasant young man. None of us imagine him capable of murder. But whether the jury will see things our way . . ."

"Surely they must!" Georgiana exclaimed. "He's so young, and he has an excellent character."

"But there is the matter of the money he was owed. Some might see that as motive."

"I suppose so. . . ." Georgiana sighed. "Well, I feel very sorry for him."

"We all do, my lady." Cooper coughed discreetly as Georgiana was about to move away. She turned back. "I wondered, my lady, whether the person had been found satisfactory."

Georgiana realized he meant the gin-sodden Mrs. Grundy. "Oh, no. I'm afraid not, Cooper."

"It is just that . . ." He lowered his voice. "Some of the staff have been expressing . . . doubts."

"Doubts?" For a confused moment, Georgiana thought he meant religious doubts. "Surely the vicar—"

"About working under Mrs. Cliffe. Now that her history is so widely known, you see . . . They feel it lowers the reputation of the house, that she should continue here. I wondered if it might be possible to remove her to a different location, at least until His Lordship returns—"

"Cooper, that's enough." Georgiana felt her cheeks flush, both with anger on Mrs. Cliffe's behalf and with embarrassment at conversing with a servant on such a subject. "I know you only mean to help, but we must give Mrs. Cliffe all our support at this time. I won't hear a word against her."

Cooper pressed his lips together, frowning. He merely bowed, however, and withdrew. Georgiana watched him walk away, offended dignity in every inch of his bearing. After the first impulse to defend Mrs. Cliffe had died away, she had to admit that he had a point. But the trouble, if there was any, had not entered into the upstairs world, and she had to trust Mrs. Cliffe to look after the downstairs one. It was unfair to meddle in her authority while she still held her position.

CHAPTER
Fifteen

Annie groaned as she looked at the pile of mending that Lady Edith's maid had put up for her. Sometimes she dreamed of it, napkin after napkin, sheet after sheet, shift after shift. It seemed deeply unfair that she should spend her life growing squint eyed and callous fingered and hunchbacked from hours of darning. While other people, just because of who they were born to, waltz at balls with royalty and suchlike.

"I should be enjoying my youth," she sighed. Resentfully she picked up the pile of mending and lugged it to the kitchen.

"How that boy can get through so much linen is beyond me," she complained to Martha, who was hosing down the sink, where she had been gutting a chicken. "He tears everything! There's a devil in that Master Augustus, I'm sure."

"Think yourself lucky," Martha snapped back. "Some of us would give a lot to have a nice clean job like a housemaid's."

"Lucky!" Annie sniffed, picking up the first piece of mending, a napkin. She didn't feel lucky. The white mountain of mending loomed at her. It meant hours of peering at tiny stitches, painstaking, fiddly work that pricked your fingers and left you with work-hardened hands. Not like Miss Sadie Billesley's hands, she thought, and threw the napkin down again.

"Where are you off to?" Martha called after her as she got up and made to leave.

"Breath of fresh air, not that it's any of your business."

Annie went to the back door and breathed in the afternoon air. Why was life so unfair? Why did she never get a chance? She glanced over to the shining motorcar that stood in the middle of the stable yard, the doors open. Why was she never riding in a car like that, instead of standing watching them go past her?

A man came out of the servants' entrance. He carried a trunk and called out behind him, "One more, James."

Annie wondered who he was, then remembered. Mr. Templeton was clearly about to leave. This was his valet.

"Off to London?" James said as he came out with the other suitcase.

"Thanks. Yes, back to London." The valet took it and put into the trunk of the car.

"Wish I was," James said with a short laugh.

He headed back into the house. Annie stood where she was. A thought had struck her like a bolt of lightning: Wish I was.

Her hand closed on Rose's letter in the pocket of her apron. She needn't stay here, needn't resign herself to a life of the same old drudgery and being passed over for better things. She had friends in high places. Why on earth shouldn't she go to London and become Rose's maid?

Her heart soared. She could see it now—the two of them riding off in motorcars to parties and dress fittings. Rose would make the best mistress, she was so kind and generous. It wouldn't be like work at all. It would be like being a lady.

She turned round and whisked back inside. She had enough saved for the train ticket. All she needed to do was hand her notice in, and she'd be away.

CHAPTER
Sixteen

London

Rose had expected to be in ecstasy at her first visit to the Royal Academy of Art's Private View. It was one of the most exclusive events of the London season. An invitation to show at the Academy's summer exhibition was jealously sought by every artist of note. But as she strolled with Sebastian through the halls of Burlington House, past dutiful landscapes and predictable portraits, she could not help but feel it all a little . . . dull.

"The Academy's lost its fire," Sebastian commented, as if he had read her thoughts. "I feel I've seen this all a thousand times over."

"I'm glad you say that. I thought it was just my lack of taste," Rose answered. She glanced around her. She had wondered if she would see Alexander Ross here. Or maybe she had hoped.

Of course, there was no reason he would be visiting at the same time she was. There was no reason to suppose he would visit at all. Young men like him were generally more interested in hunting and punting than in art.

She had danced with him twice more since the state ball and spoken to him in company. Their paths had crossed in the foyer of the opera house and the drawing rooms of important hostesses. This was the season, after all, and it was a small world. The intimacy of their first dance had never been repeated. He danced with other women, talked to other women, laughed with other women. And yet she couldn't help believing that the smile he kept for her was warmer, more genuine, than the ones he gave to other people. More than once she had caught him looking at her, and each time he had smiled as if the sight of her gave him pleasure. It was pleasant, she thought, to have a friendly face among all the unfriendly ones.

"Do look at those women," Sebastian murmured with a gentle wave of his cane toward an elegant group gathered by the work of the latest society portraitist. "More interested in each other's dresses than the pictures." He sighed. "Somehow it all seems so disconnected from what's happening outside the doors. To look at these pictures you'd think we were not living in an age of motorcars and trams and electric light." He lowered his head as if a weight lay on his shoulders. "They don't seem to see that everything has changed."

Rose glanced at him in concern. She sensed he was not his usual self, and knowing where he had been, she could guess why.

"How is Oliver? Did you see him?" she asked. "What does the barrister think of his chances?"

"Not much."

"I'm sorry." She laid a gloved hand on his. "It was such a shock to all of us. Everyone will be sorry if Oliver—"

He interrupted her. "Please, don't say it. The worst thing is, I've been called as a witness for the prosecution."

"That is most distressing, but I suppose if you can help bring to light what actually happened—"

"I know what happened," he snapped. Rose was startled by the passion in his voice. "I know Oliver isn't capable of murder, and I won't go to court to have lawyers try to make me say he is."

Rose looked at his furrowed brow, the weariness etched in every line of his face.

"You are really touched by this, aren't you?" she said softly.

Sebastian nodded.

"Is there anything I can do?"

He shook his head.

"At least—perhaps, yes," he added a moment later. "So much about Oliver doesn't make sense, Rose. There is more to his story than he'll admit, and I think—I hope—there might be clues there that would help us save him."

"He was certainly always very well-spoken for a servant," said Rose, thinking back.

"There is so much about him that is more refined than one would expect. His accent, when he's unguarded, is a long way above his class. And when I asked him about his family he became furious. He said he had none."

"That's dreadful," Rose spoke from the heart, thinking of her own mother. There was not a night she did not go to bed thinking of her and wishing she were nearby.

"If only I could find out the truth about him, there might be something that would get him out of this jam." Sebastian's brows darkened again. "But Rose, if you could ask among the servants at Somerton, find out if anyone knows anything—what his place was before he came here. His references are fakes. I looked them up and challenged him, but he wouldn't tell me a thing."

Rose hesitated. It was not exactly insulting—but it made her color faintly to think that she was still considered a go-between to the downstairs world. It was not exactly tactful to remind her of her origins, and Sebastian seemed to realize that, because he turned on her a look of such pleading desperation that her hurt feelings melted away at once.

"Please, Rose, I don't mean to insult you. If only you knew the state I'm in." He spoke quietly, but she could see from the way he clenched his cane, his knuckles white, that he was not calm.

Rose moved toward him, lowering her voice as she feigned interest in the nearest painting. "Of course I will help. I know Oliver means a great deal to you. It is good of you to look out for him so well."

Sebastian glanced at her, then replied even more quietly. "It is not 'good of me.' I have no choice." His voice was tortured.

"Please, may I tell you something? I don't know—that is, it may be foolish of me—I don't want you to despise me."

"What do you mean?" Rose asked, startled. Sebastian's manner was so strange that she almost wondered if she should call for the attendant, if he were perhaps mad, or even dangerous.

"I can't keep silent. If I don't tell someone, it will kill me."

"Sebastian, what have you done?" Rose was frightened now.

"Nothing that a million haven't done before me. Oliver and I—we—" He paused, struggling for words. "Have you ever met someone and felt at once that you understood each other perfectly? That you had such a deep connection it felt as if you were one soul in two bodies?" There were tears glittering in his eyes now. "I love him, Rose. And I can't let him hang for a crime he didn't commit."

Rose stared at Sebastian. What did he mean? Were he and Oliver related somehow? What—and then she understood. She blushed and could not meet his eyes.

"I—I had no idea." And yet it all made sense now.

"The truth is this. I was . . . entangled with Simon Croker. He was blackmailing me. Of course you know I would do anything to conceal it. Simon attacked me, and Oliver defended me. The fall was an awful accident. But Oliver wanted to protect me, and he confessed before I could stop him." He spoke as if he felt the pain of it even now. "I hope you understand. I'm not a monster."

"Of course you're not. I'll try to understand." Rose hardly knew how to speak to him. She was shocked by the story, moved by Oliver's bravery . . . and yet she felt she ought to be persuading him to abandon his unnatural tendencies. But he was *Sebastian*. He was kind, and good, and he had done nothing that was wrong—except that it was all wrong, of course it was. Every Sunday school lesson, every sermon, everything she had ever heard in whispers and giggles and shocked looks in the servants' passages, told her so. But Somerton seemed so far away and simple and innocent now. He was Sebastian—kind, good, gentle. How could he do wrong just by loving someone?

"I've thought and thought about what to do. I've gone as far as going to the police station, but I never quite have the courage to tell them the truth. My mother . . . there are times when I hate her, but she loves me and I cannot bring that shame down on her head. She has done so much to try and keep my . . . nature a secret."

"She knows, then?" Rose exclaimed.

"She guessed what kind of man I was, perhaps before I did," he said bitterly. "And then there is Charlotte. It is her last season, perhaps. I can't ruin her chances of marriage. And Michael's career would be harmed. He doesn't deserve that. Do you understand? Tell me I'm a cad if you want to. You're probably right."

"No, no, I . . ." Rose shook her head. "It is a terrible situation."

"I won't rest until I can get Oliver free, somehow. I won't let him be sentenced. I'll confess if it comes to that." He looked at her intently. "I need hardly tell you what it would do to me, to your family, if the truth about me came out."

"No, no," Rose exclaimed, feeling almost physical pain. "Of course I will tell no one."

"Thank you." He glanced back at the door just as Rose's stepmother, Ada, and Charlotte entered. The countess raised her hand and gestured imperiously to Sebastian.

"My mother calls." Sebastian made a face and walked toward them. Rose watched him join them as the countess pointed to some small bronzes with her parasol. Rose turned away, noticing a shabby-looking man loitering by the entrance to the next room for the first time. Rose wondered how he had got in, but simply stepped around him and slipped through the door. She was not really unchaperoned, she thought. Her family were nearby. She just needed a few moments to calm herself after Sebastian's news.

She had thought she was no longer in the mood for looking at art, but she saw at once that the paintings in this room were entirely in keeping with the shock of Sebastian's secret. She stepped back to look up at the four vast canvases that filled the walls of the small gallery. Not only did they dwarf in scale everything she had seen so far. They were almost abstract—not quite, that would have been trying the patience of the Academy too far—and the artist's method so bold she could almost feel the force with which the paint had been flung against the canvas. One could not call it anything as conventional as painting, she thought. It was movement, as powerful as the leaps of Nijinsky.

And yet, she thought, as she continued to gaze at them, they were somehow . . . empty. They were storms of passion with no center, no purpose, no object. She frowned, puzzled and disappointed, as she looked from one canvas to the next.

She lowered her gaze and found herself looking into the eyes of the Duke of Huntleigh. For a second she was too startled to speak. He was lounging against the door frame, watching her without smiling. Rose felt her heart flutter under his intense gaze. "Good morning," she said.

"Good morning." He straightened up and came into the room.

Rose tried to meet his gaze, but it was impossible to do so without blushing. "I was just admiring the paintings," she said.

"Do you like them?" He did not sound enthusiastic.

"Don't you?"

"They're all right. A little tame."

"Tame?" she exclaimed. "They're the wildest things in the exhibition."

"That isn't saying much."

She had to laugh. "No, I suppose it isn't. But the vigor, the confidence, the passion . . ."

He raised an eyebrow.

"And yet they're rather sad and empty, don't you think?"

He didn't immediately answer. Rose turned back to the paintings. Perhaps she had been wrong. But everything she saw there confirmed her feeling.

"Yes," she said, nodding. "Yet even for all their power and passion, I feel the artist hasn't found his subject yet. He doesn't know what he wants to paint *about*."

The duke was still silent. Rose wondered if she had said too much. After all, she was hardly an expert on art.

"They are the best things here, though," she said. "They make me feel as if I could write music again."

"You write music?" he asked quickly.

She sighed. "I used to. But there is no silence in this city, especially during the season, and I need silence to hear my music."

He made an impatient movement. "You don't have to stay here if you don't want to."

"But I do. I cannot let my father down, not after all he has done for me. And he wants me to take my place in society."

"Oh, families. How I wish they had never been invented." He added, "Stravinsky's *Rite of Spring* is being performed here in London soon. You should go, if you are interested in music."

"I wish I could, but I am sure the countess will never be persuaded to go to a performance that has been so controversial. She does only what society does, and as a result, so must we. Sometimes I feel that society is the only living thing in London, and we are just its fodder." She stopped, surprised by how far she had gone. She met his eyes.

"You have a strange knack of encouraging me to say things I didn't know I felt until I have said them," she said with a small laugh.

He gave a slight bow. "You're wrong," he said. Rose raised an eyebrow. "Society is just a machine, like a locomotive that needs feeding. You're alive. You're truly alive because you are a creator."

Rose's breath felt thin and quick, as if she were standing on top of a mountain. This was a very different conversation from any she had had with Huntleigh before—indeed, a very different conversation than any she had ever had with *anyone* before. It was so strange, she thought, that the person to whom she felt closest, the one who seemed to understand perfectly how she felt at every moment, was the one most removed from her in birth and breeding. She couldn't help but think of what Sebastian had just described to her—an understanding between two people deeper than anything that could be put into words. She managed to reply. "So only those who have the leisure to create are alive? I can't think that's fair."

"I don't mean just symphonies or landscapes. Anyone who works creatively." He moved closer, his moss-green eyes taking her in. "There's a dignity in every kind of labor—except service. No servant could ever be creative. When one is not free, one cannot create."

Rose was a little surprised by the blunt way he spoke about servants, but she was pleased that he didn't feel the need to conceal his feelings before her. She opened her mouth to contradict him, to say that she had begun composing as a housemaid herself, but at that moment something else caught her attention. Over the duke's shoulder she could see that Ada and Charlotte had entered the room. Both were watching her. Ada looked troubled. Charlotte looked angry. Rose felt self-conscious, but some defiant spark in her made her stay where she was.

"Rose." The countess stepped into the doorway behind Charlotte and Ada, smiling frostily. "I'm so glad to have found you. We were worried you'd wandered off and become lost," she said. "Ah— Your Grace!" she exclaimed, pretending to notice Alexander for the first time. "How perfect. Charlotte and I were just saying we would be so grateful for your opinion on some of these charming bronzes. I know you're quite a collector yourself."

"I'd be delighted," he replied smoothly. With a nod to Rose, he walked away toward the countess.

Rose turned back to the paintings, feeling a little embarrassed at Ada's searching gaze. The name of the artist was discreetly placed on the gilt frames. She drew closer to one and looked at it: Alexander Ross, Fifth Duke of Huntleigh.

Rose stood as still as if she had just glimpsed the head of a Gorgon. The thoughtless words with which she had criticized the paintings—told him that they were sad, empty, that he didn't know what he was painting about—flashed back into her mind. She put her hands to her cheeks, which were flaming with mortification. Oh, why didn't I look at the frame before I spoke to him! Why! she thought.

Chapter
Seventeen

It was raining as they came back from the exhibition, a spring shower that only seemed to make the sun that followed sparkle more brightly. None of it was any comfort to Rose. She had sat in total silence the whole way back, now and then burning with embarrassment as she remembered her awful faux pas. They had been getting on so well—and she had ruined it. Again and again she remembered the unsmiling expression on his face. No wonder! He had been too tactful to reply—he was as well-bred as Ada in that sense—but he must have been furious with her. As if I knew anything about art anyway! she scolded herself. She sank into her seat, miserable to her core. He must think me so pretentious, a housemaid talking about things she doesn't understand.

"It really is time that you put it on an official footing," the countess said to Ada as the cab turned into the square, their horse trotting smartly through the puddles. The feathers on the countess's hat nodded sharply.

"There's no rush," Ada replied.

"There is every rush. There are a thousand things to organize. The trousseau must be ordered, the banns published, the invitations printed and sent—my goodness, these days a society wedding is like a military campaign!" The cab drew to a halt before Milborough House, and the countess waited with impatience for the coachman to get down and open the door of the cab. Stepping down onto the pavement, she added, "People are beginning to ask questions, and that is never a good sign. You need to secure Lord Fintan, before he changes his mind."

"If he's so prone to change his mind, perhaps I shouldn't be marrying him," Ada said dryly.

"That joke was in extremely poor taste," the countess snapped. She paused to speak to the footman. "About this evening's engagements . . ."

Rose, Ada, and Charlotte walked on to the house.

"Well?" Charlotte quietly said to Rose, as they reached the porch. "What did the famous duke have to say?"

Rose was aware of the blush in her cheeks and of Ada's troubled gaze. She shook the rain from her umbrella, scattering diamond drops onto the street.

"We talked about art," she said lightly.

"And did he engage you for the next ball?" Charlotte's voice was flint.

Rose was saved from replying as the countess reached them. No, he didn't, she thought, and he probably never will again.

"It is possible to speak to a man just in a friendly way, you know," she said quietly, "without any thought of dancing with him or—or marrying him."

She walked in, but she couldn't escape Charlotte's hissed reply. "Not during the season, my dear."

The butler—Sanders, she remembered, was his name—inclined his head toward her as she removed her hat in front of the mirror.

"There is a person to see you, my lady." His voice carried just a touch of disapproval.

"A person?" Rose paused in the act of removing her hat pin and met his gaze, startled.

"I requested that she wait in the kitchen. Her name is Annie Bailey."

"Annie!" Rose was stunned. She glanced around swiftly, but her sisters and the countess had gone upstairs. What was Annie doing here, so far from Somerton? Had something terrible happened—perhaps to her mother. . . .

"I'll go down at once," she managed. She crossed the hall with hasty steps, only pausing when she realized she did not know which of the doors led to the servants' passages. Thankfully Sanders was just behind her, and smoothly guided her to the correct one.

Rose had never been into the servants' quarters at Milborough House before. The smell was the same as at Somerton—stale cooking and carbolic soap. She inhaled deeply as she went down the bare stairs. This was all so familiar, almost frighteningly so. She hurried on to the kitchen. There, at the big oak table, before a backdrop of the ovens and the gleaming copper pans, sat Annie in her best hat and only coat. She looked nervous, but the instant their eyes met, Rose could not stop the smile that broke over her face. Annie looked relieved, and then beamed herself, jumping to her feet.

"Rose!"

They ran into each other's arms. Rose hugged her friend, then stood back, smiling at her. Annie's expression as she looked her up and down made her feel a little uncomfortable. It was so admiring that Rose had to accept that she had changed.

"Annie! What a delight to see you, and what a surprise! But why—has anything happened?"

"No, no. Don't worry. I left everyone well and as usual." Annie tossed her head as if she were shaking Somerton off. "Look at you! What a fine lady you've become. Do me a twirl, go on."

Rose, embarrassed but pleased, did a twirl. Annie clapped her hands. "Oh, don't you look fine! This is going to be so much fun, Rose. I can't believe I didn't think of it earlier."

"Think of what?" Rose was aware of Sanders still watching them from the passage, and she found herself feeling a little uncomfortable. "Why are you here, Annie?"

"To be your lady's maid, of course!" Annie beamed. "I can't believe I didn't think of it earlier." Rose gazed wordlessly at Annie's smiling, happy, confident face. "You and me, Rose, we've always been friends." Annie ran on. "We'll have even more fun now you're a lady! You'll be able to help me make my way in society. I'm sure I can manage your frocks as well as any Frenchy. And you did say you missed me. . . ." She trailed off, a little uncertain.

It was impossible. Rose knew that, and she also knew as certainly that she could not say so to Annie, not now, not to her face.

"It's a good idea," she said, clasping Annie by the shoulders and speaking with all the genuine affection she felt for her. "It may be a little tricky to—but never mind, we'll think about all that later. I must go upstairs now. The countess will be wondering where I am, and we don't want her to find you here."

Annie turned slightly pale. Rose felt mean for having scared her, but it was important that Annie didn't go wandering around upstairs, getting herself into even more trouble. She had to make sure Annie still had a place to go back to at Somerton, and the best way was to keep this all very quiet indeed.

"I handed in my notice," Annie said bravely. "I did it to Lady Georgiana, to her face. I said I wasn't prepared to work below my station anymore, and I had a better offer."

Rose took a deep breath. "Well, that's . . . well, I know you can do anything you set your mind to, Annie." *And I'll help you to,* she thought, *only not like this.* She turned to the door. "Sanders."

"My lady." The butler came into view in the shadowy passage. Rose saw how Annie look startled at the authority with which she addressed him. No, Annie had not thought this through, not at all.

"Please arrange somewhere for Miss Bailey to sleep," she

said. She knew that would please Annie, being called Miss Bailey. "She will be staying here until further notice."

"Very good, my lady." The butler sounded doubtful. "Er . . . will it be upstairs or, er . . ."

"Oh, I'm quite ready to stay in the servants' quarters!" Annie said, and Rose could hear she was nervous and a little frightened. What on earth could she do? she wondered. How could she manage the situation?

As she walked back up the servants' stairs, the smell of carbolic soap and Annie's sudden appearance made her feel very homesick for Somerton.

Chapter Eighteen

Somerton

Priya walked across the sweeping lawn, away from Somerton Court's imposing walls and toward the clump of trees known as Hob's Dell. Augustus held on to the hem of her dress and toddled alongside her.

"Ice cream!" he demanded.

"We can go and find ice cream in a moment," Priya answered. "Let's go over here first. Let's see the hollow tree." She tried not to sound impatient.

"Why?"

"Because it's beautiful, and old." And out of sight of the house, she thought, hurrying on. The scent of roses swelled, heavy, from the nearby beds.

"Why?"

"Well, because it's lived a long time." She could see it now, the oak on the border of the copse. It was draped in ivy, bare branches jutting from it like a stag's antlers.

"Why?"

Priya managed to hold her tongue, even when Augustus sullenly pinched her. She knew it would do no good. Augustus would only run crying to his mamma if she told him off, and she needed him in a good mood.

She half ran, half slid down the bank to the tree. The copse was dark and green and cool in front of her. Standing on tiptoe, she reached inside the ivy, feeling around until she found the hollow in the tree that she knew was there. Her hand found something. A rectangular, heavy object wrapped in brown paper and tied with string. A book!

A smile spread over her face. She glanced back to make sure Augustus wasn't watching. He wasn't; he was paddling in the mud. She'd get in trouble for that later, but it was worth it. She drew the book out of the hole. She just had time to glance at the tooled leather cover and see that it was *A Duke for Daisy* by R. J. Peak, the romance novel that everyone in the servants' quarters was talking about, before another hand took hers.

She gasped and spun round. Michael stepped out from behind the tree trunk. Seeing it was him, Priya relaxed with a relieved laugh.

"Did I startle you?" Michael smiled at her. "I'm sorry."

"Only a little." Priya hesitated, then hurried on. "You got it for me—thank you!" She stood on tiptoe to kiss his cheek. Lately, it was only these stolen moments with Michael when she felt truly calm and happy. She didn't know what she would do without him—as she surely would be when he came to his senses and remembered his family and his obligations. For now, though, she couldn't bear to send him away as she had done so many times in the beginning, when he first began courting her.

"What was I to do? I mustn't keep you from your duke," Michael teased her.

Priya had read the first fifty pages in snatches when Lady Edith's maid had left the novel lying around, and had been able to think of nothing else for the past fortnight. Apparently she hadn't hid her obsession from Michael very well.

"I can't wait to find out what happens next." She flipped through the pages eagerly.

"My little bookworm." Michael tucked a lock of hair behind her ear. "So you're going to read instead of talk to me, then?"

"Just one chapter," Priya said with a smirk, pretending to be engrossed. Michael began trailing soft kisses down her neck. Priya's breath caught, and she lifted her face to his. Their lips met.

Augustus splashed loudly in his puddle, suddenly aware that he had been forgotten. Michael pulled away from Priya. "Here you go," he told Augustus. He produced a bar of chocolate from his pocket. Augustus took it and greedily began unwrapping it.

"That will keep him busy," Michael said, turning back to Priya. The chocolate would also keep him awake most of the night, Priya knew, but she couldn't bring herself to care. "Now . . ."

They kissed, and Priya snuggled into the warm security of his arms.

"I feel so safe when I'm with you," she murmured.

"I hope you feel safe all the time," Michael said, looking at her keenly.

"Yes, of course." She looked down at the book, then up with a bright smile. "I had a letter from my parents. My brother has won a scholarship to a better school!"

"That's wonderful! Perhaps you won't have to send your wages home, then."

"Oh no, there is the uniform to buy, a cricket bat. . . ."

"You're so selfless, to only think of helping your family," Michael told her admiringly. "I hope your brothers are grateful."

"I hope they are too!" Priya laughed, but her cheerfulness faded quickly. She glanced over her shoulder, back toward the house. The stately golden-stone mansion rose behind her on the hill. Of course she could not see at this distance, but she had a strange feeling someone was watching her from the nursery window.

"You're shivering," Michael said, moving toward her. "Here, take my coat."

She didn't have time to protest before he had draped it around her shoulders. He stood for a second, his arm around her shoulders. She looked up into his blue, rebellious eyes. He loved her. She could see that, trust it. It was as solid as the ground she walked on. If only she could tell him how uncomfortable Sir William made her feel. . . . But after all, nothing had happened, really, and Annie was no doubt right, she was imagining things. She realized that he too looked troubled.

"Is something worrying you, Michael?"

"Well, yes. It's Eton."

"The school?"

"Mother wants me to go back. I've told her I'm not a child. The Beaks order you about, and the boys are worse. Nothing but dreary Latin verbs, what's the good of that? We ought to run away together. I'll join the army, and you can come along with me. You wouldn't mind the life of a soldier's wife, would you?"

"I wouldn't mind anything by your side," she said, with a smile. "But should you be so quick to reject Eton? I think you are lucky to have the chance of going there."

"Lucky!" He snorted. "You wouldn't say that if you had to light a prefect's fire in the shivering cold at five in the morning."

Priya swallowed a smile. That was the life of any housemaid—and it didn't end at eighteen. "You will be a man soon—you already are—and men must be well educated if they are to be respected and if they are to be able to do all the work that is required of them. Think how it would look to be an officer in the army and not know all the things that the others do. You owe it to yourself to make the most of your education."

She placed a hand on his arm. Once again she thought of the shadow at the window, the shadow that she never seemed quite able to escape. "I want you to go back to school, please, Michael," she said softly. "I want to know that you are happy and—and free."

CHAPTER
Nineteen

Oxford

"And so I say to you, the education of women is more than a right, more than an economic necessity." Laurence's words rang into the rapt audience of the Oxford Union like the chimes of Big Ben. "It is a patriotic duty. Thank you for your attention."

He bowed and seated himself and, as if moved by a physical reaction, the audience leapt to their feet in a storm of applause, catcalls, and hoots. Ada rose with them, her color high and her hands clapping furiously as if they had a will of their own. For half an hour she had forgotten where she was. Laurence's commanding voice, arguing for the rights of women, had entranced her completely.

"I do admire my brother," Emily said in her ear as she applauded. The two of them had been sitting together in what had become known as the suffragettes' gallery. "As a child, he could win any argument—and that skill has never deserted him."

"It sounds like an intoxicating power to have," Ada returned. A moment later she reproached herself for not sounding more enthusiastic. "He is our strongest supporter, and we are lucky to have him on our side."

"Yes, sadly, until we have a real voice of our own, we need men like Laurence." Emily continued, "Have you read this week's editorial in *The Times* by Hannah Darford? Now, there's a woman who could take on the House of Commons."

"Yes! It was so inspiring," Ada replied eagerly. "I loved her approach to the subject—appealing to the economic argument for women in the professions. She must be a very brave woman to practice as a lawyer despite all the discouragement she has encountered."

Laurence was stepping down from the podium, and the other speakers came to clasp his hand and shake it. Ada saw him bowing his head, nodding seriously at their words, waving away a compliment with a modest smile.

"Let us go and congratulate him." Emily turned toward the exit, and Ada followed. They made their way down the stairs and met Laurence at the bottom.

Ada smiled at him as he laughingly took her arm and guided them to the door through the jostling crowd.

"What a lot of people!" he said in her ear. She could hear a slight self-conscious note in his voice and knew he knew how good he had been. They stepped out into the golden afternoon.

"You were magnificent," she said as soon as they were outside. She squeezed his arm impetuously. "You've certainly made a convert of me."

He laughed, but there was a pleased smile on his face. "My subject spoke for itself."

"Confess: you enjoy orating no matter the subject," Ada said, teasing him. "You could argue that two plus two were five and I'd believe you. You just like persuading people."

He smiled, but didn't rise to the bait. Emily glanced between him and Ada. "I am sure you two would enjoy some time alone to stroll by the river," she said. "I'll read a book in the tearooms—and pretend that I don't know you are unchaperoned, Ada."

Ada laughed and blushed. Feeling a little embarrassed, she watched Emily walk away, self-contained and controlled as a cat.

"My sister is a dear, but a little lacking in tact." Laurence smiled, and, as always, Ada was reassured by his gentlemanly air. He offered her his arm, and Ada took it.

They strolled in companionable silence down the cobbled streets. Before them the river glittered in the sun. Punts filled with undergraduates drifted down the water, the men holding lacy parasols above the girls' heads.

"With this sun and these buildings we could be in Italy." He gestured to the glowing old walls of the Oxford colleges. "Shall we go there for our honeymoon? I'd love to show you Florence."

Ada did not answer immediately. Her eye had been caught by three turbaned young men lounging on the banks among the summer flowers. Their white summer jackets were bright against their skins, and she heard a familiar lilt in their voices as they talked and joked with each other.

Ravi and I once walked on this path together, she remembered, as the leaves of a weeping willow and the pillar of the bridge came into view. That day we quarreled over Empire politics. The memory rushed over her—the sound of the water flowing lazily past, the hard kiss of a cricket ball against the bat. Ravi's expression as he walked toward her after their argument, the way their eyes had met and she had known, they had both known, that no argument mattered compared to the strength of their desire to be together. No matter what the consequences, no matter what the risks. A sunbeam dazzled her; she put a hand to her eyes.

"Ada?"

"I'm sorry." She looked up, a stab of guilt in her heart. It wasn't fair, it wasn't fair to betray Laurence. Not even in thought. "Of course, Italy would be wonderful."

He took her hand, and Ada felt his light, strong grip through her glove. "So when shall we go? September? It's the best time, after the heat and before the storms make sailing a bother."

"September?" She felt a jolt in her chest. It was May already. "I thought I'd begin university in September."

"Why not wait a year? We can be married, see Florence, see Paris, go farther if you like . . . Greece? The Acropolis? Egypt perhaps?" He was tempting her.

"Why not next May?"

"That is a whole year away. I can't wait so long." He moved

closer to her as they walked. She felt his warm breath on her neck. "You can go to university once we're married, after all. There'll be all the time in the world, once we're married."

All the time in the world, Ada thought. *All the time in the world . . . to spend with you.*

"But we must get the season over, and then Papa will be so disappointed if our wedding interferes with his shooting, and then it's winter, and no one gets married in winter."

"You're playing with me." He struck at the tree with his cane.

"Not at all. I just don't see what the rush is."

He spoke quietly, his low voice caressing. "When you have a beautiful butterfly, you'll do anything to keep her fluttering around you."

Ada was not sure she liked the comparison. "Don't you trust me?" she said.

"Of course," he said shortly.

Ada heard the annoyance in his voice. She moved toward him and placed a gentle hand on his arm. "Laurence. I will marry you. I dream of it every day. But surely you understand that I cannot simply forget my other responsibilities."

He nodded, appearing to be pacified, and she took the chance to change the subject. "In fact, I wanted to ask your advice," she said quietly.

It was a good move. Laurence liked to be needed, she knew that.

"On anything," he said at once.

"This Alexander Ross. The Duke of Huntleigh." She felt him

tense. "He and Lady Rose have been dancing together a good deal since they met at the state ball." She hesitated over her words, trying to find the right ones to explain her vague sense of unease, her concern. "You know Lady Rose is not used to society. I would not want her to be . . . disappointed. She seems very happy, happy for the first time since our father adopted her."

"I have the greatest respect for your father, but such a radical decision cannot be without consequences," Laurence answered.

Ada forced a smile. "I hope that a little more time spent in her company will convince you that my father was right in his decision to ennoble her."

"I don't doubt that Lady Rose would grace any company. I simply mistrust anything that flies so entirely in the face of convention," he added, with a gracious smile. "But I daresay you'll think me an old stick-in-the-mud."

"No—no. You are eternally reliable, and I cannot say how much I appreciate that." Her voice was almost trembling. "That was why I wanted to ask you about the Duke of Huntleigh—and Rose."

He was silent.

She looked up at him, meeting his eyes. "I can believe the Duke of Huntleigh has been misrepresented," she said. She wanted it to be true. But the look in Laurence's eyes silenced her.

"I'm afraid he has not," he replied.

A cold iron weight seemed to settle on Ada's heart.

Laurence went on. "I have known Huntleigh since Eton, and he's a bounder. His only interest is novelty. I don't believe he's ever had serious intentions toward a woman in his life, though he's been mixed up with enough of them. He was sent down from Oxford, and I understand his travels to the Continent were not of his own volition. His father was not proud of him." Laurence sounded very serious. "I am glad you spoke to me about this, Ada, because I would have had to raise the subject otherwise. As you say, Lady Rose is very vulnerable, because of her extraordinary position, and I am afraid she is easy game for a man such as the Duke of Huntleigh."

"Are you quite sure?"

"I am certain." He hesitated, then added, "May I ask if he is aware of Lady Rose's . . . origins?"

"You mean that she used to be a housemaid?" Ada said bluntly. She hesitated. "I expect so. That is, everyone knows. . . ."

"Everyone in society. But as we know the duke has done his best to distance himself from society until this year. He has few close friends now in London. It's quite possible that he doesn't know—and if he did, I think you would find his attitude to Lady Rose substantially changed."

Ada nodded silently. There was no choice. Rose had to be warned—for her own good.

CHAPTER
Twenty

London

Ada toyed with her toast, now and then glancing at Rose, who was humming to herself. Her father was reading the newspaper, a troubled frown on his face. She knew the news from Europe had been bad—there was so much anxiety about German airships. Yet it seemed incredible that the Kaiser would really move against Britain—after all, he was the King's close relative. Other things troubled her more—like protecting Rose.

"Invitations," Charlotte announced, entering the breakfast room with a handful of letters. "I intercepted Jevins. Here you are, Mama." She handed the envelopes to her mother and sat down.

The countess made her way through the envelopes with a bored expression on her face. "Cowes, the Duke of Westminster wishes us to join him on his yacht. It will be terribly boring but we must say yes. Tea . . . tea . . . another ball . . . Oh! How very provoking!"

"What is it, my dear?" Lord Westlake enquired.

The countess sourly displayed the gilt-edged invitation. Ada read the words: Bal Masqué. "Mrs. Verulam is to have a costume ball on the evening of the Royal Horticultural Flower Show."

"A costume ball!" Charlotte exclaimed.

"That does sound rather fun," Ada said.

"Yes, but the wretched woman has simply stolen the limelight once again. Of course everyone will leave town as soon as it is over, and all anyone will think about is the ball. I was hoping to make another splash before the end of the season, but no chance of that now."

"Well, as long as I get a new dress I don't mind too much," Charlotte said.

"Of course, it will be necessary. For you, at least—I can't be expected to go to the expense of dressing up Rose."

"My dear, you receive a dress allowance to clothe *all* my daughters," the earl said, with an edge to his voice. There was an uncomfortable silence. The countess looked mutinous but began to open the next invitation in silence.

"Ah, now *this* is interesting," she said, as her gaze skipped across the sprawling handwriting. "For you especially, Charlotte."

Charlotte rolled her eyes. "Do tell, Mother."

"The Duke of Huntleigh writes to invite us to his box at the opera for the new performance of Stravinsky's *Rite of Spring*."

"Oh!" Rose exclaimed, and dropped her knife with a clatter. Ada looked at her, as did everyone. Rose met their eyes and blushed.

"That is—I would very much like to see the *Rite*."

"Really." The countess made a disbelieving face. "I don't see what chance you might have had to develop an interest in ballet, but at any rate it seems you will get your wish. He most particularly invites *all* of us."

"Didn't the audience riot at the premiere in Paris?" Charlotte made a face. "I shan't wear my best hat if there's any risk of its being crushed by anarchists."

"It sounds inconvenient." The countess sniffed. "Be that as it may, it is an invitation from the Duke of Huntleigh, and so we will go."

Ada caught Rose's eye. It was clear from her heightened color and her smile that she thought the invitation was meant specially for her. Ada's heart sank. Her sister had the look of a girl in love, and it was no pleasure to think that she might have to shatter Rose's dreams.

CHAPTER
Twenty-one

The sun glinted off the discreetly jeweled pins skewering the Countess of Westlake's new hat as she descended from her chauffeur-driven Rolls-Royce Silver Ghost before Selfridges' new department store on Oxford Street. Rose, Ada, and Charlotte followed her. Rose looked up in awe at the huge building in front of her. It was their first visit to the new department store; she could see that even her stepmother was at a loss.

The countess hesitated for only an instant. A smart young man darted forward with a deep bow, and another leapt to hold the doors open. The countess swept in, her head high. Her daughters followed her. Rose gazed around at the huge space in front of her. Counters and mirrors receded to every side. Well-dressed ladies and gentlemen drifted about, fingering the cloth draped upon mannequins, examining crystal and silver. Everywhere there were busy, smartly dressed attendants. It was more like a palace than a shop, Rose thought. It was so different, so open, so new. She was suddenly very glad she had come. She hadn't been keen at first, but Céline seemed so anxious that she should go, and Rose hadn't the heart to disappoint her. Besides, she needed to find a moment to speak to Ada. Annie was still at Milborough House; something had to be done. She wished she knew what.

"Where on earth does one start?" Charlotte said aloud. "Mother?"

"Just a moment, I am trying to get my bearings." The countess turned on the spot. Rose had never seen her looking quite so lost.

"Well, do hurry, we look ridiculous standing here like sheep," Charlotte whispered sharply.

"This way." The countess advanced confidently, the others followed her, and they found themselves surrounded by china vases the height of a small man, painted with elephants.

"I don't understand. We were in a stationer's a moment ago." The countess swiveled.

"That was a different department," Rose explained. "That's why they call it a department store, because—"

"Yes, yes, very well, I am not entirely lacking in intelligence," the countess snapped.

"Mother, let's just find the roof garden. We shall be late for Madame Lucille's show." Charlotte sighed.

"I am not leaving here without this book. Everyone is talking about *A Duke for Daisy*. It's a succès de scandale. No one can guess who the author is."

"I thought they had decided it was the Bishop of Gloucester?" said Ada. "Or was it the Marquis of Rothwell?"

"No, no, it can't be Henry." The countess shook her head firmly. "He doesn't have the wit to write so much as a postcard. No, I believe it is—"

"Look, here is Mrs. Verulam," Rose said in relief, spotting a small figure swathed in silk, jet, and Barbary ostrich plumes majestically descending upon them.

"My dear Lady Westlake," Mrs. Verulam exclaimed. "Are you lost?"

The countess drew herself up indignantly.

"Absolutely not. I was simply admiring these . . . these . . ." She gestured vaguely with a gloved hand.

"Charming, aren't they." Mrs. Verulam glanced at the vases. "I bought a couple to brighten up the servants' hall. But are you not going to Madame Lucille's show?"

"We are," Ada explained, "but the countess would like to buy a book first."

"What a coincidence! So would I." Mrs. Verulam raised her parasol and gestured to an attendant, who swooped deferentially upon them. "Kindly show us to the book department," she announced. "We wish to buy *A Duke for Daisy* by R. J. Peak."

"Certainly, madam. This way, madam."

The man hurried off, and they followed him.

"But how did you know?" the countess exclaimed as she followed behind Mrs. Verulam.

Mrs. Verulam turned a pitying, amused glance upon her. "What other book exists, this season?"

As they crossed the shop floor, while Mrs. Verulam and the countess bickered politely about who the mysterious R. J. Peak really was, Rose saw her chance. She dropped back to walk by Ada's side.

"I have something to tell you," Rose murmured in her ear. Ada glanced at Rose's face with sudden anxiety. "Annie has come down from Somerton," Rose went on. "She has some idea of becoming my personal maid."

"What!" Ada exclaimed, then quickly lowered her voice as Charlotte glanced back at them. "She can't be serious. What an impossible situation it would be for both of you."

"I know." Rose sighed.

"She can't have thought it through. You, who used to be house-maids together—now she will have to fetch and carry for you, mend your clothes, arrange your dressing table, sit up waiting for you to return from balls, take orders from you directly—oh, she can't have thought it through." Ada shook her head in disbelief.

"I don't think she has."

"You must tell her to go back to Somerton at once."

"How can I? She'll think I am turning up my nose at her."

"I don't know how you can, but you must," Ada said firmly. "You are an Averley now, and you must behave like one or things will be impossible for you. Annie simply cannot expect things to be on the same footing as they were when you were both housemaids."

"But I haven't changed. . . ."

"But you have, Rose, and there is no pretending you haven't. Things are different for you now." Ada's voice softened. "I don't mean to sound unkind. Annie will have all our assistance if she wants to better herself. But you are Lady Rose Averley now, and you must live up to your name."

They walked on in silence. Rose frowned slightly. She did understand what Ada was saying, but she seemed to forget that being adopted as an Averley had not wiped out the half of her being that was plain Rose Cliffe, daughter of a housekeeper. Somehow there had never seemed to be such a distance between her and Ada as now, when Lord Westlake had raised her up to share his daughters' pedestal. As much as we love each other, we are not the same, Rose thought, and felt disappointed to have to admit it.

They stepped into a paradise of books. Signs hung above reading rooms and writing rooms where pyramids of books were carefully arranged, and people browsed here and there.

"Ah! *A Duke for Daisy*." The countess pounced and picked up the book with a satisfied sigh.

"I'm so sorry," the attendant murmured, "we have only one copy left."

"Oh, do take it," Mrs. Verulam said brightly, "I can always borrow it from my butler."

The countess turned red. Rose bit her cheeks to stop herself laughing. The countess would without doubt rather be known to wear last year's fashion than to read the same novel as a butler. However, she had no choice. She proceeded to pay for the book with a back as straight as her thin mouth. As she did so, Charlotte turned to the assistant. "Can you show me where the oil paints are kept?" she inquired.

"Certainly, madam. Just this way." The attendant moved away, Charlotte following, and their voices receded. Rose watched as the man pointed out the different kinds of paint and canvas, and Charlotte listened, nodding.

"How strange," Ada said. "I didn't think Charlotte was interested in painting."

"Neither did I," Rose said thoughtfully. She couldn't help thinking of Alexander Ross. Did he know Charlotte painted?

The attendant led them over to the lift, the countess stepped in, and the others followed. Mrs. Verulam looked about her, disconsolately.

"One feels so like a cold capon being sent up for dinner," she murmured, as the door clanged shut and the lift boy pressed the button for the roof garden.

Ada stepped out of the lift into a fresh summer's day. They were lucky it hadn't rained, she thought, looking at the rows of chairs and the red carpet spread out among decorative palms. She recognized many faces among the seated ladies; London during the season was a small place. She glanced over to the distant dome of St. Paul's and then to the crown-like spires of the Houses of

Parliament. It made her feel a little dizzy to be so high up, or perhaps it was merely the effect of the lift and the relentless modernity of Selfridges.

Rose's hand on her arm steadied her. "A little dizzy?" she asked, with a smile.

Ada smiled back. "Just a little—we are so high up. But it seems to suit you."

"Yes, I adore it," Rose said simply. She turned to look out at the birds that wheeled among the rooftops. Ada thought Rose had rarely looked so handsome, with the color in her cheeks and the light in her eyes. She wished she did not have to broach such an unpleasant subject with her. But it was her duty.

Lady Duff Gordon herself introduced the gowns. Gold pencils rippled across notepads as the leaders of fashion took notes for the greatest ball of the season, Mrs. Verulam's costume extravaganza.

Ada glanced over at Rose. She seemed intent on the mannequins parading in front of her. "I want to speak to you about the Duke of Huntleigh," Ada murmured, under cover of Lady Duff Gordon's narration. A well-known actress in a slender black velvet column latticed with pearls posed before them, turning this way and that to display the fall of the cloth.

"Alexander?" Rose inquired, and Ada's worst fears were realized.

"You are on first name terms, then?"

"It's his name, that's all."

Ada watched as another slim, elegant mannequin strolled out in front of the crowd, her summery yellow hat bedecked with a cascade of silk flowers. "I think you should be careful with him. He has a bad reputation with women."

Rose sighed. "That was a long time ago."

"Yes," said Ada urgently, "but you should perhaps take warning from it."

"The 'Zephyr,' with ruched and embroidered overskirt, is worn by Miss Elsie Delaunay," announced Lady Duff Gordon. Ada clapped politely as the young singer walked out before them, her beautiful smile displaying teeth as small and white as the pearls around her neck.

"Is this advice from Lord Fintan?" There was a note in Rose's voice Ada had never heard before. Defiance. The fear surged up inside her again. Rose was too innocent, too vulnerable.

"Laurence has known him a long time. I wish I could say he liked him."

"They're very different people, certainly."

Was that a note of sarcasm? Ada was taken aback, and a little annoyed. Her response was a touch more waspish than she meant it to be. "Yes, Laurence is trustworthy, honorable, and well-respected in society."

"And please observe, ladies, the simplicity of this gown in brocaded silk. No trimmings are necessary with such a luxurious fabric. . . ." Applause, like a flight of doves taking off. The mannequin flurried her ostrich-feather fan.

"I didn't think you cared so much for society," Rose said quietly, looking directly ahead of her at the parading gowns. "I thought you cared about more important things."

"I do." Ada sighed. "Rose, I am only trying to help. Alexander Ross has a terrible reputation."

"Because people who don't understand him talk badly of him. He was kind to invite us to the *Rite*, he knew I wanted to go, and this was the only way the countess would take me."

"I just don't want him to . . . disappoint you." Ada swallowed. What she had to say next tasted bitter in her mouth. But she had to convince Rose, had to protect her. "Does he know . . . if he knew . . ." She hesitated; it was such an unpleasant thing to have to say. "He may not be quite aware of your previous—"

Ada broke off. Charlotte was standing a few feet away, seemingly absorbed in adjusting her gloves.

Rose replied, her voice hushed and annoyed. "Please don't concern yourself. I have no expectations of the Duke of Huntleigh. I enjoy his conversation. I admire him as an artist. That is a very long way from being vulnerable to his charms."

Ada could see from the color in her cheeks and the fast, clipped way she spoke that she was upset and angry. Ada winced. This was not what she had wanted. She tried again. "Rose, you're not being entirely honest with me. I thought that as sisters—"

"And I am not sure you are being entirely honest with *me* about your feelings for Laurence."

Ada flinched as if she had been burned. Rose was right, and she could not deny it. She fixed her eyes on the mannequin passing before them and said no more.

Chapter
Twenty-two

Rose was still flushed with annoyance when they returned from the fashion show. She had never, ever been angry with Ada, and even now she felt guilty for it. But it had shocked her to hear the way she spoke of Alexander. It was so unjust, so unfair. What had the man done but be a little unconventional? The invitation he had sent was so clearly meant for her. It was so kind of him, and even despite her rudeness about his painting. He must have forgiven her for her thoughtless remarks. She felt a passionate urge to defend him, to take his arm in front of everyone and prove that she at least believed he was a good man.

But one thing Ada was right about, and she had to admit it, uncomfortable as it was. Annic had to go. As Rose handed her hat to one of the servants, she decided to go directly and speak to her. Any painful thing was best got over with quickly, her mother had always told her.

She was aware her heart was beating uncomfortably fast as she went down the steps into the servants' quarters to speak to Annie. *There's nothing to worry about,* she told herself. *I shall simply explain, quietly and gently, that she can't stay.* She had a feeling, though, that it would not be easy.

Annie was sitting in the kitchen; Rose hesitated at the door. Annie was poring over an exercise book, a pencil in her hand. Laboriously she traced the letters one by one, and her mouth shaped them as she read aloud. "M-O-N-D-A-Y."

She was learning to read. Rose hadn't imagined she could feel worse, but it turned out she could. She hesitated at the door. Was she doing the right thing? Maybe she should just run back upstairs, ignore Ada's advice. But Annie looked up, and the chance was gone.

"Rose!" Annie's smile was wide but nervous. She jumped to her feet.

"You're learning to read." Rose's voice was soft.

Annie blushed and shrugged. "I—I was just trying it out. Of course I don't need it. Just a hobby, like." She came over to Rose, her hands clasped in her apron, her cheeks flushed. "Have you spoken to the countess? Will it be all right for me to stay?"

Rose swallowed. "Annie, I . . ." She hesitated, and hated herself for being a coward. "I don't think it will work. I am sorry."

The look on Annie's face made her wince. "I don't understand." Annie held out her hands imploringly. "I know I'm not a real French maid, but I've been doing for Lady Georgina. I understand the job. I could learn quickly. Just because I can't read don't mean I'm stupid. You know that. You've seen I'm quick on the uptake when we worked together before."

Rose knew then that she had done the right thing. "That's just it, Annie. We won't be working together. I'm a lady now, and you're still a maid. You'd have to fetch and carry for me, you'd have to take my orders and it wouldn't feel right, don't you understand? You'd be working for me. I'd have to tell you off if my bathwater wasn't hot or my stockings weren't mended. I couldn't always be giving you the afternoon off. It just wouldn't work, Annie."

Annie's look of shock faded slowly, replaced with anger. Rose's hope that she would be understood faded with it. "I see. You're too good for your old friends, that's it." Annie stepped back, folding her arms. She shook her head hard as Rose tried to speak. "No, no, no. I understand you. You've forgotten where you came from, Rose Cliffe."

"But I have to learn to be a lady now, and a lady can't be a maid too, don't you see?"

"Yes, I do. I see perfectly well." Annie's voice trembled and a tear splashed onto the exercise book. Rose moved toward her impetuously, wanting to hug and comfort her, but Annie backed away. "No thank you, Lady Rose. I've learned my place. I won't trouble you again. I'll just go on the streets and be a fallen woman because there's no other future for a silly fool who trusted in her friends and lost her place—"

"Annie, don't take on so." Rose could have laughed at her

melodrama, but she knew Annie didn't see it that way. "You won't have lost your place. I'll get it back for you. My mother won't hold this against you."

"I won't go back there. They'll laugh at me." Annie shook her head, tears flying.

"Well, then I'll get you a better place. Or a better job. You won't be left high and dry, Annie, of course not. If you want to be a lady's maid I'll help you, but you working for me . . . it just won't be right, Annie. You can see that, can't you?" Annie's sobs told Rose that she couldn't. Rose moved toward her again, but Annie backed away and her sobs turned hysterical. Rose hesitated, not knowing what to do. A small scuffle behind her made her turn.

It was the tweeny, she realized, after a moment of trying to place the mousy little creature who trembled at the door. "Oh . . ." She had forgotten her name. "Can you please look after Miss Bailey? Bring her a cup of tea." She hesitated, trying to remember how Annie liked it. "Milk and two sugars. And please tell me . . . when she has decided what she would like to do."

The tweeny bobbed a curtsy and went into the kitchen. Annie had sat down and was sobbing at the table, her head in her hands. Rose paused at the door and glanced back. The tweeny's arm was around Annie, and she was whispering comfortingly to her. Annie nodded as she spoke. Rose was glad Annie was being looked after, but a stab of loneliness pulsed through her heart as she looked at the warm scene before her. It was a world she had left behind her, like a lost glass slipper in the snow, and she could never go back to it again.

CHAPTER Twenty-three

Charlotte gazed down from the window of her dressing room into sun-dappled Milborough Square. In her hands was an envelope, and inside the envelope was a stiff little piece of gilded card. Charlotte had a drawer full of such cards, all inscribed with the names of the best hostesses. Each one held memories collected over three seasons of dancing and flirtation and more. But this one was different. This was a dance card for Mrs. Verulam's costume ball. It would take place on the last night of the official London season. The last night of Charlotte's third season. Charlotte had known the season would end, of course, but somehow the invitation made it real. She had been out for three seasons and she was still not engaged. Not yet.

"Ward," she said, turning from the window.

Stella, who was folding clothes quietly in a corner of the room, looked up.

"I'd like you to take a little note over to the Duke of Huntleigh for me."

The pause before Ward replied, "Yes, miss," was just long enough to be insolent. Charlotte noted it, for future reference. For now, she simply drew out her writing case. It had simply never occurred to her that the duke might not know of Rose's disgraceful history. But the man had been out of society for so long it was hardly surprising. She began the letter.

Dear Alexander—

When we know each other so well, it seems silly to address you as Duke!

I wanted to thank you for your invitation, which we received this morning. I have been simply longing to see the Rite *ever since I first heard of it. I am so excited I can barely sleep for thinking of it.*

So kind of you to invite my stepsister Rose as well. The dear girl deserves every opportunity she can get to improve herself. As you might imagine, the season is rather overwhelming for a former housemaid, but I think she has been handling it all with admirable humility.

Now I'm going to be shockingly unconventional and extend my own invitation to you. I propose that we visit an exhibition together. There is an exhibition of Futurist art on

Heddon Street. As you know London is so far behind the European capitals in terms of art, it would be a crime to miss it, don't you think?

She signed her name, placed the letter in the envelope, and sealed it before handing it to Ward.

One could, if one was organized, kill several birds with one stone.

CHAPTER
Twenty-four

The afternoon spread golden wings over London, over the rattle of the carts and the impatient blare of motor horns, the stench of horse manure, and the stink of petrol. The Underground Railway, like an imprisoned dragon, roared and rushed through the earth, disgorging sooty, shaken passengers from its grasp. From South Kensington to Aldgate, it surged to the surface like lava.

Yes, Stella thought as she closed the back door of Milborough House behind her and walked out onto the street, her yellow-and-black best dress—one of Lady Charlotte's cast-offs—swaying with her movement, her parasol twirling as elegantly as that of any lady of fashion, all the action was under the surface. Nursemaids strolled past her, pushing baby carriages, but Stella saw past the demure caps and ribbons to the watching footmen at the railings, the whispers they exchanged, the quick, guilty kisses.

The smart set of London lived within a few square miles, and Stella didn't have far to walk to reach the Duke of Huntleigh's London residence. She crossed Milborough Square, Lanchester Gardens, Grosvenor Square—each one lined with Georgian mansions, formal and white-clad as vestal virgins—and reached the airy space known as Park Square.

She paused to laugh at a Punch and Judy show that had drawn a small crowd to the shade beneath a plane tree. The puppets jabbered and danced about.

If you kept all the strings at your fingers' ends, Stella thought, if you knew when to pull each one—you could make sweat break out on a marquise's brow. You could cause a duchess to wince, a debutante to blush. Who wanted to be a lady when you could be a puppeteer? It was very easy to steam open letters, and she had chuckled before she left at Miss Charlotte's clever strategy to shake the duke loose from Rose. But—she paused to inhale the scent of the deep-red roses that grew in the square—she had her own strategies.

Just before she left, Ellen the tweeny had come up to her holding a few scraps of red silk petals. Exactly like the torn silk rose from her mistress's dress that Stella currently kept hidden in her top drawer. "Please, miss," she had said, with a nervous curtsy. "I wondered if you knew where these belonged."

Stella had taken the silk petals and refrained from squealing with joy. She had known that they would turn up. Things always did. "Now, tell me, Ellen," she had said, turning the petals this way and that so the vivid color caught the light like drops of blood, "where exactly did you find these?"

CHAPTER
Twenty-five

Somerton

"I'm so sorry, Mrs. Cliffe," Georgiana exclaimed as she entered the drawing room, out of breath from hurrying. "I had to see Cook about the dinner menu for tonight."

Mrs. Cliffe jumped and looked up. She quickly slid the notebook she had been scribbling in under her papers.

"No, please go on with your work." Georgiana came across the room, feet sinking into the thick Persian carpets, and took the chair next to her. "I suppose you're noting questions to ask her?" She reached for the letter that lay on the occasional table, the thick yellow paper covered in firm, neat writing. "Mrs. McRory, isn't it? I see she worked for the Prime Minister. How interesting." She glanced at Mrs. Cliffe's flushed face. "Are you hot? It is rather too late in the year for a fire."

"Not at all." Mrs. Cliffe said. She was breathing rather quickly, and glanced down at her notebook again. Composing herself, she went on, "Shall we ask the lady to come up?"

Georgiana rang the bell. As she waited for Cooper, she hoped fervently that this interview would be the last one. So far not a single applicant had been suitable. The agency shrugged its shoulders and apologized; more interesting work in town, service was no longer as desirable as it once was, a national crisis. Georgiana sighed. She had enough to worry about with local crises. Priya was unwell again, Annie had handed in her notice—so strange, she had seemed such a reliable girl—Sir William had gone on a weeklong binge after his latest argument with her father, and Lady Edith had engaged a Russian spiritualist to purge her soul. All she had succeeded in doing was purging her wallet.

"Mrs. McRory," Cooper announced, holding open the door. Georgiana sat forward with a welcoming smile.

The woman who bounced through the door was as unlike Mrs. Cliffe as could be imagined. She was so short that for a moment Georgiana thought there had been a mistake and a child had been sent instead. But it took her the barest instant to see the stern, furrowed brow, the hairy chin and the determinedly pinched mouth. Mrs. McRory was small, but only in the way that a bullet is small.

"Ma'am," she said, dipping a brief curtsy to Georgiana. Georgiana had never been on the receiving end of quite such a dismissive curtsy. Without waiting to be invited, the woman strode across the floor—if such a small woman could stride; it was more the action of a tightly wound spring unleashed—and seated herself in the chair Georgiana had intended to graciously invite her to sit in. Her legs dangled, swinging in her rusty black skirts. "Shall we begin? *I* usually commence *my* interviews exactly on time."

"Er—of course. Yes, certainly." Georgiana sat back, flustered, and cast a nervous glance at Mrs. Cliffe, who was watching with raised eyebrows.

"You will no doubt want to know about my previous employers," Mrs. McRory began. She had a slight Scottish accent. "My last employer was Lord Malmesbury, but I found it impossible to continue once he had engaged a French chef. Neither my morals nor my temper could allow it. I hope, my lady, that you do not intend employing any such person."

"I think there is very little chance of that," Georgiana said, thinking of the accounts.

"My chief motivation is bringing order to the disorderly," Mrs. McRory announced. "Order to the disorderly," she repeated, rather as if savoring the thought. "I cannot abide waste. I abhor indolence. Under my guidance, servants discover in themselves heretofore untapped reserves of energy, resolution, and moral fiber. Before I rose to my present elevated position"—at this Georgiana had to bite her cheeks to stifle a smile—"I was a Good Plain Cook. Some cooks pride themselves on their ability to make a fowl last three days. *I* made a fowl last a week and then served him up as consommé to our late, lamented monarch." She smiled with a look of deep inward satisfaction. "Who honored me by saying I had produced an Unparalleled Confection of Delicacy."

Georgiana found herself speechless. She glanced at Mrs. Cliffe.

"You would be expected to arrange large country events such as weddings, shooting parties, and balls," Mrs. Cliffe said. "Does your experience in London—"

"Done it," Mrs. McRory snapped. "Maharajah of Petampore. Foreign gentleman. Required a season for his eldest daughter. Butler died. Heart attack. Ordered the entire thing myself, *including* male staff."

Georgiana rustled through the references, feeling she ought to regain the initiative. "References all in order," Mrs. McRory said. "I looked in on the laundry room on my way up and ordered the linen. Very disorderly."

"Yes, we've lost our first housemaid, Annie," Mrs. Cliffe murmured. "Well, I . . . can't think of anything more to ask, Mrs. McRory. We'll be in touch."

Mrs. McRory bounded to her feet with such energy that Georgiana was afraid she felt insulted. But as the woman jerked her abrupt curtsy and surged to the door, she realized that it was just the speed and decisiveness with which she moved. James arrived only just in time to open the door for her. Mrs. McRory, who came approximately to his waist height, looked up at him through narrowed eyes, then reached up to tap him on his shirt front.

"Stain. Disorderly. *I* always have *my* footmen wash their linen in Patchcock's Peculiar Granules. Stains vanish with Patchcock's."

She disappeared through the door, and James, looking flabbergasted, hurried after her. Georgiana managed to hold her giggles back until the door had closed behind her. "Did you ever see such a person?" Georgiana was half laughing, half admiring. "*My* footmen! I wonder what Cooper will have to say about that?"

"I should think it would shake him up a bit, and no bad thing, my lady." Mrs. Cliffe was smiling too. "He has been letting things slide while His Lordship was in London."

"You're right." Georgiana was sobered again. Making the disorderly orderly. Well, they certainly were a disorderly household. Perhaps Mrs. McRory was just what they needed.

"Her references are certainly excellent." Mrs. Cliffe was glancing through them again. "I must write to check them, of course, but really . . ."

"She's the best we have seen so far," Georgiana said, finishing the sentence.

They looked at each other and shared a thoughtful nod.

CHAPTER
Twenty-six

London

The Theatre Royal on Drury Lane was crammed with people who had heard of the dramatic reception of *The Rite of Spring* in Paris and were eager to see it repeated in London. Rose strained to hear the overture above the chatter of voices as she followed the others to the duke's box.

"I heard it was unlistenable—primitive—Nijinsky has gone too far."

"A moral scandal—unspeakably shocking—"

"Stamping and banging and not a tune to be heard!"

She squeezed between perfumed dowagers, feathers from expensive hats tickling her nose. Alexander was nowhere to be seen, though she felt her heart beating rapidly, expecting to see him at every moment.

"I am so glad the duke offered us his box," the countess said loudly as they went through the crowd. "It would be insufferable to sit in this crush."

"And speaking of the duke," Charlotte murmured behind her fan, "where is he?"

The attendant bowed as he showed them through the velvet curtain into the box.

"Has the duke yet arrived?" the countess demanded of him.

"I could not say, my lady." The attendant bowed and backed out.

"Or has been instructed not to say." Charlotte sighed and seated herself.

Rose and Ada exchanged glances as they sat down.

"I don't know what to expect," Ada said. "I suppose it will be interesting. I adored *The Firebird* and Fokine's choreography, but the *Rite* has had such a violent reaction in Paris. . . ."

"I'm sure there is something to it." Rose sat forward, her chin on her hands. She wondered where Alexander was. She longed to see him, to smile at him and have the chance to apologize for her rudeness. He must have known the countess would never have taken her to the performance without his invitation, and she was touched that he had remembered their conversation on the subject—even though she had been so unpardonably rude about his paintings.

Before they could speak of it further the lights dimmed, the curtain rose, and *The Rite of Spring* began.

Rose realized in an instant why the reaction in Paris had

been so violent. This was not the voluptuous, breathtaking beauty of *The Firebird* or *Scheherazade*. A bare and wintry scene filled the stage, the dancers moving in violent spasms. The gorgeous embroidery of fairy tale was ripped away to leave the clean bones of the story within: the merciless sacrifice of youth and beauty in an eternal, powerful rite as rhythmic as the changing seasons, or the pumping of blood through the human body. Rose couldn't repress a feeling of rising, heady, drunken excitement, as if she were hearing and seeing the future rushing toward her at the speed of the fastest motorcar.

"*Rite of Spring!*" The countess sniffed. "It's the ugliest thing I have ever seen. Spring is flowers, beauty, elegance. . . ."

And new life, thought Rose, and the savage pain of throwing off the past. But the only person who would understand that was Alexander. She was dying to hear what he thought about it, dying to tell him that she thought she understood better now, what he was trying to paint, thought she could see a way now, to make music that didn't ring as false as the laughter of the audience. . . .

The audience fidgeted, laughed, catcalled. Rose thought, angrily, that they had made up their minds before it had even begun. They had come to see a riot, not a ballet.

When the interval bell rang, the countess rose at once.

"Worse than I expected. And the wretched Huntleigh isn't even here!"

Rose jumped to her feet as the door of the box opened and

a man entered—but it was not Alexander. It was Sebastian, and she saw at once the tension and strain on his face, although he spoke lightly. "Good evening, everyone. I heard you were here, so I thought I'd make an appearance."

"About time too! Where on earth have you been for the past few days? Everyone has been asking about you."

"Are you all right?" Rose scanned Sebastian's face. She could see he looked tired and troubled.

"Not really. I've just heard that Oliver's pleading guilty."

"No!" Ada sounded shocked. "But why?"

"Oh goodness, not more of this penny dreadful," Charlotte groaned.

"I've been called as a witness and he wants to save me from going to court," Sebastian said, ignoring his sister and speaking directly to Rose.

Rose's eyes widened. Of course, if Sebastian ended up in court, the newspapers would see him as fair game. And then . . . everything might come out.

"How feudal!" Charlotte said with a laugh. "I can't imagine Ward doing as much for me."

"Well, I'm delighted that someone at least considers our feelings!" The countess sounded furious, but Rose could see that beneath her sharp voice she was scared. "You don't seem to consider what people may say—"

"I don't care what people say!" Sebastian snapped. Rose flinched, and the people around them turned in surprise.

"Hush!" the countess hissed. "Keep your voice down. Journalists are everywhere."

"Good, perhaps one of them will report the truth for once."

"Be careful what you wish for." The countess's voice was icy, but Rose heard the fear underneath the ice. She remembered what Sebastian had said at the exhibition. She had never believed she could feel sorry for the countess, but she found she did.

"I know what I want, Mother. I know for the first time what truly matters. And I am not ashamed of it. On the contrary, I'm proud."

Sebastian turned and stormed away, pushing through the crowd until he disappeared in the direction of the exit. Slowly, like water filling a footprint at the edge of the sea, the conversation flowed back. But Rose could feel the piercing glances and hear the murmurs, as if the sea were whispering rumors to curious ears.

"I've had enough of this cacophony." The countess's voice was brittle.

"Oh, no," Rose exclaimed. "You can't wish to go now—not without seeing the second half."

"I don't expect it gets any better," Charlotte sighed, following her mother out of the box.

"Better! It was wonderful." Rose turned to Ada, who was hanging back, silent. "Ada, you agree with me, don't you? The power of the rite, that poor girl dancing herself to death, sacrificing herself—"

"Excuse me." Ada's voice sounded strangled, and she rose to her feet. She pushed her way out of the box. Rose, startled and anxious, followed her. Ada moved like a sleepwalker, feeling her way to the wall, and steadied herself against it.

"Are you faint?" the countess demanded. She beckoned to a steward. "Some iced water for Lady Ada." The steward bowed and hurried away at once.

"Ada, do you feel unwell?" Rose fanned her with the program.

"I'm sorry." Ada drew a deep breath. "It was a little hot in there."

"Of course, it was."

"Just a few moments to compose myself, and I shall be able to leave."

The iced water arrived and Ada drank gratefully.

"Let's go," the countess said impatiently.

Rose could do nothing but follow her to the exit. As they made their way through the crowd its movement pushed her sideways and a strong hand steadied her. She looked up to see Alexander. She couldn't stop the smile of happiness that broke over her face. But to her surprise he seemed determined not to meet her eyes and swiftly let go of her arm. She looked into his face, searching and surprised. He was blushing.

"Your Grace!" came the countess's voice, ringing over her shoulder. Rose started and turned around. The countess and Charlotte were heading toward them.

The countess spoke first. "Where have you been? So naughty

of you to invite us and then not be there." Her words were playful, but Rose could see she was irritated.

Alexander cleared his throat, looking uncomfortable. "I must apologize, I meant to join you in the second half." Rose wondered if he was telling the truth.

"I am so grateful for your invitation," Charlotte said. "It's a wonderful piece—so new, so fresh, so modern."

Rose stared at her in astonishment.

Alexander smiled, looking relieved to see Charlotte. "I'm glad you enjoyed it. I saw it in rehearsal and it was a marvelous experience. So few people seem to have understood it properly."

"Oh, I adore anything by Stravinsky," Charlotte said firmly. "Which is your favorite piece?"

"If I had to choose, I would say *The Firebird*."

"Ah yes." Charlotte breathed, a hand playing with the carnelian pendant at her neck. "The thrill of the chase . . . Eastern decadence . . . the passion of the music . . ."

Alexander smiled, looking half embarrassed and half amused. He glanced at Rose, but then looked back at Charlotte, as she said, "So you'll join us for the second half of the program?"

"In fact, I'm afraid I've been called away—urgent business." He didn't look back at Rose. "I do hope you enjoy it, though."

He made a movement as if to leave, but Charlotte spoke again. "I've been working on that little self-portrait you saw, and it is so much improved. I want to thank you for your help."

"You're welcome," he replied. "I'm sure it's down to your talent and not my advice."

He turned to go. Charlotte darted away from her mother and placed a hand on his arm. In a voice so low that only Rose heard, she asked, "Did you receive my note about the exhibition?"

"I did," he answered in the same low voice. "I would certainly be interested in seeing it—"

Charlotte gave him a dazzling smile as she stepped back. "Tomorrow," she mouthed at him. "Send your car."

Alexander made them an awkward bow and hurried away. The crowd swallowed him up.

Rose didn't realize she was staring after him until she heard Ada's sympathetic voice in her ear. "Come on, Rose. Let's go."

"I don't understand—" Rose was still looking after him, though he had long vanished into the crowd. She felt too shocked even to weep. Was it her rudeness about his art? But no— why would he then have made a special effort to invite her to the *Rite*?

"What is there to understand? The man is clearly a cad." Ada's voice trembled, and Rose knew she was furious with Alexander. But there had to be some explanation, some reason. She began to follow in the direction he had gone, but Ada drew her back. Rose turned to her, confused. On Ada's face she saw her own pain mirrored.

"Rose, don't make a spectacle of yourself." Ada spoke clearly and with quiet authority.

"But—"

"Don't give him the satisfaction of seeing you're hurt. Walk away without looking back."

For an instant Ada was the mistress again, and Rose the maid. Rose allowed Ada to lead her away, one hand resting protectively on her arm. She glanced back once, but Alexander had disappeared into the crowd.

CHAPTER
Twenty-seven

Somerton

Georgiana was nervous as she came down the vast staircase to dinner. She could hear William's voice from the drawing room. He was clearly already more than a little drunk.

"Got a tip for the Kempton races . . . Lord MacIvory . . . fine sportsman."

Georgiana curled her lip. She knew that to William, *sportsman* meant someone who sat on the edges of sport, drinking and betting. She walked into the drawing room. Lady Edith was sitting on the sofa close to the windows, fretfully flapping at her pugs, who were gathered around her ankles. The little dogs yapped and nipped, leaping up to try to catch her draping sleeves. William, glass in hand, lolled in a chair with his back to her. Michael stood, looking as if he would like to leave the room altogether, by the door to the dining room. The potted palms cast shadows over his face, but Georgiana could tell he was scowling by the way his hands were forced deep into his pockets.

"Good evening, everyone," she said, trying to be as bright as possible. She needed at least Edith to be in a good mood if she was to get her to agree to engage Mrs. McRory. "I'm so sorry I'm late."

"Dinner is served." Cooper, who had been waiting just inside the dining room door, opened the doors with a deep bow.

"I suppose you may think it's a good evening," Edith said as they went in to dinner. The table was laid with silver and crystal, gleaming in the candlelight. "I suppose it must be quite pleasant for you with nothing to do all day but play the piano and ride and enjoy yourself." Her pugs scampered after her.

"Well," said Georgiana, maintaining her good-tempered smile as Cooper held her seat out for her, "I actually wanted to speak to you about—"

"When one is a mother there is simply nothing but trouble and distress," Edith went on without listening to her. She examined the menu with a sigh. "Dear me, Cook has so little imagination. If we had only engaged a French chef as I asked—"

William waved his empty glass at the butler, who instantly moved to fill it. "Westlake's cheap, that's the problem," he announced. "He has no idea of how a man of property must present himself." The footmen moved around the table, serving the soup course.

"As you do, you mean?" Michael said with a sneer. Georgiana

winced, but Edith was speaking over him, and William didn't hear.

"Augustus is such a sensitive child and Priya certainly has a way of managing him, but she is so nervous," Edith continued. "I merely enter the nursery and she starts as if she has seen a ghost. I sometimes wonder if she has. Indians are so attuned to the supernatural." She gave a dramatic shiver.

Georgiana did not dare look at Michael. Instead, she pushed her soup to one side and leaned forward. "Of course everything has been in so much disorder since Mrs. Cliffe handed in her notice," she said, "but I am delighted to say that we have found an excellent possibility to replace her."

"Really?" Edith did not sound convinced. "I hope she is not too expensive."

"Very reasonable, really. She previously worked for the Duke of Westminster," Georgiana said, hoping that this would impress Edith.

"Oh indeed?" Edith looked happier.

"Yes, and so if you are agreeable, I would like to write and offer her the position."

"Down, Cupid! Oh dear, no, not on the carpet—not again." Edith looked up from the pug as a footman hurried up with a cloth. "Yes, yes, that is all very well, but what shall I do about the nursemaid? I wonder if her brain is quite all right? Sometimes she seems quite lost in her own thoughts."

"She does own those, you know," Michael muttered, but only loud enough for Georgiana to hear. She knew how much it must be costing him to control himself and not speak out in Priya's defense, and she was grateful for his strength. If anyone guessed their relationship, Priya would be the one in trouble.

"So I hear you're not going back to Eton?" William boomed from the other end of the table. "That's right, lad, school is for milksops. I got out as soon as I could."

"But university—" Georgiana began.

"Oh, that's for muffs. I never went, and look at me now." His face was red, and strands of soup were caught in his moustache. "Wine, Cooper."

Georgiana glanced at Michael. The look of disgust on his face was plain. Perhaps, she thought, she would yet find herself in the extraordinary position of being grateful to cousin William.

As soon as supper was over, Georgiana rose and met Edith on the way out. "So may I engage her? Mrs. McRory, that is?" she said eagerly.

"Oh, very well. I suppose we have to have someone. But it is a great inconvenience to me, personally." Edith tossed her head and floated off in a mist of Russian scarves and a foam of slobbering pugs. "Come, sweeties. Sugared almonds for you now."

Georgiana hesitated. Instead of following William and Edith into the drawing room, she turned aside. Michael had excused himself and turned to go in the opposite direction. She followed him.

She found him in the library, standing by the great globe that she remembered her father examining so often as he worked. The oak bookcases loomed over him, a smell of leather and paper and old cigar smoke filled the room. Michael was gazing at India on the map. He looked up when she came in.

"I just wanted to say how grateful I am that you did not make a scene at supper," Georgiana said quietly. They hadn't spoken in private since their argument, and she was a little nervous about how he would react. "It must have been very difficult, but I know you did the right thing, for Priya."

Michael gave her a small, unhappy smile. "Everything I do is for her. I want to make her proud, as proud of me as I am of her."

Georgiana came closer to him, touched by the affection in his voice. "She will be. I know she will be."

"But not if I turn out like that bounder." With a tilt of a chin he indicated the drawing room, and William.

"You won't. How could you?"

"Did you hear what he said about not going to university? I don't want anyone comparing me to him."

Georgiana looked at him hopefully. Michael gave the globe a last spin. "Oh, stop looking at me like that. You were right, all right? I freely admit it."

"Oh, Michael!" Georgiana clapped her hands. "So you're going back to Eton?"

"*Thinking* about it," he said grumpily, but he caught her eye and smiled, a proper, mischievous Michael smile, the kind she hadn't seen for a long time. "To tell you the truth," he admitted, pushing his hand through his tousled hair, "I feel I've been a bit of an oaf to you. I'm sorry, Georgie."

Georgiana impetuously threw her arms around him and hugged him. A second later she drew back, blushing. "I'm so sorry—but I'm so pleased. For you and for Priya."

He smiled at her. "We'll never forget all you've done for us, Georgie. You're more my sister than Charlotte ever was, you know that."

Georgiana smiled back. She was aware of a soft bruised thing in her chest that might be her heart. But whether it was aching because she felt the pain of his love for Priya or because she wanted that love for herself, she didn't know.

She had always thought that when she fell in love, it would be obvious. But it seemed things weren't that simple. Nothing was simple at all.

Chapter Twenty-eight

London

Charlotte came down the stairs of Milborough House with the unhurried elegance of one who knows the race is already won. She cast a glance toward the mirror on the landing, and smiled. Her new Poiret hat was the smartest pink and black, a charming brooch of jet and rose amethyst set it off, and the cut of her bodice was daringly modern. She adjusted the brim of her hat just a touch, so it dipped below one eye, and arranged the coils of the necklace so the eye was drawn inward and downward.

Nothing stood between her and the duke now. The Huntleighs were an old family, and no matter how unconventional he liked to think himself, this one would never marry a housemaid. Before long, a ring—indeed, the Huntleigh parure ring—would be on her finger. Then it would be time to humiliate Laurence. It was lovely to have something to look forward to.

She went on down the steps, smiling to herself. Sunbeams poured through the fanlight and spread across the boldly tiled floor, reflecting off the gilded frames, the mirrors, the silver bowl crammed with roses that decorated the hall table. It was such a dazzling picture that for a second Charlotte could not tell where the sound of sobbing came from. She blinked, and realized there was a girl sitting on a small, battered suitcase by the door. Hardly a girl—she looked to be about Charlotte's own age. The inelegant way she was slumped, her red hands and cheeks, her common, clumpy shoes, her unfashionable dress, all proclaimed her to be a servant.

Charlotte was a little taken aback. The girl did not seem to have noticed her at all; she was sobbing too hard. Charlotte hesitated. If she went over there she might end up being wept on, and her pale-pink suede gloves would not take that well. But she could not quite bring herself to walk straight past the girl as if she were a piece of furniture. Charlotte took another, indecisive step forward.

The girl started at the sound of footsteps. She looked up, then leapt to her feet like a startled rabbit. "I'm so sorry, my lady," she blurted. She gulped and swallowed back tears.

Charlotte murmured something and made to walk past her. But the sound of the girl's muffled, swallowed sobs plucked at something in her. She knew what it was like to cry alone and try to hide it.

She turned to the girl. "May I ask"—her voice came out sharp—"what on earth is the matter? And," she added, her curiosity increasing, "who you are?"

The girl gulped and rubbed her nose with a plain white handkerchief. Charlotte watched her uncomfortably, half wishing she had said nothing.

"I—I'm Annie Bailey, my lady. Housemaid at Somerton." Her sobs threatened to overwhelm her again. "Least I w-was."

"Annie!" Charlotte was startled. Yes, of course there was something familiar about her. "But what are you doing here?"

Annie burst into fresh tears as she began to explain. Charlotte listened in astonishment. It was hard to sort the words from the sobs, but eventually she began to piece together the story. The girl had had some farfetched idea about being lady's maid to Rose, she had come down here, and Rose, unsurprisingly, had told her to go back again. Charlotte was not sure whether to laugh or lose her temper. It was too ridiculous. And yet of course one would have expected this kind of situation to arise following the Earl's insane decision to adopt his illegitimate daughter.

"And sh-she told me go to back to Somerton," Annie finished with a sniff. "I can't go back. They'll all mock me."

"Oh dear," Charlotte murmured. She was thinking quickly.

"She s-said it would cause trouble for her if I stayed."

"Oh, we wouldn't want that, would we?" Charlotte placed a hand—gingerly—on the girl's shoulder. Annie looked up in surprise. Charlotte forced a smile, trying not to think of the grease that was probably adhering to her suede glove even now.

"My dear, I can't bear to see you so upset. Anyone can see you are well turned out and would make an excellent lady's maid."

"That's just what I said. But Rose—I mean, Lady Rose— wouldn't listen."

"Extraordinary." Charlotte shook her head sadly. "She has become so headstrong this season. Almost as if she were getting ideas beyond her station." Then, as if struck by a sudden and delightful idea, she clapped her hands. "I know! Why shouldn't you stay and be *my* maid?" Charlotte had enough faith in her own taste to feel it was worth a risk.

"Your maid, my lady?" Annie gasped.

"Yes! It would answer perfectly, don't you think?"

"Why yes, b-but . . ." Annie drew breath. "Don't you already have one?"

"Yes, but between you and me she is quite careless and dirty, and dishonest too. Besides she is not as elegant as you clearly are. You obviously have a natural grace and—and modesty." Charlotte was surprised at and rather proud of her ability to make things up on the spur of the moment. Perhaps I should write a novel after I am the Duchess of Huntleigh, she thought. She quickly dismissed the thought; far too much like work.

"Do you really mean it?" Annie gasped.

"Of course I do! I am sure we can find you something to do until my maid leaves." Plenty to do, she thought. It would be very advantageous to have a girl like Annie downstairs.

"Oh, thank you, my lady! Thank you!" Annie clasped one of Charlotte's gloved hands and covered it with grateful kisses. "I can never thank you enough. Never, ever. I'd have been so humiliated to go back there."

"Please, don't thank me." Horrified, Charlotte managed to extricate herself from Annie's grasp. She didn't dare glance at the state of her gloves. "Now I must rush, and there are a few small matters I must attend to before you can take up your post. But just dry your eyes and take your case back upstairs. If Sanders asks any questions, tell him you answer to me now."

Annie was still flurrying curtsies as Charlotte sailed out through the door the footman held silently open for her. The car was waiting at the bottom of the steps, and the chauffeur, his brass buttons gleaming in the sun, leaped to open the door for her. As Charlotte hastened down the steps she was already pulling at her gloves, and as she settled herself into the motorcar's plush interior she removed them with a fastidious shudder. There were smudges on the pale pink suede. Happily she had remembered to bring a fresh pair.

"Drive on," she ordered, and as the car pulled away she tossed the gloves out of the window. They landed in the gutter and lay fluttering there with the fallen cherry blossoms, and were quickly crushed under the wheels of an omnibus.

Chapter Twenty-nine

Somerton

Georgiana watched as Mrs. Cliffe took a last glance around her room. She wondered what the housekeeper was feeling. This had been her home for most of her life, her sanctuary, her private world. The golden light shining from the well-polished oak desk, the glint of the china locked carefully away behind glass, the cushions of the rocking chair shaped to fit her body. The patient tick of the clock. Mrs. Cliffe had to be finding this parting so hard, thought Georgiana. And yet she didn't seem unhappy. In fact Georgiana thought she herself was more anxious.

Mrs. Cliffe cast a last, lingering glance around. She nodded slightly, as if to herself, and gave a slight sigh. Georgiana moved a step closer.

"That's all, my lady. I think Mrs. McRory will find everything in . . . order."

"I'm sure she will," Georgiana said warmly. She hesitated. "You will leave me your address, won't you? In case—" She almost said, *In case I should need you,* but swiftly corrected herself to, "In case Mrs. McRory should need anything."

"Of course, my lady." Mrs. Cliffe set down her valise and wrote her address in the housekeeper's book. Georgiana watched over her shoulder. It was a smart street in London. She felt relieved that Mrs. Cliffe had been able to secure a good situation.

"You will let Jackson take you to the station, won't you? I would be so pleased if you would."

"That would be an honor, my lady. It will be my first time in a motorcar."

"Mrs. Cliffe, however will I manage without you?" Georgiana blurted out.

Mrs. Cliffe turned to her with an affectionate smile.

"You're doing very well, my lady." She paused. "Just remember, always have confidence. Remember, you are the mistress here, the chatelaine, and never allow a servant to sidetrack you. Act with authority, care for the staff, and you will be respected."

Georgiana smiled her thanks for the advice.

She followed Mrs. Cliffe to the door and up the stairs, wondering where all the servants were. No matter what they thought of her past life, it was unacceptable of them to let her go without a word. She hoped they had said their good-byes privately. It would be too bad to let Mrs. Cliffe go without knowing how much she was appreciated.

They crossed the hall, between marble statues and below the classical frieze that circled the dome above them. Georgiana followed Mrs. Cliffe out of the front door, blinking in the sudden bright afternoon sunlight.

The staff were all outside, lined up as if to bid farewell to a duchess. Georgiana felt a lump come into her throat. Mrs. Cliffe paused on the top step. Georgiana, standing behind her, could not see her face, but when she spoke Georgiana could hear the smile in her voice.

"Thank you all so much," she said quietly. Then she walked down the steps with as much dignity as a queen to the waiting motorcar. Jackson stepped forward to open the door for her.

Mrs. Cliffe hesitated, and Georgiana came up to her. She had been going to say good-bye, but suddenly her heart felt too full for her to speak. She put her arms around Mrs. Cliffe and hugged her. "We will all miss you so much," she said.

"I will miss you too," Mrs. Cliffe said warmly.

Something metallic was digging into Georgiana's hip. She drew back and both she and Mrs. Cliffe looked down.

"Oh, I almost forgot," Mrs. Cliffe said with a slight laugh. She unhooked the great bunch of keys from her belt and handed them to Georgiana. They were unexpectedly heavy. Georgiana's hand closed around them, and the warmth from Mrs. Cliffe's palm stayed in her hand, like the lingering touch of a ghost, as she watched the car drive away into the distance. No matter how orderly Mrs. McRory was, it would be impossible to replace Mrs. Cliffe. The old days were gone forever.

Act Two

CHAPTER
Thirty

London

But my dear Daisy, said the good vicar, only consider the difference in your station. Is it right of you to give in to this love? What consequences will flow from such a mésalliance?

Rose, who was sitting on the sofa reading, started and let the book slip as a man's voice echoed up from the street below. A second later she knew it was only a passerby. Rain pattered against the window. She sighed. Nobody would visit in this weather.

She couldn't understand what had caused Alexander's behavior at the concert. At first she had felt utterly humiliated, certain that Ada was right about him. But now, days later, she was not so sure. She couldn't have imagined the connection between them. She could only conclude that he was offended by what she had said about his paintings. And in that case it was up to her to make amends.

She stood up quickly. What she was about to do was unconventional, she knew it, but it was also the right thing to do. Of that she was certain.

She went upstairs to her room, sat down at her writing desk, and hastily, before she could change her mind, wrote a letter. She addressed it to the Duke of Huntleigh, not to Alexander Ross.

It may seem strange for me to write to you directly, but I wanted to let you know how grateful I am to you for giving me the chance to see the Rite. I am only sorry we did not have more chance to converse. I would have apologized for my thoughtless words about your painting. I should never have said anything if I'd known that you were the artist. Please believe me when I say that for me they remain the best paintings in the exhibition.

She hesitated. She couldn't take back what she had said—she believed it. Her pen hovered over the letter, but in the end she simply signed her name and sealed it. But at least she had thanked him.

The letter sealed, she was faced with a new problem. She did not know where the Duke of Huntleigh lived, and as a single young lady she could hardly ask. She thought at once of Ada. Ada would know, or be able to find out, his address. But as she sat with the envelope in her hands, she remembered the contempt with which Ada had spoken about Alexander. She would never willingly take it to him. Her face fell as she remembered how she had carried Ada's love letters to Ravi. So much had changed since last year.

But if she could not ask Ada to deliver the letter, who could she ask? There was one possibility.

She found Céline in her room, trimming a hat. Rose paused at the door, which was ajar, and smiled. Céline looked perfectly happy, humming to herself as she tried different feathers against the felt. Rose gave a small cough, and Céline started and looked up. She jumped to her feet at once.

"My lady. I apologize, I did not see you there."

"There's no need to apologize. It was a pleasure to see you so engrossed in your work." Rose glanced at the hat. "Is that your own? It is very stylish."

"I hope not too stylish, my lady. I don't wish to appear above my station."

"No, indeed. It's simply elegant. You have real taste, I expect you know that."

Céline blushed and smiled. "Thank you, my lady. I enjoy clothes, fashion . . . I have a passion for them."

"It's wonderful when you can find employment in following your passion," Rose said with a small sigh. She was thinking of her music. Céline's questioning expression brought Rose back to earth and she remembered the letter she held.

"I . . . wondered if you would do me a small favor," she began.

She wished she were not blushing. It was not as if it were a love letter she wanted delivered. "I have a note I would like delivered in confidence."

"You can trust me, my lady," Céline said.

"Thank you. I'm sure I can." Rose came forward, and handed her the letter. Céline looked at the name on the front. Although she hid it well, Rose sensed her surprise.

"It really isn't anything dreadful," she said in confusion. "I simply wanted to thank him personally for inviting us to his box the other evening. The performance was so powerful. . . ." She was aware she was rambling, and stopped, her blush speaking for itself.

"I can certainly take this note to him, my lady." Céline bobbed a curtsy. "I am acquainted with his valet and will be able to make sure he sees it."

"Thank you so much." Rose impulsively pressed her hand. "If I can ever help you, you have only to ask."

Rose turned and left the room before she could turn any redder. Returning to the drawing room, she met the countess and Ada just outside in the corridor.

". . . Ada, I have given some thought to your costume for Mrs. Verulam's ball," the countess was saying. "I think you should go as a Greek goddess."

"If you wish—but which one?" Ada sounded weary.

"It really doesn't matter, the point is the white drapery. I think it important to keep the wedding in the forefront of Lord Fintan's mind at all times."

Ada half laughed as Rose approached. "I see you have great confidence in his affection for me."

"Affection is one thing, but distraction is another—and men are easily distracted, especially at the last ball of the season, when women will be trying to dazzle even more than usual. Besides, white suits you. You play the ingénue to perfection." The countess turned away, then back, to add, "Of course if you would allow us to place a notice in *The Times*, in the usual way, it would all be settled and there would be no need for any of this."

"And then I could go to the costume ball as a Hindu goddess with six arms and a necklace of skulls around my neck if I so desired, I am sure," Ada murmured. The countess frowned.

"There's no need to be saucy. Believe me, I would rather be organizing the wedding of my own daughter, but since you are the one who is to be married, I am certainly not going to allow any member of my family to have an engagement that is not exactly *comme il faut*. The cheaper papers have been gossiping already about your alliance, and if anything *should* happen to prevent the wedding, it would be most unpleasant."

She walked away, and Ada sighed and exchanged a long-suffering glance with Rose. Neither of them had to speak to express their feelings.

"I do wish this rain would stop," Ada said, going into the drawing room and crossing to the window. She pulled back the curtain to reveal the waterlogged street.

Charlotte looked up from the sofa where she was glancing through a photograph album. "Yes, there ought to be a law against it raining during the season," she said with a yawn.

Rose could see the pages as Charlotte turned them. It was a country house album, she realized, showing groupings of ladies and gentlemen at tea and croquet against the backdrop of a Jacobean mansion with ivy trailing from its heavy redbrick walls and dancing against the backdrop of its leaded windows. The words inscribed in fountain pen next to the mounted photograph read: Gravelley Park, 1911.

Charlotte glanced up at Rose. "Would you ring for some tea, Rose? You are closest to the bell."

Rose hesitated. Recently she thought she had noticed a certain change in the staff's behavior toward her. Somehow, if she ordered tea, it arrived late and cold. The footmen were a little less quick to open doors for her than they were for Charlotte and Ada. More than once a housemaid had failed to turn her back as she entered the room, or continued brazenly dusting. But all this, she thought, was surely in her imagination. She rang the bell.

There was a silence broken only by the rain stuttering on the glass and the lazy flick of Charlotte turning pages. A few moments later, the door opened and the housemaid entered.

"Some tea, please, Jane," Rose said.

Jane's curtsy was very brief, barely a shrug. She went out again.

"The exhibition on Heddon Street was quite shocking," Charlotte went on. "I adored it. Alexander explained all about the need for a truly modern art to represent our truly modern age."

"I'm delighted you and Alexander seem to get on so well," Ada said dryly.

Rose glanced toward the photographs again. With a brief, unpleasant shock she saw that some of the faces were familiar. There were Emily Maddox and Laurence, the two of them almost like twins, with the same sharp, shrewd expression. Then, grouped toward the back—and it was a strange grouping, like a set of chess pieces on a board—Charlotte and Alexander. They looked at the camera as if with secret smiles, seeming to say: *We share something you never will.*

"You certainly should be," Charlotte replied without looking up.

"What does that mean?" Rose spoke around the lump in her throat.

"Only that I'm saving some poor other girl from a fate worse than death. Alexander's dangerous. You have to know him to be able to handle him."

"And you think you know him." Rose couldn't keep her voice light.

"Well, we *have* known each other for such a long time," Charlotte said. She turned another page in the album. "That season was so delightful," she murmured. "Such a pity you weren't able to enjoy it, Rose. But then I'm sure you managed to have a little fun in whatever way housemaids do."

Rose turned away abruptly. She itched to slap Charlotte, but ladies didn't do such things. Rose looked at her reflection in the mirror, her large eyes, her hair piled elegantly upon her head, the rich shimmer of her kimono-style tea gown. She had a sudden violent desire to rid herself of all of it. She would never truly fit in, so why even try? If only she could be neither a lady nor a housemaid, but just herself, Rose.

"By the way, he was so surprised to learn that you were a housemaid," Charlotte added.

"You told him?" Ada's voice was sharp.

"It's no secret, is it?" Charlotte's eyes were wide and blue. "Everyone knows. At least, now they do."

Rose could see both of them in the mirror. Ada was anxious, glancing back at her as if she were afraid of her reaction. Rose was simply puzzled. Hadn't Alexander known, then? Suddenly she remembered Ada's stammered words at Madame Lucille's show. What had she been trying to say? Surely not . . . surely she had not been trying to warn her that Alexander might change his mind if he knew the truth about her background? She felt cold all over.

"What on earth has happened to that tea?" Ada said, obviously trying to change the subject. She crossed and rang the bell.

This time it was the second housemaid who arrived. She cast a glance toward Rose that was almost scornful. Rose could not respond. There were tears in her eyes and she thought that if she spoke they might fall. Could it be true that Alexander was as bad as Ada thought him?

"Agnes, Lady Rose ordered tea some time ago," Ada said warningly.

"Oh! Beg pardon, madam." Agnes bobbed a curtsy and disappeared.

"I can't think what holds them up," Charlotte murmured after long minutes had passed. "I'll go down, shall I?"

CHAPTER
Thirty-one

Agnes flounced down into the kitchen. "*Lady Rose* ordered tea," she said, mimicking Ada's voice. "Some lady! I'm not rushing. Who does she think she is? When just a few months ago she was as humble as we are!"

Annie, who was mending at the kitchen table, looked up. "Now you see what I mean?" she said. Clearly she wasn't the only person put off by Rose's airs.

"I think she has a cheek," Jane agreed, tossing her head. "She's nobody. Not a proper born lady like Lady Ada, not even a gentlewoman like Miss Charlotte."

Annie stood, smoothing down her skirts. "There, that's Miss Charlotte's buttons sewn on. I don't mind putting myself out when it's for a real lady."

She went out into the shadowy corridor, trying to ignore the stab of guilt when she thought of the old Rose, who had always stood up for Annie when Martha or James teased her. She pressed her lips together. There was no sense in being weak. Miss Charlotte had told her that, very kindly and companionably. One had to be strong if one wanted to rise in this world. As Miss Charlotte had pointed out, Rose had turned her back on her old friends very quickly, and deserved all she got in return.

The rain rattled on the skylight. Céline was standing just outside the laundry cupboard, folding shifts. Annie walked past her, then jumped as Céline caught her arm. She looked up in surprise—and flinched at the anger in Céline's eyes.

"Now just you listen to me, you silly little girl from ze country." Céline spoke in a low, furious voice. "How dare you come here and stir up trouble for my mistress. You should be ashamed! Some friend you are."

Annie jerked her arm away. "Some friend *I* am? And what about her, turning me away like a beggar?"

"Don't be so silly. She did it for your own good." She fixed Annie with a hard gaze. "Why are you hanging around here anyway?"

"Miss Charlotte told me I should stay." Annie raised her chin. "She's a real lady, unlike some."

"Lady Rose is a lady if society says she is."

"Miss Charlotte says—"

"Oh, Miss Charlotte. I see she has engaged you to spread poison about Lady Rose."

"I'm engaged as a lady's maid!"

"Are you indeed?" The sarcasm in her voice cut Annie to the core. "Well, I am pleased for you. But that doesn't make it better that you should be speaking against your friend. It's not easy for her either, you know, to be so suddenly a lady. Didn't you ever think *she* might need *your* friendship? You only think of what she can give to you."

Annie's gaze faltered, and she looked down. Rose's lady's maid was so forthright; Annie was surprised to find herself feeling uncomfortable. She tried to rally some defiance. "What does it matter to you anyway?" she muttered.

Céline folded the shift again, twice, then three times, smoothing away the creases, before replying. "I have my own plans. They are none of your business. But let me tell you, if you continue to stir up trouble for Lady Rose, I will stir up big, big trouble for *you*."

"I should like to see you try!" exclaimed a voice.

Annie turned to see Stella standing at the end of the corridor. She had a triumphant smile on her face as she came toward Céline.

"I hate to ruin your illusions of rising to be lady's maid to a Duchess, but I don't believe the Duke of Huntleigh is interested in Lady Rose."

"What makes you say that?" Céline did not sound troubled.

"Oh, never mind. Just that he's more likely to marry someone else."

"Miss Templeton?" Céline sniffed. "I doubt it."

"What Miss Templeton wants, Miss Templeton gets." Stella paced slowly toward them, smirking. "This is her third season, as we all know—she's on the shelf after this. She wants a proposal and she wants one from the Duke of Huntleigh. If you want to know what I think—"

"We don't, Ward."

Annie's head jerked up at the new voice that cut into their exchange. Charlotte Templeton stood on the servants' stairs, a little above them. Her face was flushed slightly, but the look she gave Stella was icy.

Stella and Céline straightened at once.

"Miss Templeton," Stella said, sounding terrified.

Miss Templeton ignored her. She walked down the stairs and smiled at Annie. "Bailey, have you finished my mending?" She held out her hands, and Annie wordlessly placed the dress in them.

Stella's eyes went from the dress to Charlotte and Annie. "But that mending—that's my job, Miss Templeton."

"No, Ward, it is my lady's maid's job," Charlotte said.

Céline's eyes widened.

Stella's color changed from red to pale. "Your—but—I—" she began.

Annie stood clutching the hem of her apron, feeling like a rabbit before an oncoming train. This was more than she had bargained for. She hadn't thought Miss Templeton would rid herself of her old maid quite so viciously and publicly. She could feel Stella's furious gaze burning into her.

"I've placed your reference and month's wages on your dress-ing table, Ward," Charlotte went on. "I may be *on the shelf*, in your view, but I still have my standards, and one thing I cannot abide is a servant who does not know her place." She smiled sweetly. "And now, where *is* that tea?"

CHAPTER
Thirty-two

"I have delivered the message you entrusted to me, my lady," Céline said the next morning as she helped Rose dress.

"Oh!" Rose wished she had not. She felt foolish and small for writing to Alexander. The image from the photograph album had stayed in her mind. Alexander and Charlotte had been standing so very close together in the photographs. They'd shared a whole season together. They had talked, and danced, and laughed, and no doubt exchanged secrets. Had more happened? She was not sure she wanted to know.

Rose turned to see that Céline was holding a piece of brocaded silk in crimson and gold.

"Now, my lady, if you'd like to look at this sample, which has come from Worth—"

"I wouldn't much, Céline," Rose sighed.

"Or perhaps this one—" Céline flipped the page of her fabric sample book to show a swatch of dove-gray chiffon.

"I am not really in the humor."

Céline looked at her in surprise. "But my lady has given some thought to her dress for Mrs. Verulam's costume ball?"

"To be honest, I was thinking of not going at all."

Céline stood very still, her face expressionless. Rose tried to lighten the mood. "You may have the afternoon off, Céline. It's a beautiful day and there's no sense in your spending it moping around inside with me."

"My lady," said Céline. "I must ask you to go to this ball."

Rose raised her eyebrows. "I beg your pardon?"

"I would like you very much to go to this ball and allow me to dress you as a daughter of the Earl of Westlake should be dressed." Céline's voice trembled.

Rose's cheeks flushed slightly with annoyance. Were all the servants going to be insolent to her? She had thought better of Céline. She spoke hastily. "I think you're being familiar. I dress quite properly. But you seem to want me to stand out. I don't say your dresses are not elegant, are not—" She hesitated. "My goodness, whatever is the matter? Céline, are you crying?"

Rose leapt to her feet and reached for her handkerchief. She pressed it into the maid's hand and ushered her to a chair. Céline dabbed the tears away. "Whatever is the matter? I am sorry if I upset you. I didn't mean to—"

"Please, my lady," Céline said, "You don't know what damage

you will do to me—to my dreams—if you keep on as you are doing. You are acting like a housemaid still—excuse me, but it is true. But you are not a housemaid. You are a very beautiful young lady, and I could dress you so that society would be dazzled as if a meteor had landed in their midst—"

"But I can't think of anything worse—didn't a meteor land in Russia a year ago and many people were killed?" Rose was glad to see her lady's maid's lips curve in their usual mischievous smile. She went on, "It's Charlotte who's going as the Firebird, not me. I really don't want to dazzle." She paused. "But am I to understand that it matters to you what I wear?"

"Of course it matters, my lady!" Céline exclaimed. "My reputation—" She hesitated.

"Oh?" Rose was half amused, half insulted. "So I'm your shop window, am I?"

"In a sense, my lady—yes." She looked down, then up again with a bright, fierce gaze. "My lady, I don't intend to be a maid all my life. I want to have independence, and I know I can earn it through my skill. I don't mean to leave you, but perhaps a little shop, a *boutique* . . ."

"You want an atelier!" Rose exclaimed.

"Yes, but . . . it all depends upon you," Céline said. "This ball will be the culmination of the season. Queen Alexandra will be there!"

Rose began to understand. Queen Alexandra, the widow of King Edward and mother of the current king, was a known arbiter of style. If she admired a dress, everyone would rush to buy it.

"If society sees I have dressed Lady Rose Averley more than becomingly, stunningly—I can succeed. But if you do not allow me to do that . . ." Céline bowed her head. "I have a chance, my lady, and you are it. I hope you don't object to my speaking so boldly."

"You wouldn't be yourself if you were not bold, Céline." Rose's amusement had subsided, and she was now admiring. Goodness knew Céline would need boldness if she were going to try to set herself up in business. "Well, I was thinking how useless my life is, but if I can be of use to you, if I can give you the help you need . . . well, why not? I will be your mannequin, Céline." Rose smiled. She would not allow Alexander's rejection to stop her having pleasure or helping others. "I *will* go to the ball."

CHAPTER
Thirty-three

"Thank you, Thompson." Lady Emily Maddox looked up to acknowledge the tea that the butler placed at her side. "You may leave us."

The butler melted away and Emily turned her attention back to the young woman perched on the edge of the chesterfield in front of her. Although she was clearly not at her ease in the opulent drawing room, she met Lady Emily's gaze with a hard, bold confidence. Miss Ward, thought Emily, was the kind of woman who set a great deal of store by revenge. She liked her already.

"Do please go on," she said, lifting the teapot. There was the music of Assam flowing, and the gentle shiver of china against china as she handed the cup and saucer to Miss Ward. "So Miss Templeton dismissed you unjustly."

"It was more than unjust, my lady. I was privy to all Miss Templeton's secrets. I carried messages for her, arranged assignations. Of course my conscience protested, but I did it out of a misplaced loyalty to her." She sipped the tea—the porcelain, thin as a rose petal, glowed as the light shone through it—and her eyes met Lady Emily's. She lowered the cup. "I can be very loyal, my lady."

"I am sure you can," murmured Emily, adding silently, *When it suits you.* "So you were only following her instructions when you carried this letter to the Duke of Huntleigh."

Stella set cup and saucer down. The clock distantly chimed four. "Yes, and now I bitterly regret it." There was certainly passion in her voice, but Lady Emily doubted it was the passion of remorse. "Apparently the duke had no idea that Lady Rose was once a servant. And Miss Templeton has no more obstacles in her way." Her eyelid twitched though her voice was perfectly calm. "I expect it was her plan all along."

Emily looked down at the cup and saucer in her hands. They fit together so well. Just as she had once thought she and Alexander fit together so well. That had been an illusion, most rudely shattered by Charlotte one terrible Saturday-to-Monday at Gravelley Park two seasons ago.

They had come for a jolly house party—she and Laurence travelling together, Alexander arriving after one of his jaunts to Europe, and Charlotte with Sebastian in tow—poor old Sebastian, always down on his uppers. A few other young people, some games of tennis, riding, croquet, and theater games. And dancing to the gramophone and the piano in the evenings. Emily had danced with Alexander several times that season, and had fancied herself in love with him—no, perhaps she really *had* been in love with him. At least, his dry voice, with the laugh hidden deep inside it, had made her feel all shivery, whenever she heard him speak. They had flirted. Laurence hadn't approved, but he'd had other things to occupy him—namely Charlotte Templeton.

That Saturday night, Emily, lying awake, had heard whispers and giggles and the padding of bare feet along the corridor. She had heard enough so that when Charlotte appeared late for breakfast the next day, and when Emily heard whispered arguments between them the day after that, Emily guessed at what had happened. Charlotte must have allowed Laurence to go a little too far, and now she was frightened and desperate for him to propose. But Laurence had never reacted well to pressure of that kind. He had pulled away—and that afternoon, over a game of cards, Emily had watched helplessly as Charlotte exerted all her skills of flattery and flirtation to tease Alexander out of Emily's clutches and into her own.

Emily still flushed with humiliation and rage as she remembered that afternoon. It was not that she wanted Alexander back. That was two years ago and much had changed. But she still remembered the pain Charlotte had caused her. Hatred, in her experience, endured much longer than love.

Emily set the cup and saucer down on the silver tray and looked up at Miss Ward with a pleasant smile. "Well, I do think you have been very badly treated in all this. And by chance, dear

Leblanc has just given notice—she wants to get married, of all things. May I offer you employment as my lady's maid?"

Miss Ward smiled. Lady Emily wasn't surprised. Their needs matched precisely, and it had been obvious from the start that this was why the woman had come. She must have heard of Leblanc's departure on the servants' grapevine. Gossip did travel so.

"I would be honored, my lady." Miss Ward put a hand into her reticule and drew out something grasped in her fist. She opened it to display scarlet petals, as if she had crushed a rose in her hand. "And now that that is quite understood, I think you may be interested in these. . . ."

CHAPTER
Thirty-four

Rose followed Ada out of the breakfast room. Ada stopped to collect the visiting cards that had already been left.

"'Lady Gertude, Lady Cynthia,'" Ada read aloud, flicking through them as she entered the drawing room. "Oh, what on earth can those two want? They're fooling no one by pretending they like us. Thank heavens Laurence will be here to help us bear them." She placed the cards on the mantelpiece just as Charlotte and the countess came down the stairs, dressed to go out, Charlotte a blaze of yellow and pearls, with ivory feathers in her hat, and the countess resplendent in the palest shades of gray and violet.

"I simply cannot wait," Charlotte was saying to her mother. "*In flagrante* with her butler—it's like a play!"

"Where are you two going?" Ada asked, looking up.

"The divorce court public gallery," the countess said, glancing in the mirror to adjust her stole. "It's Agatha Folsover today. I'm *so* looking forward to it."

"Don't you think it's a little cruel?" Rose said quietly. "Marriage isn't a spectator sport."

The countess ignored her—Rose was used to that—but Charlotte replied, "Nonsense. It's exactly that, and she's a fool if she imagines anything else." Her voice was acid as she continued. "Ada understands, don't you? From the trousseau to the honeymoon, it'll all be pawed over by the gossip rags."

"My dear, you sound quite jaded," the countess murmured, taking the visiting cards from Ada and glancing through them.

"Just realistic, Mother."

"I hope it hasn't put you off marriage." A note of warning sounded in the countess's voice.

Charlotte's mouth trembled slightly, but she composed herself, and when she spoke again she was her usual self. "Not at all. I'm just looking for the perfect partner to perform with." Her eyes met Rose's. "Someone who shares my artistic interests."

Rose kept her face expressionless. She was not about to allow Charlotte the satisfaction of seeing that her shot had hit home. There had been no reply to her note. Just a cold silence.

Charlotte turned right and left, looking in the mirror with evident appreciation. "I do like my new maid's taste," she said. "If she goes on this well, she'll be Lady Annie in a year, I shouldn't wonder."

She swept out, and the countess followed her. Rose and Ada looked at each other.

"I wish she had not taken Annie on," said Rose under her breath. "I suppose I should be glad, but I wonder what her motives are. The poor girl is no more a lady's maid than I'm a duchess, and I'm sure the extra work is falling on Céline."

Ada sighed. "Yes, it worries me too. However, perhaps it's a way for Annie to return to Somerton without too much embarrassment."

"You're right. I must think of it that way," Rose agreed.

"Have you plans for this morning, Rose?" Ada asked. "I hoped to find some time to write to Emily about our fund-raising dinner for the suffragettes. We want to invite Hannah Darford to speak." She turned to the newspaper, glancing at the front page. "Though with all this troubling news from Europe, I wonder if this is the moment for such an event. Laurence says there is nothing to worry about, but I'm afraid he is trying to shelter me."

"No, no plans," Rose said. Ada glanced at her, and Rose managed a smile. She couldn't weigh on Ada's spirits, it wasn't fair to her. "I shall take the chance to practice. It seems forever since I last played," Rose said. She turned and left of the room, heading for the drawing room. There was no music room here, but the countess kept a piano for after-dinner concerts.

Rose sat down at the piano and gazed at the keys. Once she would simply have begun to play, and ideas would have formed as if out of thin air. But now all she could hear was the rattle of wheel on the cobbles outside, the scraping of some maid cleaning the steps, the endless drone of the city. She placed her hands on the piano, but she did not begin to play.

A small sound behind her made her start. She turned sharply. Sunlight poured through the sash windows and bathed the walnut table and sideboard and glinted from the piano. The breeze through the open window stirred the curtain. Rose blinked as she seemed to see a ghost cowering behind it. Then she realized it was not a ghost. It was the tweeny. She looked frozen with terror, and she was holding Rose's book, *A Duke for Daisy*, which she had left behind on an end table the day before.

Rose stood up, startled. The tweeny jumped like a shot rabbit. She dropped the book with a clatter, and Rose saw that her hands were shaking. Full of pity, she left the piano and crossed to the girl.

"Please don't be afraid," she said warmly. Ellen, she remembered. The girl's name was Ellen. "I don't mind your reading it at all. I had no idea you were interested in books."

Ellen hung her head. She was so pale and washed out, Rose thought, remembering how she had rarely had a sight of sunlight when she was a housemaid. There was never time, never anything but work and sleep.

"I can't read much, my lady." Her voice was a whisper. "But the maids, they're reading it out loud in the evenings and they let me listen in. I just wanted to know what happened next. I'm sorry if I gave offense."

"You haven't, not at all." Rose was touched at the bravery it must have taken for the girl to creep up here, risking the rage of both the countess and Cook. "You may borrow it, take it away with you." She pressed it into Ellen's hands. Ellen took it, her face a mixture of terror and delight.

"Thank you so much, my lady! It is such a beautiful story." She hurried to the door, then paused and looked back at Rose with an expression of longing. "Do you think it could ever come true, my lady? That a duke could fall in love with a dairymaid?"

Rose hesitated. Her instinct was to say no, never. Hadn't she learned that over the past weeks? But Ellen was looking at her with such longing. False hope was cruel, but sometimes, she knew, people needed kindness more than truth.

"I . . . think it might," she said gently. "Maybe. It would depend upon the duke. And the dairymaid."

CHAPTER
Thirty-five

Eton

Michael hurried down the corridor toward his next lesson. Speaking was forbidden in the corridors at Eton, but in the Latin book he held was a letter, pressed like a flower between the pages. A letter from Priya.

He glanced up and down the corridor. There was no one to be seen. He knew he would be in trouble if he were late, but he couldn't wait another moment. He stepped into the shadow of a small alcove, opened the book, and read quickly.

To his disappointment the letter was short. He knew Priya had been ill, Georgiana had told him that in her own letter, but Priya hadn't replied to any of his anxious questions about her health. Instead there was light, bright chat about the servants, about her brothers and their new school, about her father's improving health. And then there was a change in the ink, as if she had set the letter aside and come back to it with a new pen. What followed was rushed and almost illegible.

I've been thinking how wonderful it will be when we're married. I am trying to hold on to that. We'll have a little house, with some climbing roses, and a vegetable garden so we needn't worry about food. Can you tell I've been dreaming of it? I try to think of it when things are difficult. I think of it so hard it floats in front of my eyes, as real as a photograph. It must be somewhere, that safe place. Oh Michael, I mustn't ramble on like this. I wish I could tell you everything that's in my heart and mind, but I know I'd regret it, so—work hard, and come back soon!

She had signed it with a flurry of kisses. Michael frowned at the letter. *I wish I could tell you everything that's in my heart and mind, but I know I'd regret it.* What did *that* mean?

He wasn't the imaginative sort, but he was sure there was something wrong. This desperate rush of words was not like Priya. He had half a mind to walk out of the school, go back to Somerton. But that would be irresponsible. He was here for Priya, he reminded himself. He was here to work hard so that they could have a happy future together. His house had never been a home, there had been no one to love—his brother and sister were so wrapped up in society, his mother distant, his father dead, just a succession of nannies and nursemaids who changed every year.

Priya was a miracle; her stories of a loving family made him feel he had come to life for the first time, her affection was all he had ever dreamed of. He clung to the memory of her, her soft lips, her silken hair, the scent of her skin. No, he had to stay here, he had to conquer his anxieties and be a grown-up. He had to think of the future, for both their sakes.

He looked up from the letter, to the pictures that hung on the wall. There were framed photographs of the famous match against Harrow in 1910. Even though he was concerned about Priya, Michael had heard all about Fowler's match, and he examined the pictures with interest.

Footsteps and the swishing of robes made him jump. One of the masters was coming. He stepped back out of the alcove quickly, and then turned back just as quickly. A single face in the photographs had caught his attention. Dark curly hair, and the distinctive Eton uniform. The camera had caught him just turning toward the lens, and the black eyes looked out of the frame at Michael with a strange intensity.

"Templeton!" called the master sternly. "Hurry to your next lesson, boy."

Michael scurried on down the corridor, but he was breathing fast with shock. It couldn't be possible. And yet he would know that face anywhere, he had seen him so many times, impassive as he held Sebastian's dinner jacket or lathered soap for the razor. The face belonged to Oliver.

CHAPTER
Thirty-six

London

Rose sat before the piano. The pages of music stirred in the breeze that came through the open door to the garden.

The music will come, she told herself. It must come. It must come back.

She tried a chord, remembering the music of *The Rite of Spring* and trying to echo it. Alexander was right, it was a masterpiece.

Oh do stop thinking about him, she told herself. As if there were not other, more important things to worry about. She turned her mind determinedly to Sebastian. How was poor Oliver feeling now? But that did not help. The tune she was playing slipped away from her and she made a small sound of annoyance. At this rate it would be time to go up to Céline and be fitted for Mrs.

Verulam's ball, and she would have wasted the hour she had for writing music.

"Why can I not *concentrate*?" she exclaimed. She jumped up, determined to close the window against the sunshine, the birdsong, the distant rattle of trains, and the clatter of carts. But before she could move, she heard footsteps outside the door, and the butler announced:

"The Duke of Huntleigh."

Rose turned in astonishment. Alexander Ross strode into the room, just a pace behind the butler. His hair was if anything longer and more tangled than it had been before, and paint stained the sleeves of his morning coat. The smile he gave her was completely disarming.

The thought shot through Rose's mind that Ada would have known how to deal with this—a cool how d'ye do, a little polite chitchat, a call for tea, a brief, distant indication that she had plenty to do this afternoon, thank you, and good-bye. But when she looked into his eyes she found herself saying, "I've missed you."

"I've missed you too," he replied so readily and with such a lack of embarrassment that she didn't even blush, though she was sure that as soon as she allowed herself to think about what she had just said—Good heavens, what had she *said*?—she would sink to the floor with mortification.

"I'm sorry to say Charlotte is out," Rose stammered. Why, she wondered, was she not angry with him? Why was she not resenting his behavior toward her? Why did her pride not demand she turn away? Simply because now he was here, standing before her, now that she was looking into his thoughtful green eyes, she *knew* that Ada was wrong. He did not care if she had been a housemaid.

"I didn't come to see Charlotte. I came to see you. I have been in Cornwall, painting, and only just received your letter on my return to London this morning."

Rose collected her thoughts. She had already made enough of a fool of herself.

"I am so sorry for my thoughtless words," she began, as formally as she could.

"Not thoughtless at all." His mouth curved in a smile. "Plenty of good thought went into them."

"But—but I was so insulting."

He waved his hand dismissively. "Yes, my pride was hurt. I'll accept that. But it only hurt because I knew you were right. The best criticism does hurt, that's how you know it's worth listening to."

"No, no, I—" she began in confusion.

He spoke over her. "My paintings *are* empty. I know it. And I'll fix it—somehow. But I don't want you to think that I'm childish and self-centered enough to ignore you because of my hurt feelings."

"Then why did you?"

"I was embarrassed." He met her eyes directly. "Not a much better reason, but when you feel you've made a fool of yourself it's hard to behave well." He laughed, and her heart seemed to soften with tenderness just as laughter softened his features. The laughter quickly faded, though, and he went on. "I was told—I hadn't known before, believe me—that you were once a housemaid—"

Rose took a deep breath. So this was it. She could see the conversation playing out in front of her, he would apologize for giving her false expectations, she would have nothing to do but stammer that it didn't matter, and try not to show how hurt she was.

"You can imagine how horrified I was."

Rose's pain gave way to anger. He had no right to speak to her as if she had no feelings at all, and she opened her mouth to say so, but he went on.

"No, no, please let me explain. I didn't know, when we were at the exhibition, and I remembered instantly how rudely I'd spoken about servants then. I don't want to remember the exact words." He winced. "I thought you must despise me. I had already sent the invitation to the ballet, but I could not bear the thought of facing you and knowing how offended you must be. Nor could I stay away."

"Oh," she said faintly. His words came back to her. *No servant could ever be creative.*

"It's not a good excuse, I know. I was so glad when I received your letter and discovered that you hadn't taken offense. I hope you will accept my apologies."

Rose fought back a desire to laugh in relief and happiness. "You haven't insulted me at all," she said warmly. "Are we friends then?" She held out her hand to him.

He took it and pressed it, smiling into her eyes. "Very much so."

It seemed perfectly natural for him to take her arm and for them to walk though the house and out into the gardens for a stroll. Rose found her pace fitted his easily. There seemed no need to talk. The distant rattle of traffic was muffled by the trees that lined the garden wall. This is as close to silence as I have found, she thought, almost startled by the realization.

"I am glad," she began awkwardly, "that you don't think . . . less of me, for what I once was."

"Not at all. I certainly do think that all this . . ." he waved a hand, his gesture including the neatly planted flower beds, the majestic house behind them, the bustle of London, ". . . is at heart ridiculous. One group of people shouldn't be supported on the shoulders of another. But I think it is all the more marvelous that you have been able to move between two worlds. I think you are very brave." He turned a serious gaze toward her.

Rose shook her head. She thought of the embarrassment she had felt at the state ball, of the insecurity she felt every day. "I am not brave. I have little choice but to accustom myself to my new life."

"But you have done that with such grace. You have managed to remain yourself despite everything."

Rose couldn't help sighing.

"You don't agree?"

"I wish I had managed to continue composing," she replied. "But I have found it so hard to work since the season began."

He raised an eyebrow. She went on, trying her best to explain as they walked among the flower beds. "When I sit down at the piano, I can't play. It's not as it was at Somerton. I feel adrift in a new and unknown sea. It feels as if I've lost my way."

"You too," he said thoughtfully.

"I know my compositions must change, just as I have changed, but I don't know what they will change into yet. What I will change into." Once again she realized that just by speaking to him she had managed to explain to herself how she felt.

"Something about your presence makes me see clearly," she said with a smile. "I never understood exactly how I felt until just now."

He turned to her suddenly, his face alight with an idea.

"Why don't we go away from here? The city, the season, the whole thing. Let's run away."

Rose stared at him, shocked at the suggestion, and the light in his green eyes. Her first instinct was to refuse, but she hesitated. What if I said yes? she thought. The bare idea made her feel as if she were in a lift like the one in Selfridges, being whisked up into the air by a force as powerful as the pull of the future.

"What—just us? Together?"

"Who else?"

"Well—I—" Rose could hardly believe he was proposing such a scandalous adventure. And yet her mind was already working, thinking, If Céline pretends I'm ill . . .

He caught both her hands, speaking to her with an energy and excitement that caught her like wildfire. "We've both lost something. You have lost your music, and I've lost my art. Perhaps we'll find it together, if we go away from here. To the wilderness."

Rose grasped one final time for dignity, decorum, discretion. "I—I don't think I'm dressed for the wilderness," she objected, looking down at her thin tea gown.

His smile widened, and she felt it catch her like fire. "No, you certainly should have a hat. We're driving."

She laughed. And laughed again. Was he serious? How could she risk everything like this? But a drive with Alexander—the thought of the wind teasing her hair, flirting with her hat, the sun kissing her skin—it all seemed so wonderful. She couldn't possibly—and yet why not? No one need know, not if she was careful. Dare I? she thought. Dare I?

"Wait here," she said, and turned and ran back to the house.

She burst into her room. Céline, who had been sitting sewing buttons, looked up in surprise. "My lady? Is something the matter?"

"Yes—no. I need a hat, Céline." She looked around the room.

"Of course. I am so sorry, I had thought you were not going out until the evening, my lady." Céline scurried to the wardrobe.

"Neither had I." Rose hugged herself, watching Céline bustle about, securing roses and ribbons. She longed to go with Alexander, longed to escape, to see what he was promising her— but she knew it was madness. She hesitated. Should she go? Was she strong enough to resist, if . . . "Céline, if you wanted very much to do something—but it seemed madness—what would you do?"

Céline turned. Rose met her keen, sharp gaze.

"Is it the Duke of Huntleigh?"

Rose's mouth opened. Céline was certainly perceptive. "Er—yes. He wants me go to go for a drive with him—alone."

Céline crossed the floor in two quick strides and settled the hat on Rose's head. Rose felt her strong, deft hands securing hatpins, tilting the brim.

"*Voilà. Parfait!* My lady, we are not in the days of Queen Victoria. This is the modern world. Why should you not go?"

"You think so? Really?"

Céline nodded firmly. "Be quick and discreet, and no one will ever know."

Rose flushed with happiness. It was exactly what she had wanted to hear.

"Thank you, Céline." She hurried to the door, took a deep breath, and went quickly down the stairs to meet Alexander.

CHAPTER
Thirty-seven

The wind rushed into Rose's face, her veil fluttering with light and speed. The duke drove fast but well, steering the motorcar through the London streets. The sun turned the Thames to diamonds and glittered across the windows of the grand houses.

"Where are we going?" Rose called over the noise of the engine.

"Away from here." He grinned. "I promise you one thing, and that's better pictures than the Royal Academy."

He pressed the accelerator and excitement fizzed inside Rose like the bubbles in champagne. Before them were the open road and the fields. She knew she should be sensible, should make him take them back to London and safety. But was it really safety?

How safe was a prison? Do I want a life like Ada's, she wondered, in which even my heart is not my own?

She clutched the edge of her seat, listening as he half spoke, half shouted, over the noise of the engine, gesturing out at the crowds that hurried home among the grand houses.

"See there—a city of seven million people. A few hundred of them act as if the rest didn't exist. They're like dreamers, wandering around in their own airy delusions. They don't even see themselves, let alone the rest of the world. Sleepwalkers, that's what I call them."

"Or castaways, that's how I feel," she replied. "Walking round the edge of my tiny island, looking out on the flat unchanging sea."

"Why don't you build a boat and sail away?"

"I try, but as soon as I've got a few planks together my maid interrupts to talk about dresses, or the butler announces luncheon, or Lady Such-and-Such arrives and I have to make polite conversation with her."

"A busy desert island."

She laughed. "Yes, and a most fashionably decorated one, with all the modern conveniences. And it's got its own tides, you know. As soon as you set out they drag you away, to dress fittings, shopping expeditions, balls, parties, Saturday-to-Mondays. . . ."

"Hateful, isn't it?" He flashed her a knowing glance. "It's a merry-go-round, and all the horses are the same, and the music never changes. . . . I dance with the same girls every season and all of them I've known from the nursery, and all of them are so perfectly predictable. Debutantes pressed out of the same mold, and not one of them has a laugh that's real. That's why I went away, to shake myself free."

"And did you find freedom?"

Alexander was quiet for a moment, running a hand along the smooth leather of the motorcar gear. "Can you feel it? The speed, the power? Nothing can hold us back, we can't be trapped by the confines of our parents' generation. Tell me, how can you ride a motorcar, feel that powerful heart beating, how can you feel London shudder and breathe with the rhythm of the trains hurtling through it, the very air split and conquered by aeroplanes, how can you feel all that, and be content to be led into dinner at a sedate pace in precise order of precedence? How can you dream beside the river as if nothing had changed, as if everything were going to go on forever and ever and ever the same?"

Rose found herself breathless. "No," she whispered. "I can't."

"We are changing and we can't stop ourselves. We're going somewhere, Rose, all of us, and I want to know where. The future has to be better than the past, hasn't it?" He looked at her, and suddenly said: "I am so glad we're on the same journey, Rose."

She laughed in confusion, startled by his sudden, almost drunken happiness.

"You've no idea what a breath of fresh air you are." His gaze traveled over her. "I have never met a woman like you before."

Rose smiled, and felt her face warm. To hide her confusion she looked out at the streets. They were leaving the houses behind as fields unfolded like green banners, the hedges dazzling her eyes with the sunlight gleaming from their green leaves.

"But where are we really going?"

"Cornwall."

"Cornwall?"

"Mont Pleasance. It's as close to the wilderness as we can get in a day. We spent every winter there, when the cold of the Highlands became too much to bear. The second duke built it for his bride." He added, with the irony she had come to associate with him, "So there has been at least one happy marriage in my family, it seems."

Rose was sure she should ask more questions. Cornwall seemed a long way away, a place she had only heard of in legends of King Arthur and the Holy Grail. Surely she should be protesting, she should be afraid, conscious of the danger to her reputation. But somehow she did not want to. She didn't feel afraid, she realized to her surprise. She didn't feel anxious. Being here, with Alexander, now, felt right. More right than anything had in a long time.

She relaxed into the leather seat. The countryside blurred past, sun and golden fields mingled with the constant roar of the engine. A weight of worry seemed to melt away like an iceberg vanishing. The sound of the engine was lulling her, and Alexander's presence was warm and reassuring by her side. She slipped into a dream, a dream in which she was at the prow of a boat, rushing forward through a dark sea, onward to an unknown destination. But she did not feel afraid, because Alexander was right beside her.

The silence woke her. She gasped in sudden fright. "Where are we?"

"It's all right." Alexander's voice steadied her. "We've arrived."

Rose struggled to sit up. The wind had half destroyed her hat, and her hair was tangled beneath it.

"Oh dear," she murmured as she tried to rescue her hat. Then she saw where they were, and all thoughts of her appearance vanished.

They were on a rocky rise above woodland, and below her she could see the stark, rugged shape of a castle. It perched upon the rock like a sea eagle. A winding path led down to it. And behind it, glittering, moving, constantly dancing . . .

"Is that the sea?" she asked.

He looked at her in surprise. "You've never seen the sea before?"

"No. Somerton is not near the coast." It was enormous, she thought, huger than she had ever dreamed. The pictures at Somerton did not do it justice.

"I suppose not. Well, what do you think of it?"

"I think it's the most beautiful thing I've ever seen." She added, "And listen—listen to it!" She smiled in wonder and delight as she realized the constant rushing and roaring was the sound of all the waves breaking upon the beach. As if that sound had opened her ears to others, she realized that she could hear through it the gentle rustle of grass, the sweet and shrill birdsong. Above the sea, gulls circled, crying like children. And behind it all, like the white canvas of a painting, was silence.

"What a beautiful place," she exclaimed. "And oh—what is the castle?"

"That's Mont Pleasance," Alexander said. "We can only reach it by foot from here. It was built to be secluded—apart from the world."

Rose gazed at it. The castle was beautiful, as beautiful as Somerton, but utterly different. There was nothing elegant about it, nothing tame. It had the beauty of an uncut diamond.

"I forget that there is so much for you to discover," he said. He smiled down at her. "I'm glad that you first saw the sea with me."

"*Because* of you," she replied. "It's a beautiful gift. Thank you." His eyes glittered as he gazed back at her. "You are so lucky to have this as your home."

A shadow seemed to cross his face. "Let's go," he said. He climbed out of the motorcar and came round to help her down.

She glanced at him as they walked down the winding path toward the castle. Alexander had not sounded proud of his home. He gave no sign of pleasure in being there as they walked under the stone arch, into the embrace of the courtyard.

Closer up, Rose could see that the castle was falling into decay. The clustered turrets were entwined with ivy. She could hear the crashing of the waves below. Espaliered fruit trees that had once grown against the sunny walls had been allowed to run wild and she caught the smell of apples crushed into the grass.

"Is there no one else here? No servants?" The castle felt so far away from everywhere else. It was almost as if the outside world had vanished.

Before Alexander could answer, a man came out of the front door. Rose just had time to see he was bearded and dressed in a smock-like garment splashed with an eye-watering combination of paints, before he waved and shouted in a French accent. "Alex! At last. You must tell me if this orange is too clean."

"Your colors are never clean," Alexander retorted with a grin. He took Rose's hand and led her across the courtyard. Feeling both terrified and elated, Rose followed Alexander and the Frenchman inside. She gasped and stood still, gazing around her in amazement.

A great wooden staircase swept up in two flights to a landing above, and on the walls hung vivid, powerful abstract canvases. The heads of boar and stag hung crazily among them in a strange clash of ancient and modern. On the walls hung swords arrayed in fan shapes, and classical statues lined the hallway, intermingled with extraordinary metal objects that seemed ripped from the heart of a steamship or an aeroplane. With the sunlight coming through the stained-glass window above the stairs and glowing from the wooden banister, it all combined to make the most original impression that Rose had ever seen. It was like looking into a different universe. And then one of the statues, dressed in a Grecian tunic, turned and stepped down from her pedestal.

"Are you no longer painting me, darling?" she asked the Frenchman. "I must have a cigarette then." She did not even glance at Rose. Neither she nor the artist took the slightest notice of Rose, and to Rose's surprise this did not annoy her. In fact, it was welcome. No one was staring, no one was listening. Rose was simply accepted, as natural a presence as the light. The French artist and his model wandered away, chatting and sharing a cigarette. Alexander led Rose up the stairs. She glanced into room after room. In some, she saw easels set up. A gray-haired, bespectacled woman in canary-yellow stockings sat at a window and typed furiously without looking up. Rose heard an opera singer's voice floating down like strands of gold from an upstairs window.

"I don't understand." Rose was breathless, both from the astonishing sights all around her and from trying to keep up with Alexander's fast pace. "Who are those people? Do they live here?"

"They do, for as long as they wish to. They're like me—they just want to paint, or sculpt, or write. And in Paris, they starve and live in hovels. I brought them all here, let them live as they want, work freely. I want the place to be somewhere that people can do something worth doing."

Rose looked at him in disbelief. It was impossible to imagine Somerton thrown open in the same way. "But this is your home. You are very generous to open it up like this."

"No, no," he said wearily. "I have to let in the light somehow."

She wanted to ask him what he meant, but he forestalled her, pushing open the great doors to a long gallery. It was still decorated in the heavy Victorian style, but the windows had been thrown open to the view of the sunlit sea. He led her down the room, past portrait after portrait.

"Are those the ancestors?" She looked up at the grim faces, from the days of armor, wigs, and ermine. The great swords that hung on the walls like guillotine blades seemed soft next to them.

"Yes. Cheerful lot, aren't they?"

Rose followed Alexander down the echoing stone hall. The last portrait had been taken down and a bare space on the wall showed where it had hung. Rose looked curiously after him, but he didn't pause, only strode on.

Room after room was filled with canvases, electric and powerful, propped here and there as if they had been done in a great hurry and forgotten about as soon as painted.

"It's wonderful, it's so wonderful," Rose could do nothing but repeat the words. "I didn't think a place like this existed."

"I knew it didn't. That's why I created it." He looked around him. "It's the place I wanted it to be when I was growing up here. People like Vincent, and Marlene . . . They can work here."

"It's the most wonderful idea. I've never seen anything so perfect." She realized how much she would love to live here, far away from London society, free as the seagulls.

Alexander turned a warm smile to her. "I'm glad you like it. I would want my wife to help me in this work."

And he walked away. Rose stood, stunned. Was that a proposal? she asked herself. Unable to think of a response, she followed him.

I should challenge him, she thought, a little angry. But she hadn't the courage to. She was afraid of breaking the fragile spell that seemed to allow them to be together. If she stopped and thought, she would remember how impossible it was for her to be here, what dreadful trouble she would be in if she was found out. She didn't want to think of that. I have till midnight, she thought, and I am going to dance my heart out.

"Come, let's look at the sea. It's the best view in Cornwall."

He caught her hand and ran with her along the hall, threw open a door, and they stepped out onto the battlements. The wind ruffled his curls as he turned to the sea. Rose, watching him, had a strange thrill of thinking that he might have been his ancestor from a hundred years before.

It was beautiful, the rocks and coves, the light glinting from the sea, the white sails of yachts on the horizon. Seagulls keening as they balanced on the wind. And the rocky maze of a garden, leading down to the sea. She breathed in the fresh, wild air. Still she rolled Alexander's strange words over in her mind. A proposal? Or just a careless comment? Perhaps I simply imagined it, she thought. Or misheard. She groped for words, anything to break the silence.

"There must be so many happy memories here for you—"

"I hate the place," he said quietly.

"But why?"

"My father. He hated everything I loved, it seemed. He forbade me to study art, drove my mother to madness, and drank

himself to death. Everything here reminds me of him." Alexander
waved his hand toward the castle behind them. "I think if I bring
my life here, my art, my passions . . . I think I will one day be able
to paint over the memories of him."

"I am so sorry," Rose murmured, remembering the last, missing portrait. It must have belonged to the last duke, the father
Alexander was doing all he could to erase.

"He forbade me to study art. We quarreled again and again.
It was only by running away, giving up everything to go to Paris,
that I could learn to paint."

"But he must have loved you." She drew closer, wanting to
comfort him and not knowing what to say. "He left you all this."

He laughed, a harsh bark. "There was only one thing he
loved more than himself, and that was the Huntleigh line, the
Huntleigh name. He would never have left the estates to anyone but me. As bad as he thought me—and he thought me very
bad—I could at least produce an heir. You see? I didn't matter at
all. His only interest in me was that I should marry a suitable
heiress and produce more Huntleighs."

Rose hardly knew what to say. It felt as if he had drawn a
curtain aside, to show her a life of such shadow and sadness that
it broke her heart to think of it.

"Then why did you come back?" she said. "Why return for
the season?"

He hesitated. "You may have heard gossip about my conduct
the season before I left. . . ."

She wanted to know the truth so badly, and he had already told her so much. "What happened at Gravelley Park?" she interrupted, hardly believing her own daring.

He shot her a keen glance. "I'm not proud of it. I don't want you to think badly of me."

"I don't want to think badly of you either," she said.

He sighed, running his hands through his curls. "Laurence invited us to Gravelley Park for a Saturday to Monday. I was—well, I was not at my best, shall we say. My father and I had just had another falling out. I had brought several bottles of Highland whisky as a gift for Laurence. Needless to say, I drank the whole of them. I hardly remember that weekend, but from what I understand, my behavior was reprehensible. I first led Laurence's sister to believe I had serious intentions toward her, only to throw her off for Charlotte Templeton. Another lady toward whom I had no serious intentions. I was a rake, and there's no denying it. I am only now trying to make amends for my behavior toward Miss Templeton, though understandably Emily Maddox wants nothing to do with me."

Rose's mouth opened in shock. "But . . . is this why you've paid Charlotte such attentions? Your previous conduct?" It was as if an invisible weight had lifted from her chest.

"Yes." He smiled down at her. "Though now that I've truly gotten to know her, it's clear that she is simply using me to make Laurence jealous. I feel a bit of a fool, of course, but at least now we are even." He laughed. His dark mood had vanished as quickly as it had come. "Come, let's go back inside. There's one more thing I want to show you."

"We ought to go back," Rose protested halfheartedly, but Alexander was ahead of her and did not seem to hear. He led her along the corridors and threw open a door. Rose saw a room hung with tapestries and shrouded in shadow. The tall windows were open to let in the sea breeze that stirred the curtains. In the center of the room, its polished wood shining so deeply that it seemed almost to glow, stood a grand piano.

Rose gasped. She turned to him, an unspoken question in her eyes. He met it with a smile.

"Yes, I was thinking of this when I asked you here." He hesitated, then added, "I wasn't telling the whole truth when I said I had no happy memories here. My mother sometimes used to play this piano. I'd like to hear it again."

Rose didn't need to be asked twice. She walked over to the stool and sat down. She ran a hand lovingly over the wood, and opened the lid. For a moment she was frightened that she would not be able to play, that just as in London, she would be lost. But the instant her hands touched the keyboard she knew she had nothing to fear.

All the new sounds she had heard since she came to London—and the cries of the seagulls outside, the steady rush and roar of the sea—mingled together in her mind and her fingers sought them out on the keyboard. She was so engrossed that she was startled when she looked up and saw Alexander close by, watching her. His eyes shone as brightly as the sunlight on the wood.

Her hands danced across the keys, and music spilled out. All the new sights she had seen—the sunlight on the sea, rippling and shimmering as if it were liquid metal; Alexander's words, *We are changing and we can't stop ourselves*—all came together in her mind like strands woven into a tapestry. That was what her music would be, she knew now. It would be change itself. It would never repeat a pattern, but always be transforming, always be weaving something new. Lost to all sense of time, she did not notice as outside the light faded from the sky, and the stars came out one by one over the dark sea.

Chapter
Thirty-eight

Cornwall

Rose woke to perfect peace. The sea's gentle sighs and the cries of the seagulls mingled with the salty breeze that blew in through the open window. She realized she was no longer at the piano, but lying on the sofa, covered in a blanket. And wrapped in Alexander Ross's arms.

Her eyes fluttered open, and she remembered the night before in a rush of fierce joy. They had talked and laughed late into the night. He had told her about Paris, until she could almost see the brash, bold lights and smell the cigar smoke mingled with the fumes of oil paint and turpentine.

"I'll take you there," he had told her. "We'll walk along the Seine, I'll show you the Eiffel Tower. It's monstrous but beautiful, just as the future should be."

She allowed herself to snuggle deeper into his arms, feeling warmer and safer than she ever had in her life. She noticed a sketchbook under his arm, one corner jutting out. Moving softly so as not to wake him, she tried to see what he had been drawing. She managed to extricate the sketchbook and looked at the drawing. The figure was a blur of movement, of light, somehow, though the light was caught in dark lines of charcoal.

She looked up to find him smiling at her, his eyes open. "I'm sorry—I was prying," she said, but couldn't help smiling back at him.

"No, don't be," he said, taking her hand. "It will be yours anyway, when it's finished." He picked up the sketchbook, looking at it thoughtfully.

"I wonder if it looks anything like the music sounded." He began stroking her fingers with his thumb. Her hand fit so perfectly in his. "I was fascinated by the way you put sounds together. I don't think I've ever heard anything like it before."

"I'm not trained, of course," Rose stammered. Her heart sped up with each brush of his skin against hers.

"But that's exactly why it's so fascinating. Your music is original. Your ideas are like you—unique."

His gaze was soft but so intense that she blushed. She was aware of the warmth of his body next to hers, the closeness of his lips to her own. She looked away in confusion, but she could still feel him looking at her, and it felt more intimate than anything she had ever experienced before.

I shouldn't be doing this, she thought. This is dangerous. This is . . .

She looked up, directly into his eyes. Gently he kissed her on the mouth. Rose melted into the dizzy, glorious feeling. Although everything she knew told her that she was behaving dreadfully, dangerously, she could not stop kissing him. It simply felt right, she thought, shocked at how easy it was to behave in ways one would not have dreamed possible.

She felt his hands at her waist, shifting her onto his lap as his lips moved against hers more desperately. She pressed her body against his. An overpowering need to erase the space between them had taken her over, and she ran her hands through his hair, deepening their kiss.

Finally she drew away, gasping for breath. Her eye caught her own reflection in the mirror. She almost laughed at the sight of herself, her hair tangled and her dress ruffled.

His breath was heavy too. "What is it?" he asked.

"I've made a mess of myself," she smiled. "If my lady's maid could see me now—" She stopped short.

Céline. The ball. It was tonight!

"Rose? What is the matter?" Alexander said, sounding anxious.

"Oh!" She gasped, a hand to her mouth, as she realized the severity of the situation. "Mrs. Verulam's costume ball. It is tonight!"

She leapt to her feet, hastily trying to tidy her hair and her dress. It would be awful to let Céline down. This ball mattered so much to her. Alexander followed her, trying to calm her.

"Does that matter? Need you go?"

"Yes, yes I must. I promised Céline." She glanced out of the window. The sun was already high. "Can we be there by this evening?"

"If we must. But who is Céline?"

"My lady's maid." She turned to him. "I'll explain in the car, but we must go now—please!"

Chapter Thirty-nine

London

Ada woke slowly and uncomfortably, becoming aware that the morning light was shining directly in her eyes. She blinked and groaned and sat up.

"Céline?" The lady's maid was standing by the fireplace, watching her, her hands wringing her white apron nervously. Ada glanced at her jeweled pocket watch, which sat on her bedside table. "Goodness, it's early. What do you mean by waking me at this time?"

"I'm sorry, my lady, but there are some persons downstairs to see you. Sanders said I should wake you, because they won't go."

Ada caught the fear in her voice at once, and rubbed her eyes, trying to wake up and make sense of the situation.

"Some *persons*? Whatever do you mean?"

Céline bobbed a curtsy—it was extraordinary to see the usually self-possessed girl so upset, thought Ada—and scurried closer to the bed.

"My lady, I think, I know it's not my place to say, but I think they want money."

"Money!" Ada sat up bolt upright, quite awake now.

"They mentioned Sir William's name."

Ada swung herself out of bed. This had to be dealt with instantly. "I see. Very well, thank you for alerting me, Céline. Please get out my most . . . authoritative dress and prepare some hot water."

"The maid's already brought it, my lady." Céline hurried away to the wardrobe as Ada went to the washstand. She had spoken with more confidence than she felt. As she washed her face and allowed Céline to dress her and prepare her hair, her heart was pattering with nervousness and anger. How dared William's creditors call here? Things must really be bad.

She took a quick look at herself in the mirror. She looked too young, but it would have to do. The countess should not know about this; that would be too humiliating. Besides, she sensed that only an Averley would do.

"My lady, there is another thing—"

"Not now, Céline."

Ada descended the stairs and went to her father's study, hoping that the imposing busts of Greek philosophers and the shelves of leather-bound histories would overwhelm the creditors a little.

The vast walnut desk was a welcome defense. She seated

herself behind it, playing with the gold pen that stood by the inkwell. If only she knew the extent of William's debts. If only she had some idea what they were going to attack her with—

The door opened and Sanders, with an air of great contempt—for which Ada was grateful—announced. "Mr. MacNab, Mr. Harrison, Mr. Smith."

The three men who shouldered their way inside were of a kind Ada saw every day through the window of her motorcar. Cockneys to a man, relying on weight and intimidating looks to bluster their way through life. Ada found herself wishing she had not sat down. It was theoretically the position of power, but they loomed over her threateningly. She forced herself not to get to her feet. She could not show she was intimidated. Instead she quickly registered the differences among them: Harrison clutching his cap and glancing about him, obviously more impressed than he liked to show; MacNab to the front, scowling, the clear ringleader; Smith in the background, an unknown quantity.

"Good morning, gentlemen," she said quietly. "How may I be of assistance to you?"

"We want to see Sir William," MacNab announced. The others murmured agreement.

"I'm afraid that is impossible. He is not in London. May I ask to what this refers?"

"Refers to?" MacNab gave a sarcastic laugh. "Eighteen guineas is what it refers to."

"Sir William backed a horse, my lady," Harrison began, wincing a little at his companion's aggression.

"I see." So they were bookmakers. Ada was hardly surprised, but a white, cold flame of anger against her cousin kindled inside her. The one thing one did not do, did not even risk doing, was bring one's family into disrepute. Her own memory of her romance with Ravi struck at her conscience, and the sparks kindled the flame. How much had she given up, so as not to bring shame on her family? And William had made it all for nothing. "Well, I am sorry to tell you that you are looking for your money in the wrong place. Sir William is not here."

"Are you Lady Ada?" It was Smith who spoke.

Ada bristled. There was a complete absence of respect in his tone. MacNab's aggression was in itself a compliment, she knew it masked fear, but this man spoke as if they were *equals*.

"I am," she replied.

"I don't care if Sir William's not here." This was MacNab again, fists clenched, leaning forward. "We must have our money and we must have it now. You can write us a cheque."

"I wish I could." Ada honestly did, it would be the easiest way to get rid of them, and objectionable as they were, she had to admit they had right on their side. "But I have no money of my own."

"No money?" MacNab's hairy eyebrows raised. "How much did that dress cost?"

Ada colored angrily. But before she could answer, Smith spoke again.

"What's the situation between you and Lord Fintan—you two engaged?"

Ada was breathless with shock and anger at the impertinence of the question. Smith pressed on. "Tell us yes and we'll be off. We don't mind waiting if we know we'll get our money sooner or later. But seems like you don't mind waiting either, according to the papers," he continued, leering. "Nervous, are you?"

Ada opened her mouth indignantly, but before she could reply, the door of the study flew open, and Laurence strode in. He was the picture of cool composure, but Ada could read the cold fury in every line of his face. She leapt to her feet in relief. Never had she been so grateful to see anyone.

"What is the meaning of this?" Laurence demanded. "How dare you speak to a lady in this manner? I should horsewhip the lot of you!"

MacNab squared up to him. "The lady's cousin owes us money. You'd do well to stay out of this, sir."

Laurence moved toward MacNab, stopping only inches from him. He towered over the man. "You know, the owner of Kempton Park is a good friend of mine. You'll find yourself permanently banned from the racecourse if you ever so much as look at my fiancée again. Do you understand my meaning, sir?"

MacNab took a step back.

Smith spoke, and his quiet, even voice had an immediate effect. "No need to upset yourself, sir. My apologies, my lady. We won't bother you again."

He drifted out of the door, and after an awkward moment Harrison scuttled after him with a muttered apology. MacNab followed more reluctantly. Ada could hear his raised voice as

Sanders ushered them away, complaining about his money.

She exhaled, a shaky, long breath, and steadied herself against the desk. Laurence stepped forward quickly to support her.

"Are you well? If you say so, I'll go after the brutes and beat them to a pulp."

"No, no, please. You arrived just in time. I'm so grateful." Ada realized she was trembling and on the brink of tears. Laurence helped her into a chair.

"Sanders was clever enough to telephone. It's unpardonable that you should have been subjected to this." He spoke through tight lips. Ada placed a hand on his shoulder, hoping to calm him.

"Please don't. There was no trouble, really. William should pay his bills."

"It's absolutely unpardonable," he repeated, and shook his head angrily. "That my fiancée should have been treated this way . . ."

Ada found herself on her feet again. The smell of the men still lingered, and she was feeling a little weak.

"You can't have had breakfast. Won't you have some with us?" She led the way to the breakfast room. "Sanders, please send something up."

"Yes, my lady." Sanders strode away. Ada entered the breakfast room and seated herself with relief at the long table. Early morning light blazed in. She reached automatically for the silver tray of post and the ivory-handled letter opener that had been placed with fresh flowers on the table. As Laurence went on talking angrily about the creditors, Ada sorted through the post, glad of something simple and mindless to occupy her while she recovered her poise. As usual, most was for the countess and Charlotte—but today there was one for her, addressed in a hand that even in her distracted state she recognized as familiar. She took the letter opener and slit the envelope open as Sanders laid the sideboard and Laurence's angry voice broke around her. The first line turned her to stone.

My dearest Ada,

She could not believe that she hadn't seen it at once—it could only have been her distraction that stopped her from recognizing instantly that the letter was from Ravi.

I wonder with what feelings you will read this. I hope they have not changed. I still think of you as I ever did, only with more pain. Business will bring me to London this summer. It is a rush and I will find it difficult to get away. But I hoped we could meet. I won't compromise you by asking you to reply to this. On the 21st August at noon I will be underneath the great clock at Paddington Station, where we parted from each other. If you can, be there too. If you cannot, I will understand. I will never forget you, but I will understand.

Yours forever,

Ravi

She clasped the letter opener in one hand, the letter in the other. She sensed that the color had fled from her face. It was as if she had opened up her heart with the small silver blade, and inadvertently ripped open a wound that had been sewn closed just a few months before. And now she realized that the pain had never gone away. She had just got used to it, that was all. The wound was very, very far from healed.

"Ada?" Laurence was leaning forward, looking anxiously into her face. "Are you well? You've turned so pale."

"I'm quite well," she murmured, "quite well."

"You are in shock, you must be. Let me fetch you some water."

He leapt up and went to the sideboard. Ada folded the letter and slid it back into the envelope.

Laurence returned with the water. Ada sipped it gratefully. He was looking at her with concern, not at the letter. That was all she needed.

"Thank you. You're so good to me." She could feel tears welling up in her eyes.

"My dear, you've been so strong." His voice was gentle. "But you must let me take over now. This situation cannot go unremedied."

She nodded. "Laurence, do you think you could . . ." She hesitated. "I would like to lie down."

"Of course. An excellent idea."

Ada got to her feet. She could hardly just leave the letter sitting there, but she didn't want to draw attention by picking it up.

Luckily Laurence turned away to ring the bell, and she was able to collect the letter and hide it in her hand. She moved to the door. Now she was back at Somerton in her mind, six months ago, at her father's wedding, clasping a note in her hand, feeling it beat within her grip as if it were her very heart.

Laurence held Ada back just before she went through the door. He bent his head to hers and pressed a kiss onto her lips. She received it like a marble statue.

"Rest, dear. I will take care of everything," he murmured.

"Thank you so much," Ada murmured, mechanically. Slowly, like a woman just awoken from a dream, she walked upstairs.

Céline met her on the landing. "My lady," she whispered.

"Oh Céline, not now!" Ada made to walk past her, but to her shock Céline caught her wrist.

"My lady, I must speak to you!" For the first time Ada heard the panic in her voice. She turned a questioning look on her. Céline was pale, and her eyes were red as if she had been crying.

"Lady Rose did not come back last night," she whispered.

Ada gazed at her, uncertain that she had heard correctly.

"What do you mean? Lady Rose went to bed early with a headache."

Céline shook her head silently. Ada opened her mouth to protest. But Céline's expression told her everything she needed to know.

Without another word she turned and walked along the hall to Rose's room. She tapped on the door. Céline was close behind her. When there was no answer, she pushed the door open and looked in. At a glance she could see that the bed had not been slept in.

Ada closed the door silently. She turned to Céline, who looked terrified, and beckoned her away into an alcove. She glanced left and right to make sure no servants were passing.

"Tell me everything," she whispered. Her anger and her fear were equally balanced.

"I—the Duke of Huntleigh came to see her. She went away with him."

"What!" Ada took a few desperate steps up and down. If this were known, Rose's reputation would be shattered like glass. "No, that's impossible. Lady Rose would never be so . . . so lost to all sense of propriety." And yet the note in her hand burned like a brand, as if it were saying, *You thought that of yourself, didn't you?*

"I am sure she's done no wrong, my lady."

"Why on earth did you not stop her? Forbid her?" Ada was talking nonsense and she knew it, but she had to lash out at someone. "Why did you not tell me?"

"I thought—I just thought—"

"You thought Rose could marry a duke and you would become lady's maid to a duchess. Well, because of your foolish scheming, you may well be lady's maid to a fallen woman!"

Céline gave a strangled sob, and her hands flew to her mouth.

Ada knew at once that she had gone too far. "Céline, forgive me. I don't know what I'm saying. I'm just so worried. . . ." She pressed a hand to her forehead. "How long have we before the Royal Horticultural Society show?"

"The cars are ordered for twelve, my lady."

"Very well. We must say that Lady Rose has catarrh, that she isn't feeling well, that you will bring everything necessary up to her, but she is not to be disturbed. That will work. Well?"

Céline nodded silently.

"Good." Ada took a deep breath. Perhaps she could still save Rose's reputation—if they were lucky.

Chapter Forty

"So Rose is still unwell," Charlotte said as she and Ada walked down the green paths in the gardens of the Chelsea Hospital, scents of summery flowers drifting toward them. "I can't say I'm sorry. It's so embarrassing having to cover up her faux pas."

Ada said nothing. Laurence's hand was on her arm, protective and controlling. She wanted to leap to Rose's defense—but she was uncomfortably aware that at this very moment Rose was committing the worst of faux pas, one so unthinkable that not even Charlotte would think to accuse her of it. One did not spend the night in the company of a man. Not even Ada had been guilty of that. She still could not understand what had possessed Rose.

She looked away from Charlotte's curious gaze, trying to distract herself by watching the crowd. Stately men in morning coats, their top hats gleaming like well-brushed horses, their watch chains glinting and buttons shining, strolled among the orchids and rhododendrons, accompanied by their wives, their figures still showing the influence of the Edwardian S-bend. The younger, elegant debutantes were pretty in their looser, freer summer dresses, and the young men up from Oxford or Cambridge who sauntered past were the picture of debonair, carefree summer. Ada felt detached from all of it. Ravi's words kept running through her head. She was afraid that she would forget herself and blurt them out loud.

"The show looks quite marvelous." The countess waved her program like a fan, her furled parasol picking out the way before her. "I'm very pleased, the hothouses at Somerton need restocking."

"It's a delightful new venue," Lord Westlake said, looking around appreciatively. "A stroke of genius to hold it here. The grounds of the Chelsea Hospital are admirably suited."

"I quite agree, my dear. It's a charming way to end the season."

Ada caught the note of affection between Lord Westlake and the countess. That at least was a relief, she thought. The gulf that Rose's adoption had created between them seemed to be healing. Perhaps the countess was finally getting used to the situation.

"I must see the Japanese dwarf trees," the countess exclaimed, surging forward into the crowds. "Come, Charlotte."

Charlotte followed her. Laurence hesitated, then placed a hand on Lord Westlake's arm. He drew them into the shadow of a grapevine.

"Sir, there has been an unpleasant incident," he said under his breath.

Ada started, for a second imagining he had somehow found out about Ravi. But the searching glance he gave her was not because of that.

"Ada is behaving very bravely, but you must know that this morning three duns came to the house, after Sir William's debts, and they upset her very much."

"What are you telling me?" Westlake exclaimed, a look of shocked anger on his face. "This is unconscionable."

"I think so too. I'm appalled that Ada was exposed to such a situation."

"Really, I—" Ada protested faintly. "I am quite all right."

"You're in shock, anyone can see it," Laurence said tenderly, his gaze protective.

"My dear Ada," her father said. "I am so sorry I was not there to shield you from such impertinence. I feel ashamed that it was allowed to happen." He scowled, and Ada felt the weight of anger that clung around his shoulders. "If I had known when I adopted William . . . but it is too late now. My only desire is to secure a future for you and Georgiana—a future for Somerton."

Ada nodded. Laurence spoke next, not to the earl, but to her. "Lord Westlake has stopped William's allowance, so we hope he will run up no more debts. But we must act to reassure people. And there is only one way to do that." His gaze met Ada's, and he took her gloved hand in his. She was aware of the thin layer of leather that separated them. "Let us set a date, Ada. It is the right thing to do. For me, for you—for Somerton."

Ada looked deep into his eyes. She saw the warmest respect, the deepest affection. She looked to her father. He had turned away discreetly as Laurence spoke, but she saw the white hair glinting at his temples. It had not been there a month ago.

She took a deep breath and drew herself up. "And Oxford?" she faltered, feeling low for bargaining.

Laurence's words tumbled eagerly over each other. "As soon as we are married. It's unconventional, but why shouldn't we take rooms there? You can attend the university. I can easily travel to London when Parliament is in session, and I shall enjoy revisiting my old haunts."

Ada looked at her father. Part of her almost wanted him to forbid it. But he spread his hands. "Once you are married to Laurence, you are his. I think women's education unnecessary, and I can't understand why you wouldn't rather be decorating Gravelley Park, but if you prefer to take a degree, why not?" He smiled. "Married women are allowed a latitude that unmarried women are not."

"And I will be the most generous husband," Laurence said warmly. "Just say when. Everything can be arranged—we can be granted a special license if necessary."

"The twenty-first of August," Ada said quietly.

It was the date that had been running through her head ever since that morning, the day Ravi would be waiting under the great clock at Paddington Station. She was doing the right thing, she knew it; and yet she felt as if two halves of her soul were slipping apart. She was too weak, too easily tempted. It was unthinkable to betray Laurence. She could never see Ravi again, and he knew that. The best thing to do was to put the meeting entirely out of her own power.

"Let us be married on the twenty-first of August at midday," she said again.

Laurence clasped her hands tightly. His voice trembled, triumphant. "You will make me the happiest man alive!"

He drew her close. Ada's father coughed and took a few hasty steps away, appearing to have become very interested in the fronds of a palm tree. Laurence held Ada's wrists so tightly that the kiss he drew her into was awkward, uncomfortable. Their lips met, and yet she still felt detached from herself, as if something divided them, or divided herself from herself.

It will take time, she told herself. But I have done the right thing.

CHAPTER
Forty-one

By the time they returned to the house, Ada was exhausted from the countess's barrage of instructions, advice, and commands about wedding preparations. Her father had announced the news at once, and there had been no other subject of conversation since.

"Your bridesmaids will be Charlotte, Georgiana, and Rose," the countess went on as they stepped down from the motorcar onto the sun-glaring pavement. "And Lady Gertrude and Lady Cynthia."

"But why?" Ada exclaimed, roused at last to respond. "I don't even like them. Nor do they like me."

"It makes no difference. I promised their mothers, and these things are very important. Now, about the conveyance. I expect we shall hire a landau, and then I think it may be best to hire a chef to arrange the wedding breakfast. We will need a special license because of the time of day, but since Laurence's godfather is the Archbishop of Canterbury, that should not be too difficult to arrange."

Ada stepped with relief into the coolness of the hall and handed her hat to Sanders. The countess's words seemed to have nothing to do with her. It was just another ball or tea dance that was being arranged, another grand society event. Was Rose back? That was Ada's only thought. She pushed any thought of Ravi out of her mind. That was over.

"Well, well, that was a delightful afternoon after all, and we have restocked the gardens." The countess swept into the drawing room, carrying her new bonsai tree. "Ah, Sebastian, do look. Isn't this a vision? I imagine the whole of the south end re-landscaped and a miniature fairyland created. I must redecorate the Russian rooms too—Japan is sure to be the next craze, if the enthusiasm for these little trees is anything to go by, and I intend to be the first to introduce it. I was lucky to secure this one—I had to practically *wrest* it from the claws of Mrs. Verulam." She placed the bonsai on the sideboard. Ada walked in after her to find Sebastian standing at the sideboard, reading *The Times*. Rose was nowhere to be seen.

Sebastian cast a glance toward the tree. "Very nice, Mother," he said without enthusiasm, and returned at once to the newspapers.

"Well, you *are* gloomy." The countess sniffed and went to sit on the sofa, her silken skirts rustling and falling into elegant pleats.

"What happened? Has your tailor disappointed you again?"

"I do hope not," Charlotte chimed in. "I was so looking forward to seeing you as Sinbad tonight." She perched in the chair next to her mother. She had been rather silent for the afternoon, but now she cast a mocking glance toward her brother. "Pale-blue silk harem pants, the rumor goes."

"Oh, do shut up," Sebastian snapped. The countess raised an eyebrow. Ada was startled, but as Sebastian continued to turn the pages of the newspapers, she began to realize what might be wrong. She stood and moved as if casually toward the sideboard. Glancing over his shoulder she saw that she was correct. The headline, in letters as black as mourning, read "Somerton murder scandal: Campbell pleads guilty, transferred to Pentonville." There was a grainy photograph of Oliver, surrounded by walls of policemen, being escorted into the police wagon.

Charlotte assumed an expression of deep hurt. "Too much champagne last night? Too little?"

Sebastian slapped the paper closed and turned to face his mother and sister for the first time. "I wish you could understand that there are more important things in the world than your wretched social merry-go-round," he said.

"That will do." The countess's voice was at its coldest. "I expect to see you in better spirits this evening, or you may consider your account at Pennycuick of Jermyn Street closed."

Sebastian's face hardened. Ada took a quick step toward him. But a sudden, violent shrilling shattered the tension. Ada started. "What on earth is that awful noise?" She covered her ears.

The countess looked baffled. "I have no idea. Is it something in the street?"

Charlotte went to the window.

Almost as soon as it had begun, the noise ended. There was the sound of Sanders speaking in the hall.

"Who—?" The countess interrupted herself with a laugh. "Of course, the telephone! I quite forgot I'd had one installed."

"Well, is it always going to make that dreadful noise?" Charlotte looked appalled. "Couldn't it play a pleasant piece of music to alert our attention, perhaps? There must be a way to arrange it."

There was a discreet knock on the door, and Sanders entered. "The telephone for you, sir," he addressed Sebastian. "Master Michael calling."

"Michael!" the countess exclaimed. "What *has* he done now?"

Sebastian left the room, and the countess and Charlotte looked at each other with deep suspicion.

"I don't see why you have to assume he's done wrong," Ada said mildly.

The countess sniffed, and Charlotte cast Ada a withering glance. "My dear, let us be realistic. He's probably been expelled again."

"If he has," the countess said, reddening, "I shall disown him."

"Oh, you wouldn't!" Ada exclaimed. But the conversation was interrupted as Sebastian raced back into the room.

"Sebastian, what has happened?" the countess demanded. "You look as if you have swallowed a jumping bean."

"I can't explain. There's no time. I have to be off— Good-bye, Mother—please make my excuses to Mrs. Verulam."

Ada looked at him in astonishment. The countess started to her feet. "Sebastian, what are you saying? Where are you going?"

"Something's come up, Mother. I'm sorry."

Sanders appeared at the door with Sebastian's hat and coat, the footman hovering behind with the cane. Sebastian snatched them and headed for the door, pulling on his coat as he went.

"Sebastian!" The countess's voice was almost a shriek. She ran after him into the hall. "Is this to do with Oliver?"

Sebastian's silence was answer enough.

"You cannot go. What will people think?" she hissed.

"I don't care. I don't care anymore." Sebastian went out the door, his hat askew. The footman who leapt to open it for him was too late. The countess took a few more steps after him, then stopped, clenching her fists. Ada, who had followed her in concern, saw her face reflected in the hall mirror. She expected to see fury in it, but to her astonishment, she saw fear. What was the countess so afraid of? she wondered. Just before the door swung shut behind Sebastian, she saw a determined, rough-looking man cross the road beyond him.

CHAPTER
Forty-two

Somerton

Georgiana came in from her early morning ride with color in her cheeks and a spring in her step. The day was perfect for riding, glorious sunshine, and she hardly felt tired at all. The country air was doing her good. Even better, Mrs. McRory seemed to have a very strong whip hand over the staff, and the servants were all scurrying around like mice who had met the cat. As she crossed the hall she spotted a letter on the table, addressed to her. She picked it up and saw that the return address was Eton School.

"Michael!" she exclaimed. With a little skip of happiness she went into the breakfast room, and seated herself to read. The footman brought tea and she read the letter as she waited for it to brew. She had been a little nervous to hear from him, but the first lines reassured her at once. He was having a "ripping time," cricket was "top hole," and even the "beaks" were "pukka." She couldn't stop a smile bubbling up, even under the solemn eye of the butler. Michael was all extremes.

But then her face clouded.

> *Please look after Priya for me. I often feel that she is not telling me everything in her letters. I suspect she wants to protect me from knowing how badly Edith treats her. I'm concerned about her—do ask after her, please, Georgie. And tell her I love her.*

Georgiana remembered with a guilty start that it had been a while since she had last seen Priya, walking across the lawn as she usually did for afternoon walks with Augustus in tow. She rang the bell and waited until Cooper came up.

"Oh, Cooper," she began. "I just wondered if you had heard anything about Priya. The nursemaid, you know. I feel a little anxious about her since she is a foreigner here, and of course quite isolated from the rest of the staff." She hesitated. Cooper was looking uncomfortable. "Is anything the matter?"

"No, no, my lady. Not at all. Only that I am afraid to say that Priya is indisposed at the present time."

"Oh dear! A summer cold, I expect?"

"Yes, I expect so." Cooper sounded ever more wretched. Georgiana sat forward.

"Are you quite sure nothing is the matter?"

"Quite—it has been a little difficult to accustom ourselves to Mrs. McRory's ways, that is all, my lady."

Alarm bells rang at once in Georgiana's mind. "I see. Is there any special trouble?"

"No, no. That is, the third housemaid has given notice."

"Oh dear," Georgiana exclaimed.

"It is regrettable, but I hope we will be able to fill her position."

"I'm sure you will." Georgiana was worried, though. It would put more of a burden on the remaining staff. "Is there anything you would like me to do? To say to Mrs. McRory?" she offered valiantly, though the thought made her a little nervous.

"Thank you, but no, my lady." Cooper sounded firm, if embarrassed. "Please do not trouble yourself."

Georgiana nodded and allowed him to leave. She was not as confident as he was—but she knew that it was never wise to meddle too much in the affairs of the downstairs world. Cooper and Mrs. McRory would have to settle their differences as best they could. She turned to her writing desk; a reply to Michael was a pleasure she would indulge at once. He would be glad to know that Priya merely had a cold.

CHAPTER
Forty-three

London

"Breathe in, my lady." Céline's soft French accent soothed Ada's nerves. She obediently held her breath while Céline laced the corset tight. She wrung her hands as she stood before the glass, hardly aware of her own reflection, slim and white as a candle.

"You've heard nothing from Lady Rose."

"No, my lady."

"I'm frightened, Céline. I can't imagine she has gone willingly. I can't think her so foolish. The duke has such a dreadful reputation. Do you think he could have harmed her, forced her. . . ." Her voice trailed off. She hardly knew what she was suggesting, only that the thought of it filled her with terror. She sat down suddenly on the bed, as her head spun. "Oh, I can't go to this ball. Not with Rose missing."

"My lady, you must." Céline crouched by her side, her face full of anxiety. "I'm sure she is in no danger."

"How can I keep lying to my father, the countess, to everyone?" Tears ran down Ada's face. "How can I lie to *Laurence*? He'll see I am agitated, he will know, and he will ask me—and what can I say?" The thought of Laurence's penetrating gaze terrified her most of all. How could she admit that her sister had gone away with a such a man as the Duke of Huntleigh? He would despise Rose, and she couldn't bear that.

"Please, my lady. You've got to be strong. We have to keep this secret. If we hear nothing from Lady Rose or from the duke by tomorrow morning, then we must tell someone. But Lady Rose's reputation is at stake. You know what that means as well as I."

Ada nodded silently. Rose, a former housemaid with nothing but her beauty and title to recommend her, needed her reputation as a gambler needed an ace. "You're right, Céline."

She stood and allowed Céline to slide the dress over her head. Céline knelt at her feet and stitched the last few pearls to the hem of the dress. As Ada looked at herself in the mirror, gleaming in the gathering shadows, she remembered another evening, when Rose had dressed her—the way her heart had pounded then, at the thought that she would soon be meeting Ravi. But that dress had been pink and gold like the sunset. This one was pure white. So much had changed, not merely the dress. She would marry Laurence, and she had to make herself forget Ravi entirely.

Ada pulled on her long kid gloves sprinkled with pearls like dewdrops, and slipped on her dancing shoes.

I look like a bride, she thought. . . . Or a virgin sacrifice.

Ada remembered that horrible concert—*The Rite of Spring*—she had gone to with Rose. That dance had haunted her dreams ever since, its cruel power, the terrified girl trapped within the circle and dancing herself to death. Sacrificed, so that the wheel of the year could turn, remorselessly, round and round, like the everlasting wheel of the seasons, the turning of dancers coupled in vast ballrooms, a world where there was no escape, no breaking of the circle ever allowed. . . .

She made a slight, desperate noise, her heart pounding.

"My lady?" Céline glanced up.

"Nothing," Ada said, managing to smile.

"There, my lady." Céline stepped back to examine her with an expert eye. "Perfect."

Ada stood and turned around in the mirror. Her thick dark hair was simply swept up, secured with a jeweled band. The dress was light to wear, yet the pearls gave it a pleasing weight when she turned, and made the silk brush her hips so the shape of her body was momentarily revealed.

"It's your work that is perfect, Céline," she said in admiration. "You are an artist."

Céline blushed and curtsied. "I love fabric, my lady. I love working with it."

"Well, we are lucky to have you. Shall we go?"

The countess met them in the corridor, resplendent in heavy gold lace, sable bands, and deep cream silk, with strand after strand of pearls falling to her waist. A huge ostrich-feather fan in her hand fluttered and flirted with the air. She looked Ada up and down.

"Very elegant, very appropriate," she commented. "It's not so important now, of course, that the date has been set and the invitations sent out."

"Invitations sent out?" Ada said, sharply. "But we only arranged it this afternoon—"

"Oh, I am always prepared."

"And whom have you invited to my wedding, may I ask?" Ada was angry, and she was also frightened. The machinery was rolling into action sooner even than she had expected.

"Just the usual people, those who matter. The Duchess of Ellingborough, of course, a few bishops, my bridge circle . . ." They went down the stairs, to join the men, who waited below.

"Ada," her father said fondly as she came down the stairs. Ada saw the affectionate expression in Laurence's eyes as he stepped forward to take her hand, and her seething anger calmed somewhat.

"You look exquisite," he told her. "As perfect as a marble Venus." He glanced to the countess and added, "And no one would take you for anything other than her sister."

The countess simpered and tapped him with her fan. "Laurence, you know exactly how to please."

"Good evening, everyone," came a voice from the top of the stairs. Laurence looked up, and Ada felt his hand tense in hers. She followed his gaze—and had to suppress an exclamation of mingled shock and admiration.

Charlotte's suppressed smile showed she was well aware of the impression she had created. Her dress glittered with rubies and garnets, heavily weighted down with gold embroidery so it flowed around her, hugging her shape with shocking closeness, flowing over the navel, where a single ruby glittered. Bands of silver and gold encircled her arms, formed like serpents, and a plumed and jeweled turban that seemed stolen from a maharajah's harem was wrapped around her golden hair.

She took her time descending the staircase. The silence was electric. Ada finally found her tongue. "You look wonderful," she said with honesty. "It's a triumph."

Charlotte bowed her head in acknowledgement of the compliment. Laurence said nothing. Everyone else murmured admiringly at how well she had captured the spirit of the Firebird.

"But where is Rose?" Lord Westlake frowned.

"She's . . . still unwell." Ada flushed and couldn't meet his eye.

"Unwell!" the countess exclaimed. "For the last ball of the season? Is she at death's door?"

"This is the second day, is it not? Has no one telephoned a doctor?" Lord Westlake looked around in concern. "The poor girl, she must be distraught at missing this."

"She—I—" Ada stumbled. She knew she had to lie, and the lie had to be good. "I believe she's feeling homesick," she said softly. "It is the first time she has been away from Somerton, and the season is such a whirl."

Lord Westlake did not look convinced, but to Ada's relief the countess joined in. "She *has* been looking very down in the mouth for some weeks. It's unsurprising, really. She isn't used to all this excitement."

"My dear . . ." said Lord Westlake warningly. The countess pressed her lips together primly. Lord Westlake turned back to Ada. "Well, I'm very sorry she should miss the fun. I know how she enjoys music. But if you really think she would rather stay here . . ."

Ada nodded. "I think she would, Papa. Céline will bring her everything she needs."

"Very well. You know her best." He turned to the door, and Sanders, who had been waiting for his nod, bowed and held it open so they could pass down the steps to the waiting motorcars.

CHAPTER
Forty-four

London

Rose tiptoed down the side passage to the kitchen door. It was late—Alexander had insisted on driving to Hatton Garden and picking a package up from a jeweler before they came here.

"It won't take a moment," he had reassured her, as they pulled up before the small shop. Rose, hugged in her cloak, had watched anxiously as he disappeared inside, leaving the engine running. To let Céline down would be terrible, after she had promised to help her. Luckily Alexander had been as good as his word, hurrying back with a faded red morocco case that he handed to her before driving them back west.

Through the window of Milborough House she could see a light. A maid was mending by the light of a candle. Rose peered through the glass, then turned to Alexander, who was just behind her.

"It's Céline!" Rose whispered. "My maid. That's lucky."

Rose tapped with the case at the kitchen window. Céline's head was bowed as she stitched. Rose tapped again. At last Céline looked up. She saw Rose, and her eyes widened. The next instant she was scurrying to her feet and running to the door. Bolts shot back, chains jangled open, and Rose tumbled in, followed by Alexander.

"Did anyone see you?" was Céline's first question, as she locked the door again behind Rose. Her second, directed to the duke, was frantic with anxiety. "How could you come here with her? Don't you know what will happen if you are seen together? You will compromise her beyond redemption!"

"Céline!" Rose, scandalized by her outburst, turned apologetically to Alexander. But the duke seemed unconcerned at being addressed so freely by a servant.

"Please calm yourself. No one saw us. It was mercifully quiet. I expect everyone is at the ball—"

Céline's eyes glinted tears. Rose put the case down on the kitchen table and clasped Céline's hands in her own. "Céline, I forgot, I am so sorry. I know I promised you this chance to show off your work."

"It does not matter, my lady," she said, looking down.

"But it does. I can't let you down like this, it isn't fair." She turned to the door. "We can still go to the ball."

"Of course!" Alexander picked up an apple from the kitchen table and bit into it casually. "I'll drive you."

"You will do no such thing, my lord, unless you want to compromise my lady. We will take a hansom cab." Céline paused, her hand to her mouth. "Oh, but the jewels—the set you ordered from Garrard. I had to send them back."

"Can't I wear my usual pearls?"

"It will ruin the vision." Céline's mouth turned down at the corners.

"Jewels?" Alexander swallowed a mouthful of apple. "You're lacking jewels?"

"They were to be amethyst and silver and rose quartz." Céline's eyes brimmed with tears at the memory. "They would have brought out the color of my lady's eyes admirably."

"Well, there's none of that in these, but would they be any good?" Alexander pointed to the red morocco case that Rose had almost forgotten. "I just had them cleaned in Hatton Garden. They're rather old-fashioned, I suppose, but they make a good show."

Céline and Rose looked at each other blankly. Céline picked up the case and undid the clasp. She lifted the lid and gasped. Light seemed to fill the kitchen. There was a stunned silence as both women gazed at the Huntleigh parure glittering like sunlight on the sea: a belt of diamonds like a garland of crystal roses, earrings in the shape of looped rings of flowers, and a tiara like a crown of light.

"I mean, if you can do anything with them," Alexander tossed his apple core into the ashes of the kitchen fire. "Of course they may not suit your vision—"

Céline snapped the case shut. "My vision," she said firmly, "shall be tailored to suit them. Come, my lady. Upstairs, and we can still be at Mrs. Verulam's before midnight."

CHAPTER
Forty-five

"So many journalists!" Lord Westlake exclaimed, disapprovingly, as their car drew up outside Mrs. Verulam's London residence. "I thought Mrs. Verulam had more taste."

Ada looked out of the window of the motorcar at the milling women with notepads and men with cameras. "I think taste is formed by the magazines these days, Papa."

They walked up the white marble steps toward the sound of the orchestra.

"It's fairyland!" Ada heard the woman in front of her exclaim, and when she stepped through the great doors of the ballroom she saw at once why.

A grand staircase of polished wood swept down to the dance floor, which was already crowded. Above them canopies of duck-egg-blue silk mimicked a summer sky, stitched with pink silk flowers to echo cherry blossoms. Entire bolts of silk of the same blue draped the walls, and on them were stenciled Japanese cherry trees in full pink blossom. Rhinestones sprinkled everywhere made the canopies shimmer as if touched by frost, and the swaying, gently billowing drapes of silk gave the feeling that the couples on the floor were dancing in a cloud. Here and there on tables and sideboards, bonsai trees were placed, and electric light streaming from the crystal chandeliers gave everything a diamond brilliance.

Mrs. Verulam, in an Elizabethan dress complete with heavy padding and stiff with gold embroidery, with Emily by her side, pretty and witty as a china-white, red-lipped Pierrette, glided forward to greet them.

"Japanese," the countess said, the corners of her mouth turning down as if she had tasted something undesirable. "How original. How very clever of you."

"Thank you, dear Fiona," Mrs. Verulam said sweetly. She glanced past her to the next guest. "Lady Edwina, how delightful!"

Ada gazed entranced down at the dancers. She had thought nothing could make her smile under the circumstances, but as she watched the costumed dancers whirling here and there in perfect control and freedom, she felt the fog of worry lift slightly. It was impossible not to enjoy the sight of jaded society belles and beaus transformed into French shepherdesses and fairy princesses, maharajahs and knights in shining armor.

"It's the perfect end to the season," Laurence murmured just behind her.

She looked up at him quickly and they shared a smile. For a second Ada felt the ice around her heart melt, and she had a sudden glimpse of how it might be. The future, with Laurence, might not be a dreary slog of duty but a thing of harmony and pleasure. They had everything in common. She took his offered arm gladly, and together they descended the staircase.

CHAPTER
Forty-six

Charlotte Templeton came to the end of her dance and stepped from the floor into an eager gaggle of suitors. But as she accepted names for her dance card, she smiled at the knowledge that Laurence, dancing nearby, was glancing at her over Ada's shoulder.

He was fascinated, he couldn't help himself. He never had been able to resist her. But she would win this game. Alexander Ross had been more than charming to her at the exhibition—two years in Paris had clearly rubbed off his corners. He was like a ripe fruit, ready for plucking. This evening she felt perfectly happy and quite ready to be friends with the whole world.

As she danced with a young lord she had known for two seasons, she followed the other couples with her gaze. One in particular stood out. Everyone had been talking about them—young Blanchford and Lady Helen Fairfax. She was strangely moved by the way they danced together, as if each were the other's Narcissus, gazing into clear water and falling in love. Once she had believed in love like that. Once she and Laurence had danced like that together. . . .

"You are smiling," said her partner gallantly.

"Oh—just remembering happy times," she replied casually. But she kept watching the two young people. One's first season, how long ago it seemed. How innocent she had been.

Stepping from the dance floor, she noticed that a small, modestly dressed lady was waiting for her attention. The lady stepped forward at Charlotte's encouraging smile.

"Miss Templeton, may I congratulate you on your most becoming gown?"

"Why yes, you may," Charlotte murmured, glancing down at the paper and pen. *"Country Life?"*

"Vogue. I'm sure our readers will be fascinated. . . ." The lady scribbled down notes as she glanced at Charlotte's dress. "May I enquire whether the gorgeous beads on the sleeves are rhinestones?"

"Carnelians." Charlotte was scanning the room as she spoke. Alexander had not yet arrived, she noted. Like him to be late.

"Is it true that you represent the Firebird, from Stravinsky's ballet?"

"It is. I designed it myself."

"Your brother, Sebastian Templeton, is not here?"

She frowned. "No."

"Much concerned with his valet's case, I am sure."

"Excuse me," Charlotte said sweetly but firmly. She stepped past the journalist and took the hand of Lord Winchcombe, who was waiting eagerly to lead her into the next foxtrot. Anything was better than spending the evening indulging journalists' obsession with her peacock of a brother, when she had gone to so much trouble to get the attention on her alone.

CHAPTER
Forty-seven

"You look worried," Laurence said as they danced. "I expect you are thinking about Lady Rose?"

Ada wanted to deny it, but it was the truth, and she knew her expression showed it.

"You are very considerate of her," Laurence said gently. There was only warmth in his voice. "It cannot be easy to have a new sister, and one so . . . unaccustomed to our kind of life. But I am sure there is no need for concern, one does get exhausted this close to the end of the season. No doubt she needs rest and will be better as soon as you return to Somerton."

Ada longed to rest her head on his chest as they turned together. Laurence was so good, and she had hidden so much from him already. She needed someone else to know, someone to share the burden, someone who could help. She knew Laurence would be a support; he had proved that with those awful men who had come after William.

"I must tell you," she murmured. "Rose has done something most unwise, I don't know who to confide in. I am frightened for her."

His hands tightened on hers. "I hope this has nothing to do with the Duke of Huntleigh."

Ada nodded, her face close to his chest. She blushed deeply, already wishing that she had not spoken. "She is with him, somewhere. Laurence, could he hurt her?"

"I have no doubt of it." Anger laced his voice. "Huntleigh broke my sister's heart. He has no shame, the cad."

Ada looked up sharply. "He makes a habit of this then?"

"He is certainly not to be trusted where women are concerned."

"I hate him!" Ada exclaimed, terror and anger mingling together. "Oh, how can he do this to Rose? He has no honor, no morals!"

"I am afraid not, but your sister must be quite mad to have gone with him."

Ada flushed, ready to defend Rose. "She is so innocent. She may have been foolish, but she would never do anything really bad."

"I believe you, but should this get out . . ." He trailed off.

Ada knew he was right.

"I am as angry as you are with Huntleigh, believe me," he continued. "Lady Rose is soon to be my sister-in-law, and this would be a great disgrace for me too, if it were to be known."

Ada was silent. She hated the humiliating note of contempt for Rose she heard in his voice, and yet how could she blame him? He was the perfect gentleman, that was what she admired about him, and Rose's behavior must have shocked him. She was already regretting confiding in him. But they would soon be married, and then wouldn't she have to tell him everything?

And just then, Ada saw the Duke of Huntleigh. She tensed, her fingers gripping Laurence's wrist so tightly that he exclaimed in surprise and pain. The crowds had parted just a little, like curtains swaying open across a stage, and she had glimpsed his characteristic shadowed, reckless face. But where was Rose? The dancers swayed back again, and he was gone.

Ada stopped dancing and turned toward the crowd, following in the duke's wake. Laurence, one hand still holding hers, the other around her waist, followed.

"What's the matter?" he asked.

"I saw him."

"Who? The duke?"

Ada knew she should not allow him to follow. There would be a scene if the two men met, she was sure. She twisted loose and turned away.

"I'm sorry!" she cast over her shoulder before she hurried off into the crowd, leaving Alexander behind.

Ada tried desperately to force a way through the crowd. It was like being caught in a thorn forest, but a forest where the trees were prickly with jewels and rhinestones. Ostrich fans tickled her nose, debutantes' giggles rang out like the chattering calls of monkeys. It was as hot as a jungle; a jungle where Ada was soon lost. She stood on tiptoes and thought she saw his curly hair, but then a starched shirt front and a whiff of cigar and sandalwood blocked her way, and by the time she had escaped, she had lost him. She turned on the spot, the light splintering from jewels and sequins, dazzling and confusing her. But a sudden brightening of the room, as if a curtain had been twitched aside to let in a ray of light, made her turn to the grand staircase. At once she saw Rose.

Rose stood at the very top of the staircase. Ada's first thought was that she looked like a waterfall caught in sunlight. Her dress was of ruched dark-silver chiffon, burnished like antique metal, falling almost to her silver slippers. It was clasped at one shoulder with a diamond brooch shaped like a garland of flowers. A diamond tiara, like a crescent moon, crowned her thick dark hair. Clasping her waist were more diamonds, and it seemed as if all the light in the room came from her smile.

Laurence gazed after Ada in confusion and anger. He made a quick movement to go after her. Huntleigh deserved horsewhipping, Ada needed protection . . . and then he saw her: Charlotte, the vivid crimson of the dress against her white skin. She stood by the silken curtains, and as her eye caught his, she smiled, and stepped behind them. The silk swirled for an instant against her body, echoing her shape.

Laurence stood frozen for a second, and then he abruptly came to life, pushing through the crowd as he headed after Charlotte, toward the swaying silken draperies. He hated himself for what he was about to do. And yet, he knew, shouldering past dowagers and debutantes, that he could not resist it. Ada was beautiful. Ada was the perfect wife. But Charlotte . . .

He reached the draperies. The silk billowed, moved by the breeze. He moved along the edge of the dance floor, unnoticed by the crowds who talked and laughed above the music. The silk had been draped over the windows and the paintings and the statues that usually lined the room, and their shapes showed like ghosts when the sail of silk fell against them.

They had played this game the first season they had met. Sometimes he wondered what would have happened if he had proposed then, when they were both wide-eyed and innocent— before he had met Ada.

A woman's curving hip and breast formed under the material, then disappeared as the breeze stirred it again. When the silk fell against it again, Laurence brushed a hand over it. Cold marble, merely a statue. He moved on, walking softly, brushing a hand against every curve that appeared until he found one that was warm, and scaled with sequins.

At Somerton

He glanced left and right. Everyone was concerned with their own little gaggles of compliment and flattery and gossip and scandal. He turned and slipped behind the silk screen, and vanished from the ballroom as if from the world.

Chapter
Forty-eight

I win again, thought Charlotte, as Laurence joined her. Her smile was pure victory, and the kiss she gave him had the arrogance of the conqueror about it. She had not misjudged him; he was as passionate as always. But then he pulled away.

"This is the end of it," he whispered harshly. "I am going to marry Ada, and when I do, I won't be unfaithful to her."

"Of course you won't, dear," Charlotte laughed breathily.

"I mean it."

"I'm sure you will suit each other perfectly." She turned away from him and walked toward the window, knowing that the moonlight made her bare shoulders gleam like marble, and her swaying walk would cause the sequins to dazzle and glimmer across her hips.

"I know you don't believe I love her." He was following like a hypnotized rabbit, she noted as she turned to face him. "But I do. She's different from you—she makes me a better person."

"Oh, does she think you need improving?" Charlotte smiled.

Laurence scowled. "That's not what I meant. She looks up to me, she admires me. She thinks of me as a hero."

"But you're not a hero, are you, Laurence?" Charlotte said. "You're a politician."

Laurence's jaw clenched. Charlotte went on. "You don't believe in female emancipation any more than I believe in unicorns. You see it as a means to win a seat, a reputation, power. Don't mistake me—I wouldn't have it any other way. A vote is just a piece of paper, but a coronet lasts forever."

"She *makes* me believe in it," Laurence said quietly. It was a tone Charlotte had never heard before, and it irritated her deeply. "I never knew how much I loved her until this season. She's so pure, so faultless, so innocent, so—"

Charlotte raised her eyes to heaven. She followed him as he backed away, out of their hiding place. Yes, she had a plan, but it was too much to let him praise Ada's *innocence*.

"You might not think her so innocent—" she began, and then hesitated as the curtain swung back behind her and she saw the ballroom. Laurence was not paying attention to her. No one was, in fact. Everyone was gazing in a single direction, toward the grand staircase, and all those who were whispering were whispering the same words.

Close by Charlotte a dowager leaned toward her friend.

Behind the flutter of her fan Charlotte heard the extraordinary words: "Is that . . . Can it be . . . Can it possibly be . . . the Huntleigh parure?"

Charlotte was struck by a strange feeling of dread, as if some awful doom were coming toward her, something of which she had only ever glimpsed the wings in nightmares. She pushed past Laurence, walked forward, making her way through the whispering, glittering crowd . . . until she saw.

Rose, descending the staircase, all eyes upon her. Rose with the happiest smile Charlotte had ever seen on her face. Rose, in a silver tunic moving like dawn light on the sea, shamelessly simple, with all the light in the room clustering at her waist and throat and shoulders and in her hair. Rose, drawing gazes toward her like a magnet. Rose and the only words in the room: "Can that be . . . Is that really . . . Am I dreaming—or is she wearing the Huntleigh parure?"

Charlotte knew when she had won, and she knew when she had lost. Any chance she had ever had with the Duke of Huntleigh was gone.

Rose, her cheeks touched with a slight blush, made her way through the crowds. Everyone was staring. Very well, she thought, let them stare. Let Céline have her chance. She could see her father in the distance, with the countess. She walked toward them.

"Rose!" her father exclaimed as he saw her.

"I felt so much better that I thought I would come after all," she said, trying not to blush as she sensed the countess staring at her.

"I'm delighted. It would have been a shame for you to miss this." Lord Westlake smiled at her kindly. "What a beautiful dress. I am no expert, but even I can see you will not lack for dancing partners this evening."

"Thank you, Father." Rose smiled, feeling warm and proud.

"And it is," he added in a lower voice, "a pleasure to see you doing yourself justice at last. I understand how difficult things have been for you. But you must always remember you are an Averley—and now, at last, you are holding your head high, as befits an Averley."

"They are the most extraordinary diamonds," the countess said, staring at her. "May I ask where you got them?"

"Garrard. The ones I ordered were not ready, so they sent these instead." Rose was impressed by the ease with which she was able to lie.

"Really. They look like family pieces to me."

Rose felt a hand on her arm and turned. Mrs. Verulam stood there, beaming nervously. Rose wondered why she was away from her post at the head of the stairs. Then she noticed the countess sinking into a deep curtsy, her father bowing, and quick as lightning realized that the woman standing beside Mrs. Verulam was Queen Alexandra.

Rose sank into a curtsy at once.

"Please, my dear, rise," the queen said. Rose did so, her heart beating fast. Had the queen noticed that the jewels were not what she said they were? She was a connoisseur of jewels. But all she said, in a voice full of kindness, was, "I wish to congratulate you on your gown. It is most elegant and remarkable."

"Thank you, Your Majesty," Rose murmured.

"May I ask, who is your dressmaker?"

There was perfect hush as every woman in the room stopped breathing, the better to hear Rose's reply. Queen Alexandra was still an arbiter of style, far more so than the king's wife, the awkward Queen Mary. Rose could hardly stop herself beaming from ear to ear in a most unladylike way as she replied in a voice loud enough for all to hear: "I am most fortunate in my lady's maid, Céline Duplessis, Your Majesty."

"How charming. I do congratulate you both." The queen smiled and moved away, Mrs. Verulam following behind her. Rose sank once again into a deep curtsy. *Well, Céline,* she thought, *I have given you your chance, and I wish you luck.*

As she stood, Rose saw her reward. Alexander walking toward her, smiling. She took his hand and let him lead her out onto the dance floor.

CHAPTER
Forty-nine

Céline smiled as she watched from behind the screen that separated the cloakroom from the ballroom. Lady Rose had finally found her feet, she thought. She had seen the potential at once, and as she had expected, it had just taken one dress—the right dress at the right moment—to place her in her rightful position, at the center of attention. Yes, with a little tending, Lady Rose would blossom and take her place as a leader of style and fashion.

Behind her, maids pinned up fallen hems and reattached corsages, tidied hair and sent their mistresses out again glowing as if new. Céline realized that a number of the ladies were whispering and glancing at her as their maids worked. Hiding her smile, she turned and went back to where Ada's opera cloak hung. Stella, who was nearby, gave her a sour look.

"I hope you are enjoying your new position," Céline said.

"Very well, thank you. I am delighted to have bettered myself," Stella replied.

Céline heard the venom in her voice, and didn't have to fake her smile. "I'm glad you are suited to it," she replied demurely.

"Are you Lady Rose's maid?" a ringing voice demanded. Céline looked round to see a formidable woman, ostrich plumes nodding from her bandeau, a wattle decorated with diamonds hanging below.

"*Oui, madame.*" Céline dropped her eyes modestly.

"Quite extraordinary what you have done with Lady Rose. I must compliment you." She lowered her voice, to the volume of a muted foghorn. "How much are you paid, may I ask? I am sure not more than you are worth, but possibly less . . . ?"

Céline mentally rolled her eyes. Frenchwomen were so much better at this kind of thing.

"I am very happy with my position, my lady. However . . ." Céline hesitated, seeing a group of ladies coming toward her in a determined floating mass of tulle, then continued as soon as they were within earshot.

"I shall be opening my own atelier very soon, on Hope Street."

There were gasps. Lady Gertrude shouldered her way to the front of the crowd.

"Will you be selling the gown Lady Rose is wearing?" she demanded.

"The 'Arrival'? I most certainly will, and several other of my own original designs."

There was a moment's silence, and then the crowd of ladies descended upon her in a shrill blizzard of excited questions. Céline, swelling inside with pride, worked to maintain her most modest and dutiful expression. She knew her career had truly begun, and tasted a sweetness that was all the more pleasant for the bitterness of Stella's expression.

CHAPTER
Fifty

"I'm so hot." Rose fanned herself as the dance came to an end. "Isn't there anywhere cooler?"

"I'm sure we can find somewhere," Alexander replied.

He drew her through the crowd, toward the silk curtains. As she passed through, they rippled and billowed against her skin. She saw a flash of red sequins on the ground. Behind, a shadowed alcove was lit by moonlight through a large window.

Rose went to the window, gazing out over the moonlit lawn edged by a dark line of trees. Alexander followed.

He was very close to her. She could smell his sweat, the sandalwood of his scent, the crisp linen of his shirt. They had been this close when he had kissed her before, and yet this felt different somehow. This was not Mont Pleasance. This was the real world.

I would want my wife to help me in this work, he had said. Had he meant it as a proposal? She felt his hands on her waist and turned around. The look in his eyes made her heart pound.

"This is the most perfect night," she began, trying to somehow put her joy into words. "Thank you for . . ." Her voice died away as he lowered his face toward her. She felt her breath quicken, and closed her eyes. His lips brushed her cheek, then her neck—the lightest of touches, as if a butterfly's wings were beating against her skin. He took her hands and drew her against his chest without speaking a word. They clung to each together in the moonlight, the strains of the distant orchestra floating around them.

It was only a moment, but it seemed to last an eternity. And in some way, she thought, remembering what he had said about memories haunting a room, it *was* an eternity. She knew she would never forget this moment. She remembered what he had said, the hinted proposal. For the first time she allowed herself to believe in it. He loves me, she thought as their hearts beat together, her head swimming with the wonderful delight of it all. He really does.

She lifted her head, waiting for his lips to touch hers, but instead he started, and stepped back. Rose instinctively turned to look behind her.

Ada was standing there, silhouetted against the curtains.

From the shocked expression on her face, Rose knew she had seen them together.

"I am so sorry, am I intruding?" Ada addressed Alexander in an icy voice.

"Not at all," he replied easily, releasing Rose's waist.

Ada looked at Rose. Rose flinched at the expression in her eyes.

"I would like to speak to you, Rose, if it is convenient."

Alexander bowed to them both and moved away. He looked back before he returned to the ballroom, and Rose had the comfort of seeing him smile at her. Then she was left alone with Ada. One look at Ada's face told her that all was not well.

"I have been looking for you everywhere." Ada's forehead was creased with anxious irritation.

"I—I felt much better," Rose began, "and I—"

"What were you thinking?" Ada interrupted.

"What do you mean?" Rose realized for the first time how distraught Ada was.

"You know very well. How could you go away with him, how could you do anything so insane!"

Rose flushed. "Céline told you then?"

"She had little choice when you did not come back. We were frightened for you! How can you arrive like this, so coldly, as if I had not been crying my eyes out with worry—"

"I'm so sorry. I didn't think—" Rose moved forward to take her arm, feeling suddenly guilty.

Ada stepped back. "I had to lie to—to everyone."

"Everyone?" Rose caught the hesitation.

Ada blushed. "I told Laurence the truth."

"How could you!" Rose felt as if she had been slapped. "I never, ever told your secrets!" she whispered, furiously.

"Rose, I was terrified! I had no idea where you were, and that man—I expect you don't know he betrayed Emily Fintan."

"It wasn't like that—"

"And you have his side of the story, of course."

"I trust him."

"Do you? Are you then engaged?"

Rose was breathless with surprise. "That is very blunt," she managed at last.

"And that is not an answer. Are you ashamed to answer me?"

Rose met her gaze fiercely. "No, I have done nothing to be ashamed of."

"That at least is a blessing. But has he proposed?" Ada's voice was sharp with anxiety.

Rose took a deep breath and said carelessly, "If you must know, he has not. A man and a woman can be friends. And I am no fortune hunter."

"Oh Rose, as if I said you were!" Ada exclaimed with exasperation. "But if you are not engaged, what do you mean by wearing that?" Her glance took in the diamonds. Rose looked down at them in surprise.

"Why should I not? He lent it to me. It's only for one evening."

"One evening where the whole of society will see, and will leap to the assumption that you are to be the next Duchess of Huntleigh! No other rumor is now flying around this room. No other words will be printed in the gossip pages of the magazines tomorrow!"

"Well, let them say what they want."

"You say that because you don't know what it is to be cast out of society. And when they find that you are not to marry him, you *will* be cast out, because your reputation will be destroyed!"

Rose was frightened now, but she was also angry. With Alexander, she had glimpsed a world where reputation's brittle shell didn't matter. Where you could be different, yet still valued and beloved. "No, I don't know what it is to be cast out of society. You forget, I was not in it until a few months ago. And if this is what it is to be in it, I think I can very well do without."

She turned and walked away, pushing aside the curtain and returning to the ballroom. But she knew in her heart, as the searching glances turned to follow her, that Ada was right. Everyone here expected her to marry the duke—everyone except herself, who knew that he had just had the perfect moment to propose, and hadn't.

She looked for him as she went through the crowd. She caught a glimpse of golden-red hair, but it was a silken scarf thrown over a dowager's shoulder; hurried toward a broad back, but it belonged to a stranger whose shirtfront stank of cigar smoke—and then she heard his voice. She was blocked from him by the backs of Lady Cynthia, Lady Gertrude, and Lady Emily.

"All the titled heiresses in the room at your disposal," Lady Gertrude was saying. She was clearly trying to sound as if she were amused, but her voice was a little too shrill. "And you choose the illegitimate housemaid. So *original*, Alexander."

"Oh, does gossip spread so fast these days?" Alexander sounded annoyed. Rose tried to step forward, but another group of young ladies moved in front of her blocking her way. Rose felt as if she were back at the beginning, back at the garden party in Milborough House, being squeezed out, cold-shouldered.

"Isn't it obvious?" Lady Emily said, her voice dripping poison. "He's marrying her exactly because she *is* a housemaid. Isn't that right, Alexander? I remember you saying to me a long time ago that you would only marry to spite your father."

Rose felt as if she had been slapped.

"I did say that, didn't I?" Alexander chuckled humorlessly. "You seem very informed on my feelings—and very keen to marry me off."

"Haven't you proposed?" Lady Emily demanded, as Lady Cynthia and Lady Gertrude exchanged malicious, delighted glances.

Alexander gave her a polite, icy smile. "Reports of my marriage have been greatly exaggerated."

He strode away through the crowd, leaving Rose standing, her face white with shock, tears forming in her eyes. Lady

Gertrude turned, caught her eye, nudged Lady Cynthia. Rose didn't wait to see the triumphant, sneering looks on their faces. She turned away and pushed through the crowd in the opposite direction away from him, blinded with tears of humiliation and anger.

Act Three

CHAPTER
Fifty-one

Somerton

"And so," the countess said with a small sigh, as she seated herself on Charlotte's bed, "another season ended. As soon as this wedding is over, we must talk about what we are to do with *you*."

Charlotte flushed. She met her mother's eyes in the glass above the dressing table. The sun was setting over the woods and fields that surrounded Somerton Court. Its dull copper blaze, reflected in the mirror, turned the diamonds in her hair to rubies.

"I did my best," she replied. Trust her mother to bring this up, the very first evening they arrived back at Somerton. She did not need reminding that her plan to snare Alexander had failed.

"And it was not good enough, was it?" The countess's eyes were sharp as ice. "Three seasons, and no proposal."

"Plenty of proposals, Mother."

"None that you accepted. And none *this* season." The countess leaned a little closer toward her. "If I didn't have more faith in your good sense, I would say you were in love."

Charlotte gave a slight laugh as she fastened the tiara in her hair. "I feel like a whelk, mother, and you're the pin. But don't worry, no matter how deep you dig, you'll never find a heart."

"Good," said the countess. "Because you can't afford one. You are getting old, and you no longer have the novelty of a debutante. Next season it will be harder than ever for you to attract proposals."

Charlotte pressed her lips together, hard. She knew that nothing would annoy her mother more than silence.

The countess waited, then when her daughter did not reply, rose abruptly to her feet. She looked in the cheval glass, one hand playing with the strands of pearls around her neck. "Well, luckily you have a mother who loves you and wants the best for you." She glanced at Charlotte. "I have the perfect solution. Young Blanchford."

Charlotte frowned, unable to think who her mother meant. Then her eyes widened as she remembered. "You can't possibly mean that babe in arms who has only just left Eton? Why, mother, he doesn't even shave yet!" She laughed. "Do you take me for a cradle snatcher?"

Her mother shrugged. She turned this way and that, to admire the flow of her gown in the glass. "Say what you like, he has a very comfortable fortune and will inherit the title. Everyone knows his father is on death's doorstep."

"That's something, but he needs a nursemaid, not a wife." Charlotte shook her head again, dimpling a smile as she fastened her necklace. "Besides, you're not terribly well informed. He and Lady Helen Fairfax are an acknowledged item."

"They were," said the countess.

Charlotte stopped fiddling with her jewelry and turned around in her seat to look her mother in the face. The countess's smug smile told her that she was serious. "I don't understand you. They were so very much in love. Nothing would have separated them." Charlotte was surprised at the anxiety she felt.

"Oh, a word in the right ear at the right time," the countess said, waving a hand.

"Do you mean to tell me that you engineered their separation?"

"You put it so bluntly. The important thing is that young Blanchford is now available."

Charlotte breathed out sharply. A headache had begun to pulse. She spoke quickly, without looking at her mother: "Well, I think that is disgraceful. And I certainly will have nothing to do with Blanchford. The whole thing is unpleasant, Mother."

"Hah!" The countess laughed in a mixture of surprise and anger. "You are a fine one to talk, my little schemer."

Charlotte paled, all of her anger and humiliation rising to the surface. She would never stoop so low as this—she, at least, had enough pride to meddle only with people who would do the same to her without a second thought.

"They might have been left in peace," she said furiously. "It was their first love affair and they might have been happy, had you not come along."

The countess tutted dismissively. "Nonsense, they'll get over it. You'll have Blanchford, and be grateful. He will be at the wedding and you can secure him then. He was simply overwhelmed by you in your Firebird gown, the poor boy, and besides, weddings are such delightfully romantic occasions. Every single man there thinks naturally of the moment when he will find a sweet companion to share his life."

"Delightfully romantic indeed, with the two parties' solicitors picking over the contract in the wings!" Charlotte laughed sarcastically as the countess moved to the door, her gold chiffon evening gown sweeping and catching the sunset rays.

The countess turned at the door to add, "By the way, I'm a little concerned that you gave Ward notice so brusquely."

"She deserved it," Charlotte snapped defensively.

"I'm sure she did, but there are more . . . sensitive ways to handle these things." The countess opened the door. "Don't be late for dinner. Lord Westlake has asked Sanders to open the '98 Dom Pérignon now that Ada and Laurence's union is official."

The door snicked shut behind her, and Charlotte was, finally, alone. She took two or three deep breaths to calm herself, and reached for her scent bottle. The odor of violets always calmed her. But the crystal bottle was empty.

Charlotte started to her feet and went to the bell. She placed her thumb on it and kept it there. After a couple of moments she heard running footsteps in the corridor. The door opened, and

Annie stood there, breathless, nervous, and looking as if she had been asleep.

"You rang, miss—" She ducked as the scent bottle flew over her head and shattered against the wall.

Charlotte took a couple of deep breaths. The sight of her maid cowering calmed her. "My scent bottle was empty," she said coldly. "Your job, you stupid girl, is to keep it filled. What am I to do with you?"

Annie, still crouching on the floor, whimpered an apology.

"Get up," Charlotte told her. "You have one more chance. If you disappoint me again, you can find a new job. Now, get out of here, find a broom, and sweep that up."

Annie, curtsying and trembling, scurried away.

Charlotte turned away, breathing more slowly, her rage subsiding. In its place, as if it were a sea receding, was left a bleak despair. She contemplated her array of scent bottles and cases for jewels, fans, and gloves, all lined up before the mirror. They were her army, a glittering, velvet-lined, musk-scented army. And this season, they had all been roundly defeated.

But Charlotte still had her greatest weapon. And she could not wait one single moment longer to use it. After so many defeats, she needed a victory.

She rose and crossed to the secretaire in the corner of the room. She opened it and drew out a letter she had begun a long time ago. She smoothed the paper and reread the words she had written.

Dear Sir, she read, feeling her breathing already calmed. She had forgotten entirely about Annie's failings. *I think you will be interested to know the full details of Lady Ada Averley's relationship with a young Indian student, Ravi Sundaresan, which began in the Spring of 1912. . . .*

A small smile crossed Charlotte's lips as she leaned over the paper to finish the letter.

CHAPTER
Fifty-two

In the privacy of the broom cupboard, Annie released the tears that had been building up. No one had ever thrown anything at her before, though she had heard much worse tales from other maids, and she knew that if you wanted the reference, there was nothing to do but grin and bear it. But from Miss Templeton—*her* Miss Templeton, who had been so kind, so considerate, who had dismissed her own maid in order to employ her—she had never expected such a thing. She had only drifted off to sleep for just a second—the journey from London had been so tiring, what with keeping track of all Miss Charlotte's luggage—and running into town to buy new scent had just slipped her mind.

Annie felt a hand on her shoulder and turned with a gasp to see Céline.

"*Ma petite*, what is the matter?" Céline asked, concern in her voice.

Annie sobbed out an explanation. "I only just forgot the scent. There's so much to remember in this job. I wish she had never given me this chance, I do. I never thought she could be so unkind." Annie sniffed.

Céline's expression was sympathetic. "This is a hard life," she said gently. "Even with the best mistress in the world. And Miss Templeton is not the best mistress in the world."

"But she was so kind before, so nice—" Annie sobbed.

"I do not like to say it, but I am almost sure that she engaged you because she knew she could encourage you to make trouble for Lady Rose."

Céline sniffed wordlessly. Rose would never throw anything at me, she thought. Never, ever.

"But where am I to get more scent this time of night?" Annie was on the brink of sobbing again.

"Is it Nuit de Violettes?"

Annie nodded.

"I'll fetch you some from Lady Rose's bottle," Céline said. "She won't mind—won't even notice, I shouldn't think."

"Will you?" Annie managed a smile. "Thank you so much. You're kind."

"We servants have to *stick together*, isn't that the English expression?" Céline smiled back as she handed Annie the dustpan and brush.

Annie watched her go, her heart full of grateful warmth. *Yes,* she thought, *yes we do*—and she remembered Priya saying something very similar. Annie hadn't seen Priya since they had arrived back at Somerton, and for some reason that troubled her. Things were clearly going to be very different under Mrs. McRory; and though she had barely had a moment to speak to her old workmates, she could sense already that the mood in the house was different altogether than it had been under Mrs. Cliffe. Everyone seemed tense and unhappy.

CHAPTER
Fifty-three

"Not long now, my lady," Céline said encouragingly, as she tried the veil on Ada before the mirror. It was a waterfall of fine silk tulle embroidered with delicate rose-gold orange blossoms.

Ada, staying obediently still at the heart of a web of tacking thread and pins, managed a smile. The invitations—mostly to people she had never met—had been sent out, and cordial acceptances received. Wedding gifts were flooding in; she already had more silver candlesticks than she knew what to do with, and her new monogram was on more things than she had thought possible. Somerton was full of the scent of orange blossom and roses, the frantic footsteps of the maids rushing to prepare the guest rooms, the butler's cloth squeaking over the silver as it was polished within an inch of its life, the landau—so rarely used now that motorcars had taken over most of the stables—being cleaned and polished, the chandeliers being dusted and redusted, and all kinds of delicacies being prepared in the kitchen.

But what made all feel so terribly real was the clipping from *The Times* that was slipped into the corner of her mirror. Her gaze returned to it again and again.

Engagements. 21st August. Lady Ada,
eldest daughter of the Earl of Westlake, to Laurence,
Lord Fintan. Ceremony at St. Anne's, Palesbury.

The twenty-first of August. A mere week to go.

"It's perfect, my lady," murmured Céline, still looking at the veil.

"Yes," Ada said, and her voice sounded small and tired. "It's perfect."

Was Ravi already in London? She thought he must be. Was he thinking about her? Or was he too busy? Did he want to meet merely out of nostalgia? Had he seen the announcement in *The Times*? Would he be waiting for her under the great clock as she said her vows? She wished her head did not ache so much. Lately it had been hard to sleep.

In the mirror she could see the bridesmaids being fitted behind her, Gertrude, Cynthia, Rose, Emily, Charlotte, and Georgiana rising like Venuses from a sea of tulle and chiffon. She glanced at Rose, who had been quite silent so far, her chin raised high as Sarah finished some last stitching at the neck of her gown. The uncomfortable position was an excuse for silence, but Ada wondered if something more was troubling her. Ada knew that Rose had heard nothing from the Duke of Huntleigh since the ball.

"Ada, have you heard?" Georgiana turned to her, almost tripping on the trailing satin hem of her dress. *"The Illustrated London News* is saying you have diamond clasps to your corset! It's not true, is it?"

Ada had to laugh, though she blushed as well. "Of course not. How can they print such vulgarities!" It was extraordinary, she thought, how much attention her forthcoming wedding had attracted. "I don't understand why they think people will want to read every last detail of my trousseau."

"But of course they will." Emily turned this way and that, admiring the fall of ivory chiffon. Gold net glinted beneath, muting the sheen of pink satin. "You are the Earl of Westlake's daughter, and my brother is a lord. It's a real-life fairy tale."

Ada's smile was forced. And it ends on the stroke of twelve, she thought. Every time she closed her eyes, she could see not Laurence standing at the altar but Ravi standing under a clock in the midst of a busy train station. Standing there where she had kissed him good-bye . . .

"This is the most beautiful dress I've ever worn." Georgiana spun on the spot, billowing waves of cloth floating from her. "I'm so pleased you have taste, and don't want to make your bridesmaids look as they're dying of consumption, as some brides seem to."

Ada laughed. "Of course I don't. It's the start of your coming out, and I want everyone to see how beautiful you are."

"I wonder who the next of us to get married will be," Emily said, meeting Ada's eyes in the mirror.

"You, perhaps."

"I don't think so." Emily's laugh was light as snow. "I'm married to the cause. I thought Charlotte would have had a proposal *this* season. . . ." She turned a sly glance toward Charlotte, who kept her smile fixed. "But perhaps Lady Rose will be next at the altar?" she murmured.

Rose gave a quick gasp of pain.

"I'm so sorry, madam!" Sarah exclaimed.

"No, it was my fault—I shouldn't have moved." A drop of blood welled on Rose's shoulder, and Sarah moved swiftly to dab it away and keep it from staining the material.

"You had such a triumph at Mrs. Verulam's ball," Emily continued. "We're all awaiting the outcome with bated breath."

Georgiana was listening, eyes wide. "What has happened? Rose, are you engaged?"

"I—" Rose blushed.

"Oh, Rose, tell me!" Georgiana fairly bounced up and down while Annie desperately tried to hold her dress in place. "You've had a proposal and you never let me know? You are mean!"

"Don't tease her," said Ada anxiously.

"I hardly know how you can bear to wear rhinestones after experiencing the real thing," Gertrude said. "It was such a very particular attention the Duke of Huntleigh paid to you. I'm sure he has proposed, and you are simply being modest in not telling us."

Ada opened her mouth to try changing the subject, but Lady Cynthia stepped in. "Come now, Rose—you can tell us. After all, we are all bridesmaids together—it makes us practically sisters." She raised her head like a snake about to strike.

"Did the duke propose to you?" Emily's voice stabbed again. "He must have done, of course. . . ."

"Certainly the alternative doesn't bear thinking about," murmured Lady Gertrude.

Rose could no longer avoid their eyes. She looked down, and Ada ached as she saw the hunted expression on Rose's face. Ada knew then that she had been right, that Alexander Ross had merely been trifling, and she wished desperately that she could protect Rose. But there was no protecting her now. If he didn't propose, her reputation would be ruined.

A piercing shriek from the upper stories interrupted her. The maids started, Charlotte and Georgiana exclaimed, and Emily swung around in the direction of the noise, looking astonished.

"Goodness, what was—" Ada's words were drowned out by more shrieks, crashes, bangs, howling. She looked around at the others, but the ladies and their maids all met her gaze with equal mystification.

"Can the kitchen cat have got in with Lady Edith's pugs?" Georgiana said, clutching her dress together, looked around.

"It doesn't sound like the cat, my lady," Céline murmured.

Ada listened, and this time could make out distinct voices,

shouting at each other. One was Augustus, and she could tell he was in the throes of a tantrum. The other was Lady Edith, in no less of a state.

"It sounds as if someone is being murdered. How many more valets have the Averleys to lose?" Emily murmured, with a look on her face as if she had smelled something bad.

Ada found herself furious. How dare Edith embarrass her in front of her soon-to-be sister-in-law? "I must go up at once," she said, hurrying to the door.

"I shall come," Georgiana followed her. "I don't understand it," she added in an undertone as Rose joined her. "We haven't had such a scene ever since Priya arrived."

"Oh, do let us join the party," Lady Cynthia exclaimed, following them. "I'm dying to see what can have caused such a noise."

Ada hurried up the stairs, followed by the other ladies, trying to hide her annoyance at Cynthia and Gertude's obvious desire to witness a scene. As she went up flight after flight, the voices grew louder and clearer. Augustus was in the midst of a tantrum, in which only the words *No!* and *Mine!* could be discerned, and Lady Edith was ranging up the full chromatic scale from "Darling, darling, calm yourself! Toodles, my sweet pet!" to "Your father will whip you for this, see if he doesn't, spawn of Satan!" Ada reached the nursery corridor to find two maids cowering just outside the door, which was ajar. They hastily turned to the wall as Ada approached.

"Lady Edith, what is the matter?" Ada demanded, opening

the door fully. She gasped as she saw a scene of devastation: the rocking horse shattered beyond repair, Augustus writhing on the hearthrug, and spilled food and broken china everywhere. Lady Edith was stretched out in the rocking chair, her smelling salts pressed to her nose, murmuring faintly about the Four Horsemen of the Apocalypse.

"The poor boy . . . Evil spirits must have corrupted him. . . ." Edith wept.

"But where is Priya?" Georgiana exclaimed.

"Well may you ask!" Lady Edith revived enough to say indignantly. "That dreadful woman, the pygmy—"

"Mrs. McRory?"

"Yes, she has sent Priya away without notice!"

"But why on earth!" Ada exclaimed. "Whatever she has done, it cannot merit this."

"No, how am I to manage?" Lady Edith began to weep again. "None of the maids can handle him like dear Priya could. She had some magical way about her. And good nursemaids are not to be found nowadays, not without paying a most outrageous price—"

Ada left her without another word. Closing the door on the scene of devastation, she paused and spoke to the closest maid, Sarah. "Have you any idea why Priya has been given notice? It seems extraordinary. I understood she was more than satisfactory."

The maids glanced at each other uncomfortably.

"I think Mrs. McRory is the best person to explain, my lady," Sarah murmured at last.

"I see!" Ada did not see at all; the mystery thickened. Mrs. McRory had acted beyond her authority, and if the housemaids were refusing to tell her what was going on . . .

"Well, I don't!" Georgiana exclaimed angrily. "How dare she intrude into the realm of the nursery? She knows very well that Priya reports directly to Lady Edith and Sir William. I shall speak to her at once. See that Lady Edith is brought some strong tea and smelling salts immediately," she said to Sarah, and marched toward the stairs.

Ada looked after her sister in astonishment and then smiled with pride. Perhaps it had been a good thing to leave Georgiana behind, after all. She certainly seemed to have grown up and developed a healthy amount of authority. Mrs. McRory had better have some excellent explanation, Ada thought.

CHAPTER
Fifty-four

As Georgiana reached the baize door, it swung open, almost hitting her in the face. James started, a look of horror on his face.

"Beg pardon, my lady, I didn't expect you!" He was clutching an immense gleaming silver tureen.

"Please don't apologize. Is Mrs. McRory here?" She walked ahead without waiting for an answer. The servants' corridor was a hive of activity; she could smell silver polish and hear the cook shouting at the tweeny for not making the wedding cake icing stiff enough. The staff who saw Georgiana in her bridesmaid dress marching toward the housekeeper's room did double takes. A maid scampered out of the kitchen, saw Georgiana, gasped, and reversed at speed. Georgiana glimpsed the rose-pink garlands the maids were stitching at the kitchen table, the towering bulk of the wedding cake. Cooper she glimpsed in his pantry, dusting off the best vintages.

"Mrs. McRory!" she demanded, marching into the housekeeper's room without the courtesy of a knock. The housekeeper was almost invisible, lost among a fortress of accounts. "I demand to know why you have dismissed Priya. I find it extraordinary that such a valued and essential member of staff has been sent away without even a reference."

Mrs. McRory, who had bobbed up from her chair as soon as she entered, pinched her mouth to the size of a pea and raised her eyebrows. "Valued and essential—*hmmph!*" She sniffed.

"I *beg* your pardon," Georgiana exclaimed, shocked at her disrespectful attitude.

"Oh, no, my lady. If that is the kind of person the Averleys consider valued and essential, well, very well, but I had no idea that was the kind of household I was entering and I certainly think, my lady, if it were not for your youth and my great regard for your esteemed father—no, not a moment longer, indeed, my lady, not for all the tea in China!"

Georgiana swayed slightly under the onslaught. "I don't follow in the slightest," she said. "Are you trying to suggest that Priya was in some way guilty—"

"Guilty! Oh yes, doomed and damned, my lady, no matter what latitude the gentry may allow themselves—and indeed I am no stranger to such shocking revelations—but in this house, I certainly felt myself safe from— But clearly, no better than London!"

Georgiana took a deep breath. All she could make out was

that Mrs. McRory thought Priya guilty of something dreadful. Perhaps something had been stolen, and they were blaming the foreigner.

"Whatever is missing," she said quietly, "I can assure you I have the greatest confidence in Priya, and I am sure she is not to blame."

"*Hmmph!* What's missing cannot be returned, my lady."

"Broken, then—"

"*Hmmph!* Shattered beyond redemption, but it's her own fault!"

"Mrs. McRory, if only I could speak to Priya, I am sure we could clear this all up—"

"You'll have to look for her in London, then. She left on the first train."

"What do you mean?" Georgiana exclaimed. "Why? How? Is there anyone to meet her?"

"Oh, she has a friend all right, though if he'll look after her now—well, some are lucky and some not so lucky." Mrs. McRory nodded savagely. "And now, my lady, if you will forgive me, I have a wedding to organize."

Georgiana found herself most politely buffeted out of the door.

She stood, blank and confused and angry, in the servants' corridor. What could Priya possibly have done to deserve this? What would Michael say? He had asked Georgiana to look after Priya. And now . . .

Georgiana turned and went to the stairs, fists clenched, mind working fast, ignoring the servants who peeped at her from the kitchen. She could speak to her father, beg him to use all his influence to find Priya. But London was so big! She had only passed through it once, on her way back from India, but she recalled the steam of the railway station, the roaring of the traffic, the hustle of the crowds. How could anyone find one girl there?

As Georgiana reached the steps, she met Annie coming down them. The housemaid's eyes widened as she saw her, and she at once drew back, flattening herself against the wall to let Georgiana pass.

Georgiana hesitated. She recalled all Mrs. Cliffe had told her about preserving a proper boundary between servant and mistress, but these were special circumstances. She cleared her throat and, unable to conceal her embarrassment, said, "Annie—er—excuse me—but I must ask you something."

"Yes, my lady." Annie's whisper was almost inaudible, and she did not look up.

Georgiana moved closer, glancing behind her to make sure no one was listening to their conversation. She spoke in an undertone. "I must be terribly stupid, but I don't understand what Priya is supposed to have done. Has something very valuable gone missing? Whatever it is, I am certain she could have nothing to do with it—"

Annie raised her eyes to her.

Georgiana stopped, struck by the startled look on Annie's face. "What is it, Annie? What has happened? Please tell me. I am responsible for everyone here, and if there is any way of helping Priya I must do it."

"M-my lady, didn't you know?" Annie whispered. "Priya's *in trouble*. She's pregnant, miss."

Georgiana stared at her in horrified disbelief.

Michael, she thought. She turned on her heel and ran up the stairs without another word to Annie. Two thoughts stood out with the brightness of headlights. She must write to Michael instantly, and she must hide this scandal from her family. If Priya were ever to be able to return to Somerton, the secret must be kept at any cost.

CHAPTER
Fifty-five

Palesbury

"Georgiana, are you quite all right?" Ada asked as they sat in the carriage, on their way down the lane to the church. Green hedgerows rose to either side and the sky was bright with sunshine, the air full of summer birdsong. Behind them in the second carriage were the earl, Charlotte, Lady Gertude, and Lady Cynthia, who had arrived that morning.

Georgiana started. "Yes—oh yes." She knew she sounded distracted, but hurried on. "I was just thinking that it does seem so strange to have a rehearsal."

"I certainly wouldn't like to attempt it without one." Ada smiled at her sister. She wasn't fooled by Georgiana's act, but she was touched by her brave attempt to seem unconcerned. It was clear that her little sister had begun to feel responsible for the staff at Somerton, and the bad news about Priya had shaken her.

"Yes, but it makes me think of a stage play," Georgiana said, with a small sigh. "I suppose I always thought that weddings just . . . happened." She waved her hand vaguely.

Ada exchanged an amused glance with Rose. The countess sniffed.

"And I never imagined there was so much for the solicitors to do," Georgiana continued.

Ada looked down. Georgiana had touched a sore spot. No matter how much Laurence assured her that the legal matters were simply a matter of convention, she disliked all the wrangling between Mr. Hobbes and Mr. Branford greatly.

"I think you have a mistaken impression of marriage in general, Georgiana dear," the countess said. "Probably from reading novels. A marriage among important families is the union of two grand estates. Naturally there is a good deal of legal business to conclude."

"That's just what I mean, it's as if Gravelley Park and Somerton are getting married, not Laurence and Ada—"

Georgiana stopped short as Rose frowned and whispered, "Georgie!"

"Oh, I am sorry, Ada—I didn't mean—I know you love each other very much, and I didn't mean to imply—" Georgiana exclaimed, blushing in anguish.

"Of course I know what you mean," Ada said soothingly, but she couldn't stop herself flushing red. Georgiana had a knack of stumbling upon the truth. To her relief, she saw the gray stone spire of the church coming up before them. As they turned into the churchyard she could see that Laurence's motorcar was already there, a startlingly modern sight next to the comfortable old country church, with its honeysuckle-wreathed lych-gate and the carefully tended gravestones gathered around it. She descended, looking around for Laurence, and Rose followed, while Gertrude, Cynthia, and Charlotte got down from the other carriage, fussing about their dresses.

Lady Emily was standing with the rector by the doors. As she walked up the winding path toward them, smiling a greeting, Ada saw another woman, by the looks of her a lady's maid, standing discreetly to one side. A flash of yellow hair showed under her hat.

"Isn't that Ward?" Rose exclaimed. "What is she doing here?"

"Yes," said Ada, following her gaze. "You're right." She glanced back at Charlotte, who was walking behind them up the path. She too was looking at Ward, and Ada noticed that her face seemed pale.

Emily wore a smart walking suit, clearly made in Paris. She smiled as she greeted them. and the rector murmured modestly and hung back.

"Good morning," Emily said as they reached her. "Laurence drives so fast, we've been here for half an hour. He's inside, inspecting the memorial stones. He is a keen amateur historian, as I'm sure you know."

"Let's join him." Ada took Emily's arm and turned to the church. The countess hung back, staring at the maid, who had stepped forward to follow them.

"I see you have employed Ward," she said.

Emily turned to follow her gaze. Her smile was quite genuine as she replied, "Yes, I was surprised Charlotte let her go. She's an excellent lady's maid. Very knowledgeable . . . about all kinds of matters."

Arm in arm, Ada and Emily walked into the church.

Chapter
Fifty-six

Charlotte twisted the ribbon of her reticule through gloved fingers as she followed the others into the church. Stella Ward, here! And in the service of Emily Fintan, of all people. She could feel her heart hammering under her corset, anger and fear drumming through her veins. She couldn't hide it from herself. Ward had outplayed her. Charlotte had been so concerned with attacking Rose and Ada that she had forgotten to defend herself.

Laurence came down the aisle toward them, the verger one obsequious step behind him. He took Ada's hands in his own, but Charlotte barely listened to their greetings. She risked a quick glance behind her. Ward had followed them but remained at the rear of the church. As she watched, the maid seated herself in one of the pews at a respectful distance from the ladies and gentlemen.

"Miss Templeton, would you be kind enough to move slightly to the left, which will be your position on the blessed day itself. . . ." The rector's voice intruded, and Charlotte turned around. She smiled sweetly and stepped to the left to allow Ada to move forward. She glanced again to the pew at the rear of the church where Ward sat, her head modestly bowed, as she waited for her mistress. The hat shaded her face.

The rehearsal wore on, and Charlotte hardly managed not to scream in irritation as the organist played "The Voice That Breathed O'er Eden" over and over again. *Think!* she told herself. There had to be some way to bribe or bully Ward into holding her tongue about her and Laurence. Her mother's elegantly straight back was turned, but she glanced back once, and the expression on her face left Charlotte in no doubt that she understood the gravity of the situation.

Ada and Laurence stood together in front of the altar while the rector fussed around them, positioning them like two mannequins. Laurence looked awkward and irritated, Ada pale and silent. She followed the rector's instructions with docile obedience.

But I know the truth, thought Charlotte, allowing her gaze to run over Ada, allowing her fear to metamorphose into anger. *I know what a hypocrite you are. You kissed that Indian boy. Perhaps you went further. You imagine you can preserve that mask of icy virtue, you imagine you can smile at Laurence while never letting him know the truth, that you're not as pure as he fondly imagines. Well, I shall whisk*

*away the veil. I shall expose you for what you really are—no better than
the rest of us.*

Charlotte held her reticule tightly. The letters were in there,
stamped and addressed. When they left the church she would
have nothing to do but slip them into the postbox at the gate and
let Her Majesty's Royal Mail do the rest for her. If only she could
stop thinking about Blanchford and Lady Helen Fairfax. The
image of them dancing together, perfectly in love, kept recurring
to her, and it plucked her conscience uncomfortably. If I have the
chance, she thought, I will make sure that whatever misunderstanding my mother caused between them is cleared up.

The rehearsal wore on, the rector timing the procession down
the aisle with his large, unfashionable pocket watch. Through it
all Charlotte was aware of the figure at the back of the church—as
ominous as the grinning skeleton with a scythe that leant against
one of the old memorial stones set into church wall.

"Finally over," the countess sighed, smoothing a wrinkle
from her impeccable gloves, as she turned away from the couple
at the altar. She paused by Charlotte, and murmured: "Rather
worrying, don't you think? I hope you have been discreet."

"Of course I have. Do you take me for a fool?" Charlotte was
aware that she sounded guilty.

"Not in the least. I don't feel the need to repeat our conversation of the other evening." She raised an eyebrow and walked
down to the carriage.

Charlotte followed, hating her mother. But then she clutched
the silk tassel of her reticule, aware of the letters inside it. No,

she couldn't hate her mother. But she could hate Ada. Ada, who thought she could break all the rules and get away with it. Ada, who was going to marry Laurence.

As she drew near the group, Charlotte heard Lady Emily's mischievous giggle. They had been friends once, and Charlotte had ruined their friendship just to spite Laurence. Had it really been worth it?

The women had not noticed her. Ada stood a little to the side, Rose and Georgiana beside her. Gertrude and Cynthia leaned in eagerly, like the geese on the pond pecking for worms. Emily had something in her hand—Charlotte saw a flash of scarlet silk. The sight stirred a sudden memory in her. She stopped dead.

"But, my dear Emily," Gertrude was saying, her voice sharp with greedy curiosity, "what *are* you suggesting? You can't possibly mean—"

"All I can tell you is what my lady's maid said." Emily's voice dripped with malice. "She tells me that undressing Charlotte that evening she noticed that one of the silk roses on her dress was torn. Well, it seems that one of the maids found the missing petals in the laundry room, of all places! And more than that, she says she saw how they were torn. . . ."

Charlotte felt herself turn cold. Into her mind's eye flashed the image of a Lalique vase about to meet a marble floor. Her reputation, her last chance—her last season—were about to shatter. In an instant she realized that everyone she had ever called a friend over the last few seasons had become her enemy. The man she loved had become an opponent. Even her maid had betrayed her. She was completely alone.

"Oh, but that rose belongs to me," Ada said.

Lady Gertrude's face fell. Lady Cynthia raised an eyebrow. Emily stared at her speechlessly.

"To you, Ada?" Rose asked.

"Yes." Ada reached out and plucked the crumpled petals from Emily's hand. "It was my corsage on the evening of the countess's garden party. I noticed that I had torn it somehow that evening. I have been wondering where the lost petals had got to."

"But the maid's story—" Lady Gertrude said hopefully.

Ada shrugged, meeting her eyes levelly. "Perhaps the petals were left in the laundry room for Céline to fix. Who knows? Besides, as we all know. . . ."

"Servants have such vivid imaginations," Rose finished. She and Ada exchanged a slight smile.

Emily's mouth twisted as if she had tasted a lemon. Charlotte stood behind them, thunderstruck, silent.

"It certainly is true, one cannot trust a word a servant says," Lady Cynthia said, nodding wisely.

Lady Gertrude still looked disappointed, but she turned away with a shrug. One by one, the others followed her down to the carriages.

Charlotte was left alone. She stood in the midst of the gravestones, halfway down the path that led from the church to the waiting carriages. She opened her mouth, then closed it again.

For the first time in her life, she had no idea how to behave, what to think, what to say. Ada had saved her reputation. There was no denying it. But why? And . . . what had she done to deserve it?

Her mother looked out of the carriage and beckoned. Charlotte started as if recalled to life, and walked down to the carriage.

"Do hurry, dear, we have so much to do," her mother said as Charlotte reached the carriage door. "Didn't you say you had letters to post?"

Charlotte hesitated a second before replying.

"No, there's no need. I have changed my mind," she said. Only the heightened color on her cheekbones betrayed the confusion within as she took her place in the carriage next to her mother.

CHAPTER
Fifty-seven

Somerton

Ada felt tired as she entered Somerton on her way back from the church. Yet she knew she had to hide her fatigue. She should not make things difficult for the staff, she told herself. Her job was simple: to walk where she was led, to smile when she was expected to, to say *I do* at the right moment. And in return she would make her family happy and have her greatest wish fulfilled, to study at Oxford.

Ada saw Cooper carrying a large parcel to the blue sitting room.

"Not more wedding gifts!" she exclaimed. "That is—how lovely. Who is it from?"

"Lord Fintan, my lady," Cooper said.

"Oh!" Ada was startled. She followed Cooper in. Despite

her father's objections—"It looks like a floor of Selfridges"—the countess had followed the fashion and turned the room into a kind of shrine. Silver, jewels, boxes made of rare woods, crystal vases, gold scent bottles, exquisite paintings and bronzes—all had been catalogued by Cooper and formed a glittering display. Ada hovered as Cooper unwrapped the package. She sniffed as a familiar scent wafted out: old paper and leather bindings.

"How wonderful!" she exclaimed as she saw a set of volumes in tooled leather revealed. Another glance told her they were the collected Greek playwrights, and a very little more inspection that they were rare editions from the reign of Queen Elizabeth. She couldn't suppress a squeal of delight.

Cooper handed her the card that came with it. Ada recognized Laurence's elegant handwriting at once. The words were not romantic but they made her smile:

A small payment on account, that you may be sure I will keep my promise.

She understood at once. The books were to promise her Oxford and her studies. Laurence had a knack of not pressing her, and yet reassuring her. He was so admirably discreet, so good at saying exactly the right thing.

"Dear Laurence," she murmured.

She crossed the room, still gazing at the card, hardly aware of James standing guard at the door as stiff and dutiful as a guardsman.

Laurence is perfect, she told herself. Laurence is perfect.

Out of nowhere, Ada felt a breathless catch in her chest. It was as if an invisible corset inside her ribs were being laced tighter and tighter. She turned, and with quick, tight steps walked across the room, the card still pinched in her fingers, and out into the hall. She was aware of James watching her with concern. She swallowed.

I am feeling a little out of sorts, she told herself. There is no need to alarm the servants. Ada took a gulp of air and headed at random across the hall to the library. She walked in and stood with her head leaning against the shelves, inhaling the comforting smell of books, trying to calm herself.

"Are you quite well? May I ring for a glass of water?"

Ada started upright. She hadn't realized there was anyone else in the room, but there was, a ladylike woman, about thirty, in a well-tailored tweed walking suit. She had just risen from the window-seat her gloved hands clasped around a leather handbag, and she was looking at Ada with gentle concern.

"I— No. That is, yes, perhaps a glass of water. Thank you." Ada was startled out of her nervous fit. The woman crossed smartly to the bell and rang it. She turned back with a smile.

"I surprised you. I'm so sorry. You must wonder who I am and what I am doing in your house."

"That question did cross my mind, yes." Ada's returning smile was warm. The woman seemed both well-bred and pleasant.

"Of course. My name is Hannah Darford. I am here to see Mr. Templeton."

"Hannah Darford!" Ada exclaimed. The lady smiled enquiringly.

"I *am* sorry, but we know each other—at least we have corresponded." Ada crossed the floor to her and clasped the woman's hand, shaking it warmly. "I am Lady Ada Averley. You were kind enough to agree to speak at our fund-raising dinner—"

"Lady Ada, of course! I had not realized you were so young, forgive me."

"I admire you so much," Ada went on enthusiastically. "It is so wonderful to see a woman making her voice heard. I wish I could join you in your campaigning."

"Do you?" Miss Darford's eyes twinkled. "Well, please take my card. Should you ever wish to visit us, please do—though I understand you will be married soon, and that of course will take a good deal of your time."

Ada took the card. She looked up as she heard someone enter the room. Sebastian stood there, his face flushed with excitement, his eyes sparkling with a light Ada had not seen in them since Oliver's arrest.

"Miss Darford, I presume? Hello, Ada." He gave her a brief nod, and returned his attention to Miss Darford. "Can you come with me now? If we're lucky we can still be in time."

"I came here for no other purpose." Miss Darford crossed to him with the stride of a confident woman.

Ada found her tongue just as they were leaving the room. "Sebastian, you're going somewhere?" She hurried after them.

Sebastian didn't stop walking, but spoke hastily over his shoulder. "We are. It's an emergency, Ada. I'm sorry."

"But—" Ada was so startled at his sudden decision that she hardly knew what to say. She ran a few steps after them, and paused as Thomas handed them their motoring dusters and hats. "In the motorcar? Is it—are you—will you be long?"

Sebastian was opening the front door of the house, not even waiting for Thomas to do it for him. "A day or so," he called back to her.

"But the wedding—" Ada ran after them again, catching the door as it swung shut. She almost shouted. "You will be back in time for the wedding, won't you? It is the day after tomorrow! And you are best man!"

Sebastian was climbing into the motorcar that stood ready, engine humming. He revved the engine as Ada spoke, and his reply was almost lost in the noise.

Miss Darford leaned over the passenger-side door, smiling as she held her hat on, the motoring goggles making her look like some kind of benevolent insect.

"I hope we'll be back in time for your wedding, Lady Ada!" she called. "It's a most urgent matter—and our very last chance."

Ada stood speechless as the car drove away with a thunder of crunching gravel. She put a hand to her head, which she felt in danger of losing.

Of course, she remembered. Tomorrow is Oliver's trial.

CHAPTER
Fifty-eight

Palesbury

"Forward," grunted the policeman, and Oliver walked forward, through the iron door of his cell and into the short dark corridor that led to the courtroom. The handcuffs around his wrists weighed him down and chafed with every step. The policemen who flanked and surrounded him formed a wall of dark blue, forcing him to walk at a slightly faster pace than he could manage, shackled. It was a murder trial. He knew that and wasn't surprised at the treatment. Still, he seethed inside with anger as the policeman behind him shoved him again in the small of the back.

He blinked as they came from the darkness of the cells into the murmuring light of the court. The public galleries were crowded. Oliver looked up and glanced around, and spotted the men with their hats placed in front of them on the bench, how they moved quickly to touch the crown or the brim. Hidden cameras. He had heard of the trick, and he could hear the scrape of ten or twenty pencils against notepads, beneath the whispers and coughs. The press would have a field day. He was glad again that he had kept Sebastian out of it—but, glancing around, he still felt sick with disappointment when he didn't see Sebastian's face watching from the gallery.

"Sit," the policeman ordered, and Oliver shuffled into the prisoner's box. The gate clanged shut behind him. Another prison. He stared at his manacled hands, trying to disregard the fact that he was the focus of all attention. Even though he had told Sebastian not to come—warned him not to—ordered him not to—he wanted him there more than anything.

"All rise," announced the clerk. There was a thunderous rustle as the whole court stood. Oliver stood with them, and glanced up toward the judge's bench. The judge saw a small, elderly man, drowned in a gray wig and red robes, making his way awkwardly to his seat. Oliver almost wanted to laugh at the absurdity of it. He glanced once toward the jury—a typical cross-section of London life—then down toward the benches where his counsel sat. And then he saw her. Hannah—here? He thought for a second he had said it aloud.

"Be seated," the clerk boomed.

Oliver sat. He felt almost as if his legs had been cut out from under him. He stared straight ahead. He could not see her from his seated position, but he was sure—the thumping blood in his head told him—that he was right. It was his sister. He knew she had wanted to train as a lawyer, but his father had always forbidden it. Was it just coincidence that had brought her here? How could she possibly know? He had done everything he could to disappear, to hide from his hated father, to change his identity. They could not have found him. He would rather die than return to his father's house.

There was some whispering and murmuring from the benches. The judge looked up as Mr. Brompton edged toward him and with a bow handed up a folded slip of paper. The judge took it, opened it, read it. Oliver knew he might be imagining it, but he thought he saw the judge start, as if he had been suddenly caught on a fishhook. He ducked his head to look over his spectacles, first at the paper, and then toward Oliver in the prisoner's box. Oliver met his gaze, uncertain what it meant. The judge's face now gave nothing away.

The judge folded up the paper and passed it to another wigged gentleman who stood nearby. There was some whispered conversation. The public gallery shifted, restless. Oliver glanced around. Was this how things were supposed to go?

The judge rose to his feet. "Case adjourned," he announced, and a roar of disappointment surged up from the public gallery.

The clerk seized his gavel and banged it irritably. "Order," he called, "order."

Oliver stayed where he was, too startled to react. His first feeling was one of anger and resentment. How could they spin out his torture like this? Let them sentence him and get it over with. But then, as the policeman unlocked the door and urged him to his feet, he felt a wild, reckless sense of relief. Something had happened. An object had fixed in the toothed wheels of justice and brought the whole thing to a halt. But what? Had it something to do with Hannah?

Oliver looked over his shoulder as he was led away, searching for her face. He saw her at once, pushing her way through the crowd with authority—and this time, just behind her, his face alight with anxiety and hope and love, he saw Sebastian.

"Sebastian!" he gasped. He wrenched out of the grip of the policemen. Sebastian broke into a run. The courtroom had nearly emptied, but some people were still filtering out of the public galleries. They turned to look as the two young men ran into each other's arms.

"It's going to be all right," Sebastian said. Oliver felt his arms tighten around him. "Why didn't you tell me who you were, you idiot? Never mind—Hannah has arranged everything, she's a marvel. You'll have to go back to prison now, but we'll get you off, see if we don't."

"I thought you weren't coming," said Oliver, as tears filled his eyes.

Sebastian cupped his face tenderly, and his voice was fierce and gentle as he said, "You bloody idiot."

Oliver heard Hannah say sharply, "Sebastian!" and then the policemen dragged him away. He let them shove him back into the cells. He didn't care when they pushed him and laughed, muttering coarse names. He had heard all those before, anyway. What mattered was that Sebastian had come, had saved him. Now everything was going to be all right.

CHAPTER
Fifty-nine

Hannah, her arm locked in Sebastian's, steered him through the crowd and out of the court. Sebastian, happy and dazed as he was, was able to appreciate the way she contrived to make it seem as if she were leaning on him for support, when in fact she was directing his footsteps. It must take some character, he thought, to be one of the first female lawyers to have qualified and practiced in England.

"That was extremely unwise," she murmured to him sharply.

"I daresay. I expect they will gossip anyway."

"Gossip is one thing. Did you see that man touch his hat to you as you embraced Oliver?"

"No." Sebastian was surprised. "Why should he have done that?"

"The gentlemen of the press conceal cameras in their hats. The technology has advanced to such a degree that excellent photos—snapshots—can be taken quickly and in secret. We will have to follow him, and bribe or bully him into giving the photograph back."

She nudged Sebastian sideways and he found himself almost falling through a side door, down steps, into the glaring light of the afternoon. To his right, some kind of a rugby scrum appeared to be going forward. Another glance told him it was the press, baying around the exit as the police van carrying Oliver emerged.

"How long will he have to stay locked up?" Sebastian exclaimed.

"Not long, I hope. We'll wait till the fuss has died down. With my connections I'm sure of getting a retrial with the right judge. He'll be acquitted, I'm sure of it. No one wants to send the Chief Justice's godson to the scaffold. Now, there goes our man."

She strode out into the road as a man clutching his hat onto his head with both hands walked swiftly away from the crowds.

"Hold up!" Hannah hurried after him. Sebastian followed. The man looked around, then broke into a run. Hannah did so too, and Sebastian followed. As they reached the corner, Sebastian recognized the man who had been following him for so long.

"We want to buy that photograph you just took!" Hannah shouted to him.

"I bet you do. Every Fleet Street editor is going to say the same." The man backed away, grinning.

"Name your price," Hannah insisted.

"Thank you, but I'd rather try it on the open market."

Hannah tutted with impatience. "For all you know that negative may show nothing. The angle was a difficult one. We'll buy it sight unseen. If you refuse us you may have a worthless shot of the crowd on your hands."

"May do." The man was walking away backward. A tram rattled by, and as it slowed, he jumped on. "But I think I'll take my chances."

Hannah stared after the retreating tram. "Damn," she murmured.

Sebastian caught her arm. "Oh, who cares? He probably has a worthless shot, as you say. How could anyone take a decent photograph at that distance and at such short notice?" He felt himself humming with excitement like a turning engine. "Oliver's saved and that's all that matters. Let's celebrate. Haven't we a wedding to go to?"

Hannah at last looked away from the vanishing tram, and answered his smile, though her eyes remained troubled.

"Yes. I daresay you're right. It's simply that it's a loose end . . . and as a lawyer, I dislike loose ends."

CHAPTER

Sixty

Somerton

Rose came slowly down the stairs. Tomorrow was the wedding, and she would have to see Alexander. Unless, of course, he did not come.

The words she'd overheard still ached, like a bruise in her heart. She had thought she was loved for herself. But it seemed that even to him, she was just a housemaid—that being a housemaid was the most important thing about her, and always would be.

She paused on the landing, and looked at herself in the gilt-framed mirror that hung there, between a grand Titian canvas and a bust of the Emperor Augustus. Her eyes were the same, her face was the same, as when she had worn a maid's uniform in this house. All that was different was the outside, the dress she wore, the gloves and the jewels. And yet that was all people saw.

The truth was clear to her. Even if he did propose, she could not accept. She could not marry someone who was only interested in what she was, not who she was. It felt almost a relief to have decided that.

Reaching the ground floor, she heard the gramophone blaring out ragtime and a rich male voice singing along with it. Astonished, she picked up her pace. She entered the drawing room and saw Sebastian, a bottle of champagne in one hand, waltzing with a cushion from the ottoman. She burst out laughing despite herself. "Sebastian!" she exclaimed. "What on earth has come over you?"

Sebastian turned round, beaming at her. "The very best of news. Oliver's trial's been put off—we hope to get him clear altogether. It should be possible. Good God, Rose, do you know who he is?" He was clearly dying to share his news. He dropped the cushion and vaulted over the ottoman to whisper in her ear. "Lord Hammerman's son—you know, the banker. His real name's Daniel, but I prefer Oliver—don't you?"

"Lord Hammerman?" Rose exclaimed. The name was synonymous with gold, and with the Hammerman Ruby, presented to Queen Alexandra. "The one who died recently? So he's not really a servant?"

"Far from it. His godfather's the Lord Chief Justice." Sebastian tossed down another glug of champagne and danced on the spot. "Have a glass with me, Rose, celebrate."

"I daren't," she said, laughing and glancing at the door. "But that lady who came here—"

"His sister, Hannah Darford. She took her mother's name when she began to practice law. A remarkable woman, I'll say. It was all down to her that we managed it. I contacted her after Michael told me about a picture that he saw at Eton of someone who looked just like Oliver. Michael was right. It was Oliver. I raced down there, demanded to know who the lad was. 'Oh yes, Daniel Hammerman. Expelled—awkward, rather.'" Sebastian lowered his voice. "Can you believe the story? He got into some entanglement with another boy, it all came out, they expelled him. His father disowned him, and Oliver decided to make his own way in life. But now old Hammerman's dead, and his mother and sister are free of the tyrant. They'll welcome Oliver back with open arms. Daniel, I should say. Damn it, I'll never remember."

"I'm so glad!" Rose exclaimed. "Everyone will be so pleased—not that they can know the truth, of course, though Ada might—"

"Ada!" Sebastian exclaimed. "Almost forgot the reason I came back. How is the old girl? Nervous?" He grinned. "It'll be you to the altar next, I'm sure, won't it? I hear Alexander Ross paid you particular attention this season." Rose forced a smile. Sebastian looked at her more closely. "Is everything all right, Rose?"

"Of course. I'm so happy for you and Oliver. I truly am." She trembled on the brink of telling him everything that was weighing on her, but Cooper's slight cough interrupted her. She turned to the door. Cooper inclined his head.

"The Duke of Huntleigh," he announced, as Alexander Ross entered the room.

Rose's heart sank. She could not answer his warm smile, and was glad when Sebastian went forward to greet him first. It gave her a chance to collect herself.

"Good morning," she said coolly when he turned back to her. "What a delightful surprise, we were not expecting you until tomorrow."

"I wanted to speak to you in private." He glanced at Sebastian.

"I think I'll go for a walk," said Sebastian at once. "A pleasure to see you, Huntleigh." He went to the door, and as he stepped out, turned to raise an eyebrow at Rose. Rose knew what he was thinking, and couldn't summon up a smile to answer him.

Alexander glanced at the chair. "May I sit down?"

"Of course," Rose said awkwardly. She wished he would simply leave, and not give her the pain of this conversation. She crossed to the bell. "I shall ring for tea. It's a long drive from London—no doubt you are thirsty."

"Oh, don't bother with that." He waved a hand dismissively.

"Very well." Rose returned to her chair. She seated herself upright on the very edge, painfully conscious of the contrast with the last time they had met.

"I think you know why I've come here," he said. There was a note of excitement in his voice, and he quickly got up and strode about the room. "I never thought I would be a married man, but when you meet the right woman, it seems natural, doesn't it?" He waited for her reply.

Rose did not respond. She did not trust herself to speak calmly.

He went on, sounding awkward, "I know I said I'd never do anything so conventional, but that is why we are so perfect for each other—you are anything but conventional, Rose." He laughed. "My father would be turning in his grave if he knew I were to marry a housekeeper's daughter."

Rose flinched.

Alexander, not seeming to notice, went on. "I thought we could get married in Paris, then travel down to the south of France—see the places where the Impressionists painted, then on to Morocco, perhaps. We needn't invite anyone unless you'd like to."

"Excuse me," Rose said, interrupting him. She was astonished at his arrogance. "I think you neglected to say something."

Alexander looked startled, then he smiled. "Oh—of course. If you'd like me to do it the usual way. . . ." He got up and knelt on one knee in front of her. With what Rose thought of as a mocking flourish, he bowed, and said, "Lady Rose, will you do me the honor of accepting my hand in marriage?" He reached into his pocket and drew out a blue velvet box. He opened it, revealing a diamond ring set in an intricate white gold band. It was like a star in a blue velvet night.

"Pretty, isn't it?" he said. "From the parure. Will you marry me, Rose?"

Rose could control herself no longer. She started to her feet, trembling with anger and sorrow. "No. I will not."

Alexander stared at her in astonishment. Slowly he got to his feet, as she went on.

"Your self-confidence—your condescension—is breathtaking. Did you not for one moment entertain the idea that I might not accept you?"

Alexander slowly put the ring back in his pocket. "Well—honestly, Rose, no I didn't. I thought we understood each other."

Rose tried to calm herself, to speak reasonably. "And I thought that you loved me."

"I do!"

"No, Alexander. You are not seeking to marry me for love, but for hate. Hatred of your father."

"I beg your pardon! How can you assume you know what I think, what I feel?" He sounded angry now too.

"I heard what you said to Lady Emily."

"Lady Emily!" He sounded astonished. Rose, infuriated, opened her mouth to speak again, but he interrupted her. "Do you not realize that if you do not marry me, there will be no way out for you? Rose, for your own sake, for the sake of your reputation—"

"How dare you assume that I would marry you for that reason alone!" Rose could not hold back her fury.

"But—"

"I won't marry just for reputation's sake. And I am not merely a convenient way of rebelling against your father. I would not marry any man on those terms, and I will not marry you."

She pushed past him and ran from the room.

CHAPTER
Sixty-one

"Rose," Georgiana said, as she came out of the music room. "Did you see if the post has come yet—" But Rose hurried past her, a handkerchief pressed to her eyes. Georgiana's voice died away, and she watched in astonishment as Rose ran up the stairs. A few moments later she heard a door slam.

Georgiana stood where she was, uncertain what to do. Part of her wanted to go after Rose, but a more urgent voice told her to go downstairs and see if Michael had replied to her letter. The instant she had posted it she had regretted wording it so harshly; but as the days passed she had decided she had not been half unkind enough. Priya, alone, pregnant and in London, was in the worst possible situation. The more she thought about it, the more furious with Michael Georgiana became.

"So stupid of him!" she exclaimed to herself as she went downstairs.

"E-excuse me, my lady."

Georgiana turned as she heard the timid whisper. She hadn't even noticed Annie standing in the hallway. It was so surprising to be spoken to first by a housemaid that she didn't answer right away. Annie glanced left and right, then moved toward her.

"I'm sorry, my lady—but I have a message. From Master Michael."

Georgiana took a step toward her at once. "From Michael?" she said in an undertone. "But why has he spoken to you? I don't understand. Where is he? Is he coming home?"

"He is home, my lady. He asked me to let you know he was outside, in the kitchen garden. He didn't want to come inside, for fear—"

"The coward!" Georgiana exclaimed. Annie shook her head.

"No, my lady, please—I wanted to speak to you before. I think I know what happened, Miss, to Priya. And it wasn't Master Templeton. He swears it and I believe him."

Georgiana looked her keenly, but Annie seemed distraught enough to be telling the truth.

"Then who—" She hesitated. She was aware that she had already hinted at far too much about Michael and Priya's relationship, and she was wary of giving more away.

"My lady," Annie whispered, twisting her hands nervously in her apron strings, "I have to tell you, for it's been weighing on my conscience. Priya said something to me before she went to London. She was afraid, so afraid, and I just—" Annie broke off, looking desperate with remorse.

Georgiana turned cold. "Afraid of what?"

"Of Sir William, my lady."

"Oh no," Georgiana whispered. A wave of guilt swept over her. She should have known—she should have seen it. She was responsible for the staff. Could Priya have been hiding this secret all along? And Michael—she had promised him she would look after Priya.

"I must go out to him," she said aloud. She turned to the door, leaving Annie standing where she was. Almost at a run, Georgiana hurried down the corridor and out into the courtyard, without pausing for her hat or gloves. When she saw the gate to the kitchen garden standing open, she broke into an outright run. She caught the wrought-iron gatepost and swung round it, almost into Michael's arms. They gazed at each other, Georgiana breathing fast.

Michael was the first to speak. "I have to go to London, to look for her. I only wanted to see you to swear it wasn't me. I haven't slept since I got your letter, I came at once."

His face was white and dirty, streaked with tears. There were smudges of oil on his Eton uniform.

"I couldn't go to the house for fear of being caught and sent back to school. I've been lurking about here for hours until I found Annie." He went on, his voice shaking with passion. "She told me about William. I'll kill him."

"Michael," Georgiana began, frightened because she could see he was serious.

"You must tell me where he is."

"Michael, no." Georgiana was surprised by the authority in her own voice. She faced Michael commandingly. "What we must do is find Priya. That's the most important thing. William can wait."

"You're right." He ran a hand through his hair, leaving grease marks. "I'll go to London at once. Annie says she talked of going to look for a boat back to India, among the lascars in the East End."

He turned away and began walking through the bushes in the direction of the road. Georgiana followed him, hurrying through the bushes, twigs and grit getting into her thin shoes.

"Wait—but how will you get to London? And—how did you get here?"

Michael turned to her, a thin smile touching his lips for the first time. "I stole a beak's car. Headmaster's, actually. Not really stole—I'll bring it back."

"Michael!" Despite her worry about Priya, Georgiana was scandalized and delighted. "They'll expel you without a doubt."

He shrugged. "It doesn't matter. Nothing matters except finding Priya—and killing William."

Georgiana caught his arm, frightened by the determination in his voice. "You must let me come."

"You?" Michael shook his head. "I'm sorry, but you'd be no use. Besides, your chest is bad. You'd catch your death of something in the East End, and your father would never forgive me."

Georgiana swallowed her pain at his harsh voice. There was no sense in arguing now. Priya needed them. "Nonsense—my chest has been better for months now. Besides, if she's going to the lascars, you'll have to talk to them to find out about her. I don't suppose you speak a word of Bengali."

Michael opened his mouth, then shut it again.

"Exactly," said Georgiana in triumph. "But I do. Our *ayah* was Bengali." She paused an instant to let this settle in. "You need me, Michael. Now hurry up—let's go."

CHAPTER
Sixty-two

Ada paused in the corridor, glimpsing Charlotte in the drawing room with Cooper. Charlotte's back was turned, but Ada heard her saying, "And the guest rooms, are they prepared? I am sure Lady Ellingborough would like fresh flowers in her room, and Laurence I expect will like a room to compose himself for the wedding as soon as he arrives."

"I'll see to it at once, miss," Cooper replied.

Ada drew a slight breath of surprise: Charlotte, helping with the preparations? It was unprecedented. Charlotte turned around, and Ada was struck by the expression on her face. Instead of the usual sulky, mutinous look, it was softer, and strangely self-conscious.

"I'm sorry, I overheard, and . . . are you really helping? I'm so grateful. It is a lot of work." She spoke warmly, and was rewarded by Charlotte's slight blush.

"I want to help," Charlotte said awkwardly. She showed Ada the notebook she held. "I was just cataloguing the wedding gifts. You have received a beautiful set of porcelain from Mrs. Verulam."

"That's wonderful," Ada said.

Charlotte hesitated. As Cooper moved discreetly away, she spoke in a rush. "I overheard you and the bridesmaids when we were at the church. I'm grateful for your rescue."

"Oh . . ." Ada found herself feeling awkward. It had been such a natural thing to do that she had not thought about it since. "It was nothing. Emily sometimes allows her mischievous spirit to run away with her. I am sure she did not realize the damage her gossip could cause."

"Yes, but after we have so often been on . . . not the best of terms . . . it was a generous action on your part." Charlotte seemed equally awkward, and Ada thought with amusement that Charlotte seemed much happier when she was in conflict with others.

"I . . . I would like to be a better sister to you, in the future, if you'll let me." There was a slight note of pleading in her voice.

Ada, astonished but delighted, smiled at her. "That's a very kind and wonderful thing to say," she said. "Nothing this year has made me happier."

"Not even when Laurence proposed?" Charlotte's voice had a strange half laugh, half sob in it.

Ada noticed and was puzzled. She forced a smile, and spoke quickly to avoid showing her mixed feelings about her wedding. "I am sorry that this season didn't bring you joy also," she said. "I know your mother is very keen to see you settled, and it must be tiring, sometimes."

Charlotte shrugged coldly, and Ada had the sense that a curtain had been allowed to fall back. "Oh," her stepsister said, lightly, "I am used to it." She turned and walked quickly out of the room.

Thoughtfully, Ada watched her go. Perhaps Charlotte's heart was not as ironclad as she liked people to think.

CHAPTER
Sixty-three

London

Michael pulled the motorcar over to the side of the road. Georgiana gazed around them in shock, and covered her mouth and nose. It stank of open sewers.

"Are you sure this is the right place?" she whispered. The houses around her were half collapsing, slipping down into the mud of the Thames, propped up by shanties and shacks from which barefoot, dirty children peeped. A small crowd had collected at the end of the street, staring at them.

"This is where they directed us to." Michael's face was grim. He got out of the car. "Come on."

Georgiana hesitated. She was tired from the long drive. It had taken all day, and she was frightened by the place where she found herself. She almost felt that she had left England and ended up in a foreign country. The green fields of Somerton seemed so far away. But she could not let Priya down now. She had taken responsibility for Somerton and that meant all the staff too.

She got down and, holding her skirts as far out of the mud as possible, followed Michael across the street and into the shadowy maze of houses. The sun seemed to cut out here, and the faces peering at them from doorways were no longer children, but adults. Georgiana sniffed as she smelled something familiar: *roti*. She glanced to the side and saw an Indian man crouching inside a house, cooking the flat breads over a small fire. He stared at her with blank curiosity. Georgiana looked away hastily, then remembered what they were there for.

"Michael." She pulled his sleeve. "Let me ask that man if he's seen her."

Michael followed her across to the crouching man, who watched them approach with the same wary, emotionless stare. Georgiana licked her lips; for a moment she thought her memory would desert her, and then the words came back to her.

"Please . . . girl, my age, smaller than me . . . pregnant . . . you have seen her?" she fumbled in Bengali. She tried to describe Priya, her hands working as much as her tongue as she described the way Priya would be dressed, the shape of her face. The man shook his head slowly. Georgiana's face fell. It was impossible to tell if he did not know, did not understand her, or did not want to understand her.

"Someone must have seen her," Michael said. "We must keep looking. A girl like Priya would stand out here."

Georgiana nodded. She didn't say what she knew Michael was thinking: a girl like Priya might stand out and come to harm.

They made their way down the street, asking everyone they saw. None of the lascars had an answer for them. The children giggled behind them, following them deeper into the slum. Georgiana felt panic rising inside her. How would they ever get out? *Would* they ever get out? She tried to force herself to breathe calmly.

Then she spotted something that made her shriek in excitement. "Michael—look!" She pointed toward a pawnbroker's window. There hung a gray woman's coat.

"It's hers. I know, I've seen her wear it when she goes to the village." She rushed over and fingered the cloth. "See here, I remember this darn. These people must know something!"

Michael turned to the pawnbroker, who was watching them nervously. "How did this coat come here? We're looking for a young girl, an Indian girl, who would have arrived in this neighborhood not long ago. She would have been smartly dressed."

The pawnbroker shook his head. "We'll pay for information," Georgiana said, perhaps too eagerly.

The pawnbroker smiled, showing bad teeth. "You put your purse away, my dear. This is a bad neighborhood to have money in." He turned and called into the back, "Rachel!"

A thin, big-eyed girl came forward from the darkness in the shop. She looked twelve, but Georgiana realized that the girl had to be close to her own age.

"You tell her, miss. She's as likely to have seen her as me."

"Did you see this lady?" Georgiana quickly described Priya to her.

To her joy, Rachel nodded. "I did, miss, yes. She came and sold that there coat. I gave her a shilling for it."

"Where did she go then? Did she tell you what her plans were?" Michael demanded.

The girl hesitated, rubbing her bare foot along her thin shin. She glanced at the pawnbroker. Then she shook her head. "I don't know, miss. I'm sorry."

"Well, did you see which way she went?"

Rachel gestured with her chin toward the dankest of the small alleys that led off from the square.

Georgiana's heart sank. "Thank you. You've been a great help." She pressed a shilling into the girl's hand and turned away.

Michael strode down the alley, then hesitated, and turned back to offer Georgiana an arm. Georgiana took it gratefully. Clutching each other nervously, they went into the darkness.

There were fewer people here to ask. But at last Georgiana knocked on a door that opened to reveal three Indian men, one with a long white beard and a serene expression, the others very dark and silent.

"We're looking for a girl," Georgiana began without much hope. As she came to the end of her description, the man with the white beard shook his head.

Georgiana's heart sank still further. They couldn't have come all this way, had this stroke of luck of finding her coat, only to have the trail go cold.

She looked around, not knowing what she hoped to spot. A couple of grubby, peaky little urchins still watched her from the corner. They whispered to each other and looked at her. One advanced, as wary as a city pigeon.

"Miss," he began, speaking from a safe distance. "Was you looking for the Indian girl?"

Georgiana stared at him. She could barely believe what she was hearing.

Michael recovered first. "Yes, we are. Can you tell us where she is? Have you seen her?"

The urchin nodded. He rubbed one foot against his shin. "Gizza penny?" he suggested.

Georgiana fumbled in her purse and handed him a shilling.

"Cor, thanks, miss!" The urchin's eyes widened, and he popped the coin in his mouth—not having any pockets. "I saw an Indian girl go in there." He pointed toward a lumberyard, dank and depressed looking. "She went in that shack."

He scampered off. Georgiana and Michael looked at each other and then at the lumberyard. It was deserted and dank. Old planks and salvaged bricks were piled together in heaps. The gate was locked and chained, but Georgiana walked closer and saw that the chain was rusted through.

"You think she could be in there?" She looked into the forbidding place. There was a shack, certainly, but it was so tumbledown looking that it hardly provided shelter. "But why would she go there?"

Michael shook his head and pulled the gate open. It opened

with a squeal of hinges. They went through, and Georgiana followed Michael, fearfully, to the shack.

Michael pulled open the door. Georgiana's eyes grew used to the darkness. There were old planks lying about, puddles of dank water, some old barrels and sacks in the corner.

"Oh, she can't be in here," she exclaimed, horrified. "Michael, come away." She tugged at his sleeve, and then froze as something on the sacks moved and moaned faintly.

"Michael." Priya's weak voice floated toward them. Then she began to cough, great racking coughs that shook her whole body.

"Priya!" Michael gasped, and ran forward to take her in his arms.

Georgiana followed.

"Don't—don't let him in—no, no!" Priya gasped as Michael lifted her up.

"There isn't anyone here, just us," Michael soothed her. But Priya pulled away, and Georgiana was shocked by the terror in her eyes.

"I must hide!" She lapsed into Hindi, her eyes glinting white in the dim light.

"What's happening to her? Is she mad?" Michael sounded terrified.

"Delirious." Georgiana put a hand on her forehead. "Oh, she has a fever. Quick, we must get her out of here."

Together they struggled to get Priya out of the shack. Rain had begun to fall. Michael swept Priya into his arms and Georgiana followed them out of the lumberyard. Her dark hair hung down, soaked in the rain.

"But where shall we take her? What shall we do?" Michael was half sobbing as they reached the road. Georgiana could not cry. She was too frightened for tears. Priya's face was white and she seemed barely conscious, her head lolling on Michael's shoulder. Now and then she coughed, a racking cough that seemed to rattle her bones like a sack of scrap metal.

"We must get a cab." Georgiana waved to a boy who was kicking a stone in the gutter. "Get me a cab, be quick." She pressed a shilling into his hand and the boy took off at speed. "Oh, I hope he comes back!" She turned to see Michael leaning against the wall, holding Priya's head between his hands.

"She can't hear me. She's hardly breathing," Michael said. "Georgie, what are we going to do?"

Georgiana looked round at the sound of hooves. A cab was coming toward her, the driver looking half inclined to drive on at the sight of them. She had to be firm. She had to forget how afraid she was, forget that she knew no one in London, and act like the chatelaine of Somerton Court. She summoned up all her strength and stepped boldly out to claim the cab. And then she knew where to go.

"Take us to Lordswell Street, number twenty-three," she told the driver as he jumped down. "And quickly—the lady is unwell."

They scrambled into the cab and she helped Michael steady

Priya as they jolted along. She was cold and her pulse was so weak that for one terrifying second Georgiana thought she was dead.

"Priya, listen to me. Can you hear me? It's over, you're safe. You'll be safe now," Michael kept repeating. Georgiana did not interrupt, but she wondered to herself how safe Priya could ever be now. Her gaze kept returning to Priya's stomach. How could she not have known? She pressed Priya's hand, rubbing it, trying to drive the warmth back into it. She did not think she would ever forgive herself for letting this happen.

CHAPTER
Sixty-four

The cab drew up outside a large, respectable house with railings all around it. Georgiana, looking out of the window, was glad that Mrs. Cliffe had found employment in what seemed to be a good family.

"Are you sure this is a good idea? What if her employers object? Or send us away?" Michael asked as he got down from the cab, still holding Priya in his arms.

Georgiana paid the fare and followed him down. "They mustn't," she said firmly.

She went down the steps into the dim yard in front of the house. Through the smudged window she could see a woman in a black-and-white uniform moving about in the kitchen. She tapped on the glass.

The woman looked up, startled. It wasn't Mrs. Cliffe. Georgiana steeled herself for another round of persuasion. The woman came to the door, pushing back stray wisps of hair under her cap with red fingers. She unlocked the door and looked out.

"Yes, what is it . . . miss?" She looked from Georgiana to Michael and Priya with growing uncertainty.

"We must see Mrs. Cliffe," said Georgiana. She summoned all her dignity, all her breeding, and drew herself up straight and ladylike as she had seen Ada do. "It is a matter of the utmost urgency."

The woman looked at Priya again.

Georgiana took her hesitation for disapproval, and jumped in. "I don't have time for quibbling. The young lady is extremely unwell. If Mrs. Cliffe is at home, we will see her now. If not, we will wait in her parlor."

With a level of daring that astonished her, she pushed the door open. The woman backed away, and Michael put his foot in the door before she or the footman, who looked up from his newspaper in astonishment, could leap to close it. Georgiana saw her way straight before her, past the kitchen table—the place was much smaller than Somerton—to the opposite door and the tiled servants' corridor. She marched straight ahead as if she owned the house, holding the doors open for Michael and Priya to follow her. The woman followed them.

"But—" she began.

Georgiana interrupted her—never let a servant sidetrack you, impose your authority at once. "Is that the housekeeper's room?"

She pointed to the most imposing-looking door on the corridor. There were few to choose from.

"Yes, but—"

Georgiana strode forward, rapped on the door, and pushed it open. A cozy, warm room greeted her, twinkling with polished brass, an arrangement of flowers on the windowsill, the china locked away in a majestic glass-fronted cabinet. Two chairs faced each other before the fire, and there was a couch below the window. Michael strode forward without invitation and laid Priya upon it.

But the woman who rose, startled, from behind the desk, was not Mrs. Cliffe.

"Yes?" she said. "May I help you?"

Georgiana found herself speechless. Could she have got the address wrong? But plain as day, it had said number twenty-three. Mrs. Cliffe, then, had made a mistake.

"I'm terribly sorry," she began.

"This lady and gentleman were desirous of seeing Mrs. Cliffe," the woman behind them piped up.

"Oh?" The woman's eyebrows lifted. She spoke to Georgiana in a quite respectful voice. "I am Mrs. Drayton, the housekeeper here. I shall see if Mrs. Cliffe is at home, miss. Who shall I say . . . ?"

Georgiana gazed at her open mouthed.

Michael answered for her. "Mr. M-Michael Templeton and Lady Georgiana Averley," he managed.

"Of course. Please do sit down, my lady, sir—the young

lady looks very unwell." With a glance of concern at Priya, Mrs. Drayton went quickly from the room.

Michael slumped into one of the chairs by the fire. Georgiana dropped into the chair opposite. They stared at each other wordlessly.

The cook hovered. "I'll bring you some tea . . . and should I not fetch the doctor, my lady, for the Indian lady?"

Georgiana finally found her tongue. "Yes—yes, please do!" She twisted round in her seat as the cook was leaving and called after her. "Excuse me—am I to understand this is Mrs. Cliffe's own house? That she is mistress here?"

The cook gave her a look as if she had just escaped from Bedlam.

"Yes, my lady," she said. "If I may be so bold, I don't quite understand why you didn't call at the *front* door. The butler, Mr. Heath, would have been most willing to assist you."

She bobbed a curtsy and fled, leaving Georgiana not sure whether to laugh or cry.

"My lady!"

Georgiana jumped to her feet as she heard Mrs. Cliffe's voice and the rustle of taffeta. She took in the fashionably dressed woman before her, a piece of paper and a pen clutched in her fingers, as if she had just come from her bureau. For a mad second Georgiana thought this could not be Mrs. Cliffe—and then she saw Rose's features reflected in her eyes and her welcoming smile.

"Please, please, sit down—I insist that you not rise," Mrs. Cliffe exclaimed. She knelt down beside Priya. "Oh my poor girl." Her shocked tone showed that she had understood the situation. "I am so sorry. How could this have happened? I suspected before I left that the staff were hiding something from me, but I had no idea it was this—I could never have suspected it." She sounded as if she were holding back tears. "Has someone sent for the doctor?"

"I have, ma'am," said the cook, who hovered at the door.

"We can do nothing now but keep her comfortable until he arrives," Mrs. Cliffe murmured.

"Thank you so much," Georgiana managed to say. "I was so anxious that we would be turned away . . . but Mrs. Cliffe, this is your house? How—I don't mean to be rude, but—how . . . ?"

Mrs. Cliffe's handsome face was touched with color. Georgiana followed her gaze to the paper she held. It was half blotted. In the other hand she was still holding a fountain pen.

"You write," she began, slowly. "You write and . . . have had great success." She looked around at the housekeeper's room. On the desk lay a book, open. The title was well known to her: *A Duke for Daisy.* The flowing inscription below read: *To Mrs. Drayton, from a grateful employer.* It was in Mrs. Cliffe's familiar handwriting.

Light broke over Georgiana as if dawning over the hills around Somerton. "Why—you're R. J. Peak!" she exclaimed.

Mrs. Cliffe's expression, half embarrassed, half proud, confirmed it completely.

CHAPTER
Sixty-five

"Why doesn't she wake up?" Georgiana whispered.

They had been sitting by Priya's bedside for what felt like hours. The light had died from the sky and night had fallen. Priya seemed to have disappeared into the pillows and blankets; in the dim light she almost seemed to be no longer there. Only her thick black hair flooding across the pillow was the same as before. A hush hung over the close room.

Michael shook his head. His fingers were wound into Priya's; he had not taken his eyes from her. "I'll marry her," he said, "I'll adopt the child as my own."

Georgiana glanced at him sharply. Her first thought was to ask if he had taken leave of his senses. His mother would never allow it, and he was not yet of majority. But the expression on his face made her think twice about speaking her mind.

"Of course," she said gently instead.

"I'll get a job, in a factory or something. We can live cheaply. It won't matter, none of it—not the money, or anything. I'm sick of it all anyway."

Georgiana wondered what exactly he meant by "it all." Money, his mother's nagging, Somerton? Her? She tried not to feel hurt. Priya was more important now. She glanced toward the door for the thousandth time—and this time, as if in response to her prayers, it opened and Mrs. Cliffe entered with a small, balding man carrying a doctor's black bag.

Michael half rose, still gripping Priya's hand. The doctor motioned them to be seated, and hurried to Priya's bedside. He took her hand and felt her pulse. Georgiana watched his face anxiously, but not a smile or a frown escaped him.

"Has anyone given her something to eat or drink?" he asked briskly. He opened his bag and Georgiana winced at the sight of it, remembering her own weary illness.

"She's had a few sips of hot, sweet tea, with brandy," Michael answered.

"Very good." He reached out his stethoscope. "And not conscious? Not waking?"

They shook their heads.

"She is . . . in the family way," Mrs. Cliffe murmured. "She can't be too far along."

"I see." He hesitated. "Perhaps you should leave, sir. I am going to do an examination."

"I'm not leaving her," said Michael. "You can do what you have to with me here."

The doctor glanced at Mrs. Cliffe, who nodded slightly.

Georgiana could bear it no longer. She should have known. She should have seen. It was her duty to care for the staff. She turned and went from the room, and stood shaking with silent sobs on the landing. The maids slipped away as she approached, but Mrs. Cliffe followed after her. Georgiana felt comforted to feel Mrs. Cliffe gently clasp her shoulder.

CHAPTER
Sixty-six

Somerton

"My lady."

Rose had been sitting in the dying light that came through the window of her dressing room. Her eyes were fixed on the dark shadows of the trees swaying against the horizon.

Céline's gentle voice repeating "My lady" finally reached her.

Rose sighed and sat up. "Yes, Céline."

"It is time to dress for dinner." Céline's voice was soft with sympathy, and Rose knew that she knew what had happened, or at least, guessed. What did it matter? she thought. Nothing seemed to matter at all, now.

She stood obediently and allowed Céline to begin undoing her tea gown. The maid's deft, gentle fingers unhooked and untied. Satin whispered to the floor.

"I hear the Duke of Huntleigh was here this morning," Céline said. She was standing behind Rose and Rose could not see her expression.

Rose had meant to answer with a casual, careless word or two. Something to convey that she cared as little as possible. But instead, faced with Céline's kind discretion, she could not hold back a great sob. She covered her face with her hands, shocked at herself, but the tears escaped through her fingers. All the misery she felt came flooding out of her.

Through it she felt Céline's hand on her shoulder, gently guiding her to sit on the bed. She was saying something quiet, soothing—*There, there*, perhaps, or *It will be all right, my lady*. The words did not matter. Rose heard only the kindness.

"Oh Céline," she gasped, realizing it as she spoke: "I am so utterly miserable."

Céline knelt before her, gently detaching Rose's fingers from her face to dab at it with a muslin handkerchief. "What happened, my lady?"

Rose struggled to conquer her sobs. "Alexander was here."

"And did not propose?"

"He did."

"But then—"

"I refused him." Rose began to sob again.

"My lady—why on earth?"

"Oh Céline, don't ask. I am so humiliated, so confused. He does not love me, he loves the idea of hurting his father by marrying a housemaid."

She pressed a hand to her mouth again, stifling sobs. Céline knelt silent, thoughtful. Rose managed to explain what had happened, through her tears. She felt a hand press her own, and then Céline spoke again.

"My lady—may I ask a personal question? Do you love him?"

"You know I do, Céline. I can hide nothing from you." Rose managed a smile.

"Because . . ." Céline rose to her feet. "If you love him, if you know your life would not be complete without him, I do not think you should let a little petty pride stand in the way of your happiness."

"Pride!" Rose looked up, shocked and angry.

"*Bien sûr.*" Céline began folding the tea gown, making neat pleats of the satin. "You have rejected him because he hurt your pride. But the passion of pride grows cold very quickly, while the passion of love can keep you warm for a lifetime."

"Céline, I don't think you can have understood me. It is not I who am proud. He insulted me."

"How, exactly, did he insult you?" Céline inquired. She placed the tea gown in the drawer and settled the silk rose of the sash on top of it with a pleased, small nod to herself.

"He—he—" Rose floundered. "He said that his father would turn in his grave to see him marry me."

"I should think he would, from all I have heard of him. "

"But he only wants to marry me to have revenge on his father."

"Nonsense, my lady, if you'll pardon me." Céline shook her

head firmly. "You are more sensitive than you should be."

"But—" Rose looked up at her pleadingly. "I overheard him at the ball saying to Lady Emily—"

"A woman whom I have no doubt the duke greatly esteems and to whom he only speaks his most honest feelings, especially in public and within hearing of all of society."

Rose surprised herself by laughing.

"*Non, eh,* mademoiselle?" Céline pursed her lips against a smile. "Is it the truth that you have been thinking about these words of his since the ball? That you have convinced yourself that the self he shows to Lady Emily is more real, more true, more honest, than the one he shows to you?"

"Oh, Céline, I have been an absolute fool, have I not?" Rose put her head in her hands.

Céline hummed a small tune to herself, but Rose looked up and caught her eye.

Rose laughed again, but this time the sound was more painful. "I suppose you are right. I have rejected him out of silly pride, without thinking, just because I didn't want to seem the kind of woman who marries anyone whether there's love or not, just for their fortune. Because I knew people would say that of me if I married him without having his love." She got up and paced to the window. Outside, the last light was fading from the sky, the shadows were lengthening across the fields, and a skein of crows flew past overhead, trailing their harsh voices like the songs of Thames boatmen. "But what can I do to put things right?"

"Summon him back," Céline said immediately. "Send a message to Mont Pleasance. Say that you were wrong and you will marry him. It does not matter how things began between you. What matters is how they end—in happiness or in sorrow."

"But I couldn't. What if he didn't answer?"

"My lady, if you care, it doesn't matter how much you risk. Risk everything if only you are honest with your heart."

"You don't understand, Céline. I must have hurt him as badly as he hurt me. I do not know if he will even come for Ada's wedding tomorrow. I do not know if I will ever see him again at all." Rose put her hands to her face as she realized again just how badly she had mistaken her own heart. "Oh Céline, I am such a fool!" She began sobbing again, and Céline's hand on her shoulder could not comfort her.

Chapter Sixty-seven

London

Georgiana paced up and down in front of the window. It was late at night and she had not slept, but she did not feel her exhaustion. Her nails were bitten to the quick. Mrs. Cliffe stood by her, arms folded, an anxious, serious look on her face. Both were listening for any sound from inside the room, but there had been nothing but a deadly silence.

"I can't bear it," Georgiana spoke brokenly. "I should have stayed with Michael. I am such a coward."

Mrs. Cliffe reached out and clasped her hand. "You are no such thing. You are a brave, brave girl, my lady, and I am proud of you. It was my responsibility to care for the staff, and how much more so when the girl was young, and from a foreign land.

But my lady, have you forgotten that your sister's wedding is tomorrow?"

"Oh my goodness!" Georgiana exclaimed. "You are right, and I am bridesmaid. I cannot let Ada down."

"Of course you cannot!" Mrs. Cliffe exclaimed. "Never you worry, dear. Michael and I can look after Priya. You have a sleep now, and tomorrow early my man will drive you to the station and you can catch the first train. Collins, my maid, will go with you."

"There's no need," Georgiana protested.

"Nonsense." For an instant Georgiana was reminded of Mrs. Cliffe as the housekeeper of Somerton Court, not the successful author. "No Averley daughter shall travel unchaperoned, not if I have anything to do with it!"

CHAPTER
Sixty-eight

Somerton

Charlotte hurried after her mother as she swept through the reception rooms, Cooper and Mrs. McRory at her heels.

"I don't like that wreath there at all, it obscures my portrait," the countess announced, pausing in the drawing room.

"I'll have it moved at once, your ladyship," Mrs. McRory replied.

"Good. For the rest, this room is charming. Is everything in order for the breakfast? The guests will be arriving very soon, and we don't want to keep them waiting."

"Everything is perfectly in order, your ladyship," Cooper stepped forward to say. "We are ready to serve as soon as you give the word."

"Excellent." The countess led them on, back through the drawing room, into the blue room and the Chinese room, and out into the hall.

"My lady, Lord Fintan has arrived," Cooper announced. "He is in the conservatory."

"Already!" the countess exclaimed. "I hadn't expected him for an hour at least. Charlotte, go and meet him and tell him that Ada will be there as soon as she can." She swept toward the door.

Charlotte stood where she was.

The countess glanced back. "Well, go on, girl."

Charlotte turned and allowed Cooper to lead the way. Her heart was beating uncomfortably fast. A tête-à-tête with Laurence was exactly what she had hoped to avoid. It was going to be difficult enough to conceal her feelings as it was. She steeled herself as Cooper opened the door of the conservatory and announced, "Miss Charlotte Templeton."

Laurence looked around, startled. He was as handsome as ever, dressed in his morning coat. She was reminded of the first time she had seen him.

"Charlotte." He came closer to her as Cooper withdrew. "You truly can't help yourself, can you?" he said softly, and raised his fingers to touch her cheek.

Charlotte jerked her head away. She was not sure she would be able to hold back tears.

"Ada is just dressing and will be down as soon as she can."

"I see. You've made certain we would have ample time to say

good-bye, then," he said with an air of contempt. Yet he moved forward, wrapping his hands around her waist possessively. They wandered upward, but she pulled out of his grip.

"I don't want to say good-bye," she whispered.

Laurence made an impatient noise. "I've told you. I won't keep on with this—with us—after I'm married."

"That's not what I mean. I don't want to say good-bye the way you want to."

Laurence stepped back, frowning at her.

"Just a few weeks ago . . ."

"I know." Charlotte pressed her hands together, desperate to explain and yet not sure how to find the words. "But things are different now. I feel . . . I have been unfair to Ada." She spoke hastily, awkwardly. Suddenly it seemed important to tell the truth. "What happened in the past happened, but let us end our relationship here."

He smirked. "Righteousness doesn't suit you, Charlotte."

"What does it matter? Laurence, we are both to begin new lives now. You with Ada, and I—alone. But I would like us to be friends. You know, as we used to be." She held out her hand to him, meaning him to shake it.

Laurence moved forward, more gently this time, and she thought he was going to take her hand. He did, but then he pulled her toward him and kissed her on the mouth. Charlotte tried to protest, but she realized she had not the strength.

It was a strange kiss, gentle and affectionate. It reminded her of their first kisses, before their relationship had become a competition, twisted out of its natural shape by the constant scrutiny and demands of the world they lived in. She closed her eyes upon the tears she hadn't shed and suddenly it was three years ago, and she was so much younger, so much stronger, and light as a feather. She surrendered and gave in to his embrace.

Chapter
Sixty-nine

"Where has Charlotte disappeared to?" the countess exclaimed as she reentered the hall. She pointed at Ward, who had just come up from the servants' quarters. "You. Go and find Miss Charlotte. She should be in the conservatory. Remind her that there is no time for idle chitchat, she is needed to help me."

Stella hesitated. She was ready to refuse; after all she was no longer in the countess's service. But, seeing the countess's commanding finger, she didn't quite dare. She turned away, annoyed with herself, and walked with quick irritation to the conservatory.

She was glad, though, she thought, that she was no longer working at Somerton. Downstairs, two kitchen maids were in tears, and the first footman was threatening Mr. Cooper with his notice, all because of that slave-driving Mrs. McRory. No,

Stella was certainly better off where she was. She made her way through the palm trees, following the rippling of water and the rustling of leaves. The path led her around corner after corner, until she came to the fountain, and saw—

She gazed in astonishment at the sight. Lord Fintan she did not recognize immediately, not until she saw Miss Charlotte's golden hair, and then it all rushed upon her with the cold clear shock of a wave of fresh water. Lord Fintan was kissing Miss Charlotte Templeton!

She let the leaves fall back at once. She was almost trembling in shock. So it was still going on! The horrible knowledge rushed upon her that she had had a chance to destroy Miss Charlotte entirely, if she had only realized it. If she had only realized that the information she held was live, was current, instead of old news!

Her mind raced. They had not seen her, and as a result there were many possibilities. She chose the simplest and most effective one. Going back out to the hallway, she caught the arm of a maid who was rushing by with armfuls of tulle wreaths laced with orange blossoms.

"Go upstairs," she told the girl, "and tell Lady Ada that Miss Charlotte wishes to see her urgently in the conservatory. Never mind those garlands—I shall take them to Mrs. McRory. Go on now. Hurry up."

She gathered in the bundle, and watched as the maid scampered off upstairs. Then, the white garlands held carefully so as to prevent them dirtying on the floor, she went off to find Mrs. McRory.

CHAPTER
Seventy

Ada hurried downstairs, shaking loose a pin that seemed to have become tangled in her hem as Céline was fitting her dress. What could Charlotte want now? she wondered. There was so much to do. The veil was not to Céline's perfect liking, and now there was a footman in tears over something Mrs. McRory had said or done—and the guests would begin arriving any moment.

Only six hours left, said a small voice in Ada's heart. *Tonight, you will be a married woman—married to Laurence.*

She pushed open the glass doors to the conservatory, wiping away a strand of hair in the heat. Half running, she went through the conservatory, looking for Charlotte. She caught a glimpse of white muslin through the green fronds and headed toward it.

"Yes, Charlotte," she began, brushing the palm leaves out of her way, "what is it—"

She stopped dead. The words froze on her tongue. An unbelievable sight met her eyes. Charlotte, in Laurence's arms. Laurence kissing Charlotte. A moment later she would register the gentleness with which Laurence cradled Charlotte's body, the soft helpless way in which Charlotte seemed to melt into him. But for now, all she saw was the man she was to marry—in just a few hours' time—kissing her stepsister.

Laurence saw her first. He gave a horrified, strangled gasp and released Charlotte. Charlotte's eyes focused on Ada, and she clapped a hand to her mouth, stifling a shriek.

Ada broke the silence. She looked at Charlotte. "Is this what you meant by being a better sister to me?"

The color drained from Charlotte's face. "I am sorry—I never meant—" she gasped. She turned and ran from the room.

Ada heard Charlotte sobbing as she went. Ada looked back at Laurence. He was standing very still, a frightened expression on his face. She suddenly realized how very frightened he was, all the time. The fear had always been there beneath his veneer.

"I can explain," he began.

Ada laughed shortly. "Please do. It seemed quite straightforward to me, but perhaps . . ."

"I love you." He advanced gingerly.

"Please," Ada said coldly. "Spare me. Simply explain why you were kissing m-my bridesmaid. My sister."

Laurence took a deep breath. A politician's voice rolled out of him. "I will admit I was kissing your sister, but Ada, you have kept me at arm's length. If only I had been able to satisfy my natural urges through the . . . normal channels, I would never have fallen for Charlotte's persuasion."

Ada stepped back as if he had dealt her a physical blow. Her hand flew up as if to ward his words off. "Laurence!" she exclaimed. "I could forgive anything but this. Are you truly trying to blame me for your lack of self-control?"

"I love you, Ada, and you never let me near you. Who's to wonder if I stray?"

"I don't want to hear it." Ada turned away and walked toward the house with quick, nervous steps. "Tell me you love her, tell me you find me unattractive, tell me anything honest, but not this!"

"Ada!"

"No, I can't hear another word." She half ran from the conservatory. Laurence ran after her.

He was desperate, she could hear it in his voice. "Ada, please, forgive me! Ada, this makes no difference to us, does it?"

"I don't know. I must think!" Ada left him at the bottom of the stairs. Her head ringing with the shock of what she had seen and heard, she raced up to her room, and shut the door behind her.

CHAPTER
Seventy-one

Georgiana clasped her hands together to stop their trembling as she sat in the pony trap, rattling up the drive toward the white cliff of Somerton Court. Of all her many escapades, she was sure this was the one that would land her in the most trouble. Breaking a window was one thing, climbing the oak tree at the end of the drive and getting stuck up there was another, but going to the worst parts of London with no warning, in a stolen car, and staying away a whole night? She felt faint at the thought of the reaction that awaited her. But she had had no choice. The longer she looked at it the more certain she was that she and Michael had done the right thing.

"Do you think my father is home yet?" she asked the groom anxiously.

"He is, my lady. Back an hour ago," answered Jevins.

Georgiana swallowed. As they came up the drive she could see that not only was her father's Rolls there, but several other cars as well. The wedding guests had begun to arrive. Ada would be under immense stress already, on the eve of the most demanding day of her life, and she had made it worse. She wondered how she would face her.

The pony trap drew up in front of the doors and Georgiana hopped down. The groom gave her an understanding grimace.

"Good luck, miss," he said.

"Thank you Jevins. I'll need it." Georgiana turned miserably toward the house and walked up the steps. To her surprise there was no one in the hall. In the distance she could hear shouting voices, and a moment later recognized them as her father's and Lord Fintan's. A door slammed, and she caught a snatch of their words.

". . . Never, as a father, have I ever been so enraged. . . ."

Georgiana stood stock-still, confused and nervous. What could be going on? As she listened, the servants' door flew open and Cooper came out, almost at a run.

"Oh my lady, is it you?" he exclaimed, clearly flustered. "I thought James would be up here, and when I realized there was no one to receive visitors—"

"It's quite all right, Cooper. I can see that everyone is under a strain." Georgiana handed him her hat. "What is going on? Have the guests arrived?"

"They have arrived, indeed, my lady, but the family are—are occupied and not able to see them." Cooper's stammer told Georgiana he was hiding something. She frowned.

"Cooper, what has happened? You must tell me."

"Well—to be honest, my lady, it's all of a kerfuffle." Cooper's eyes bloomed with tears. "Things were proceeding in an organized manner, though that Mrs. McRory is a Tartar, and one or two of the staff have told me in confidence they'll be giving notice as soon as the wedding is done, for they weren't happy about what happened to Priya—and in all honesty neither am I entirely confident in my conscience about that young lady—but now there seems to be some disagreement between Lord Fintan and His Lordship."

"Disagreement!" Georgiana was shocked, and at once conscious of how embarrassing this was, in front of her guests. "The settlement was arranged a month ago—but I shouldn't be speaking of this to you, Cooper." She remembered herself quickly.

"No, indeed my lady, and certainly not in the public hallway," Cooper reproved her.

"Georgiana!" came Rose's voice. Georgiana turned quickly. Rose was standing on the landing, and she came down the stairs with hasty steps as she spoke. "There you are at last."

Cooper melted discreetly away. Georgiana steeled herself for a telling off, but Rose hurried on, speaking in a low voice as she reached her. "Have you any idea what is going on? Ada is locked in her room, Céline says she won't even allow her in to dress her. Charlotte is locked in *her* room, and I am certain I heard her sobbing through the door. Father and Laurence seem to be having a dreadful argument in the library, the countess is beside herself, and I have been desperately trying to entertain two bishops and a lord, all of whom are most offended that Lord Westlake has not yet arrived to welcome them." She put a hand to her forehead. "I just don't understand what is going on."

"Neither do I!" Georgiana was astonished—it seemed no one had even realized that she and Michael were gone, and no wonder, if things were in such a confusion.

"We must see Ada. If she is having doubts—" Rose hesitated. "I don't know what is in her mind, but we must go to her. She needs us now more than ever before."

"Of course we must!" Georgiana exclaimed. She took Rose's hand and together they ran up the stairs to Ada's bedroom.

Céline was standing by the door, tapping gently. "My lady," she called softly. She looked up in relief as Rose and Georgiana came toward her.

"Thank you, Céline, you may leave it to us now." Georgiana stepped past her to tap at the door. Céline retreated.

"Ada," Georgiana knocked. "Ada, dear, it's us—Georgie and Rose. Your sisters. Please let us in? We want to help. Whatever it is, we want to help."

She listened to a long silence. Her heart trembled. What if Ada didn't reply? What could be making her behave so strangely? But then she heard a soft footstep, and the sound of the door being unlocked.

She breathed a sigh and glanced at Rose. Together they opened the door and walked in.

Ada was standing by the window. She seemed to have been looking through some old letters, for she had a small wooden box, of Indian make, open before her on the dressing table. She closed the box and turned to face them. Next to her, the wedding dress on its stand, a massy, delicate cloud of ivory, seemed like a ghostly mirage, a headless version of Ada. She stood to one side of it, slight and pale. She looked as if she had been weeping.

Georgiana raced across the floor. Rose was right behind her.

"My dear Ada," Georgiana exclaimed as she put her arms around her sister. "What can be the matter?"

Ada's smile fluttered on her face for a moment.

"Dear Georgie," she said. She sounded washed out as a day after rain, but she didn't cry. "I suppose nothing is the matter, really—everything has worked itself out. At least, I understand a good deal now that I didn't before, and I suppose that is for the best."

"What do you mean?" Rose asked.

Ada shrugged. "Only that Laurence doesn't love me. He loves Charlotte. I found them kissing in the conservatory."

Georgiana was speechless. Then she gasped. "What! Oh no, it can't be—it can't be. He loves you dearly. I know he does."

"I could never have believed it." Rose sounded equally shocked. She put an arm around Ada. "You know I never quite believed he was good enough for you—but I never doubted Laurence loved you beyond all things."

"I think he loves me in a way," Ada said calmly. "But he isn't brave enough to be honest with himself about what he truly wants, about who he truly is. He wants a version of me that doesn't exist. He wants a version of himself that doesn't exist. And I—I want the truth. Mirages won't do for me. I have realized that now."

Rose sat down suddenly on the bed. "But what are you going to do?" she said, looking up at Ada. "The wedding is today. Can you go through with it, knowing what you know?"

Ada was silent.

Georgiana turned to her. The entire horror of the situation now struck her. Do what she might, Ada was faced with a terrible choice. "Ada?" she said. "What are you going to do?"

Ada shook her head.

"I don't know. I must have time to think." She looked up at Rose. "You were right all along. I knew you were, but I didn't admit it. I was as cowardly as Laurence, in my own way. I didn't understand him, and I didn't understand myself. I am sorry."

"Oh, Ada, you must never apologize to me!" Rose got up and put her arms around her. Holding her close, she said, "I have so much to apologize for too. I was caught up in my own emotions, I didn't see that you were struggling. I should have been there for you, I should have been a better sister."

"You have always been the best of sisters—both of you," Ada said warmly. She hesitated. "And . . . if I have been the cause of any misunderstanding between you and the Duke of Huntleigh, I am very sorry. I took my assessment of his character from

Laurence, but now I—I think my source may not have been the most reliable judge."

Rose shook her head sadly. "He's gone," she said quietly. "I made my decision, and it's over."

Ada looked at her in sudden surprise. "He proposed, then?"

Rose nodded. "I rejected him," she said, her voice trembling.

"Oh dear, all these unhappy love stories!" Georgiana exclaimed. A few months ago, the season had seemed so full of promise, she had dreamed of beginning her own first season. And now . . . now it seemed that nothing was that simple. Love could end even though it was true love. Love could be false love, or the wrong kind of love, or love that came at the wrong time to the right people, or at the right time to the wrong people. She had thought it as solid and immutable as a diamond, but it seemed to be as changeable and varied as the weather.

"I must think," Ada said. "I must be alone, I hope you understand."

"Of course we do," Rose said, and Georgiana echoed her. Together, they left the room silently.

CHAPTER
Seventy-two

London

Michael paced back and forth across the sickroom. He had had little sleep, and had been waking every hour to administer the medicine the doctor had left for Priya. All sense of time had fled from him, and he sometimes thought he was dreaming as he walked.

"Michael . . ." Priya's voice was feeble and hoarse, but she had spoken. She was awake.

He threw himself forward, kneeling at her bedside. He pressed her hand. Her thick eyelashes fluttered like shadows on her cheeks. "Priya!"

"It's all right," she whispered. Even now, she was comforting him.

"Are you thirsty? Can I get you anything?" he asked. "The doctor will be back soon. You're safe now, nothing will harm you again. I promise."

He was desperate to protect her. Her fingers tightened on his. His eyes filled with tears "Priya, I want you to know that I'll kill William."

"No! You must promise not to."

"Why should I?" He saw her flinch, and lowered his voice. "Damn it, I will, but I don't understand why you want to protect the monster."

"It's not him I want to protect. It's you. I don't want to see you go to prison. I couldn't bear that. Promise me you won't do anything foolish."

Michael could hear the fear and panic in her voice. He swallowed. "Very well, I promise."

"Thank you." Her head fell wearily back on the pillow and he saw her smile faintly. "We'll have a little house, won't we, Michael?"

He clutched her fingers. "Yes. With a garden for the child to play in."

"And there'll be fruit trees. And enough room for my parents when they grow old."

"Plenty of room for all of them, and your brothers too." He could see the house in his mind's eye. The roses growing around the door, the hens pecking in the yard. Maybe a swing hanging from the apple tree . . .

A look of sudden pain crossed her face, and she groaned. Michael saw terror in her eyes. "The baby," she gasped.

Michael leapt up and rang the bell. He threw open the door and shouted down the corridor: "Get the doctor! Quick! Now!"

CHAPTER
Seventy-three

Somerton

Rose stood silently as Céline busied herself with putting the finishing touches to the delicate folds of her bridesmaid's gown. To her right, Georgiana, being dressed by Annie, was just as silent, and Rose could see, when she glanced into the mirror, the furrow of anxiety between her eyebrows. She felt pained by it. Georgiana was too young, she thought, to be burdened like this.

Céline and Annie seemed to sense that something was wrong, for they hurried about their work silently. Rose could take no pleasure in the dress. All her thoughts were with Ada, all the thoughts she could not speak aloud in front of the maids. What would Ada do? What would she decide?

As if reading her mind, Céline murmured, "Perhaps Annie and I might go and see if Lady Ada is ready to be dressed yet, my lady. It will take some time to get the dress quite perfect."

Rose hesitated. They had left Ada alone an hour, and it was now nine o'clock. She knew Céline was right, but she hated to hurry Ada. "I suppose you must," she said reluctantly.

As soon as Céline and Annie had gone, Georgiana sat down on the bed, her face the picture of misery. "Oh, Rose, what will we do?" she asked in an undertone. "I don't want Ada to marry that awful man now. Of course I don't. But how can she refuse? The guests are downstairs!"

"Calm yourself. I'm sure Ada will make the right decision." Rose went toward her and pressed her sister's hands between her own. "And it—it isn't always necessary, you know, to marry for love. . . ." Her voice failed her, and she could not meet Georgiana's candid eyes.

"Isn't it? Do you really think that?" Georgiana's voice had a note of bitterness in it, and again Rose winced to hear it.

She knew Ada had a hard choice ahead of her. Could she truly marry Laurence under such circumstances? If she did not, how would the family escape Sir William's debts? She longed for Ada to refuse to marry him, but she knew that even if the financial situation were not so pressing, Ada would have little support in such a decision. No one was so foolish, she had learned, as to think that in society one married for love.

"No," she said in a low voice. "But if Ada chooses to marry Lord Fintan, we mustn't judge her. We must support her."

There was a quick knock at the door, and Céline came in. She looked frightened, and she held an envelope in her hand.

"My lady, I could not find her," she began. "She was not in her room. It seems that she has dressed herself, and perhaps she has simply gone for a walk, but . . . this envelope was on the dressing table."

She handed the envelope to Rose, who took it. It was addressed to their father. A thousand thoughts rushed through her mind. Of course, Ada could just have gone for a walk. But then why leave a note? Her fingers trembled and the writing moved before her eyes. She looked down. Georgiana was gazing at her with wide eyes. "We must take this to Father," she said, only just managing to keep her voice from shaking.

As she went out of the room, Rose's foot knocked against something by the door. She looked down to see a corner of white paper, protruding from under the carpet. Georgiana and Céline were just ahead of her, and she bent to pick the paper up. It was a second envelope, and this one was addressed to her, also in Ada's handwriting.

"Rose, are you coming?" Georgiana called back to her.

Rose slipped the envelope that was addressed to her into her pocket and hurried after them. Her heart beat uncomfortably fast as she went down the stairs. She could hear the raised voices of the guests as they milled in the reception rooms. The study door was ajar and she followed Georgiana in.

Laurence, a frightened, mutinous expression on his face, was standing behind Lord Westlake's great desk, almost as if it were a defense. The earl and countess were having a furious whispered conversation by the fireplace. Rose heard the countess say,

". . . can make no difference," and the earl reply, "My dear, have you no sensitivity at all to her feelings?"

"Father, Ada isn't in her room," Rose said, coming forward, holding out the envelope Céline had found. She kept the other hidden behind her back. "There may be a normal explanation, but . . . this was left on the dressing table."

Her father's expression showed at once that he understood what the note might be. He ripped open the envelope and read in silence. Laurence came forward anxiously and hovered at his side.

"My goodness, don't keep us all waiting! What has happened?" the countess demanded.

"Here, read it—you may as well all know. I see no way of keeping this quiet." Lord Westlake threw the note into her hands and clapped his hands to his face, rubbing his forehead hard. He sighed and paced away. "Damn it, I can't blame her. I am an example of what happens when you marry without love."

Georgiana and Rose exchanged a look and moved to read over the countess's shoulder. Rose took in the few lines at a glance:

Dear Papa, Please forgive me. I have gone away to think. I will shall be staying with Miss Hannah Darford in London. Laurence should marry Charlotte. I think they will be happy together. Love, Ada

Rose could hardly repress a smile. She knew it was a catastrophe—knew that this could plunge her family into financial ruin—but she could not help it. She was glad, glad that Ada had rebelled against the life planned out for her, had followed her heart.

"Damn it, how dare she!" Laurence exclaimed.

"How dare *she*?" the earl roared at him. "Your behavior, sir, was scandalous, improper—"

"I don't try to excuse myself, but it's no reason to act in such an insane manner," Laurence retorted.

"But what are we to do?" the countess interrupted, sounding as close to hysterical as Rose had ever heard her.

"Do about what? Ada appears to have done everything that needs doing; I see nothing we can do in response," the earl replied.

"Do about the wedding, I mean! She simply cannot do this. She may not do this. I forbid it!"

"But she has done it," Rose said. Her hand closed on the other note, the one addressed to her. There was something more to the story, she was sure.

"Well, she must be brought back again! I am not facing all our guests and telling them there is to be no wedding—"

"Is to be no wedding?" the Duchess of Ellingborough said, sweeping through the door. "But I distinctly understood that I was invited to the wedding of Lady Ada and Lord Fintan. Has something untoward happened?"

CHAPTER
Seventy-four

Cooper hovered in the doorway of the drawing room. Tea had been served, and served again, and he could see guests beginning to glance at the clock with hungry expressions. He glanced to the breakfast room, where James and Thomas were shifting from foot to foot, glancing toward the door.

"Why aren't they going in to breakfast?" he moaned under his breath.

"Cooper, what is the matter? Have you any idea why the breakfast is not being served?" The rector hovered by his elbow, anxiety sweating from him. "At this rate we shall be late for the service."

"I am afraid, sir, I am as much in the dark as you are," Cooper murmured back.

"I don't see Lord Westlake anywhere. Or, for that matter, the bride and groom."

The Duchess of Ellingborough sailed into the room. Cooper heard her ringing tones as she addressed the vicar. "It seems there is not to be a wedding after all. It seems quite unreasonable, after I have taken the trouble to come from London. Young girls these days hardly seem to know what they want."

"No wedding!" The vicar looked scandalized. "It can't be true. I must speak to the countess at once."

Guests crowded around the duchess.

"My dear Lady Ellingborough, can this be correct, is the wedding really off?"

"What a terrible shame!"

"No wedding," Cooper repeated in horror and disbelief. "Oh dear, oh dear, oh dear." He fled back to the servants' quarters. His first thought was how Mrs. McRory would take the news. He nearly fell over Martha and Annie, who were right behind the baize door.

"Oh sir, is it true? Is Lady Ada really in London?" Annie gasped.

"You—er—you shouldn't be eavesdropping," Cooper tried but failed to maintain his dignity. "In London? What is she doing in London? Who said that?"

"Martha said Tobias said—" Annie began, then shut her mouth quickly as Mrs. McRory loomed behind them.

"Cooper? What is happening out there? Why are the guests

not at breakfast? This is most disorderly. I have done my part and I expect you to do yours."

"I don't know why they're not at breakfast," Cooper said. "I have tried, Mrs. McRory, but there appears to be some delay."

"Delay! Not in *my* household. You must make them go into breakfast."

"H—how?" Cooper asked.

"Oh Mrs. McRory, they say there's to be no wedding! What are we to do with all the cake?" Sarah burst out.

"No wedding?" Mrs. McRory gave her a disbelieving glance, gathered her skirts in her hands and charged forward, through the baize doors. She looked this way and that, just as Cooper saw Georgiana and Sebastian hurrying past. Mrs. McRory sallied forth.

"My lady, a word, if you please."

Cooper, Annie, and Martha watched with bated breath through the crack of the door. Mrs. McRory blocked Georgiana's way, her arms folded.

"I must know, my lady: Is there to be a wedding, or isn't there?" she asked with dangerous politeness.

Sebastian and Georgiana looked at each other.

"There . . . will . . . probably be a wedding . . . we think . . . as far as we know . . . at the moment," Georgiana stammered.

Mrs. McRory turned several shades of purple and Cooper was almost sure small jets of steam burst from her ears. "Then I must say, I have no further desire to serve in this household, thank you very much, my lady." She rose onto her tiptoes and shook her finger in Georgiana's face. "A wedding is the kind of event that should definitely occur or definitely not occur—there is no such thing as being probably married, you think, as far as you know at the moment. There may be in France. But I am glad to say I know nothing of such disorderly matters. Good day, my lady. I wish you the greatest success with your search for a new housekeeper."

"Mrs. McRory, you don't mean to say you're giving notice!" Sebastian exclaimed.

"I am indeed, sir."

"Hooray!" exclaimed Cooper, then clapped a hand to his mouth. The door swung shut just as Mrs. McRory swiveled to glare at him. Martha and Annie stared at him in disbelief, then broke into giggles. Cooper flushed, but he couldn't stop himself from smiling.

CHAPTER
Seventy-five

London

Michael, seated in the armchair in Mrs. Cliffe's sitting room, swayed as he tried to stay awake. The doctor had been in with Priya for a long time—Michael could not have said how long exactly—and Michael had been pacing back and forth until finally exhaustion had forced him to sit down. Now he drifted in and out of heavy, tangled dreams. At one point he opened his eyes to find that someone had brought him tea and toast—not that he had the stomach to touch it. He heard footsteps and whispering in the corridor, and once a maid peeked around the door at him. But it was hard to know what was real and what was a nightmare.

All the things he had seen in the last twenty-four hours came rushing back to him as soon as he closed his eyes. Emaciated children, dead-eyed women, Priya's pale face and distended stomach as she lay like a corpse in that awful shack. He jerked awake at the sound of gunfire, but it was just a cart rattling by over the cobbles.

Mrs. Cliffe was in the room, standing by the window, her arms crossed as if to defend herself.

"How is she?" he managed to ask.

"I've heard nothing." Her face was pale, and she had shadows under her eyes.

"You must prepare yourself," she was saying, but then he slipped back into sleep, into the horrors of dream. Something had slipped through his fingers, something small and essential, like a key.

He woke with a start. "Where—!" he started to cry out, his voice slowed as if it were struggling through thick mud.

"Mr. Templeton?"

The doctor's voice jerked him awake once again. Dazed, drunk with exhaustion, Michael sat up. The doctor was looking at him anxiously. Mrs. Cliffe was crying, her handkerchief pressed to her face.

"I am sorry," the doctor was saying. His sleeves were rolled up, and he looked pale and drawn.

Michael shook his head. The man didn't understand. He didn't care that the baby was someone else's. He only cared about looking after Priya.

"I want to see them."

"Sir, I don't advise it." The doctor's face was very pale. "I am so sorry."

"It doesn't matter," said Michael, sitting forward. It seemed important to make the doctor understand that he wasn't ashamed of Priya, but proud of her bravery. "I'm going to marry her, you see. Then I'll adopt the child, and no one will care."

They stared at him in silence.

"Michael," said Mrs. Cliffe. She came up to him and put her hand on his shoulder, a soft, motherly touch. "My dear, do you know what has happened? Do you understand?"

Then Michael began to realize, and pushed Mrs. Cliffe blindly away, because he knew only one thing could have broken through her decorum and allowed her to treat him with such tenderness. If he pushed her away, it might not be true. He might not have to see the future before him blown up, leaving a gaping shell, a hole, devastation.

The doctor cleared his throat. "I am so sorry, sir. I am afraid they are dead—both dead."

CHAPTER
Seventy-six

Somerton

"I distinctly heard there was to be no wedding!" Lady Ellingborough announced, her voice carrying through from the drawing room all the way into Lord Westlake's study over the excited chattering of the guests.

Lord Westlake looked around at his family. "We must make an announcement," he said.

"But what on earth can we say?" The countess had gone quite white.

"The truth. There will be no wedding today."

"But what about the creditors?"

Her husband shook his head and shrugged. "Ada cannot be forced to marry against her will—and I would not attempt to force her, not in these circumstances. We shall have to find some other way of holding back the storm."

Rose followed her father out into the corridor. He spoke casually, but she knew that matters were serious.

"My dear friends," Lord Westlake began, clearing his throat as he went into the drawing room. "You are so good to have come here today. But I have a sad announcement to make. . . ."

Rose could wait no longer. She stepped aside, into the shadows of the hall. Half hidden by a display of ferns and potted palms, she tore open the envelope and opened the folded slip of paper. She read the note hastily.

It was not from Ada, though it was addressed to her. It was from Ravi, addressed to Ada, and dated the previous month:

My dearest Ada,

I wonder with what feelings you will read this. I hope they have not changed. I still think of you as I ever did, only with more pain. Business will bring me to London this summer. It is a rush and I will find it difficult to get away. But I hoped we could meet. I won't compromise you by asking you to reply to this. On the 21st August at noon I will be underneath the great clock at Paddington Station, where we parted from each other. If you can, be there too. If you cannot, I will understand. I will never forget you, but I will understand.

Yours forever,

Ravi

The twenty-first of August—today! Rose thought. Ada had told half the truth—she had gone to London. But, Rose realized, a smile breaking across her face, she had gone to meet Ravi. There was no doubt of it. Rose's heart beat faster. She felt a surge of triumph on Ada's behalf.

A strong hand caught Rose's arm. She looked round, startled. It was Alexander.

"Rose—I must speak to you," he began with desperate speed.

Rose was breathless with confusion. She automatically tried to struggle away, but he drew her to one side. "Please, it won't take a moment. Where does this door go?" He pulled open the closest door and bundled her inside. Rose found herself overwhelmed with the smell of polish.

"The boot cupboard," she said with a strangled laugh.

"Oh good lord." He looked around at the tiny wood-paneled room, with Lord Westlake's well-worn hunting boots lined up in rows. "I'd hoped for something more romantic. Well, this will have to do." He ran a hand through his hair. "Rose, I'm sorry. I was an arrogant fool yesterday. I don't know how you didn't slap me."

Rose couldn't find words to reply. He has come back, was all she could think. He has come back.

"I—I brought you something," he said, fumbling with the package he held. "Something better than a ring." He held it awkwardly out to her. Rose took it. It was not heavy; she could feel a frame. She tore open the paper. Inside, she saw a canvas, a painting.

"Oh!" she exclaimed.

It was the sketch he had begun at Mont Pleasance. Now it was developed. She saw herself, but, more than the simple lines of her face and figure at the piano, she saw the whirls and tides and giddying swirls of music. He had caught the power of her imagination in color and movement, and as she looked at the canvas, she wasn't sure that it wasn't moving before her eyes, rocking like the sea swaying against the shore at Mont Pleasance, like the two of them dancing together that first night, when he had said, *Alexander Ross . . . I flatter myself you could get to like him.*

He was speaking to her, his voice low and sincere. Rose pulled herself back from the spell of the painting.

"I want you to know that it isn't true, that you are wrong. I don't want to marry you to hurt my father. I want to marry you because you make me feel like that." He pointed to the painting.

She gasped out a half laugh, half sob.

"I know," she said. "I'm sorry."

"Don't apologize. Just say you'll marry me."

"I will, I will—but Alexander, this . . . this is the most beautiful thing anyone has ever given me." She struggled to compose herself, but it was no good. Tears were flowing freely down her cheeks. Alexander moved in closer, and hesitantly cupped her face in his hands, brushing away her tears.

Alexander looked at the painting as if he hadn't seen it before. "Yes," he said, sounding surprised. "It is good, isn't it?"

"Even better than the pieces at Mont Pleasance." She looked at the painting again, and she was more sure than ever as she said, "It's stronger. It has more purpose. It seems to know what it is, what it wants to be."

"You're right," he said. He took her hand. "That's because

you inspire me. And Rose, I flatter myself that I inspire you too. See how we bring out the beauty in one another? We ought to be together—and that's what I should have said yesterday, when I made such a mess of things. Rose, an artist needs light to paint by and you are my light. That's what I should have said. Rose, will you marry me? Can you say yes with a smile this time? I don't think it counts if you're crying."

"Yes," she said, smiling at him through her happy tears. "Yes, I will."

A second later, she was in his arms, his lips pressed to hers, and she relaxed into his embrace, as strong and gentle as the sea's rocking waves. Rose, dizzy with happiness, rested her head on his shoulder. This is forever, she thought, and she knew she was smiling, happier than she had ever been in her life.

"Mont Pleasance needs you to make it my home," he murmured into her ear. "We'll make a music room, shall we? Just for you."

"I can't wait," she murmured back. "With a view over the sea?"

"Yes, and I'll teach you to swim. If you think the sea is beautiful from a distance, wait until you're in it on a summer's day!" His eyes gleamed, and he grinned at her.

Rose laughed. Then she started as she heard angry voices in the corridor.

"What was that?" Alexander said, startled. "I thought the guests had all left."

"Yes. It sounded like . . ." She hesitated as footsteps raced past. "Michael. But I thought he was at Eton. . . ."

The next moment she heard a scream of fear echoing down the corridor. It was Georgiana's voice.

Alexander darted past her to the door and opened it, shielding her with his body. Rose looked around him. The oak door to the library was open, and for a shocked moment he thought she could see Michael and Sebastian fighting. A second later, as she raced after Alexander toward them, she realized that they were not fighting; Sebastian was trying to restrain Michael. Michael's real target stood cowering in the corner by the massive stone fireplace, his drink-reddened face blazing with fear and anger. Georgiana, looking pale against the oak paneling, pressed her hands to her mouth, while Lady Edith appeared to have slipped into a faint. The countess, her face white, had collapsed onto the sofa next to her.

"What has happened?" Rose exclaimed. She went to Georgiana at once, and put her arms around her.

"He killed her!" Michael roared again. He did not sound like himself; his voice was ragged and hoarse, and when Rose turned to him she was shocked by the shadows under his eyes. He struggled to pull himself loose from Sebastian's grip.

"I don't know what you're talking about!" William blustered.

"She's dead," Georgiana said, sobbing, collapsing into Rose's arms. "Priya's dead—and so is the baby."

"What!" Rose exclaimed in horror. She turned to Alexander,

who looked as troubled and confused as she felt. "I don't understand. What has happened?"

"It's very simple." Michael seemed to have gained some control over himself. He shook Sebastian off and stood, swaying slightly, his gaze fixed on William. "He took advantage of Priya, he got her with child, and in fear she ran away. Now they are both dead—and he is guilty." He pointed at William.

"I don't know what you are talking about!" William shouted back. "Lies, lies all of it. She probably had some lover in the village."

"She told me it was you," Michael replied.

"And you believe her?" William sneered. He stepped back hastily as Michael lunged toward him, hands out as if to throttle him. Sebastian and Alexander both hastily grabbed Michael's arms. This time Alexander reached Michael first and held him back.

"Is this true?" Lord Westlake spoke for the first time. His voice was ominous. "William, do you deny it?"

"I do," William said furiously.

Rose, not knowing what to think, looked from William to Michael and back. William could not meet her gaze.

"Because if it were true, no matter what the cost, I would disinherit you," Lord Westlake said.

He spoke calmly, but Rose could see in his clenched fists that he was under great pressure. Frightened, she glanced at Alexander, but he was using all his strength to stop Michael from attacking William.

"It is true, it is!" Georgiana sobbed. "Priya would never lie!"

"All servants lie," said William contemptuously.

"Watch your mouth, or I'll let him kill you," Alexander said quietly. His eyes glinted with fury. William backed away nervously, straight into the fire tongs, sending them clattering to the floor. He jumped and glanced at the door as if planning escape. Rose followed his gaze, and saw that Annie stood in the doorway. She held a tray of tea, and stood as if frozen with fear.

"Annie!" she exclaimed. "No one wants the tea now, thank you—please, please leave us." She could not imagine the damage to the family if this scene was reported below stairs.

But Annie did not move. The teacups on the tray rattled as she trembled, but she took a step forward bravely. "If you please, my lady—my lords—" she began, her voice tiny as a scared mouse, "I think what Master Michael says is true."

"Who the hell cares what you say?" William began furiously.

"Silence," roared Lord Westlake. Rose jumped, and Annie whimpered. Lord Westlake strode forward.

"Annie, you have always given excellent service. *I* care about what you have to say," he said to her quietly. "I want the truth, no matter how painful it is to hear."

"P-p-p-" Annie sputtered, trembling. She licked her lips and began again. "Priya told me that Sir William was trying . . . trying to take liberties with her. She was afraid. She asked me what to do about it. I'm so s-s-s-sorry that I didn't listen to her." She began to cry, and all the teacups and the teapot on the tray she held echoed her rattling sobs as if in sympathy.

Rose swiftly crossed to her, took the tray away, and put her arms around the girl, soothing her. With her face turned away, Rose only heard what happened next.

Her father spoke in a dead silence, clearly directing his words to William. "I have endured your gambling, I have endured your reckless spending and your drinking because I believe that an estate of this age and distinction should remain in family hands and you, sadly, were my only heir. But this is the last straw. I would rather allow Somerton to go to strangers than have people say the Earls of Westlake were bad stewards."

"You cannot take a housemaid's word above mine!" William said furiously.

"I would trust a good servant above a bad master any day. That is what you do not realize, William, what you do not understand. We are *all* family here. We owe those who serve us protection, and if we fail in that duty we are not fit to be masters."

"Damn it!" William exploded. "The girl was a tease, always—" He broke off, and without another word he ran for the door, pushing violently past Michael and Alexander as he went.

"Let him go!" Lord Westlake said as Sebastian moved to follow him. "I will write to my lawyer at once."

"But," said the countess, speaking for the first time, her face still white as paper, "what will you do about Ada? William's debts still remain." She put her head in her hands. "I will never be able to show my face in society again."

"I do not know. I know only that Ada cannot marry a cad, and that I will not leave Somerton to a bad master."

"I don't quite understand," said Alexander. "Excuse me, but are you saying the estate is bankrupt?"

The countess turned as if seeing him for the first time. There was silence. Rose knew that no one was willing to admit the family's debts before a stranger. But he was not a stranger to her.

"It's true, I'm afraid," she said quietly. "Ada's marriage was the one thing that could have saved it."

"Oh nonsense. Don't worry about money, sir," Alexander said, addressing Lord Westlake. "I'll sell a couple of Rubenses. We need the space anyway."

Sebastian let out a strangled laugh. The others looked blankly at each other. Only the countess began to smile as if understanding.

"That is very kind of you, but I could not accept—" Lord Westlake began formally.

"Not from a stranger, no, but since I intend to marry Rose, I'll be family. Oh—sorry—one usually asks permission, doesn't one, but I must say I don't care a fig for your permission. I have Rose's, and that's enough for me."

He smiled around at the astonished faces. Rose couldn't help laughing out loud at the expressions they all wore. She stepped up to Alexander and kissed him on his cheek. It was going to be the greatest fun to spend the future with him.

Chapter
Seventy-seven

London

Ada looked out of the window as the train drew into London. Fields gave way to a sea of roofs, the towering cliffs of tenements, the glint of the river between them. In just a few moments, they would be face to face. And then . . . ?

The train carried her into a tunnel. She gazed at the reflection of her own face in the window, pale and calm. She had expected to be nervous, to be frightened. After all, she had done something shocking. She had thrown over Laurence and with him all the expectations of society. She had perhaps lost her chance at Oxford forever. And yet she felt perfectly serene and calm, as if she were rushing joyfully forward while remaining perfectly still at her center, perfectly steady in her heart. She had never felt so certain that what she was doing was right.

The station opened around her, and the train drew slowly and noisily to a halt. Ada followed the guard to the doors. He opened them to her and tipped his hat as she got down. For an instant she stood completely alone in the busy rushing tide of people. Then she began to walk toward the clock. She could see it hanging like a great moon above the humming, busy station. It was five minutes to twelve. Her train had arrived just in time.

What would happen when she met Ravi? She did not even know. Perhaps she was chasing a dream, but her heart was open, ready, waiting. It had been many months since they had seen each other. Both of them had changed. Would it be the end . . . or a new beginning?

People crossed her path, hurrying to appointments, love or work, destiny or fate. Their journeys were not hers; she could not follow their paths. She had only her own path to follow, her own life to shape, as if she were casting before her in the dark. The clock only told her there was little time to live, little time to decide, and the hands of time went only one way.

She tried to see between the rushing figures, men and women, hats and coats and the trolleys full of luggage crossing the space between her and her goal. For a moment she thought he was not there, that she had come all this way for a mirage. And then she saw him. She saw him, saw the light in his tiger eyes, and she knew he saw her. Her heart began to thunder in her chest.

No. Not yet over.

She began to run.

EPILOGUE
One Year Later

London

The shop on Hope Street advertised itself only by the small brass plaque at the door, on which was inscribed *L'atelier*. No one had to ask whose atelier it was; not since the last ball of the season, when the new Duchess of Huntleigh had made her now legendary entrance. Céline had a small clientele, but it was worth it to maintain exclusivity. One wall of the town house had been knocked through so that the fashionable women who found their way there could see into the well-lit workroom beyond, where twenty or so dressmakers were assiduously stitching the beautiful, modern gowns that had made Céline the most sought-after couturier of 1914.

There was no saleswoman. Céline prided herself on serving each customer personally. She only handed them over to her assistant, Mme. Bercy—currently kneeling at the feet of the Countess of Carnarvon, adjusting the hem of a blue velvet evening coat worked with abstract lilies in gilt-metal thread—when she was satisfied they had chosen exactly the outfit that would make them look spectacular. It was a matter of pride to her that she never allowed a customer to walk away with a dress that did not suit them, no matter how much they wanted to buy it. Some considered her impertinent—after all, she was a mere tradeswoman!—but most were glad to take advantage of her professional judgment. They never regretted it.

Her eye was caught by a slight imperfection in the line of one of her favorite new designs, the "Sphinx." She beckoned the model over, and spent a few moments adjusting the kimono-like folds of sable and dull gold that formed its complex geometry.

"It is a beautiful dress," the model commented, watching the way the heavy material swung. "A triumph."

"Thank you, *ma chére*." Céline straightened up and examined the result with her head on one side. "But it is not a dress for a *jeune fille*. It will be hard to find the perfect woman to wear it."

The doorbell jangled, and Céline looked up to see a new customer entering, the woman's lady's maid one step behind. Céline took the customer in at a glance. She was an attractive woman, who appeared young until one saw the streaks of gray in her thick dark hair, and the fine lines around her eyes and mouth. The modest, uncertain way she glanced about her showed that she was not nobility. Her clothes were respectable but not inspired. Céline wondered who she could be. She was too old to be a theatre star, but certainly attractive enough to have been one once. New money, then, but not the usual kind, who thought that bad manners stood in for good breeding, and whose dress was usually chosen with display rather than taste in mind. Céline was intrigued.

She went over to greet the woman, smiling encouragingly. The smile she gave Céline in return was sweet and grateful, and Céline was suddenly sure that she had seen her face before.

"Madame is looking for something in particular?" she asked.

"Yes." Her accent confirmed Céline's suspicion that she was new money. "A dress for an evening party. My publisher told me that you were the best dressmaker in London."

Céline couldn't help but smile at her innocent enthusiasm. So many women came in here blustering and cheapening the gowns.

"I am honored. Madame is a writer, *alors*?"

"I have written novels." The woman hesitated again. "It is a dinner in my honor, in fact," she went on, blushing. "I have been anonymous so far, and my publisher wishes now to reveal me to the press and the public. I must make a good impression."

Céline was far too professional to let her surprise show on her face. To ask questions was of course impossible, but she at once wondered if this lady could be the mysterious R. J. Peak.

"Well, madame," she said, "may I ask you to step behind this screen and remove your hat and dress please."

The woman hesitated, then obeyed. After an appropriate length of time Céline joined her behind the screen. The woman stood blushing nervously in her satin slip. Céline examined her for a few minutes in silence, walking around her twice, so as to get the best possible impression of what she had to work with.

"You have excellent lines," she announced finally, "and wonderful poise to the head. Moreover, your complexion is very youthful."

"I fear you flatter me," the woman said.

Céline shook her head firmly.

"I never flatter. It is bad for business. One may sell a dress on flattery, but when the customer realizes it does not suit them, they do not return."

"I see you have found that honesty is the best policy." The woman smiled.

"*Oui*, madame." Céline returned her smile. "Trust me; you could wear any gown fearlessly. But this is not *any* party, is it?"

"No," the woman agreed. "That is precisely the problem. My publisher wishes to *present* me, almost as if I were a—a—gown myself. Do you understand? They wish the press to be impressed with me as an author. And for that, I cannot simply look like myself. I must present an image of someone they would like to see as an author. Am I explaining myself well?"

"Very well," Céline nodded. *And you have explained something else too,* she thought. Something about this woman's quiet intelligence—as well as her understated beauty—reminded her strongly of the Duchess of Huntleigh—or, as Céline still thought of her, Lady Rose. Could they be related some way? she wondered.

"I hope you have some ideas, because I have none. I must admit I am not used to high society," the author said with a blush.

"Plenty of ideas, madame. Never fear, we shall make you look like an author." She glanced around the screen and beckoned the closest model forward.

Céline went to work, explaining the gowns as the models posed and turned to show off their various cuts and colors. The author seemed pleased to have someone take the difficult business of styling her off her hands, but shook her head at most of the dresses.

"They are charming, but—"

"But you want to appear something more than merely charming." Céline nodded.

They saw dress after dress, but either Céline or the customer dismissed them. Too young, too sweet, too frivolous. Not suitable for an author who wished to appear mysterious, alluring, intelligent. But when the author saw the *Sphinx* she exclaimed in delight.

"Oh, that is beautiful. So elegant." She reached out to touch the woven silk, and the model turned obligingly so that dull gold rippled into sable and back again as the light caught each thread alternately. She looked at Céline. "You don't agree?"

Céline liked the woman, but the "Sphinx" was a demanding dress. She was not immediately certain that she would have the necessary character to wear it. Still, she nodded to the model to step out of the dress.

"We shall try it. But, madame, if it is not perfect, I will not sell it to you. I hope you understand."

"Perfectly. I understand my own professional sphere, and I trust you to understand yours."

Céline fitted the dress to the woman's shape, letting out some seams and tightening others. She did her very best, hoping she would not have to disappoint her. But as soon as she stepped back and saw the full effect, she knew the match was made. This woman, with all Rose's character, but with the added confidence of age, was perfect for the severe, sensual lines of the *Sphinx*.

"It is so modern and so artistic!" the author exclaimed, turning this way and that before the mirror. The dress moved as if it were part of her body. "It makes me think of light on desert sand."

"I was inspired by the shadows cast by ruins of ancient Egypt," Céline told Mrs Cliffe. She stepped back, considered the dress, and knelt to adjust a fold. A distant shout from the street made her glance up. There seemed to be an unusual number of people thronging outside. She tried to block it from her mind as she concentrated on making the gown look perfect.

"Madame, I cannot make a better suggestion," she said finally, getting to her feet. "This gown makes you look beautiful, but powerful also. Like a—what is the word—*une lionne*. A lioness."

"It is simply wonderful." The author turned from side to side, admiring herself in the mirror. "And not too frivolous."

"No, indeed, a younger woman would be dominated by it, but for you it is perfect. It will only enhance the mystery around you. Now, you simply need some jewels—nothing too childish. Besides, I am sure pearls will be *démodé* very soon."

Céline stepped outside the screen and looked about her. They did not strictly sell jewelry, but she kept some pieces she had collected in the antiques markets of Paris around her, displayed on fragments of marble statues. One caught her eye at once: large, roughly shaped turquoise beads mingled with brass. She picked it up, then hesitated. There was much more noise outside than usual. Céline heard running footsteps and muffled shouts. Through the front window she could see that the street was unusually crowded.

"What is that disturbance in the street?" she asked Mme. Bercy quietly.

"I do not know, madame. A lot of people seem to be coming out of the houses and offices."

"Hmm!" Céline was annoyed. She did not want Hope Street to be seen as the kind of place where a public brawl might occur. It was bad for business. She went back behind the screen.

"Try this," she told the author, handing the necklace to her.

The author fastened the necklace around her neck. Instantly Céline knew it was the right choice. It intensified the color of her eyes. The woman turned to the mirror, and smiled.

"It's wonderful," she said. "Just what I was hoping for."

Céline left her to dress and went out into the shop. The volume of noise outside was even louder than before.

"Are they still making trouble?" she exclaimed in annoyance. Madame Bercy made an apologetic face.

"Well, I shall not have it." Céline marched to the door, and jerked it open. The noise and glare of the summer street hit her as she stepped out.

A crowd was gathered in the small cobbled street. From the newspapers that were being passed around, she gathered that it was focused on the newsboy. All everyday business seemed to have ceased; the flower sellers had abandoned their stalls to pore over a copy of the *Mirror* together, the pub had emptied onto the street and knots of men stood about, talking animatedly. A sudden fear snatched at Céline's heart. Something of national importance had clearly happened. The next moment, another boy ran into the street, a bundle of newspapers tucked under his arm, and one held flapping above his head.

"Read all about it! Great Britain at war with Germany!" he shouted.

"What!" Céline gasped. She ran to him at once.

Handing him a penny, she took the paper. The print was still wet, but she hardly noticed the marks it left on her gloves. The first glance at the front page had shocked her breathless. *Great Britain declares war on Germany,* read the headline. *Germany invades Belgium with airships.*

"War!" she exclaimed, unable to believe it. Her thoughts flew at once to her family in Lille, so close to the Belgian border. She quickly read the news report. There was no doubt about it, the news was genuine. The royal family had acknowledged it. Of course, there had been rumors, whispers, fears. But she had been too busy establishing the business to pay much attention, and besides it had seemed so unlikely. She felt as if she had stepped out of the door of L'atelier and into a nightmare.

"Oh!" exclaimed a voice close to her. She turned, to see that her new customer had followed her out and was reading the newspaper over her shoulder. She looked terrified.

"It is such awful news," Céline began.

The author pointed at a smaller headline. *British Warship reported sunk by German fleet.*

"My daughter. She is on honeymoon in Egypt."

In a flash, Céline knew that she had been right. She had received a postcard from Lady Rose only the week before, from Alexandria. This woman must be her mother. She understood her terror at once; with the seas a battlefield, British citizens abroad would be in a difficult, even dangerous, position.

Without another word, the author turned and hurried to her motorcar, where her lady's maid was already waiting for her with the ribboned parcels.

"I am so sorry—I do hope she will be safe." Céline followed her, anxious both for Lady Rose and for her customer, who seemed on the brink of tears. Unconsciously she placed her hand on the open window of the motorcar. "Please try to be calm. I am sure this will all be over very soon."

The woman seemed hardly able to speak for fear. Instead she

touched Céline's hand in a quick, instinctive gesture of shared understanding.

The motorcar drove away and Céline was left standing in the street, wondering what the future would hold.

Almost before her motorcar had drawn up outside her house, Mrs. Cliffe was opening the door. She stepped out as soon as it was stationary and was halfway up the path before the butler, who had come down to meet her, could reach the car.

"Has there been any message from Rose?" she asked him at once. From his expression she could tell he had heard the news of war.

"Yes, ma'am—a telegram."

Mrs. Cliffe ran into the house, Mary rushing along behind her with an armful of parcels. She saw the telegram at once, stark and white on the hall table. Her hands shaking, she snatched it up. Egypt was an Ottoman protectorate, and the Ottomans would be on the side of Germany; she knew that. Egypt could easily become a battle zone. She tore open the envelope and scanned the message.

WE ARE SAFE STOP NO SHIPS DEPART PORT SAID
FOR FORESEEABLE FUTURE STOP PLEASE DO NOT
WORRY STOP LOVE ROSE STOP

Mrs. Cliffe breathed out a sigh of relief. Tears trembled in her eyes. The butler came up to her, concern on his face.

"Madam, is everything—?" he began. Mrs. Cliffe understood that he was too tactful and aware of his position as her servant to finish the question.

"She is safe for now." Mrs. Cliffe dabbed the tears from her eyes with her handkerchief. "But I do not know when we shall see her again."

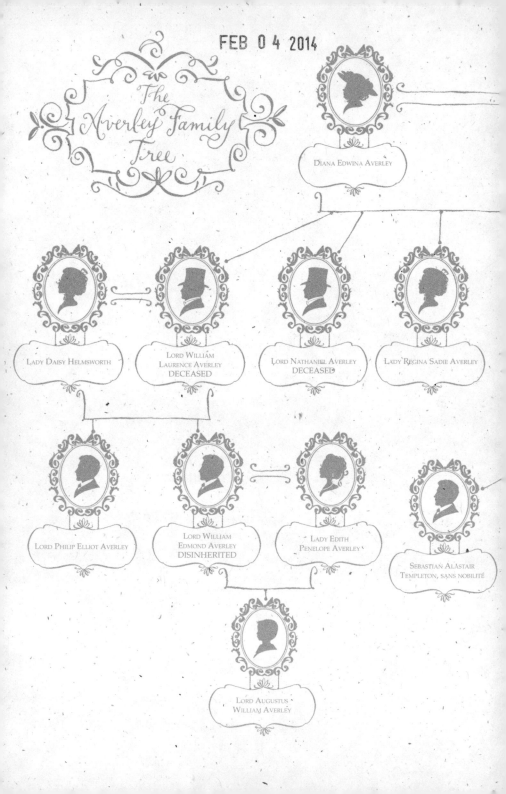

FEB 0 4 2014

The Averley Family Tree

Diana Edwina Averley

Lady Daisy Helmsworth

Lord William Laurence Averley
DECEASED

Lord Nathaniel Averley
DECEASED

Lady Regina Sadie Averley

Lord Philip Elliot Averley

Lord William Edmond Averley
DISINHERITED

Lady Edith Penelope Averley

Sebastian Alastair Templeton, sans nobilité

Lord Augustus William Averley